A Secret Service

Joy Jenkins

Girl Power Galaxy

Paperback edition, December 2020
Printed in the United States of America
ISBN 978-1-7361896-0-3
Cover Design by Benjamin Dehart
Library of Congress Control Number: TXu002152401
Visit JoyJenkins.com

To Gracie Face for being the best friend, sister, roommate, writing partner, reading cheerleader a girl could ever ask for.
Wuv vu!

Chapter 1

The mahogany grandfather clock in the Principal's office ticked impatiently, its dark wood echoing that of the imposing desk in the opposite corner. Carter slouched in her chair, legs crossed, arms folded, her expression one of mild amusement. She had seen this office before.

"Mr. Owens," Principal Withers said. "I appreciate you taking time out of your schedule to be here today."

Carter glanced at her father: his rigid, military posture, his immaculate black suit.

"I know you must have a busy day with the President, so I will come right to the point. Your daughter," Principal Withers shot a look at Carter as she busied herself by picking a piece of imaginary lint from her wrinkled uniform, "dislocated a young man's shoulder."

Carter raised her hand. "Technically, sir, he dislocated his *own* shoulder."

Beside her, Carter noted the tightness around her father's lips, the squinting of his eyes, the twitch in his eyebrow. She had seen that face before.

"As I was saying, Ms. Owens is lucky Zac Warren's shoulder is healing. Carter has already served her punishment for her actions while you were out of town. But I wanted to be sure to bring this to your attention since this was her first offense." He cleared his throat pointedly. "That is, her first *physical* offense. Detention was assigned but should this happen again, Carter would be facing suspension. Possibly expulsion."

Carter met the Principal's gaze straight on.

"Thank you," Carter's father said, never once looking at Carter, "for bringing this to my attention. I assure you this will not happen again. Was there anything else?"

"No, that was all," Principal Withers said, rising. "If you will excuse me, the water main at Thomas Jefferson Academy burst last week and we are receiving one hundred of their students this morning. I have a hectic day ahead of me."

"Good day," Carter's father said, as the two men shook hands.

Snatching her messenger bag off the floor, Carter slung the strap over her head and followed her father. The stiffness in his shoulders, the staccato tap of his shoes, the avoidance of his gaze spoke volumes. Only when they stepped out of the school and walked towards the parking lot did Carter dare to speak.

"So..." she said.

"Carter, what were you thinking," her father said.

He spun on her, making her stumble back a step.

"I thought..." she took a breath. "I thought we needed father-daughter bonding time. So I picked the most annoying kid I could find. Believe me, half the school was thanking me."

"Carter, Zac Warren could have pressed charges. I taught you self-defense to defend *yourself*, not so you could use it on some politician's son."

"Seriously?! Captain, do you think I did this for *fun*?"

Her father crossed his arms, staring down at her. "I

don't need to remind you that you *dislocated* a student's shoulder."

"The guy was beating up on a girl! I couldn't just stand by and let that happen." She folded her arms, mimicking her father's posture. "You taught me to help the little guy."

"So you dislocated his shoulder to stop him?" he asked, trying to poke holes in her defense.

"Not at first," Carter said. "I tried to talk him down. But when that didn't work, I put him in a lock. I clearly told him what the consequences would be if he tried to move. Unfortunately, he didn't listen."

Breathing in, her father looked up at the cloudy sky while Carter watched him. After a moment passed, her father relaxed his shoulders.

"Sarge," he said, turning his gaze back to her, "why didn't you inform a teacher?"

Carter sighed. "It wouldn't have made a difference. You know the kind of guy. If someone didn't stop him he would keep finding victims. You know I'm right."

Her father weighed the truth in her words and what he knew about his daughter. "Unfortunately, I do know. But that changes nothing. Next time, when talking someone down doesn't work, let a teacher handle it. Don't resort to violence. Understood?"

"Understood."

Moving toward the door to his black SUV, Carter's father hesitated. Carter tensed.

"What is it?" she asked.

Letting out a heavy breath, he met her eyes. "Sarge," he said, his voice rough. "I think it's better to tell you now than tonight." Carter's stomach clenched as she crossed her arms. "I know it's unexpected and I said I would be home for the next two weeks but I'm leaving again tomorrow. Four-day trip."

Throat tightening, Carter kicked at a pebble. When she looked up, she saw an apology in her father's eyes.

"So you're leaving again? I'm getting the feeling you

don't like me," Carter mocked. "You keep finding reasons to leave. Sometimes I think you like this President guy more than me."

Her father squeezed her shoulder affectionately. "It's only four days, Sarge." He tilted his head down, holding her gaze. "We can't afford a lawsuit, so I need you to stay out of trouble while I'm gone."

"If I did stay out of trouble then when would we ever have these lovely times together?"

Her father pulled out his keys. "I think we can find a better way to spend our time. How about this: when I come back we can go to the shooting range. Or do one of the training courses with some of the guys."

"Anderson still pissed that I got the jump on him in our last round?"

"You're an eighteen-year-old girl and he's a trained Secret Service agent. You answer that."

Carter tapped his chest with her finger. "I'm *your* eighteen-year-old daughter. Anderson should have remembered that."

"His mistake."

Her father wrapped her into a tight hug. A crushing weight filled Carter's chest as she held onto him with a silent ferocity. When he pulled back, he laid his hands on her shoulders.

"Remember, I'll always find you. That's a promise and a threat."

She gave him a teasing smirk. "So you're saying I can't run away with my Marine boyfriend?"

"Not funny," he said.

"I thought it was. Besides, your promise would be more impressive if there wasn't a tracker in my necklace."

He gave her jaw a playful nudge with his fist. "Nevertheless, you have my promise. Now promise *me* you'll stay out of trouble."

Carter tossed up her hands in the air like he had asked her for the moon and the stars in a duffle bag. "You take the fun out of *everything*. Yes, you have my promise."

"Good," he said, kissing her forehead.

He climbed into the car and rolled down the window. Carter planted her crossed arms on the rim. "Remember, you're signed up to take a bullet but that doesn't mean you have to take one in the chest. I'll take a superior father over a hero. Heroes suck."

Chuckling, her father started the car as she took a step back.

"I let Maggie know about the trip so you'll have company," he called out. "I love you, Sarge."

"Love you too, Captain," she responded, saluting him as the SUV pulled away.

She stayed frozen, watching the car disappear into the river of traffic. Turning back towards the school, she gripped the strap of her bag, her carefree expression dropping away. As she cut across the parking lot, a man wearing a black suit climbed out of a town car. Spotting Carter, he paused and shook his head.

"If it isn't Carter Owens," he said.

Releasing her death grip on her bag's strap, Carter smirked, "Anderson." She nodded to the back of a mother and son heading away from Anderson's car. "On carpool duty, I see. Do you and your fellow soccer moms wear those suits or are you trying to start a trend?"

Anderson grunted in annoyance. "Hey, I heard your old man is abandoning you again."

Carter shrugged even as her throat tightened. "Nothing new there. You don't have to worry about me, Anderson." She started walking backward. "Unlike *some* people I know, I can take care of myself."

Chapter 2

As Carter reentered the school, she dodged around a group of students in the middle of the hallway blocking traffic. Approaching her locker, she eyed the gangly, bespectacled boy who stood immobile next to it, his mouth open. He was staring at the polished boy with a self-satisfied smile standing at the center of the group: Mason Douglas.

Studying the gangly boy's face, Carter felt as if she knew him from somewhere. He wore a Thomas Jefferson maroon blazer, marking him as one of the new transfer students, so she doubted they had crossed paths before. His brown hair stuck out in places as if he were a cartoon character and his uniform looked a size too big. When she noticed the cuffs of his blazer, she paused. They were frayed. Just like hers.

"Hey," she said to the boy, "you won't make it far here if you go around staring at people. It's weird."

"What?" The boy shook his head. "I wasn't...it's not...I'm not staring..."

Carter faced her open locker. "Right, my mistake."

The boy pushed his black framed glasses up his nose. Which Carter noted were fake. As if unable to stop himself, the boy glanced back at Mason. "Okay, I know I was staring but it's strange." He stared down at his shoes and mumbled, "I never expected to see him in person."

Carter didn't think the First Son was ever worth seeing in person.

"Well, now you have," she said. "I'm guessing you found his All-American Boy Veneer isn't as shiny as it is in photos."

The boy nodded, looking back toward Mason. "Yeah, he's not what I expected."

Carter snapped her fingers in the boy's face. "The staring thing is weird, remember? Besides, you don't want Mason's attention, in my experience it usually isn't a pleasant thing."

The boy frowned. "You're *not* a fan of the President's son?"

Carter shrugged. "Let's just say that I've known Mason for four years, I've known you for four minutes and I already like you better."

The boy froze. For a second, Carter thought the stunned boy might pass out from disbelief.

"Really?" he asked.

"Yeah," Carter said. "But that all depends on how the next four minutes go."

To Carter's surprise, the boy smiled and held out his hand. "I'm Link Evans."

If her dislike of Mason made this boy breathe easier, Carter had a feeling they would get along fine. She shook Link's hand. "Carter Owens."

When she saw Link twist his head to glance at Mason, she grabbed a stack of textbooks from her locker, and pushed them into his arms. "Hold these a second, okay?"

The top book slid sideways and Link scrambled to keep the load balanced. He read the title of the top book. "You take advanced chemistry, too?"

"Yeah," Carter said, adding a stack of notebooks to Link's pile so she could get to her history textbook. "It's extremely bor-" she choked off her last word, noticing how Link perked up. "So...you like chemistry?"

"It makes sense to me. Everything has a way it should be. An order it goes in," he said, his words tumbling out. "There are aspects of that in math but I feel like it's too restrictive, there's not enough experimentation. Also, I love seeing how combining two different elements can produce a vastly different result!" He pressed his lips together and shrugged as if trying to downplay his enthusiasm. "It's kinda like life, you know?"

Carter was struck by the thought and the fact that this boy could do more than stumble over himself. "I honestly never thought about it that way," she said. "But if you like the subject, you'll like Mr. Rojas. He does a good job of explaining everything so that it makes sense and it's not a completely different language."

Taking back her notebooks from Link, Carter dumped them into her locker. "So...your school's water main burst, huh?"

"Yeah. We all got a notice this weekend. Mine said I wasn't going back and had to come here instead." As he spoke, Link surveyed the hallway, his gaze hesitating on Mason. Carter punched his arm and Link cringed, rubbing the sore spot.

"Ow! What was that-"

Carter cocked her head in silent accusation and Link winced. "Right, staring. Sorry."

"And if you learn not to stare, you'll find that Hamilton is just like Thomas Jefferson," she said. "There are people you'll like." She mockingly gestured to herself making Link chuckle. "And there are people that, if I were you," she stared at Mason then focused on Link. "I would avoid like the plague."

"All right," Link said, nodding to her advice. "Then are you the *only one* who doesn't like the First Son?"

As Carter opened her mouth to answer, a new boy in a maroon blazer appeared from the dense throng, stopping beside Link. Link straightened at the boy's sudden presence. The boy glanced from Mason to Link.

"You ready to go?" he asked.

"Yeah," Link said. He gestured from Carter to the newcomer. "Carter, this is Donovan."

Where Link was a pale, thin, rumpled boy, Donovan was a lean, tan athlete. Link slouched, while Donovan had a careless air but a stance that said he was prepared for anything. The pair were night and day.

To top it off, Link seemed to retreat into himself as if his friend's presence made him become invisible. The smiling boy from a second ago faded.

Something didn't fit.

Carter knew she wasn't going to like Donovan.

Donovan said nothing to Link's introduction but instead gave Carter a brief nod. Somehow he made one gesture both a greeting and a dismissal.

"Come on, we should get to class," Donovan said to Link.

Link pulled out a crumpled piece of paper from his pocket. "We have..."

"A.P. History with Philips," Donovan said, cutting Link off. "That's in the..."

"West Wing," Carter jumped in, annoyed with Donovan for not letting Link finish his sentence.

For the first time, Donovan gave Carter his full attention. The intensity in his dark blue eyes unnerved her. She had the distinct impression he was memorizing the defining points of her face. He studied her like she studied him.

"You have A.P. history too?" Link asked, unaware of the silent appraisals. "Can you show us where it is?"

Carter nodded. "Sure."

Link perked up, his expression as open and eager as Donovan's was closed off.

"You don't have to," Donovan said, cooly. "We're

fine on our own."

Seeing Link deflate, Carter took a step forward, eyes locked on Donovan. She had no intention of leaving Link, Donovan would simply have to give in.

"I can show you, it's not a big deal," Carter said with the smile of a stewardess.

"We wouldn't want to inconvenience you," Donovan said, gently tugging Link backwards.

Carter raised her eyebrows. "You understand it's not a crime to accept help, don't you?"

"I do."

"I can help," she said. "It's a new school and a confusing layout."

Donovan held her gaze, unyielding. "I have it memorized."

"You know about the two staircases on the second floor where only one leads in the right direction?"

"Yes. I know."

The bluntness in his tone told Carter to leave them alone. Retreating a step, she held up her hands in surrender.

"Okay then," she said. "Good luck with the closed off hallway on the second floor and figuring out that detour." She noticed Link's face fell and he frowned at the floor in disappointment. "Link," she said. Link raised his head. "I'll see you around."

As Link offered a half-hearted wave, Carter spun on her heel, heading towards the West Wing. Behind her, she heard the rhythm of a whispered argument. Halfway down the hall, Link hurried up to her, Donovan settling in beside him.

"So you walk by the history classroom?" Link asked.

"Not at all," Carter said. Link paused. "It's my destination."

"Well then it would be stupid for us not to walk with you," Link said.

Carter peered around Link to Donovan with a victorious smile. "Yes, it *would* be stupid."

Laughing, Link gestured from his friend to Carter.

"Donovan, *this* is Carter."

"Donovan, do you have a last name or are you 'Just Donovan'?"

Though Donovan's expression didn't change, Carter strongly felt he didn't find her jab funny.

"Keller," he answered.

"Like the Senator?"

"Yes, like the Senator."

Carter nodded. Senator Keller didn't have a son. She ignored the misdirection, putting it aside for later contemplation.

As she guided them through the school, she watched how the boys' maroon blazers drew surrounding attention. But similar to their contrast in appearances so were the responses they received from the other students. Donovan with his confident stride, garnered long, curious looks, while Link barely merited more than a passing glance, nothing more than Donovan's shadow.

For his part, Donovan didn't react to the attention. Beside him, Link spotted the glances given to his friend unfazed, seemingly accustomed to it.

"So," Carter said looking for another hole to poke at, "am I to pretend that your friendship isn't strange or are you going to offer a plausible explanation?"

Clearing his throat, Link tugged on his backpack straps as if his burden was too heavy. "It's not that strange. We live in the same building. He keeps people from beating me up."

"In turn," Donovan said, "he helps me with homework."

The explanation came smooth, rehearsed, and false. Flipping around, Carter faced them as she continued to walk backwards. "Yes," she said, "because anyone freely taking A.P. history needs help with homework."

Link flushed while Donovan remained unflustered. Carter continued her backwards movement, not at all bothered with the students she bumped into, too focused on the two boys before her. Storing away their reactions and the lie, Carter directed them down a crowded hallway lined with polished maple wood lockers and gleaming trophy cases showing off the prestige of the school's athletic division.

By the time they reached their history classroom, Carter hadn't puzzled out the dynamic between the two.

Putting it aside, she halted outside the doorway, facing the flow of students.

"Aren't we going in?" Link asked.

"You can. But I'm going to watch the show."

Curious, Link sidled closer to Carter. "What show?"

Carter searched the crowd until she spotted a familiar boy and girl.

"Jonathan and Macy are going to break up," Carter said. "Wait for it."

As Jonathan's gaze followed a passing girl, Macy rounded on him.

"I knew it! You're cheating on me!" Macy screamed.

The fight dissolved into tears, hysterics, pleas, and angry shouts before two teachers broke the couple apart. Carter chuckled as a teacher escorted Macy to the office, her makeup smeared down her face.

"How did you know?" Link asked, half-grinning.

"Easy. I noticed her stiff shoulders, tight lips. The distance between them. His scowl and wandering gaze," she explained, hoisting herself off the lockers. "Besides, it's Monday and that's what they always do."

"Seriously?"

"Yeah, I figure it's their way of keeping the romance alive. 'Cause really, after the first initial attraction, what do they have in common? Other than the fact that neither of them can send a text without an abbreviation or an emoji."

As Link started laughing, Carter smiled, something she had done more often that morning than most. When they entered their history classroom the teacher, in his early thirties with gray eyes and a once broken nose, flicked his gaze at them. He began to lower his eyes when he snapped them back up at the sight of Link and Donovan. Carter frowned at the hint of surprise and confusion that darted across her teacher's narrow face.

"Morning, Philips," she said.

Mr. Philips cleared his expression as he gathered up a stack of papers and gave Carter a curt nod.

"Hello, Carter. New students, I see." He waved towards the rows of desks. "Find a seat anywhere."

The bell rang as Carter slid into an open desk. When she looked back at Mr. Philips, she found a frown edged between his thick brow, his eyes on Link.

Chapter 3

An untouched sandwich sat on the table in front of Carter as she amused herself by assessing her peers relationship dynamics. The seats around her lay empty. A reasonable explanation could be given by the trash cans behind her but Carter knew better.

A tray clattering on to her table snapped her from her observations and she glanced up at Link.

He settled into the spot beside her, Donovan taking the seat next to him. Carter eyed them.

Despite the increased number of students, spots at more noteworthy tables remained available. Carter had no doubt Donovan's good looks could get him a seat at any table, Link would be the tagalong that had to be accepted. Yet they sat with her. And the trash cans.

She had to be missing something.

"You're sitting with me," she said.

Link nodded as he picked up a fry. "Is that a problem?"

"No, most people just avoid it. I'm guessing the reasons are pretty obvious."

"Is it cause you're blunt, observant, and have no problem voicing your thoughts?"

Carter widened her eyes in mock shock. "Is that why I haven't won 'Most Approachable'? And all this time I thought it was the trash cans."

Link snorted. Holding in a pleased smile, Carter scanned the room. Across the way, a gaggle of girls whispered amongst each other while throwing glances Donovan's way. One of them nudged her friends until she eventually stood. The girl stopped before Carter's table.

"What do you know?" Carter said. "Maybe I will win 'Most Approachable' this year."

Link ducked his head, hiding his laughter in his fist. The girl glanced at Carter but with an emotional expression as if Carter were furniture. Having received this look countless times over the years, it had lost its sting.

"Hey, Donovan," the girl said, flashing him a perfect smile. "I know you're new here. I wanted to let you know there is room at my table." She hesitated then gestured to Link. "You...can come too."

Link sighed as he picked at a chicken finger. Donovan didn't even raise his head from his salad.

"We're fine here," he said.

The girl paused, confused.

"Are you sure?" she asked.

Carter leaned on the table. "I'll come."

This time the girl shot Carter an acid glare before spinning on her heel and storming off.

"Huh," Carter said. "I wonder why she didn't accept my offer," she shrugged. "Mystery for the ages."

"Yes," Link said. "They'll be working on that one forever."

Carter peered at Donovan who worked on his salad like nothing around him mattered.

"Why didn't you say yes?" she said.

When Donovan locked eyes with Carter, she

wondered why he enjoyed mimicking a blank wall.

"Think about it," she said. "You'd be surrounded by girls happy to give you their attention, fawning all over you. You would be the King of the Cafeteria Court. Also, it would be the most interesting part of my day. My prediction: the red-head would have spilled something on you and tried to wipe it off with her hand. It's a tactic she's used before."

Link brightened. "Maybe you should go, Donovan. I wouldn't mind seeing that."

Still emotionless, Donovan managed to scream his annoyance at Link. He returned to his lunch, the subject laid to rest. Having no other choice but to go along with this, Link followed suit. Carter studied her two strange companions. Knowing Donovan would be the harder nut to crack, she aimed for Link.

"Why do you wear fake glasses?" she asked.

Link choked on his bite, eyes watering as Donovan froze for a fraction of a second. Taking pity on the coughing boy, Carter handed Link her water bottle and he swallowed two big gulps.

"How do you know my glasses are fake?" he rasped.

"Because I have an above average IQ and your lenses don't bend the light like prescription glasses. Now, why the fake glasses?"

Link fidgeted with the black frames, eyes never meeting Carter's, tension in his shoulders, glancing at Donovan. Clearly this was a touchy subject.

"You really don't have boundaries, do you?" Donovan asked, stepping in.

"Boundaries are for people who aren't smart enough to see their way around them. Now…"

Link played with his food. "I just feel comfortable in them."

"Okay, ignoring the glasses then."

Half-smiling, Link stared at her. "I'm starting to understand why the table was empty."

"No one told you to sit here."

Her blasé remark managed to ease the discomfort in Link and his smile widened.

"I take the blame for that," Link said. "Because so far you've been the most entertaining part of my day."

"That's a first," Carter said, mildly pleased they didn't scare easily. "Since you don't appear to be leaving, why not tell me where you stand on the social ladder?"

The two boys exchanged looks, Link startled, Donovan setting a new record for never moving a facial muscle.

"I thought your bluntness might explain the empty chairs," Link said. "But now I'm thinking it's your lack of conversational skills. You know, normal people start off with topics about pop culture or hobbies when making friends."

The question hadn't seemed odd to Carter in the slightest but apparently Jefferson Academy didn't have the status problems that Hamilton Prep did.

"First off," she said, "in the half day you've interacted with me has the term 'normal' ever been connected to me in your mind?" Link nodded in acquiescence. "Second, pop culture is dull. Third, I don't need to be told about your hobbies: Donovan boxes and you play video games."

Link looked stunned and Donovan betrayed a hint of surprise, Carter took the success for what it was.

"From the state of Donovan's scarred knuckles he obviously takes an interest in boxing. Possibly kickboxing based on his physique. As for you, you have the calluses on the pads of your thumbs that come from hours spent playing video games."

Neither boy spoke.

"So," she said, "that brings us back to your social status. For example:" She pointed to a curly haired girl across the way. "Daughter to the British Ambassador. That boy is the son of a Supreme Court judge. The idiot with the pink tie is the son of the White House Press Secretary."

Link surveyed the cafeteria with new eyes. Donovan did the same, though what he felt remained unrevealed, to Carter's growing irritation. No one had that much control of their expression.

"Where do you rank then?" Donovan asked, though Carter had the distinct feeling he already knew.

"Compared to everyone else, my father is only 'The Help', 'The Underling', 'The Gun For Hire'," she said, keeping her tone light.

"What is he to you?" Link asked, curious.

Carter folded her arms against her chest, creating a barrier. The images of a black suit, folded hands, and an earpiece filled her mind.

"The shield," she said quietly. Before Link could comment, Carter rushed ahead of him. "What do your parents do?" She jabbed an accusing finger at Donovan. "And don't lie this time. You're not Senator Keller's son."

"I never said I was."

"No, but you implied it. Besides, the only child Senator Keller has is an illegitimate daughter who is his chief of staff." At Link's disbelief and Donovan's motionless state, Carter frowned. "Did you not know that already? Seriously, they have the same oval face shape, bent nose, and tight mouth. Changing her hair color doesn't change facts."

Shaking his head, Link fiddled with his glasses. "How do you know that?"

"Because I have two eyes and a brain." Carter nudged Link's arm. "So…?"

He blinked, coming out of his astonishment. "Uh…it's just my mom and me. She's a pretty big lawyer. As for my dad…well, he's not a part of my life."

Link tore a fry in two.

"I get that," Carter murmured.

"Just you and your mom then?"

Memories of a suitcase, empty doorway, icy air, and red tail lights made Carter's stomach turn over. She curled her fingers, burying the images. "No, my dad and me."

Link held her gaze, offering an understanding smile. Pulling back, Carter focused on Donovan, not acknowledging Link's sympathy.

"What about you, Donovan?" she said. "What do your parents-"

The question broke off as Mason Douglas, shadowed by his Secret Service agent, moved past their table.

"Owens," he said. "Don't look now but people are sitting at your table."

When Mason glanced at Donovan then Link, he paused for a breath, uncertainty flickering in his eyes. Beside her, Carter sensed Link freezing. She cocked her head, putting herself in the line of fire.

"Mason, I was bound to make friends at some point," she said. "They're new so you can't blame them for not knowing about my status as a social pariah."

Mason eyed the pair again. "Maroon blazers. Transfers. Word of advice: this one is not worth your time."

"Funny," Carter said, plastering on a smile. "That's what I said about you."

A hard glint came into Mason's gaze, as he curled his lips in a patronizing manner. "You know Owens, you can be a real pain in the a-"

"Oh, I would watch what you say next," Carter said. "Because I could get in a good swing before Smith tackled me." Grinning, she leaned to the side, making eye contact with the silent, Secret Service agent. "Hey, Smith. How's it going?"

The agent pressed his fist to his mouth. From the corner of her eye, she saw Link relax, his lips twitching with a smile.

"Owens," Mason said, all his feigned civility fading. "Do you ever shut up?"

"I don't know, I haven't tried yet. I don't find it as easy to turn off my brain but I am open to tips. I can imagine you have a lot."

Mason glared at her, face reddening. Poking fun at The First Son was far too entertaining and far too easy. To top it off, Link seemed to have forgotten his shock.

"I suggest a blue tie to go with that shade of red," she said. "It will downplay the color."

"Owens, you b-"

"Yes, Mr. President?"

Mason clenched his fists at his side, vibrating with anger. Seems she'd hit a nerve.

"All those things you're thinking about," she said, recognizing his want to dispel his frustration. "I would rethink them. I have no problem punching the President's son. Also, I know Smith is so bored he would let me get in a few good hits before stopping me."

Over Mason's shoulder, Carter caught the flash of a smile right before Smith coughed out a laugh. Without another word, Mason strode off. Link let out a breath and Carter bumped her shoulder with his.

"I think a beautiful friendship is in the making, don't you?"

Chapter 4

The jingle of the bell rose above the tumult of The Sunshine Deli as Carter stepped inside. The interior was overrun by a soccer team of boisterous boys. Behind the deli counter, a woman in her early thirties bustled about, instructing her workers. "Nate, I need more lettuce. April, warm up the sourdough rolls. Anthony, I need more slices of salami."

The woman smiled, completely at ease with the mayhem taking over her establishment. Carter skirted the boys and caught the woman's brown eyes which brightened in response. With a nod of acknowledgment from the woman, Carter found an open booth in the back and plopped into it.

Tuning out the madness, she dug into her bag taking out the homework she hadn't finished. A spread of notebooks and textbooks filled the table by the time the noise had died down. A napkin followed by a cookie landed by the page Carter was working on. The rich scent of chocolate wafted up. Dropping her pencil, she picked up the offered gift and slouched down in the booth.

Maggie let out a sigh.

"I have a fifteen-minute break," she said. Strands of her auburn hair fell out of her ponytail. "Now: how is my favorite customer?"

"I don't ever pay," Carter said, biting off a piece of cookie.

"Fine, how is my favorite freeloader?"

"I think 'adopted daughter' has a better ring to it, don't you?"

Maggie blushed, the color warming her almond skin. "I believe for that to ever happen your father would have to actually ask me out." She tapped Carter's hand. "Now tell me. How was school?"

"Fine," Carter said. "We got a new group of students today. Apparently, their school had a water main burst. Anyway, now we have a hundred new kids crowding the hallways."

Intrigued, Maggie rested her chin on her fist. "And...what did you make of them?"

"Five were politician's kids, one has parents going through a rough divorce, another has a drinking problem, and another has an eye vision problem that's not being dealt with."

Beaming, Maggie playfully nudged Carter's arm. "Look at you making friends!"

Carter looked around as if she were not in the right dimension. "Why in the world would you assume that? That's just what I observed. I only talked to two of them."

Maggie huffed in exasperation. "Did you make friends with them or did you interrogate them?"

"Like I would do that?"

Maggie raised her eyebrows, disbelieving, which made Carter grin.

"I walked with them to class and they had lunch with me," Carter said.

Her smile fell away as she stared out the window. The street lights began to pop on, illuminating the sidewalks and the patches of dead leaves stuck in the gutters.

"There's something…off about them. I can't figure out what their deal is."

"Not everyone has a deal, Carter."

It was Carter's turn to look disbelieving. "Not everyone has to have a deal but everyone does."

"Were you at least nice to them?" Maggie asked.

"When have you ever known me not to be nice?"

When Maggie offered a flat expression, Carter went on. "They walked with me to class and then sat with me at lunch. So that means one of two things: one, they have seen past my rough exterior to the warm-hearted young lady that I am," Maggie snorted. "Or two, they are both insane and found my observant mumblings intelligible."

"They sat with you, huh? What are they like?" Maggie asked.

Carter sank back in the booth, brow furrowed in thought. "They didn't make sense. They introduced themselves by saying they were friends because they lived next door to each other. Part of it rang true, but…"

Carter drummed her fingers on the tabletop, while Maggie watched her, amused.

"Link says Donovan keeps bullies away in turn for help with homework. But Donovan takes advanced placement classes for all his subjects. Why would he need Link? Another strange thing is that Link is smart but he is constantly overlooked because of Donovan. It seems to bother Link but he doesn't do anything about it. He lets himself be ignored and hides behind Donovan."

Mulling over Donovan, Carter gazed onto the street. A couple walked by, the light overhead making their silvery hair glow. "Donovan…is a complex puzzle. Throughout the day he received a lot of attention. Although he seems to dislike it, he doesn't discourage it. It's like he uses it as a shield to mask something else."

Carter let out a breath. Donovan was unreadable to a frustrating extent. No normal person had that much control over their emotions.

Maggie placed a hand on Carter's arm. "Hon, was there anything about them that you liked?"

Confused, Carter frowned. "Of course. They don't scare easily."

Maggie laughed, a bright, clear sound. Her laughter faded as the bell rang and a new flood of customers swept in. "That's my break over. I'll have your sandwiches ready at the counter."

After taking her time with the last of her cookie, Carter packed up her things. At the counter Maggie set down two wrapped sandwiches. Carter tucked them under her arm.

"Tell Steve to come home safely," Maggie said.

Something inside of Carter's chest squeezed at her heart. "Will do."

Leaving the deli, Carter jogged across the road, skipping over a crack in the pavement. The narrow lane she entered was hemmed in with shoulder-high fences, the backyards hidden from sight. Carter turned into a gap between the wooden barriers where her house lay isolated. The metal staircase creaked as she ascended to the apartment above a garage.

She dropped her keys into the chipped ceramic bowl, stepped out of her shoes, and bumped the door shut. The lone photo on the wall fell, landing on the carpet with a muted thump. Dumping her backpack on the couch, Carter picked up the fallen frame, pushed the loosened nail back into the wall, and rehung the photo, not glancing at the picture behind the glass. Changing out of her school uniform into sweatpants and an old Navy SEAL t-shirt, Carter sank onto the living room couch. She curled her legs underneath her and fingered an edge of the fraying couch cushion.

Instead of pulling out her homework, she stared around at the sparse apartment. On the dining room table were stacks of paper in neat military order. Proudly displayed on the refrigerator was Carter's best target sheet from the gun range. The living room walls held faded patches of paint where multiple family photos once hung, blank now except for the single framed photo - a gift from Maggie. In the photo, Carter and her father sat on opposite sides of a booth in Maggie's deli, laughing, unaware the photo was being taken.

Carter stared at the lone frame until the light faded and she finally turned to her homework. As time slipped by, textbooks and notebooks slowly spread out across the couch around her.

When she heard the rattle of the outside staircase, she snatched up a pencil. She sent it flying as the door swung open.

"Heads up!" she warned.

Her father snatched the pencil out of the air, scowling at her. "Is that any way to greet your father?" he asked, adding his keys to the bowl.

"Don't worry, I calculated it so the eraser would have hit you. It would have startled any attacker just enough for me to take them down."

"Why throw it at all?" her father asked, nudging the door shut.

Slipping out of his coat, he draped it over the one armchair. When he unbuttoned the top button of his shirt, Carter felt as if he were discarding the Secret Service agent side of him

"You're wearing different shoes than this morning," she said. "It made your tread sound different."

"There was an incident with the British ambassador and a pond." He removed his tie and added it to the pile on the back of the chair. "It could have been Maggie stopping by."

"No, it couldn't have," Carter said. "She wears sneakers and doesn't have your whisper tread."

As her father headed to the kitchen, he tossed the pencil back at her. "Whose daughter are you?"

"Yours. I have the blood work to prove it."

Her father chuckled and Carter sank back into the

well-worn couch. "Anything interesting happen at work?"

"Yeah, but it's classified," her father said. "Anything interesting happen at school?"

"Yeah, but it's classified."

When her father raised his head over the rim of the refrigerator door, Carter offered him a toothy grin. Shaking his head, her father retrieved the sandwiches. He bumped the fridge door closed and tossed one wrapped sub to Carter. She swept away her chaos of notebooks and papers to allow him access to the couch.

With a sigh, he settled down beside her. After they had tucked away most of their dinner, Carter shifted, facing her father. He paused, reading the question building on her tongue.

"Are you planning to ask Maggie out?" she asked. Her father turned back to his food. "Because I would fully approve."

Her father swallowed his bite, a wrinkle forming on his brow. "Sarge..."

"You should be aware that I believe she's already adopted me in her mind. How else do you explain the free food?"

Her father dragged a hand through his hair, disrupting the neatly combed strands. "Sarge, it's complicated."

"I don't see how? It's been four years since the divorce." Carter squeezed the wax paper into a tight ball. Letting out a breath, she pushed aside the memories of her mother. "I don't want you to die a lonely old man."

"I won't," her father said. He cocked his head, offering her an affectionate smile. "I have you. You're all I need. My world is complete."

Carter snorted and threw the bunched up wrapper at his head. He caught it.

"I'm running away with my Marine boyfriend, remember?"

All levity was wiped from her father's face. "Still not funny. You'll date a Navy SEAL or no guy at all. I want you to be with someone that can keep up with you as well as protect you."

Carter gave a sharp salute that was drenched in mockery. "Yes, Captain, as you say."

Her father stared at her, only half-amused. Collecting the trash, he headed into the kitchen. "Finish your homework and we'll do a quick gun assembling quiz. I have to pack for tomorrow's trip."

The playfulness was sucked out of the room. Controlling her expression, Carter reached for her abandoned computer. At her silence, her father glanced back.

"It's only four days," he said, gently.

Carter said nothing, staring at her computer screen. Her father crossed the room and kissed the top of her head. "I'm sorry, Sarge."

"I know."

Chapter 5

Carter glared at the blanket of gray clouds as her father stopped the SUV at the school steps. A mix of navy and maroon blazers surged towards the front doors, a parade of faceless students.

"It's only four days, Sarge," her father said. "I'll be home Friday. I'll let you know if that changes."

By the time Carter stepped out of the car and turned back to her father, she'd successfully hidden her emotions away.

"Sounds good," she said. "Remember, you only have six months left on the job. There's really no point in getting injured now. Let one of the newbies take the bullet. Or pick Anderson. I never liked that guy."

Her father chuckled. "I love you, Sarge."

Carter felt her throat tighten but she plastered on a convincing smile. "I love you too, Captain."

After shutting the door, Carter trudged up the stairs, unable to keep the smile in place. At the top, she watched the SUV get swllowed up by the sea of cars. A chill wind whipped around her and she felt the bite of cold in her chest. Students brushed past her, urging her to move.

Layers of voices filled the crowded hallway as she made her way through the throng. Someone forcefully knocked her shoulder and annoyance sparked inside her. The culprit was a muscular boy with golden-brown hair and a face designed to smirk.

"Owens," Lucas said, loud enough to draw the attention of his friends. "Did you ever realize your father is already dressed for his funeral?"

Ice invaded Carter followed by a flash of fire as the boy's friends laughed. Carter held onto the fire, needing it.

"Lucas," she said, feigning curiosity. "I saw your car outside, did your dad get a two-for-one deal with Bentley?" Lucas stared at her, confused. "Because it's the same car he got his mistress."

Tense silence pulsed from Lucas and his friends, all of them glowering at Carter. Lucas curled his fists, his mouth made a thin, hard line. In response, Carter took a step forward, unmasking her anger.

"Do it," she whispered. "I'm dying for a reason to punch someone."

Lucas hesitated, his fury faltering under doubt as Carter knew it would. Some dogs were all bark.

"Pity," she said. "I thought you might be up for a challenge."

Lucas crossed his arms as his friends nudged him. "You know, normally I would. But my family has a rule about hitting the underprivileged."

"Funny, my family has that same rule except about the mentally deficient."

Carter walked away before Lucas could reply, though one of his friends yelled a name at her, which she ignored. It was a title she'd been called before and would again.

Inside her chemistry classroom, she settled in at her table, dumping her satchel onto the top. A shadow fell across the surface as Link took the seat next to hers.

"I'm impressed," she said. "Most people don't come looking for round two."

Though she said it, Carter couldn't ignore feeling hopeful.

"I figured you have to run out of punches sooner or later," Link said.

"You would think that, wouldn't you?"

"Should I be ready to block?"

Under Carter's scrutiny, he fidgeted but didn't back down.

"You tell me?" she said. "Got something more to hide than fake glasses and a weird co-dependency on Donovan?"

Despite the quick 1-2 jab, Link laughed. "You don't really pull your punches, do you? Is there something wrong with having a friend?"

"No. And I have a Navy SEAL for a father. Pulling punches is not something I was taught."

Link bounced a pen on his knee, a nervous tic. "It's a new school and Donovan is the only person I know here," he said evenly, though Carter detected defensiveness in his tone.

"All right, we'll stick with that answer. Where is your bodyguard, anyway?"

Adjusting his glasses, Link blinked at her, baffled. "What do you mean, bodyguard?"

"Donovan. You described him yesterday as the person who kept the bullies away. Hence my use of the title bodyguard."

Carter noticed as Link relaxed.

"Right. He's two rows back."

When Carter twisted in her seat, Donovan locked eyes with her. She gave him a brief nod but he didn't respond. Though she was accustomed to students not talking to her, his lack of expression felt like something other than dislike. What it was she couldn't tell. The bell rang and the last trickle of students, including Mason Douglas and his Secret Service agent, filed into the room.

When Link followed Mason's progression to the back of the class, Carter elbowed his ribs.

"Right, staring. It's weird," he said.

"Phones away," Mr. Rojas said, cutting off Carter's reply. "If I hear one ring or ding it's mine."

***

A clash of voices and footsteps greeted Carter and Link as they stepped out of their chemistry classroom. Before Link could ask, Carter leaned against a set of lockers to wait. The wood vibrated along her spine as students slammed doors shut. When Donovan appeared, Carter headed off to history, Link scrambling after her. Donovan followed but with more control than a floundering puppy like Link.

Sharp laughs cut through the thick layer of noise, followed by a weak protest. Carter halted, searching for the source. Further down the hallway stood a semi-circle of boys, facing a set of lockers. Without giving an explanation, Carter approached the group. Behind her, Link and Donovan exchanged glances before going after her. Another protest reached Carter as she stepped up to the gang of boys.

She flicked the ear of one. When he turned around, Carter forced herself into the center of the huddle. Slumped against the lockers cowered a scrawny, freckled-faced boy with oversized glasses.

"Hey, Edmond," she said.

He lifted his eyes to her. "Hey, Carter."

Crossing her arms, Carter put her back to Edmond, facing the semi-circle. The group instinctively edged back a step. At the center stood Lucas. Clearly he hadn't taken well to Carter's earlier verbal takedown.

"Good morning, gentlemen," she said. "A little early for this much testosterone, isn't it?" She focused on the boy next to Lucas. "Hey Zac, how's the shoulder?"

Zac rolled his shoulder reflexively as if he could still feel the pain of it being wrenched from its socket.

"Hurt pretty bad when the nurse popped it back in, didn't it?" Carter gave a careless shrug. "I offered to do it for you."

Lucas raised a hand, silencing Zac's retort. "This is none of your business, Owens. Leave," he commanded.

Raising her eyebrows, Carter nodded, ignoring the unspoken threat. "True, but *you* have no business getting into *Edmond's* business. So I have decided, since none of us is minding *our own* business, I'm going to get involved in *this* business."

The boys all exchanged looks, trying to see if their companions understood. The fact that they didn't, didn't surprise her. They were all idiots.

"Look, Owens, this is between us and Edmond. You should leave before you hurt yourself."

The comment was laughable, but Carter didn't laugh. Instead, she met each set of eyes.

"Look, I like Edmond," she said. "And I don't like you. If you continue to bully him I'm going to explain how this will go down."

She pivoted to the boy on the left. "I'm going to break your nose because I don't like your face." She pointed to Zac. "I'm going to dislocate your other shoulder, just to make them even." She gave Lucas a sickly sweet smile. "I'm going to break your wrist, taking away your baseball career. And finally you, Finch," she said, spinning towards the last boy. "I'm going to bust your ankle because I don't like the way you walk." As if they offered no danger to her at all, she slid her hands into her pockets. "Now, how does that future sound to all of you? And please feel free to look amused, skeptical, or patronizing. I would have all the more fun wiping the expressions off your faces."

As she finished speaking, she leveled a hard glare at Lucas. He flinched as if she had already struck him, but didn't move. Some people didn't know when to quit. Carter flexed her fingers, anticipation making them tingle. The energy crackling around them snapped when Lucas smirked.

"You know what," he said as if he found the whole situation amusing. "We are going to leave because I would hate to make that face of yours any uglier." He retreated a step. "See you around, Owens."

The boys laughed as they started to leave, their minds already forming the story into where they came out on top. As Finch passed Carter, he smacked her on the butt. Anger seared through her. In the time it took Link to suck in a breath and Donovan to take a step forward, Carter had seized Finch's hand and forced it backward. He dropped to one knee, as she kept his hand in an iron grip. Bending forward, she stared at him as if she could tear out his soul.

"Touch me again and you will find out how fast I can break five of your bones without breaking a sweat," she said, her voice as sharp as a knife.

Finch winced, face turning white, his lips pressed together.

"Understand?" Carter asked.

Finch nodded frantically, his eyes narrowing in pain.

"Good."

She released him. When she faced Edmond still slumped on the floor, her anger slipped away. With a sigh, she helped him up.

"Ed, what did we talk about?" she asked, exasperated.

Embarrassed, Edmond pushed his glasses up and dusted off his disheveled blazer. "Sorry, Carter."

"A couple of push-ups. You can even put the calculus book beneath you so you can read. It would just give you leverage. Or an ounce of confidence. Either one at this point would help you."

Edmond gave a jerky nod that made his glasses dip. Carter shrugged, aware she fought a losing battle.

"All right, I'll see you in A.P. Calculus," she said. "Try not to get beaten up until then. You're the only partner I have in that class. I would hate for that to end because of your untimely demise."

"Thanks, Carter," he said, smiling shyly.

"Yeah."

When she fell back into the current of students, Link rushed to catch up with her, Donovan close behind.

"Bad morning?" he asked. "Or are you the defender of the weak?"

Carter shot him a sideways glance and shrugged noncommittally. "I don't like Tuesdays. This one in particular."

"Any reason?"

She stopped but said nothing. To her silence, Link raised his eyebrows, prompting her to go on. A few seconds passed, in which the truth hung in the air between them, the image of her father's disappearing car and the waiting empty apartment.

"None whatsoever."

Puzzled, Link looked to Donovan before resuming his spot next to her.

"All right," he said. "We'll stick with that answer."

At the echo of her statement from earlier that morning, she glanced at him. Link's joking smile made her own lips curl in response.

"I guess I deserve that," she said.

When they entered their history classroom, Mr. Philips greeted them.

"Link, might I have a word?" he asked, waving him forward.

At her seat, Carter slid down, observing Mr. Philips as he talked to Link.

"What did he want?" she asked as Link plopped into his spot next to her.

Link widened his eyes, mockingly. "What? You didn't read his lips and know what he was asking me?"

She rolled her eyes. "I read your lips but not his,

genius."

"Can you do that?"

Carter tilted her head from side to side. "It's a work in progress. What did he want?"

"It was nothing, just some assignment."

The shrill clang of the bell acted as a physical force, shoving the late comers inside and to their desks.

"Class, before we get started," Mr. Philips said. "I want to remind you that this Friday we are visiting the National Museum of American History. The paper you write on the topic of artifacts and their importance will be a big percentage of your grade. Make sure you are there. Now, let's continue with the Johnson administration."

Chapter 6

Every time Carter walked through the thick oak doors into the library, she felt like she stepped into another world. The noise of the hallways faded as the doors swung closed, encasing her in a silence that smelled slightly of musty paper. The library was two stories high with endless rows of bookshelves and long rectangle tables. She knew every inch.

"Carter, you haven't been writing your opinions in the margins of my books have you?" The sweet-faced librarian in her forties eyed Carter over the top of her round spectacles.

"Only in pencil," Carter said.

Books thudded to the desktop as Diana gawked at Carter.

"Kidding," Carter said, leaning on the counter. "It was in pen."

Diana let a breath out through her nose, trying to reprimand Carter without saying a word. It didn't work, mostly because even verbal reprimands had little effect on Carter.

"You know I'm joking, Diana," Carter said. "I would rather shove my opinions down other people's throats than put them on paper somewhere they can be ignored."

Mollified, Diana retrieved the fallen stack of books, adding them to the return cart. "You know you are a strange girl."

"You say it like it's a new revelation."

"No, an old one that is refreshed frequently."

Carter laughed, garnering a few accusing glares from the already studying students. "Are you going to accept Mr. Rojas's offer of a date?"

Diana fumbled with a second stack of books. "What makes you think he's going to ask me for a date?"

"Well, for the obvious reasons that he's taken up running, combed his hair, and kept your note."

Flushing, Diana methodically neatened a stack of papers. "What note?"

"On his desk is a biography about Edison," Carter said. "One that you found for him. Despite the bookmark indicating that he is halfway through, a post-it note with a message from you remains on the cover. Why leave it there? The most likely reason is that he likes seeing your name written at the bottom."

Despite her attempt at seeming unfazed, Carter noted the twitch in Diana's lips.

"Also, I have a feeling he's going to ask you out today."

Diana jerked her head up, flustered. "Today?" She patted her graying black hair. "Why would you say today?"

"Because not only is he wearing cologne but he's also bought a new tie."

Trying to hide a smile, Diana bustled about her desk, doing nothing and looking busy at it. "Do you do anything other than observe people, Carter?"

"Is there something else I should be doing here?"

"One might think school is for learning," Diana said.

"Well, people have been wrong before. About Mr.

Rojas: my advice is to say yes but don't comment about how his tie clashes with his shirt."

"You know, he could simply want to look nice." Even as Diana voiced the denial, she tucked in the edge of her shirt into her skirt and pressed out a wrinkle.

"Possibly," Carter said, seeing Mr. Rojas approaching through the glass panes of the library doors. "But that wouldn't explain why he's coming here now."

With a squeak, Diana spun towards the doors as Mr. Rojas walked through, nervously straightening his tie. The clash of the green with his gray shirt still made Carter wince, but maybe love was color blind.

"Hi, Diana," he said.

Blushing, Diana fixed her glasses. "Hi, Michael."

Completely entertained by the awkwardness of the two faculty members, Carter rested her chin in her hand. Mr. Rojas cleared his throat and smoothed down his tie again.

"I was," he cleared his throat again. "I was looking for a biography on Tesla, do you have one?"

Diana deflated but smiled all the same, though it was strained. "Of course."

"I believe it's on the second story," Carter said. "In the back, where it's secluded."

Scarlet, Diana hurried out from behind her desk. "I'll show you." She considered his attire as they headed off. "Is that a new tie?"

Mr. Rojas peered down at it, self-conscious. "It is. Do you like it?"

Diana nodded and Mr. Rojas glowed. When they had disappeared, Carter shook her head. That only took two years to finally happen.

At an empty table, she dumped her blazer on a chair and pushed up her shirt sleeves. Tilting back, she draped one leg over the corner of the table, putting the fraying ends of her pants on display. She watched the other students, making mental notes. One table down, a boy was bent over a textbook, scowling. As he ran his pencil along the text, he dragged his hand through his hair. Carter watched him, but the book remained stuck on the same page.

Further down a quartet of girls sat chattering, unaware of the world beyond themselves. On the edge, a dark-haired girl smiled and nodded along. The gossiper beside her tucked a stray strand of hair behind her ear and her companion mimicked the action unconsciously. Carter studied the girl's uniform. The edges of the blazer had been trimmed in dark blue velvet, mirroring that of her friend. Even the small necklace that peeked out below her starched collar was the same. Interesting: a girl with wealth, beauty, a high social standing yet insecure. Daddy issues.

Eventually facing she had assignments due, Carter dumped out a mess of notebooks onto the table. Picking a subject at random, she left the table to find the corresponding textbook. As she yanked a large tome from the shelf, two voices floated towards her.

"…what can you tell me about him?" a tenor voice asked.

"Left-handed. From a well-to-do family," a deep masculine voice answered. "See how his collar is ironed but the rest of his shirt is wrinkled? Someone ironed it, but his nervous tendencies ruined the rest of it. Which explains why only one side of his hair is disheveled."

Intrigued, Carter leaned against the bookcase.

"I would guess he's about a B average student and that's only because he studies as much as he does. He struggles with understanding the material."

"How do you figure that?"

The voice clicked into place: it was Link asking the questions. Logic suggested Donovan was the one analyzing students. It appeared he could talk after all.

"He's been on the same page for the last ten minutes," Donovan continued. "He studies but doesn't know how to do it well. His parents aren't overly involved in his life or else they would have hired a tutor for him."

Carter recognized that he was analyzing the boy she'd been watching only minutes before. Following that thought, she realized Donovan drew all the same conclusions.

"What about that group? The dark-haired girl on the end," Link said.

Carter crept to the end of the row and poked her head around. Both boys faced away from her. Donovan lounged against the barrier of books, his ankles crossed and his hands hidden in his pockets. Even as he appeared at ease, Carter could sense an alert energy about him. Beside him was Link, absentmindedly scratching the back of his leg with his foot, wrinkling his pants.

"Something in her past has caused her to go looking for acceptance in others," Donovan said. "I would wager this comes from a childhood rejection. She's attractive, but she can't see it herself. Look at her mannerisms, they are exact mirrors of girls around her. She even mimics trends of girls around her, becoming copies of them. Besides, she also seeks the approval of guys."

Carter stared, bemused by how he was echoing her thoughts.

"How-" Link started.

"She approached me after A.P. Lit."

"Okay, What do you-"

Unable to hold herself back, Carter left her hideout. Donovan heard her footsteps and shot his hand out, quieting Link with a grip on his arm. As she passed them, she spun around and walked backward.

"Her father is the childhood rejection by the way," she said. "Ran off with the nanny when the girl was eight."

Link's eyebrows jumped to his hairline while Donovan clung to his mask of indifference. Seeing that they weren't going to comment on the statement, she made a retreat. She returned to her table and opened her textbook, but couldn't focus, mulling over Donovan's ability to dissect people.

A minute later, she jumped as a stack of books dropped beside her. Grinning, Link flopped into the chair next to hers. Donovan gently placed his books down across the way.

"Again you're sitting with me," she said.

"Yup," Link said, flipping open a notebook.

"And like your glasses, we're going to ignore what I just overhead?"

"Yup."

Link never once looked at her, but Carter got the sense he was enjoying himself. Donovan, as always, seemed both completely detached from their conversation and completely aware of what they were saying. When nothing else was forthcoming from her companions, Carter studied them.

Their introduction of how Donovan relied on Link for homework help was disproven as he raced through advanced mathematics like he already knew the answers. Carter twirled a pencil across her fingers, hitting a wall on why Donovan and Link would lie and how they were truly connected.

A group of girls waltzed into the library, their laughter flitted around them like butterflies. The sound drew Link's attention. Carter watched as he paused on one individual. A girl with thick ebony hair, porcelain skin, and luminous black eyes. He followed her path as she claimed a table with her friends. Feeling Carter's gaze, Link ducked his head. When he eyed the group again, she spoke. "Link, you can go talk to her, you know."

He started. "Talk to who?" he asked, tugging on his already loosened tie.

"The girl from our history class. The one you've been staring at."

Link squirmed in his seat. "I wasn't…She's not…I'm not…I don't know anything about her."

"A problem easily solved."

"What do you mean?" he asked, hesitant.

In answer, Carter held up her pencil. Link knit his eyebrows together. Donovan remained immune to the topic, but the speed in which he worked slowed. As Carter rose, Link's eyes widened.

"What are you going to do?" he asked, panicking.

"Getting you information on Amy. The girl you keep looking at."

Link grabbed her arm. "Carter. Don't."

She smacked her pencil against his wrist and he released her. She paced away from their table and made a slow progression towards the cluster of girls. She traversed the perimeter of the girl's table in a zig-zag pattern, listening.

When she had all she needed, she crouched down behind Amy's seat and slipped the pencil from her pocket. She stood and the girls fell silent. Most wore the customary looks of distaste Carter had grown to know, only Amy appeared inquisitive.

"Sorry, I lost my pencil," Carter said.

Dismissing Carter, the group returned to their conversation. Except for Amy.

"I know you," she murmured.

"We have history together."

Recognition brightened Amy's eyes. "You were the one that helped me with Zac when he got..." She flinched at the unwanted memory. "You dislocated his shoulder."

"Technically, he dislocated his own shoulder." Amy chuckled. Carter backed up as she pointed to Amy's notebook. "Good luck with pre-calc. The textbook is in the fifth row, towards the back."

Amy paused in bewilderment, but Carter continued to walk away. When she dropped back into her seat, Link stared at her, waiting. His leg bounced. When she didn't speak right away, Link shoved her arm. "Well?"

"So you do want to know about her?" she asked.

Link scowled, his leg picking up speed. Carter

stretched, savoring the way Link eagerly wanted to hear what she learned. Donavon continued to write equations, though he angled his head towards her.

"Fine, her name is Amy Howe. Senior. Right-handed. Organized. She's taking French, A.P. history, A.P. lit, and physics. Smart but struggles with pre-calculus." She nodded to Link. "That will be your way in." She rocked her chair back on two legs. "At least one parent is a journalist because she takes notes in shorthand. She prefers cats over dogs. Doodles hearts on the edges of her paper. Doesn't like being pushed around and puts up a decent fight. Currently does not have a boyfriend."

Link gaped at Carter as Donovan stilled, his pen hovering above the page. Across the way, Amy shifted, leaning forward about to stand. Carter jabbed Link, snapping him from his shock.

"The pre-calc textbooks are on the top shelf, fifth row, towards the back," she said. "Go take one down. She'll come to you." When Link didn't move, she pushed him to stand. "You understand calculus, offer to help her. Go."

Amy slid her chair back and rose, but paused as one of her friends said something. Carter prodded Link again. Finally understanding, he spun around, toppling over his seat and darting away without righting it. As he ducked into an aisle, Amy sauntered towards the lane Carter had indicated. Breathing hard, Link got there and grabbed one of the textbooks. Letting out her breath, Carter slumped in her chair, watching as Amy tucked a strand of hair behind her ear and said hello.

"The boyfriend information?"

Only then did Carter realize that Donovan had raised his head.

"They were making comments about the attractiveness of certain seniors. Amy mentioned that if Bennet Knight were to ask her out she would say yes."

Donovan had no reaction to the deduction. "Puts up a decent fight?"

Carter draped her crossed ankles on Link's fallen seat. "I helped her out of a conflict with Zac Warren. She was doing surprisingly all right for herself before I intervened and popped his shoulder out of its socket."

Donovan nodded and dropped his head, fighting back a smile.

Chapter 7

Jumbled conversations buzzed around Carter as she sat in a booth at the deli. Homework conquered her table, a battlefield of books and papers. The complexity of calculus halted as a cookie plopped down onto her textbook, dusting it with golden crumbs. Blinking herself out of the trench of mathematics, Carter straightened, arching her back.

"Sorry, girly," Maggie said, sliding into the seat across from her. "Big rush, couldn't get away. Now I am all yours."

Maggie's brown hair had fallen loose from its ponytail and a smudge of mustard dotted her cheek. Picking up the cookie, Carter eased back into the booth.

"What do you want to do tonight?" Maggie asked, tidying up Carter's mass of notes.

Carter broke her cookie in two and shrugged.

"How about, since it's just us girls, we do something fun?"

With a chunk halfway to her mouth, Carter hesitated. "Dare I ask what your version of fun entails?"

"Oh, you know," Maggie said, waving a careless hand. "Painting each other's nails, braiding our hair, watching a fun romantic movie."

"Remind me how long you have known me?" Carter said.

Maggie laughed, erasing the strains of work on her face. "Well, I thought this would be something I could do because I haven't the faintest clue how to clean a gun or assemble a bomb."

Carter let out a derisive snort. "Please, like my father taught me how to assemble a bomb." A wide grin covered her face. "I learned that online."

"Very amusing. But how about just a romantic movie then?"

With a groan, Carter dropped her head back. "Those things are terrible! The girl characters are weak and pathetic. They rely completely on the male to do everything and don't even try to protect themselves."

A twinkle came into Maggie's eyes. "And is that why I came over the other day to find you had fallen asleep to one of those stupid movies?"

Glowering, Carter crossed her arms. "Yes, I was not watching it. It merely came on after I fell asleep."

Lips squeezed together like she was keeping a secret, Maggie nodded. "Of course. It's not because, although you deny it, you still have some girl in you."

Carter lifted her chin. "I will neither confirm nor deny that statement."

"Fair enough," Maggie said. "We can decide what to do later. Now tell me how was school? Are you still talking to those two transfer students or did you scare them off?"

As Carter finished off the last of her cookie, she frowned. "Surprisingly, they sat with me again. There is something about them that's...puzzling. I don't know what it is but I will figure it out. The fact that they are still hanging out with me leads me to believe they enjoy pain."

Maggie slapped Carter's arm. "You should be nice. They probably just see how wonderful of a person you are."

"To that, I will refer to my previous question: how long have you known me?"

Maggie softened with memories. "Long enough to know that you are fiercely protective of your father and love him more than anything in this world. That kind of girl still has a heart."

"Or part of one, at least," Carter said.

"Maybe they can help you find the other half," Maggie teased.

Carter wiped the crumbs off her fingers like she was trying to discard a bad dream. "No need. We all know it left four years ago in a taxi."

The glimmer of playfulness in Maggie's countenance fell away, leaving behind something sober and sympathetic as she laid a hand on top of Carter's.

"Hon, you know…"

Carter balled her fingers and Maggie retracted her hand.

"A movie sounds fine for tonight," Carter said. "You choose. I don't care."

Maggie nodded, her smile sad. A bright chime from the bell floated over the deli and Carter glanced at the entrance before ducking her head, grateful for the new arrivals.

"You have customers," she said. "And I should finish this."

As Maggie exited the booth, Carter picked up her pencil and fell back into the world of calculus. Among the difficulty of numbers, she could suppress her memories. A few minutes later her phone rang, yanking her out of her work. A smile spread across her face as she saw the name on the screen.

"Hello," she answered.

There was no response on the other end, only the faint sound of someone breathing. Carter turned to stone as fear coiled in her chest, panic crashing over her. She gripped the phone.

"Listen," she said, her voice hard as steel. "Whoever you are, if your name isn't Steve and you don't have a daughter named Carter, then the only thing you should say next is you just happened to find this phone. Because I swear if you say my father-"

"Carter, how were you planning to end that sentence?" her father asked.

Relief washed over her like a bucket of cold water. She went limp, the tension and panic escaping her body in one quick moment. Shaking, she buried her face in her hand.

"Captain," she breathed out.

"Sarge, are you alright?"

Taking in a deep breath, Carter raised her head. "Of course, I'm fine. Why didn't you say anything when I answered?" she asked, struggling to keep fear out of her voice.

"I didn't hear you. I was still waiting for you to pick up."

"Right. Okay."

"You sure you're all right?"

Carter laughed, though she knew it came across as forced. "I'm fine."

"So you threaten everyone who doesn't answer right away?"

Her smile returned. "Only the ones I like."

"Okay, How was school?"

"Fine. I managed not to punch five people."

A laughing sigh whistled across the line. "Carter, I would hope that you would manage to not even come close to punching five people."

Even though she knew he couldn't see her, she made an apologetic face. "Would it help if I said they started it?"

"No."

"Well, then I will strive to do better next time. How's

the trip going so far?"

"As well as expected. We are dealing with…"

Sinking back into the booth, Carter let out a quiet breath, resting in the comforting rhythm of her father's voice.

Chapter 8

Outside of the National Museum of American History, Carter laid stretched out over three steps, sunglasses on and hands stuffed into her coat pockets. The conversations of her classmates clashed with the rushing of cars nearby. Carter knew they stared at her in bemusement but she didn't care. In her coat, her phone buzzed and she answered it.

"Hello," she said, blandly.

"Sarge, did I wake you?" her father asked.

"Yes."

"Carter, you're supposed to be at school."

Carter fought against a smile. "Dang, I knew there was some reason I set an alarm. It's too late to do anything about it now. I'll just skip today I guess. It's not like I actually learn anything there."

"Sarge, get out of bed. Now," her father said, his voice firm.

A bubble of laughter bounced around Carter's stomach.

"Calm down, Captain. I'm not actually in bed. I'm at

the National Museum of American History."

"Why are you there?"

"I'm protesting the government letting idiots voice their opinion on the internet."

"Carter."

Despite the reprimand, Carter heard the hint of amusement.

"I'm on a field trip with my history class," she said.

"Did I sign off on this?"

"Yup, right after you signed over all the bank accounts to me."

"Carter-"

"You should really read the fine print. And if you're calling to let me know you're not coming home today, then you should expect to have to pick the front door lock when you get back, because I will have changed it."

Her father chuckled softly making Carter lose her battle against her smile.

"I'll be home tonight. You don't need to change the locks just yet."

Carter felt the constant knot in her chest relax. "Should I expect you coming home in a car or dropped out of a helicopter?"

"Car. If I'm pressed for time: helicopter."

"Okay, I'll see you tonight. Unless I get bludgeoned with my own sign by the idiots of America."

"If you can't defend yourself against a couple of idiots, then maybe you deserve to die," her father said.

"Very true. See you later, Captain."

"Love you, Sarge."

Carter savored the words, storing them away. "Love you too."

After pocketing her phone, she returned to ignoring the world and the odd looks from her peers. A chill breeze brushed her face, carrying with it the hint of a familiar cologne. Footsteps approached her and she smirked.

"You do realize that if you keep hanging out with me

people will assume we're friends," she said, without opening her eyes.

"The thought did cross my mind," Link said, sitting down beside her. "How did you know it was-"

"You always smell like soap and Donovan wears a subtle but distinctive cologne," Carter said.

Donovan took a seat next to Link, saying nothing. Which was no surprise to Carter. In the week she'd interacted with the pair she wasn't sure he'd said more than a hundred words. Squinting against the glare of the white steps, Link eyed Carter's strange position.

"Why are you laying like that? It looks uncomfortable," he said.

"This is nothing. Trying sleeping on a rock ledge."

"Favorite pastime?"

"My father's idea of a fun outing. Before the rock ledge, there was a twelve-mile hike with a pack that weighed as much as me. Let's just say I've learned to adjust to uncomfortable situations."

Link opened his mouth to respond, but Mr. Philips cleared his throat, clipboard in hand.

"Everyone should be here now," their History teacher said. "I'm going to take roll and then we will move inside."

As he listed off names, shouts of 'here' were echoed back.

"Lucas Benton?"

"Here," a mocking tone said.

Carter grimaced. "I hate when our classes are combined."

Link nodded vaguely.

"Link Evans?"

He raised his hand. "Here."

Talking over whispered conversations, Mr. Philips continued down the roll.

"Amy Howe?"

"Here," a sweet feminine voice said.

Link swiveled his head around, searching for the

source.

"Donovan Keller?"

"Here," Donovan said, his deep voice carrying over the hum of chatter.

"Do you feel that?" Carter asked.

Both Donovan and Link focused on her, Link furrowing his brow.

"Feel what?" he asked.

"Fifty sets of female eyes shifting to Donovan," Carter said.

Link started to laugh but choked off abruptly. "How could you possibly know that?" he asked, astonished. "You weren't even looking."

"Because in a school where they've grown up with most of the guys in our class, Donovan is new and intriguing," she said. "And we're in open territory. I predict after the roll is finished some girl will come say hi. They will also leave crushed when Donovan gives them his signature blank stare."

Link grinned but tried to hide it when Donovan stared at him.

"Carter Owens?"

"Present in body but not in mind or spirit," she said.

"Understood," Mr. Philips said, before going onto the next name.

As the final 'here' was given, their teacher called for everyone's attention. "Alright," he said. "We are going to take a guided tour of the museum. Stay with the group. If you are found wandering off, you immediately get an F on your essay. Is that understood?" As he scanned the collection, students bobbed their heads and muttered assent. "Okay, let's go. Stay together."

Waving everyone forward, he led the way up the steps to the museum. The mass of students surged forward, clusters branching off and finding safety in their packs. Carter stood and carelessly brushed herself off. The trio barely made it a foot before three girls circled Donovan, herding him up the stairs.

"We've heard about a million rumors about you," one of them said. "We want to know which ones are true."

Carter laughed at the strain around Donovan's mouth. "Should we save him before he's mauled?"

"Nah, he's tougher than he looks," Link said.

Leaving Donovan to find a way to fend for himself, Carter and Link fell in behind the group. Carter paused at the appearance of a black SUV stopping at the curb. As doors opened, five men in black suits with earpieces filed out.

"Who-" Link started to say.

"Apparently Mason is coming on this little field trip," Carter answered.

In confirmation, Mason hopped down from the first car and the men created a barrier around him. As the group ascended, Carter brightened seeing an agent on the side with a shaved head and skin a few shades darker than Carter's. Carter fell into step beside the agent, Link trailing next to her.

"Hey, Curtis," she said. "Who did you piss off to get stuck on babysitting duty?"

The tall, muscular man grinned at Carter. "Pleasure seeing you as always, Carter."

Curtis's attention snagged on Link, surprise flickered across his face. Noticing, Carter jabbed a thumb towards Link.

"This is Link," she said. "No threat there."

As if to further this statement, Link waved cheerily. Curtis nodded to him, a hint of puzzlement lingering in his gaze.

"Are you doing the training course this Saturday?" Carter said.

"Anderson still mad you got the drop on him?" Curtis asked, amusement wiping away his previous thoughts.

Carter shook her head, exasperated. "You would think he would understand I have almost as much training as he does."

"I'll be there."

Carter eyed the circle of agents, then Mason. "There's not that many of you here. Is this trip really secure for Wonder Boy? He might open his mouth and someone will want to shoot him."

Curtis chuckled. "Don't worry, the museum is closed to the public. And if anything happens, we know where there's a secure location to take him."

Carter thought it over for half a second. "The basement level air-controlled rooms where they store the vulnerable artifacts, am I right?"

Curtis shook his head, impressed. "Sometimes it's alarming how much you know."

"Steve's daughter, remember?"

"Of course. Is Steve home yet?"

"No, but he should be tonight. If he's not, I'll kill him."

"I have no doubt."

The noise of the busy street vanished as they passed through the museum's entrance. The main atrium expanded on all sides, showcasing three floors of balconies. The murmur of student voices and the scuffing of shoes on tile resounded through the space. As they followed the rest of the class, Mason turned to Carter, his smile dripping smugness.

"Owens, it's cute how you're trying to get to me through my agent but it won't work," he said.

She trailed her eyes up and down, her expression bored. "Careful Mason, your ego is showing," she said. "Remember, you're in public. If your future constituents hear you, they might realize that you are a narcissist."

"I thought that was a prerequisite for being a politician?" Mason said, winking.

"Only if you hide it, which you're not."

Curtis nudged Carter. "Maybe for safety's sake you should walk further up?" She raised a skeptical eyebrow. "I'm saying this for his sake. You should walk further up."

With a resigned eye roll, Carter sent Curtis a final

grin. "See you Saturday," she said, walking backward. "Try not to strangle him when he gets annoying. I hear you don't get a good reference letter when that happens."

Curtis saluted her. When Carter spun back around, Link edged closer.

"Do you know everyone?" he asked, glancing back at the barrier of Secret Service agents.

Carter shrugged and took in the pieces of history frozen in time. "Kind of. I do training courses with my dad and his buddies."

"Another fun outing your dad chose?"

"No, this is a favorite pastime of mine."

Donovan appeared, a slight frown marring his features. At the crack in his mask, Carter regarded the crowd of students.

"Did you kill the three girls and stash their bodies in that closet?" she asked. "Because they do eventually find those things." Donovan schooled his expression back into impassivity. She held up her hands like he was arguing. "Just asking."

***

The tour guide's flow of facts filled the room, only half of it being absorbed. Carter made a slow circle, from one display case to the next. Halfway around the room, she looked away from the first Apple computer to the entrance and paused. A beefy man in a janitor's jumpsuit approached Mr. Philips and shook his hand. Oblivious, Link bumped into Carter.

"What is it?" he asked, following Carter's line of sight.

Still staring at Mr. Philips, Carter waved her hand in a dismissive gesture.

"Nothing," she said. "Mr. Philips is just talking to a former military soldier."

Confused, Link scowled at her. "How-"

"See those scars at the base of his neck?" Small inch scars ran along the man's skin down to his shirt collar. Link nodded slowly. "It's from shrapnel."

After a second, she continued her study of the artifacts.

"Alright," the tour guide said, "let's move on."

As the group entered the next section of the museum, Carter branched off, leaning over the glass cases. Link and Donovan joined her, their level of interest in what the tour guide said about the same as hers. Link jumped between reading the plaques to tracking Amy through the crowd. After he searched for her for the eighth time, Carter rounded on him.

"Just go talk to her," she said.

Startled, Link blinked at her. "What are you talking about?"

Carter glared at him. "You would think a week would be long enough for you to stop asking dumb questions."

Letting out a shaky, embarrassed laugh, Link ducked his head and adjusted his glasses. "Right." He found Amy again but made no sign of going to her.

"It went well helping her with a couple of calculus questions, didn't it?" Carter asked. Link agreed. "Then go talk to her."

Link fidgeted but didn't move.

"Link, if you don't go talk to her right now I will punch you. And I should remind you, I punch like a girl. A girl trained by a Navy SEAL."

When he lifted his head, she held up a fist. Hastily brushing off his jacket, he stumbled over to Amy. Donovan stood beside Carter, his hands stuffed into his pockets, watching Link go. The tour guide droned on, the prattle of information ringing off the stone walls and only heard by a few eager students.

"I still don't understand why you two are hanging out with me," Carter said, giving him a sideways glance.

"You understand I'm a social pariah, right?"

She spoke but didn't really expect an answer, this was Donovan after all. Mr. Walking Statue.

"Of your own making," he replied.

"What makes you say that? I could simply be misunderstood."

"You talk too much to be misunderstood."

Carter spread her arms out. "Then I'm an open book and people reject me for who I am."

Before she had even finished her sentence, Donovan shook his head. "You're too blunt for people to get close to knowing you."

She studied him, the cogs of her mind whirring, curious that when he finally spoke, it was to argue with her. He held her gaze; a cool, intelligence in his eyes. Finally, she broke away. A cluster of girls moved across their path, admiring looks sticking to Donovan.

"Well, maybe I'm too blunt," Carter said. "But that hasn't stopped either of you from hanging out with me. Bringing me back to the fact: you realize associating with me will damage your prospects of friends." She paused. "Okay, it wouldn't affect you but it will affect Link."

"What makes you say that?"

Carter gestured to Donovan's body. "Your good looks, athletic physique, and impassive, moody exterior will draw girls to you. Apparently, they find it irresistible."

The corner of Donovan's mouth twitched. "I'm moody?"

"You come off seeming moody. Which is not the same."

"You don't believe I'm moody?"

Facing him, she laughed, causing the classmates closest to them to exchange odd looks, which Carter ignored.

"I know you're not moody," she said. "You're too in control of your emotions. It's part of the persona you are conveying."

Though he finally faced her, he betrayed nothing of

how he felt about her deduction. "I convey a moody persona?"

"No," she said, pointing at him. "You convey a persona of being uninterested, in control, and better than everyone else. Moody, to the unintelligent observer. The first part is faked, the other two are real."

"What makes you think that?" he asked, evenly.

"I've studied people long enough to know when they are faking it, putting on false personalities. Seriously, I go to high school with politician's kids."

Donovan gave no reaction. "Carter, did it ever occur to you that I'm a shy person and I'm not comfortable talking to people I don't know?" he asked.

"Not even for the tiniest of seconds."

"Why not?"

"The majority of shy people struggle with reading social cues and have low self-esteem. You have neither."

"Maybe I'm introverted then."

Carter pointed at him, relieved she found a crack in the armor. "You didn't say introverted, you said shy. Which you could be, but something about your persona isn't real." She cocked her head. "Which leads me to believe you are hiding something."

"Do you have this feeling about everyone else, or just me?"

"Oh, everyone is hiding something. What, is usually easy for me to see. With you, it's not." Carter took a step towards him, challenging. "What are you hiding, Donovan Keller?"

He stared her down, his blue eyes battling hers. "Why do you force away friendships, Carter Owens?"

They remained that way, eyes locked. The tour guide called for the group to continue on and the room began to empty. Link made his way over to them and paused.

"What did I miss?" he asked.

The tension vanished as Donovan broke away.

"Nothing," he said. "We should move on."

***

Carter slammed her fist into the punching bag, sending it swaying. Sweat beaded on her forehead and ran down her temples. Music blared through the apartment, keeping time with her heartbeat. Outside the sky was a wash of darkness, lights from the neighboring buildings shining into the night. She spun and brought her leg up, kicking the taut leather. As the bag came back towards her, she hit it again.

The front door opened and closed but Carter barely registered it. A second later, her bedroom door swung open and her father stepped inside. At the sight of Carter in her uniform pounding away at the punching bag, he smiled. He shut off her music, the walls still vibrating with the last beats. Carter didn't acknowledge him, her features screwed into tight concentration. Pulling out a chair, her father sat down, resting his laced fingers on his stomach.

"How was school?" he asked.

Carter twisted around and slammed her elbow into the bag.

"Interesting," her father said. "Do you want to talk about it?"

The response was a quick 1- 2 punch to the worn material.

"Feet closer together. Swing from your core, not your shoulder."

Carter made the adjustments and hit the bag again.

"It's about a boy," her father said. "That's a new one."

Rounding on him, Carter set her hands on her hips. Strands of hair fell into her face, which she ignored.

"How do you know that?" she asked.

"You forget who taught you to read people. And the fact that I've been reading you your whole life." Carter knitted her eyebrows together. "Your form is sloppy and your punches lack concentration. Your mind is not in this. Do you want to talk about it?"

Carter ripped off her gloves and threw them on the bed. "How do you trust someone you know is lying to you?"

As her father's forehead wrinkled, he leaned forward over his knees. "Are they lying or withholding information?"

Carter tossed up her hands. "Is there a difference?"

"Yes, someone might withhold information about their past or who they are to protect themselves. That doesn't necessarily mean they're lying. You sense the withheld information and take it as lying."

"But how is it *not* lying?"

Her father gave her a straight forward gaze. "Sarge, have you told these people about your mother?"

Carter froze, curling her fingers into tight fists. "No."

Her father raised an eyebrow. "Why not?"

Sinking onto the bed, she swept her hair away from her face.

"In order to gain trust, you have to be willing to give it first."

She nodded solemnly. Softening, her father sat back in her chair.

"Now," he said. "What did I miss?"

A smile crept onto Carter's face as her eyes held a flicker of surprise and disbelief. "I think I made friends."

Chapter 9

S arge."

Carter rolled over in her bed, facing the doorway. She winced at the light where her father stood outlined in the door frame. Moaning, she twisted away. Her father crossed to her bed and shook her shoulder.

"Sarge."

Shrugging off his arm, Carter buried her face in her pillow. "Don't you know you're supposed to knock before coming in?" her voice muffled. "That way I have enough time to kick the Marine out of my bed, so he can be half-dressed and out the window by the time you catch him."

"Why do you think I don't knock?"

Carter peered blearily up at him. "So you're saying kick him out of my bed in the middle of the night? Got it." She sank back into her blankets. "Now, what do you want, old man? I thought we were celebrating your homecoming by sleeping in."

Her father glanced at the clock.

"We did," he said. "It's 6:30."

"I've changed my mind. I'm not happy you're home."

"Understood. Now get up. We're going for a run."

Carter gripped the blankets tighter, cocooning herself. "Have fun. Let me know when you get back. We can hang out or something."

With one strong yank, her father tore the blankets from her hold. A chill swept over Carter and she curled into a ball. Her father took hold of her arm. On reflex, she shot her leg out but hit only air. She brought her free arm around, her hand forming a fist as she swung at her father's face. He easily deflected the blow and hauled her out of the bed. Struggling, she flailed her arms and legs. He dropped her and she hit the worn carpeted floor.

"Are you up?" he asked.

Jumping up, Carter grabbed her crumpled blankets and scrambled into her bed. Without a word, her father left the room. She snuggled down into the warmth. A second later her father's footsteps echoed in the hallway, along with the sound of water sloshing in a pot. Carter twisted around as he entered her room. Adrenaline shot through her and she jumped out of bed. Her father smiled.

"You're up. How about a run?" he asked.

Glaring, she shoved him out the door.

"I'll be ready in five. Child protective services will be here in ten."

"Just enough time for us to slip out before they get here."

Spinning around, Carter kicked the door shut in his grinning face. Two minutes later, she emerged from her room, dressed and hair pulled back. Her father stood in the living room, stretching. After gulping down a glass of green power shake, Carter groaned and joined him. Her sleepy muscles protested.

"How do you feel about running to the Capital today?" her father asked, rolling his shoulders.

"As long as it means you bust an ankle on the steps, sounds great," she grumbled.

"I'll take that as a yes. You ready?"

As she straightened, she nodded. "I set the pace this time."

As they stepped out into the morning air, the crisp cold sent goosebumps racing over their arms. Light peeked on the horizon as mist blanketed the world. They descended the metal staircase and headed towards the road, the quiet of the neighborhood thick around them. Carter grinned up at her father.

"Try to keep up, old man," she said, taking off running.

Chuckling, her father fell into step beside her.

***

As Carter exited her room, she combed her fingers through her damp hair, before tying it into a ponytail. The sound of the shower running filled the small apartment. She headed to the living room but paused. Down the hall, her father's bedroom door lay open.

Backtracking, she walked to the doorway, freezing. Before her lay a simple double bed, made with military neatness, bare walls, and a desk covered in tidy stacks of paper with a lone picture frame.

After a second's hesitation, Carter crossed to the desk. Without disturbing the rest of the items there, she lifted the photograph. A family of three smiled up at her. Her father's arms were wrapped around the ten-year-old version of herself. Her mother wore a wide smile and rested against her husband, her hair windblown. Carter gripped the frame.

"I remember that day," her father said, behind her. "It was perfect."

Forcing her fingers to relax, Carter set the frame

down. "Sure."

Spotting a nearby stack of photos, she picked up the top one, studying it.

"What is this?" she asked.

The picture held a close up image of part of a face. She held it closer, something familiar about it. Her father peered over her shoulder.

"That's President Douglas," he said, moving away.

"Care to explain why you feel the need to have close up images of his face?" she asked, perusing the stack and finding more images of the President's features.

"With plastic surgery being what it is today, it's possible for people to alter their face to match the President's. They could possibly try to make a switch. It's very unlikely, but we prepare for everything. The photos are of details that could not be copied. Like the freckles in his eyes, which is a family trait, or his birthmark."

"Interesting."

"You ready?" her father asked.

"Yeah," she said, setting down the stack and following him out of his room. "You made me run twelve miles on barely any food. Child services will be hearing about this."

"Is that so?" her father said, opening the front door.

"They'll add it to the list of abuses." She faced him as he locked up. "Don't you know that you're not supposed to drop your kid on the floor?"

Her father donned a thoughtful expression. "That wasn't in the rule book."

Though the sun had woken up the world, their neighborhood remained in stasis, except for the occasional bark of a dog or rushing of a car.

"You're not supposed to raise a kid by reading a military training manual," Carter said.

"Really?" Her father grinned. "I thought it was turning out well."

"Is this your subtle way of telling me you raised me

to be an assassin? Because I'm fine with that."

"I was going for a girl able to protect herself but assassin works just as well."

As they walked out of the lane, her father draped an arm around her shoulders. Carter elbowed him in the ribs, making him chuckle. They headed for the deli, the sun giving off what little warmth it could. The bell rang overhead and Maggie glanced up from the crossword on the counter. A welcoming smile cut across her face, brightening her eyes.

"You two hungry?" she asked, laying aside her pencil.

Folding her arms, Carter slipped free of her father's embrace.

"Starved doesn't begin to describe my current state," she said. "This morning was filled with far more abuse than I believe I should be put through. Captain here made me run twelve miles on only a power shake."

Maggie winked at her before her gaze eased to Carter's father. "I guess that calls for lots of food then. How was your run?"

Staring up at her father, Carter smiled smugly. "Do you want to tell her how I completely destroyed you, or shall I?"

Appearing unruffled, he crossed his arms.

"It went well," he said.

"He doesn't want to admit to the fact that he is starting to weaken in his advanced years," Carter said.

Her father rested a hand on her shoulder and gave it a light squeeze.

"How about this, Sarge," he said. "When you're thirty-nine, I will get an eighteen-year-old to run with you."

Carter scoffed. "Please, you've let yourself go, Captain. I don't plan on making the same mistake."

Hooking his arm around Carter's neck, her father rubbed his hand over her hair. In retaliation, she jabbed her elbow into his side and spun out of his grip. Hair fell in front of her face as she lowered to a crouch, fists raised, eyes taunting.

"You think you're fast enough, old man?" she asked.

Before Carter could act on her words, Maggie took up a position between the two of them.

"Did you want food or not?" she asked.

Carter rose and carelessly brushed away her hair.

"I see what's going on," she said, pointing between her father and Maggie. "You didn't want to see him humiliated."

Shaking her head in amusement, Maggie returned to her food preparations.

"I'll have food ready in a few minutes," she called out.

Carter's father spun her around and directed her to a booth. "Maybe next time, Sarge."

"Sure," she mocked. "You just didn't want to embarrass yourself in front of Maggie."

She slid into the booth, her father taking the opposite side.

"Don't worry," she said, giving him a wide smile. "I'm sure she'll still like you. Though maybe think a little less of you."

"We're not discussing this."

"We're not discussing anything. I'm stating the obvious."

***

"Sarge, did you get that?" her father asked.

Carter stood in a huddled group with seven men, all three times her size and a head taller than her. They crouched inside a wide room, on a lot covered with empty houses. The walls were riddled with cracks and the paint fell away from the walls. The smell of decay lingered in the air from the grimy floorboards. Carter didn't want to be anywhere else.

"Sorry, Captain, I wasn't paying attention," she said, grinning.

Chuckles rippled through the group of men as her father frowned.

"Joking," she said. "You act like I haven't done this a million and one times."

She released the clip to her pistol and checked the paintballs. After she reloaded it, she cocked the gun, each motion smooth. "I scout out ahead of the group. Locate where the enemy is holding the hostages. Then when you are all in position, we breach the house."

Curtis laid a hand on Carter's father's shoulder."Were you planning to tell us that when you leave the service Carter is taking your place?"

Carter laughed along with the men, happy to be one of them.

"Now that I'm convinced you were paying attention, we can move out," her father said. He surveyed the men. "Blue team: move to the East quadrant. Red Team: North. Green Team: South. I'll take West. Sarge, comm in when you have the location. Let's move out."

The group split off into pairs and dispersed. Carter cut across the living room to the kitchen, attaching a suppressor to her gun as she went. She breathed in the smell of must, feeling completely relaxed. She nimbly cut a path to the back door, avoiding the shards of faded blue tile that dotted the floor. Easing the back door open, she slipped from the house.

A weedy backyard lay before her. With a quick glance, she jogged across the yard. The metal of the link fence was icy as she grabbed the top and vaulted over it. She dropped to a crouch when she hit the dirt, dust coating her boots. Moving to the edge of the alley, she sidled along the houses, keeping her eyes open for movement, her gun half raised. She lifted her wrist and whispered into her comm set.

"Hey, Curtis, how did babysitting go?" she said.

Static crackled in her ear and a second later Curtis's deep voice came through clear. "You know I don't talk about the people I work for," he said, a smile in his voice.

She peered around the corner of a house, noting the crouched figures of her fellow team members. "That's because if you did, Hamel's innocent ears wouldn't be able to take it."

Faint snippets of laughter rang in her ears. Before Hamel had the chance to retaliate, Carter's father spoke.

"Enough chit-chat. Stay focused. Sarge, head for the red two-story, a block North. I saw movement," he said.

"Copy that," Carter said.

She squeezed her gun and quickened her pace. With practiced ease, she navigated her way through the maze of faded houses, run-down backyards, and narrow alleys. Growing closer to the red house, she slowed, approaching it with cautious steps. Tucked into an alley across from her target, she kneeled to the ground and scanned the windows.

"I'm in position," she said.

Static. Then her father's voice. "See anything?"

"Negative. Holding."

For a long moment, nothing within the house moved. Then a shadow passed behind the blinds in one of the first story windows.

"We have movement," she said. "Checking perimeter now."

She slid out from the alley and moved to another one facing the back of the house. As she crouched checking the surroundings, a man in all black appeared. Without hesitating, she fired. The paintball exploded on the man's chest before he raised his weapon. The man looked at her with a set mouth.

"I've never liked you, Carter," he said.

She shrugged, indifferent. "Next time, Davis. Or not."

The man sat down, legs outstretched, and she walked past him, raising her wrist.

"One hostile eliminated," she said. "Affirmative, this

is our target."

"Good work, Sarge," her father said. "Teams fall in.

Hold at twenty yards. Sarge, we need the number of hostiles and their positions."

"On it."

Carter cleared the perimeter and stopped beside the house. She pressed her back against the chipping paint wall, splinters poking her spine. Inside her chest, her heart pounded. Her fingers tingled with a familiar rush of adrenaline. She crept along the house, spying in through cracks and gaps in the blinds.

"I have six hostiles on the bottom floor," she whispered.

"Good. Red team, give me information on the second floor," her father said.

Static filled her ear as she waited.

"We have three hostiles on the top floor in the South room, along with two hostages," a gruff voice said.

"Alright. Sarge, can you gain access to the second floor?"

Carter looked up, searching for an access point. Peeking around the corner, she scanned the wall.

"Drainpipe on the North side of the house," she said. "Farthest from the current location of the hostiles."

"Okay, climb it. Blue team, get into position and lay down cover," her father said.

Blue team voiced that they were in position, "Carter, we got your six."

"Copy that." Carter inched toward the drainpipe, straining to hear shouts of alarm. Unnoticed, she gripped the thin metal brackets. Achingly slow, she climbed, aware of every squeak and protest the pipe let out.

"Blue team, am I clear to enter?" she asked.

"Affirmative," Curtis said.

She eased the window open, flecks of paint sticking to her palm. Gripping the side of the window, she tucked her leg over the lip and pulled the rest of her body inside. She dropped to the floor, landing on the balls of her feet.

She crouched in an empty bedroom with faded green walls, the odor of mold tickling her nose.

"I'm in," she said.

"Get into position and when I give the order, take down the hostiles," her father said.

"Affirmative. Moving into position now."

At the door, she gently turned the knob, cracking it an inch. The hallway beyond was empty. She widened the gap and checked both ends. Breathing out, she stepped into the corridor. The floorboards shifted under her weight but made no noise.

Heart hammering and body coursing with energy, she made her way to the hostiles' location. Outside the room, she held her position, gun at the ready. Her voice barely made a sound as she relayed that she was in position.

"On my mark, we breach," her father said.

She took in a deep breath and edged towards the door handle. Holstering her gun, she pulled out a small canister from her pocket and put one hand on the door.

"Now!"

Carter kicked the door open, yanked the pin out of the canister and sent it tumbling into the room. She swung away as a flash of white light burst in the room and an explosive bang rang out. As she darted into the room, she whipped out her gun. With three quick pulls, she shot the hostiles, red paint splattering their chests.

Below her, she heard the sound of footsteps thundering on fractured floorboards and the ringing of shots. The three men before her let loose angry strings of curses as they blinked the spots of white from their eyes. Boots pounded outside the room and a second later her father appeared, followed by Curtis. Her father jostled her shoulders affectionately.

"Well done, Sarge," he said. "Hostiles neutralized and the hostages are alive."

She nudged him in the ribs as the rest of the team filed into the room.

"Sometimes I wonder how you do your job without

me," she said, grinning, feeling that every second of loneliness at school was worth it for a moment like this.

The men laughed. Carter threw her fist into the air. "Beers are on me!"

Chapter 10

Is this normal for you?" Link asked Carter. "Finishing the project halfway through the period?"

Mutterings and hushed arguments of students crowded the room, the worst of them bringing Mr. Rojas's assistance. At the table opposite, green liquid spilled over the rim of a beaker, filling the air with an acrid stench.

"Pretty much," Carter said.

"What do you do then?" Link asked.

"Sometimes I do other homework assignments. Mostly, I just watch everyone else and laugh."

"Why?"

The answer seemed obvious, student dynamics, especially in stressful situations, amused her.

"See those two?" she asked, pointing to a pair of students across the way.

When Link found them, he responded in the affirmative.

"She is taking this class to bump up her college application," Carter explained. "He is taking it because his parents signed him up for it. They have the best interactions. Watch."

They studied the pair in silence. A few minutes later the boy knocked something over and the girl rounded on him, glowering.

"Randy!" she shouted. "For once in your pathetic existence can you please try to do something right?!"

"If I did, would you make out with me?" Randy asked.

With a threatening glare, the girl returned to the experiment.

"You are so immature. I can't believe I got stuck with you," she said.

Randy proceeded to examine the inside of an empty beaker.

"I see what you mean," Link said.

"One time, she told him he should apologize to the world for being alive."

"Do you know something about everyone?"

"Mostly, yeah."

"Even the teachers?"

"Sure. They are even easier to read than the students." Carter jerked her head to the front of the class. "Mr. Rojas has taken up running in the last four weeks."

"How can you possibly know that?"

"I've been in this class for more than six months. He's lost about 10 lbs, you can see it in the way his shirts are too baggy for him."

"Okay, what else?" Link said, his interest piqued. "What about our PE teacher, Mr. Danes?"

"He is recently divorced and sees his kid on Wednesday nights."

"How do-"

Carter raised her hand, wiggling her fingers. "He still has a tan line from his wedding ring. We have a James in our class which every Thursday he calls Jamie. I'm guessing that is the nickname for his son."

Pulled into her knowledge, Link leaned forward.

Carter found it strange how something that managed to annoy so many of her peers made Link like her more.

"Mr. Philips?" he asked.

"He used to be in politics, even worked on a few senator's campaigns. Something happened though. I think he was blackballed."

"Why do you think that?"

"In the back of his room, he has multiple photos with prestigious politicians and he will talk in depth about modern campaign strategies. But he left working in politics abruptly a few years ago - none of the photos are dated more recently than five or six years back."

"The blackballed thing?"

"That is easy. Instead of bragging about his political connections, as most people would in his place, he avoids the subject entirely."

Impressed, Link nodded. "Interesting."

"Most people are when you try to learn their secrets."

At that, Link looked away, gazing out over the classroom. When Carter did the same but found nothing new to see, a thought struck her. "Want to see something more interesting than secrets?"

At the sight of Carter's devilish grin, Link drew back, hesitant.

"Why do I get the feeling that what you are about to do might end with someone's arm broken?"

A laugh tumbled out of Carter.

"Because you aren't as clueless as you look. And don't worry, not this time."

Without an explanation, Carter went over to the supply closet and collected a couple of ingredients. Back at the table, she deposited them before Link, who eyed them. Before she started working, Carter glanced at Mr. Rojas. He sat at his desk, head bent as he marked papers.

As Carter combined two powders and put them on a mesh square, Link watched her warily. Carter tossed Link a mischievous wink as she put the mesh on top of a metal tripod. When she reached for the Bunsen burner,

Link took a cautious step back.

"Should I duck and cover?" he asked, shying away.

Taking out a pair of sunglasses from her bag, Carter slipped them on.

"Not at all," she said, in a careless tone. "This won't hurt you a bit."

When she lit the Bunsen burner, blue flames flared into life, the heat of it warming Carter's skin. Still holding the Bunsen burner, she looked at Link.

"You might want to close your eyes though."

The warning made Link pale and Carter grin. As he cringed and snapped his eyes shut, Carter placed the flame underneath the tripod, burning the bottom of the mesh. For a breath, nothing happened. Then a flash of white light exploded inside the classroom. The room erupted with students crying out in shock and panic.

"What was that!"

"I can't see!"

"What happened?'

"Was it lightning?"

Using the moment of disorientation, Carter switched the burner off, swapped it with another student's, and replaced her sunglasses in her bag. She tapped Link on the shoulder and he pried one eye open. Seeing that everything was back to normal, he gazed around.

A smile appeared as he took in all the stunned and confused students. When Carter glanced back at Donovan, hoping to see some crack in his mask, she found him blinking his vision clear. As his eyes focused, they landed on her as if he already knew she had been the cause. She tipped an imaginary hat to him.

"How did you learn to do that?" Link asked.

"Easy, YouTube."

Mr. Rojas stepped into the middle of the classroom. Still working the stars from his eyes, he banged his leg on a table's edge on the way and grimaced.

"Everyone, calm down," he said. "It was just a mishap. Nothing to be alarmed about. Continue with your projects, you still have a few minutes left of class."

As Mr. Rojas finished talking, Carter swept away the last traces of evidence, leaving the table clear of her crime. Students turned back to their partners but no one returned to their work, their conversations filled with speculations. Massaging his bruised thigh, Mr. Rojas stopped at Carter's table.

"Ms. Owens."

"Mr. Rojas."

"If I touch your Bunsen burner, what will I find?"

"A cold Bunsen burner, I expect."

Cautious, Mr. Rojas held two fingers inches from the burner. After a second he tapped it, jerking back as if prepared to be burned. Upon discovering it cold, he frowned.

"Crazy what happens in chemistry sometimes," Carter said, with a mocking grin.

***

Just beyond the classroom doorway, Carter paused. When Link and Donovan trailed out, she fell into step beside them.

"You know, if you keep hanging out with us people will think we're friends," Link said, echoing her words.

"The thought did cross my mind," she replied.

Link shot her a teasing grin. As they rounded the corner towards history, an alarm blared through the school. The shrill siren beat against eardrums, making students wince. Half a second later, metal shutters slammed down over the windows. A girl shrieked. Voices reverberated off the walls, panic mounting as transfer students swirled around, shouting for answers.

Carter turned to explain the lockdown to Link and Donovan but found the space beside her deserted. Spinning around, she searched the sea of frantic students.

Above the alarm, the static of the intercom crackled to life.

"Students," Principal Withers said. "Please return to your homerooms in an orderly fashion. I repeat, return to your homerooms."

Ignoring the order, Carter ducked into the closest vacated classroom, but couldn't see either Link or Donovan. She caught the edge of a maroon blazer. Trying not to smile, she crossed to the back of the room and peered over the teacher's desk. Huddled on the floor were Link and Donovan.

"You know, I never pegged either of you as being the skittish type," she said. "Okay, I might have expected it from Link but not Donovan."

Though Link blushed, Donovan showed nothing at all. As usual. Carter pointed back towards the doorway. "Are we going to head back to homeroom or shall I join you down there? Who knows? It might improve my reputation to be found on the floor with the school's new hot guy."

Donovan worked his jaw in annoyance, which made Carter laugh. Any response from him felt like she'd won a battle.

"I'm not sure even that could improve your reputation," he said.

"Probably not. Come on. They have to make sure everyone is accounted for."

Looking embarrassed as well as pale, Link stood. "Does this happen often?"

"No, but it wouldn't surprise me if this is a test," Carter said, leading them back into a mostly empty hallway. "We have them every so often, you know, to check response time. How fast does the military show up."

"What?"

"You do realize the President's son goes here, right? The second the alarm goes off, an alert is sent to the military and they send out a response team. This is one of the most secure schools in the country."

"Oh," Link said.

The alarm still rang down corridors, urging even the most stubborn back to their classrooms. Carter glanced at her phone. "It's a good reaction time, even with the new students."

The chemistry room buzzed with excited chatter as speculations on what caused the alarm flew around. When Carter and Link took their seats, Link surveyed the other tables.

"He's not here," Carter said, reading his unspoken question.

"Who?"

"Mason."

"How do you know that?"

Carter gave him a mischievous grin. "I have my ways. Let's just say I know the second that alarm went off Smith grabbed Mason and took him to a secure location."

"You're not going to tell me where that is?" Link asked.

"Technically, I'm not even supposed to know. So...no, I'm not going to tell you. Just know that, unfortunately, he's safe."

***

When Carter, Link, and Donovan entered the cafeteria the noise felt doubled after the temporary lockdown. All anyone talked about was how the school felt eerie with the shutters down and the sight of the military checking the interior.

Before Link or Donovan could face the chaos of the lunch line, Carter offered a part of hers. Link snatched up Carter's bag of chips, breaking it open but stopped as Amy strolled past their table. He followed her path, the chips completely forgotten.

"She thinks you're cute," Carter said, snapping Link from his stunned state. "You should go have lunch with her."

Link blinked, coming back to himself. "What did you say?"

"Go eat with her."

Though Link stared at where Amy now sat with her friends, he shook his head, shrinking away from the thought. "No. I'm fine."

"Don't be stupid. Go sit with her. You like her, don't you?" Link shrugged unconvincingly. "You helped her with math homework and talked to her at the museum, you have your in. Go take it before the guy at the next table takes it."

Link straightened, scanning the neighboring tables to Amy's, trying to pick out the guy in question.

"Which one?" Link asked, still searching.

"Why should I tell you? It's not like it matters to you since you aren't going."

Past Link's shoulder, Carter saw Donovan press his lips together, trying to hide his amusement.

"Tell me who it is," Link said.

Carter held Link's gaze, opening her mouth as if to spill the truth but snapped her jaw shut and shook her head. "Nope, if you're not going to do anything about Amy, then he should at least get a chance. Who knows? It might be fun to watch him flirt with her. You know, hear how she laughs at his stupid jokes."

As Carter talked, Link wavered with indecision until he nodded to himself, his resolve solidifying. He stood abruptly but didn't move, eyes pinned on Amy.

"You might find simply saying 'hello' will go a long way," Carter said, encouragingly.

Awkwardly, Link climbed over the bench and headed towards Amy, faltering in his tracks once but finding the determination to go on. Carter and Donovan watched in silence as Link hovered behind Amy, then tapped her shoulder. When she smiled up at him, Link relaxed, a goofy grin sliding into place. Amy scooted over and Link managed to take the seat beside her without bumping her.

"Not a single guy at the table next to Amy's even looked over when she sat down," Donovan said.

"I know that and you know that, but Link doesn't need to know that," Carter said.

"Why, then?"

"I knew he would find it more painful to watch someone flirt with Amy then having to go over and talk to her."

Carter felt a moment of pride when Amy laughed and touched Link's arm, making him blush.

"Why help him at all?" Donovan asked.

Carter arched an eyebrow at him. "You mean because I'm such a cold-hearted person I couldn't possibly want to help someone else?"

When Donovan remained silent, Carter looked away. "I know I come off harsh and blunt but that doesn't mean I don't care." She felt Donovan study her profile. "Besides, Link has lived in the shadow of your good looks for so long he's forgotten that he's attractive in his own right. He just needed a push towards a girl who wasn't interested in you."

Across the way Link laughed, knocked something over and fumbled about. To her credit, Amy didn't act concerned, merely helped him.

"He's lucky to have you as a friend then," Donovan said.

Carter snorted. "Well, that has got to be a first."

Chapter 11

When Carter stepped out of the locker room, dressed in her gym uniform, weak sunlight washed over her. She welcomed the touch of warmth, tired of the cold. Around the track students stood together, waiting to get the class over with. Moving to one side, Carter stretched. As Mr. Danes blew his whistle to start class, Link and Donovan joined her.

"All right class!" Mr. Danes said, cutting through the conversations. "Today you are running a mile and then playing a friendly game of flag football."

The class let out a round of groans as if this wasn't what they'd done every Monday since the beginning of the year.

"Okay, get to it!"

Mr. Danes blew his whistle and the class sluggishly moved into action. Carter slapped Donovan's arm with the back of her hand and nodded to an eager group of girls.

"Might want to watch out," she said.

When Donovan followed Carter's line of sight to a

group of girls, they all smiled and waved at him. Carter couldn't fault them for their attraction, Donovan made gym clothes look appealing.

"Better get running," she said.

Breaking away from the trudging pack of students, Carter took off, the voices of her peers fading behind her. Around the track, the first glimpse of spring's arrival appeared in the blossoming trees and the dots of green peeking up through the deadened leaves, looking like hope.

Before long Carter lapped her classmates. She weaved in and out of the gossiping groups of girls. The boys all looked at her, some impressed, others dismissive. As she neared where Link and Donovan ran side by side, she slowed. She spun around and continued running backward.

"That's all you got?" she asked, looking Donovan up and down. "Based on your muscle tone I expected a better display of physical endurance."

A twitch in Donovan's jaw was the only response she got. For a boy made of stone, she took it as an accomplishment.

"Come on, Donovan," she said. "Scared for the first time in your life that a girl might actually be better than you?"

Donovan met her gaze with cool indifference.

"You only have to race me one lap."

Still, Donovan didn't look inclined to quicken his pace.

"All right, later slowpoke."

Spinning around, Carter increased her speed, outdistancing them. As she came around the curve she heard the sound of pounding footsteps racing up behind her. She laughed and pushed harder. Donovan inched closer to her. Carter forced her muscles to work faster, keeping ahead of him.

They cut through layers of dawdling groups, dodging around them. They were neck and neck as they came to the end of the lap. As they raced towards where they had started Donovan pulled ahead. They bolted over the starting line and staggered to a halt. Slightly breathless, Carter closed the distance between her and Donovan, grinning.

"I didn't think you had it in you," she said. "That's me wrong for once."

The barest hint of sweat formed on Donovan's forehead.

"I didn't think you would be able to keep up," he said, the first ever smile breaking across his face.

The smile transformed him from closed-off to friendly. It almost made him look human, Carter was shocked to admit.

"You wouldn't be the first male to think that," she said as she started walking again, Donovan beside her. "You know something, Donovan?"

Reverting to his usual state of being, Donovan looked at her but said nothing.

"You're kind of cute when you're flirting."

The tiniest flash of surprise darted across Donovan's face and Carter felt gratified. "Come on," she called back as she jogged away from him. "Link must be lonely."

Donovan caught up with her, hiding away his emotions once again. Carter glanced sideways at him and he met her gaze.

"Did you have fun?" Link asked in a bored tone as they reached him.

Carter slowed to match his pace, which was that of an elderly man.

"Yes," she said. "I've been curious to see if Donovan flirts and now I know. Totally worth losing the race for."

Link laughed and Donovan flexed his jaw.

***

By the time the shrill whistle punctured the air, Carter, Link and Donovan already sat on the field waiting as the rest of the students trickled in.

"I'm going to break you up into teams," Mr. Danes said.

"This should be interesting," Carter said.

With students having to be told twice which team they were on, the process was painfully slow. When the class was finally divided, Carter landed on the team opposite Donovan and Link.

"Be careful," she said, heading away from her companions.

"Why?" Link asked.

She pointed to Donovan. "I was talking to him. Mr. Danes might have said flag football but that doesn't mean some of these girls haven't been looking for the opportunity to tackle Donovan."

Link snorted at the image and Carter gave Donovan an encouraging salute. Though with her team she stood on the edge, blocked from conversations by walls of turned backs.

"I have finally put it together," a feminine voice said to Carter.

"I'm proud of you, Amber," Carter said, without looking over. "This shows promise for your future."

"Donovan," Amber went on as if Carter hadn't spoken. "Only sees you as one of the guys. Because looking at you," she eyed Carter pointedly, "no one could see a girl worth noticing."

"Like how when your father looks at you he sees disappointment instead of a daughter?"

Amber sucked in a breath and Carter didn't care. If she wanted to fight dirty, Carter would fight dirty. Over three years at Hamilton Prep had taught her that.

Amber took a step closer to Carter, finally garnering Carter's attention. "At least my father is still around while your mother saw you only as a mistake."

Anger flared inside Carter and she narrowed her eyes

at Amber. "I would step back if I were you," she said with deceptive calm.

At the furious glint in Carter's eyes, Amber swallowed and retreated. Carter stared out on the field, breathing out slowly, barricading herself against a torrent of memories. As if coming to her aid, Mr. Danes blew his whistle, calling the teams together. By the time Carter joined the lopsided huddle, she had her composure back.

As the huddles broke apart, the class fell into an awkward formation. Half the students seemed distracted by their friends while the other half played half-heartedly. When they set up for the last play, Carter crouched down facing Link, his team in possession of the ball.

"Hey, stranger," she said.

"You look familiar," Link said. "Have we met?"

When the ball was hiked, Link took off running, darting around Carter. She easily kept pace with him. The ball spiraled through the air and Link snagged it, sprinting for the end zone, Carter hot on his heels.

As she reached for the flag around his waist, she missed a step and crashed into him. They both tumbled to the ground, rolling over each other. When they eventually came to a stop Carter ended up on top of Link, both of them laughing. She pushed herself up and stared down at him. His glasses had come off and lay a few feet away.

Carter froze, her face inches from Link's. For the first time, she could clearly see his eyes. Trapped within the hazel color were brown freckles. With his features for once unobstructed by glasses, Carter saw a different face entirely. Images of a familiar, famous face flashed in her mind, making Link's features take on a whole new meaning.

A strong arm wrapped around her waist and hoisted her up.

"And you said I was the one who needed to watch out for girls tackling me," Donovan said.

Still locked in her realization, Carter reacted by instinct. She brought up her left elbow to hit Donovan but he blocked the move. She took hold of the hand wrapped around her waist and spun out of his hold, twisting his arm. Donovan countered the move and in a split second had her in a lock. Carter felt her heart ram against her chest, recognizing the move. A defensive military move.

Donovan released her and they both took a step back. Everything fell into place. All the puzzle pieces Carter knew she missed, she now had. All the interactions and stories that didn't fit together all made sense. How she hadn't seen it before shocked her. Link retrieved his glasses and slid them on.

"You all right, Carter?" he asked.

"Of course, fine. Sorry about tackling you," she said, reeling.

Link winked at her. "It's not the first time some girl has used that tactic to get close to me."

Carter forced a smile and Mr. Danes blew the whistle.

"Class is dismissed for today. Go change," he said.

The class let out sighs of relief as they headed towards the locker rooms. Carter jogged ahead of the group. Link looked to Donovan but Donovan watched Carter disappear inside, frowning.

Girls had barely started taking off their uniforms by the time Carter finished changing. Slamming her locker closed, she rushed out of the locker room. Out in the hallway, she leaned against the wall beside the boys' locker room, waiting.

When Link appeared, she grabbed his wrist and dragged him towards the girl's bathroom. She pushed him inside and locked the door. Link stumbled against a stall then righted himself. He turned back to Carter, an amused smile playing across his face.

"You know I had a dream exactly like this," he said.

"Really?" Carter said. "Did it end with me stuffing

your head in a toilet? Because that would be uncanny."

She checked each stall, before coming back to Link who remained by the door, both curious and lost.

"You want to explain to me why you literally dragged me in here?" he asked.

Someone tried the door handle then called through the door.

"Carter, let Link go," Donovan said.

Carter ignored him and stepped closer to Link. She studied his face, her conclusions solidifying. Link fidgeted, pushing his glasses up his noses. The nervous tick. She felt stupid for not putting it together the first time she'd seen him do that.

"Carter?" he asked hesitantly. "You going to give me an explanation?"

"I know who you are," she murmured.

Link chuckled awkwardly, brow tight with discomfort. "I hope so, we've been hanging out for the last week."

Carter ignored his comment. "You're President Douglas's son."

Chapter 12

L ink tensed, staring at Carter. After a long silent moment, where Donovan knocked on the door again, Link burst out laughing. Carter blinked and took a startled step back. This was not the reaction she expected.

"You think that…" Link bent double, laughing.

"Carter, open the door," Donovan called out.

Carter stood there, struggling between surprise and worry. Was it possible he didn't actually know? Link straightened, the end of his laughter sitting on his lips.

"Does this mean I can walk around acting like a jerk and people will still have to be my friends?" Link asked, teasing.

More knocks resounded through the bathroom, Donovan's growing frustration apparent in the heavy thuds.

"Link, do you honestly not know?" Carter asked.

Link tossed up his hands, exasperated. "Carter, you can't be serious? Me? Be…" Link shook his head, laughing again.

Carter didn't move, didn't speak. How could she tell

him that he'd been lied to, that his best friend wasn't truly his best friend but his bodyguard?

"Funny one, Carter," Link said, shoving Carter's shoulder playfully.

He unlocked the door halting Donovan's pounding. As Link stepped out of the bathroom, he threw a single furtive glance at Carter, his eyes holding a flicker of panic.

He slipped out, the door swinging shut behind him. The bell rang, jolting Carter. She darted into the hall. A storm of bodies crowded her sight. She shouldered her way through the mass in search of Link and Donovan. But as she burst out of the entrance, they were gone.

Carter stood on the steps replaying Link's look and she had no doubt he knew exactly who his father was.

***

When Carter stepped off the bus, she still wore a troubled frown. Behind her, the doors clunked shut and the bus rumbled away, leaving her alone on the quiet street. In the sky, the sun dipped towards the horizon. Burying her hands in her pockets, Carter headed for the deli.

Conversations muffled the ding of the bell over the door but Maggie still noticed Carter's arrival, greeting her with a wave. At her normal booth, Carter slid across the seat and peered out the window. A family of three walked down the street, the young daughter holding both of her parents' hands. Carter turned away from the happy smiles, contemplating the tabletop.

A napkin followed by a cookie, dropped in front of her but she hardly noticed, lost in her thoughts.

"Hey, girly," Maggie said, poking Carter's arm in concern. "What are you thinking over there?"

Finally, Carter lifted her head. "I was thinking over

why people do what they do?"

Maggie offered her an understanding smile. "Thinking of your mom?"

Carter stiffened, as she instinctively curled her fingers in. Maggie placed one hand over Carter's clenched fist. "You understand that what she did was terrible and you didn't deserve it, right?"

Pulling away, Carter crossed her arms, staring out on the neighborhood. Knowing and believing were two different things. But she wouldn't admit that. "I was thinking about something else."

Maggie backed away, her smile tight with sympathy. "Of course. What brought this line of thinking on then?"

Carter let go of some of the tension in her muscles, safe in a new topic.

"School. I discovered why I thought something was off about Link and Donovan."

"Oh, and what is that?"

Carter opened her mouth but stopped, the panic in Link's eyes coming to mind. He knew who he was. The panic wasn't for hearing the truth but having the truth come out. His secret wasn't for her to share.

"They just kept hanging out with me because they actually enjoyed my company," she said, popping a piece of the cookie into her mouth. "Not something I'm used to, that's all."

Beaming, Maggie slapped Carter's hand. "I knew they liked you!"

"Maggie!"

At the call from one of her workers, Maggie sighed and stood up. "Looks like I'm needed. Come over in a few minutes and I'll have sandwiches ready for you."

Carter ate the rest of her cookie while watching the sun melt behind the houses. At the counter, Maggie handed over two wrapped sandwiches.

"Tell Steve hi," she said.

With a nod Carter left, the noise of the deli dying away as she jogged across the street. When she stepped into the apartment, she paused. In the fading light, it looked bare. Trying to disperse the emptiness, Carter made more noise than needed, dropping her bag on the kitchen table and bumping the fridge door closed after stowing away the sandwiches.

Standing in the kitchen, she gazed over the living room. The appearance of a feminine touch had disappeared over the years. Silky throw pillows were now worn. Knicknacks had been broken or removed. Only brighter squares of paint spoke of family photos that had been removed. With memories pushing against the locked door in her mind, Carter sank into a chair and dragged out her homework.

***

Lost in homework, Carter didn't hear the door open or see how her father paused in the doorway, noting her position at the dining table. When he approached, Carter snapped her head up. Like a broken dam, questions about Link's true identity and it's secrecy flooded her tongue.

"Do you want to talk about it?" her father asked, gently.

The question derailed Carter's thoughts and she tried to connect what he referred to. "Talk about what?"

He took a seat next to her, studying her with caring dark blue eyes. "You're doing work at the table."

Carter found the connection but didn't want to acknowledge it. "Is that a crime?"

"No, it just means you don't want to be in the living room. Which means that you are thinking about your mother and you don't want to look at the empty spots on the wall."

Carter shrugged and leaned back in her chair, trying to appear unconcerned. "Nope, it just means that I wanted proper support for my back. The couch is too soft." Her father didn't break eye contact and Carter knew he wasn't convinced. "Not everything has to have a deeper meaning, Captain."

"No, but you forget that I've known you your entire life. I know what certain things mean." He crossed his arms. "Do you want to talk about it?"

Carter hesitated for a second. But what point was there in talking? It was in the past. What was done was done.

"There's nothing to talk about," she said. She smiled mockingly. "I can move into the living room if that would make you feel better."

Despite her blasé attitude, her father didn't back down. "It's okay to talk about it, Sarge. You know that."

Carter picked up her pencil, needing him to stop prying.

"Yup," she said. "But there's nothing to talk about. We should have another gun assembly race. I think I could beat you this time."

For a brief moment her father didn't reply, then he nodded, letting the subject drop.

"All right, but if you lose again don't get mad at me."

"Ha," she said. "I'm not going to lose. You're getting arthritis in your advanced years, old man."

Her father ruffled her hair. In retaliation, Carter grabbed his wrist and twisted. Her father punched a nerve cluster on Carter's bicep, deadening her arm.

"Ow!" Carter said, cupping her arm with her non-numb hand. "I always forget that move!"

Her father smirked at her as he grabbed a water bottle and drank.

"I'll teach it to you after dinner. You hungry?" he asked.

"If I could feel anything, I might be."

"It's only your arm, you're fine."

As he opened the refrigerator door, Carter grabbed a pencil and threw it at his bent form. Her father raised his head. She shrugged.

"I was annoyed," she said.

He rested his arm on the refrigerator door. "I hope that's not what you do when you're annoyed with your teachers?"

"Please. I stick to correcting them in front of the whole class and selling their test answers." When her father scowled, Carter gave him a toothy grin. She wasn't sure there was anything more entertaining than making her father annoyed. "Just kidding, like I would promote idiots getting ahead in the class just because they have money."

Sighing, her father shook his head and grabbed the sandwiches.

"How's the arm?" he asked.

"Still numb," she said. "If I can't do my homework because of this, then my bad grades are on you. I hope you're happy for single-handedly destroying my future."

"Did you really have that bright of a future?"

She glared and her father grinned, finding his own entertainment in her annoyance. Like father like daughter, she guessed.

As they fell to eating, Carter's thoughts about Link's true identity resurfaced. She darted her gaze to and away from her father. He took these glances in stride. When Carter's curiosity couldn't be held back any longer, she spoke. "So, did you know that President Douglas has an illegitimate son?"

Carter's father hesitated for a fraction of a second before he went on eating. She dropped her sandwich, feigning shock. "I hope you have a better poker face than that when you're with the President. Because that was just embarrassing. Might as well have screamed that you knew."

Lowering his sandwich, her father held her gaze, serious. "Carter, what do you know?"

She pointed to him with an accusatory finger. "Better yet, what do you know, Captain? And how come you didn't tell me this juicy gossip?"

Her father pushed aside his sandwich and leaned on the table. "Carter, I'm serious. How did you come by this information?" he said, his voice taking on an authoritative tone she hardly ever heard.

"Calm down, Captain," she said, raising her hands in a placating gesture, unaware that her arm had stopped feeling numb. "He goes to school with me. Well, just started going to school with me. He originally attended Jefferson Private High school. The water main burst and he was in the group of transfer students. I've been hanging out with him for the last week. I made the discovery today. He wears glasses to obscure his face and his hair is dyed brown. But he has the same freckles in his eyes and his features are too similar. His name is Link Evans."

Her father nodded as Carter finished and leaned back in his chair, drumming his fingers on the table. "All right."

"So you knew?"

His fingers stilled. "Of course, I'm on the President's detail. I need to know everything about him, which includes things in his past that could compromise him. Who else at the school knows?"

"As far as I'm aware, I'm the only one," she said.

Her father stood, eyes distant, already running through precautions in his mind. "Okay, I need to make some calls."

Carter twisted in her chair as he walked away. "He won't have to go somewhere else, will he?"

Her father stopped. "Why?"

Carter shifted uncomfortably.

"He's one of the only two friends I currently have. And if he goes, Donovan goes," she said.

"We'll see," he said.

As he left, Carter sank back into her chair, her appetite gone.

Chapter 13

As Carter hopped out of the SUV, her father spoke.

"Sarge," he said. "It goes without saying that this information is a matter of national security."

Planting her hand on one hip, Carter popped it out. "But I wanted to tweet about it!"

When her father chuckled, she dropped her hand. "He's staying at Hamilton then?"

"As far as I know, yes."

Letting out an inaudible sigh, Carter felt the tangled knot in her stomach relaxed.

"Keep an eye out for him," her father said.

As Carter clicked her heels together, she saluted. "Roger that, Captain."

Her father nodded curtly in reply then winked. "I'll see you at home, Sarge."

"Unless I'm forced to take a bullet for a certain someone."

"Being his friend, or making sure he gets to a secure location while you wait for backup to arrive, is more along the lines of what I meant."

"Then the same goes for you. I love you, Captain."

"Love you too, Sarge."

Forcing herself not to watch her father vanish into traffic, Carter jogged up the front steps, needing to get out of the cold morning air. Inside the scent of Italian espresso warmed the halls as did the mass of moving students.

As Carter approached her first period, someone jostled her and she bumped into another student as a result. Link stumbled but Donovan righted him before any damage could be done. Seeing Carter, Link tensed while Donovan scrutinized her. Both reactions confirmed what Carter had discovered.

"Sorry about that," Carter said, trying to break their worry.

"You seem to have a knack for running into me," Link said, relaxing.

"It seems I do. I'll have to watch out for that. I wouldn't want you getting the wrong idea and thinking I liked you."

When Link laughed, Carter could sense his self-assurance: he still believed she didn't know. For the moment, she decided to not bring up the subject. The middle of a packed hallway wasn't the place to discuss the topic of his parentage.

"Did you finish that essay for history yet?" Link asked as they headed to class.

"Last night, why?"

Link frowned and scratched the back of his head. "I'm having trouble finding a good reference book."

"I'll help you find one in free period."

"Thanks."

Carter nudged his shoulder with hers. "What are highly intelligent friends for?"

At their seats in chemistry, Carter dropped her notebook onto the table then looked to Mr. Rojas. She raised her eyebrows in surprise.

"Well, well, well," she said.

"What?" Link asked.

"Mr. Rojas," Carter said, feeling a laugh tickle her throat, "went on a date."

Link studied their teacher who leaned back in his chair, smiling at nothing. When Link burst out laughing, Mr. Rojas frowned at him and Link hunched over, trying to hide.

"Okay, that one I could see," he said. "Do you know who?"

"The librarian, Diana."

"Good for him."

When the bell rang, the door opened again admitting Mason, closely followed by Smith. Though Link worked to appear unaffected, Carter could still see the tension in his shoulders. Another confirmation. By the time Link looked to Carter, she acted as if she hadn't noticed his reaction and Link let out a breath.

***

As the trio cut their way to history, Carter grew more and more aware of Donovan watching her. She knew it couldn't be for her stunning good looks. That only left his worry that despite her never mentioning it, he still suspected she knew the truth. Meeting his gaze head-on, she raised an eyebrow.

"Keep looking at me like that, Donovan, and I might think you are flirting with me," she said.

Nothing. Absolutely nothing. Carter wondered if he ever got tired of not acting like a normal human being.

"Is there a reason for your increased curiosity with my facial profile?"

Donovan was saved from replying when they nearly ran into Amy. Link faltered in his steps, avoiding a collision by Carter taking hold of the back of his blazer, yanking him back.

"Hi, Amy," Carter said, cheerily.

"Hi," Amy said, though she only saw Link.

On his end, Link looked like he'd swallowed his tongue and might be on the verge of throwing it back up. Carter elbowed him in the ribs.

"Hi," Link blurted out, much too loud for the close quarters.

Amy only smiled. "Hi."

When the pair remained unmoving and uncommunicative, Carter stepped in. "Link, she's a perfect option!"

Link widened his eyes at Carter in panic, not knowing her train of thought but clearly afraid of whatever it might be.

"I'm sorry?" Amy said, baffled.

"Link, you were just saying how you wanted to sit by someone in History that was smart. Let's switch places and you can sit beside Amy. I'm sure she wouldn't mind."

"I wouldn't mind at all," Amy said, gazing up at Link.

"Yeah?" Link choked out.

Carter blamed Donovan for this version of Link, too many years of never interacting with girls had created this babbling idiot. Luckily for Link, Amy seemed to be attracted to babbling idiots.

"Yeah," she said.

***

The library held a silence crowded with busy minds and covert conversations. Carter, Link, and Donovan all sat at a table, absorbed in their studies. The peace broke when a group of four girls pushed through the doors. Carter noted that three of them were the same girls who had circled Donovan at the museum. The girls sent

Donovan smiles as they found their own table.

"I'm really impressed they still manage to get oxygen to their brains when they dispel so much of it panting over Donovan," Carter said.

Link snorted.

"Does it bother you that I attract so much attention?" Donovan asked.

He asked the question in an emotionless tone but Carter noticed the hint of a smirk in the corner of his mouth.

"Not at all," she said. "Where else would I find my amusement if I didn't get to watch girls who have never heard the word 'no' get rejected by you?"

Shaking his head, Donovan stood.

"I need a book on Samuel Adams," he said. "Where would I find it?"

"What makes you think I know that?" Carter asked.

"Because you're a smug outcast. I have no doubt this library has been your second home."

Carter couldn't be annoyed with facts. "Second story, 8th row, top-shelf."

When he left, one of the girls smoothly detached herself from the group and followed him. Carter swiveled towards Link. With the girl distracting Donovan, Carter had time.

"Link," she said.

He lifted his head, acknowledging her.

"Why did you lie to me?" she said.

Though he fought to remain neutral, Carter saw him tense.

"What are you talking about?" he asked, strained.

Carter leaned in close, dropping her voice as she held his gaze. "Yesterday. Bathroom. President. Ring a bell?"

Link lost his composure and glanced about the library, flashes of panic, fear, and anger darting through his expression.

"Link, I'm not stupid. You should know this by now. Just admit I was right."

Jerking upward, he grabbed Carter's wrist, tugging her towards the library doors. Outside, he led them to the closest bathroom and stepped inside. He released his hold and Carter leaned against the door, crossing her ankles and sticking her hands in her pockets. Dragging his hand through his hair, Link did a quick sweep of the stalls before spinning on Carter, his face hard.

"What do you want, Carter?" he asked, every muscle taut.

She lifted a shoulder. "I want you to admit my conclusion of who your father is was correct."

"That's all you want?" he said, his voice edged with anger. "You want me to admit it? Fine." He glared at her. "I'm the President's bastard son. Is that what you wanted to hear?"

Link balled his hands into tight fists. Carter straightened, shame creeping up her neck.

"Link, I just-"

"Isn't that what you wanted me to say, Carter?"

Carter swallowed, guilt coiling in her chest. "Link-"

"What?" He took a step forward, eyes blazing. "Do you want me to tell you what it's like going to the same school as your half brother and having the reality that he gets to live the life you could be living shoved in your face every day?"

The pain in his voice was a punch to Carter's stomach. "No-"

"No! You just wanted to be the person who figured it out. Who was smarter than everyone else."

"Link-"

"What are you going to do now, huh?" He stared at her, looking a little wild around the eyes, as if every terrible outcome of this conversation played in his mind. "I've admitted it, are you going to plaster it everywhere?" Carter opened her mouth but he went on. "Do it. Show the world how smart Carter Owens is for seeing what nobody else could. Do it! Make it so that I have to move. So I have to rip up my entire life because you had to be the brilliant one. Do it, ruin my life!"

The accusations knifed Carter, making her rigid. "I would never-"

"No? Really?" He jabbed the air in front of her. "Donovan said it, you're an outcast. You're telling me that you wouldn't use this information to make your life a little easier?"

"I wouldn't!" she shouted.

"Liar!" Link shook his head, hurt in every line of his face. "You wouldn't blink at using me. You're just like everyone else."

"I am *not* like everyone else!" Carter yelled, furious.

"Yeah, you are!" Link yelled. "Why should I think that you wouldn't use this?!"

Angry, Carter slammed his chest. "Because if you actually believe that then you really are a bastard!"

Chapter 14

Link dropped his shoulders, the fight leaving him in a breath. "You're right, Carter. That's exactly what I am. I don't matter, I never have."

Carter grabbed his arm. "How can you say that? Of course you do!"

"No, I don't." He yanked his arm out of her hold. "Not to anyone, not to you.

Shouldering passed her, Link left the bathroom, rushing back to the library. Carter closed her eyes, hating herself, hating her tongue, her anger. Cursing under her breath, she flung the door open and sprinted after Link as the bell rang overhead. By the time she reached the library, Link already had his backpack on, Donovan at his side.

"Link, wait," she said.

Using Donovan as a barrier, Link escaped into the torment of students, leaving Carter to watch them disappear.

***

Carter leaned over the coffee table in her living room, all the pieces of a 9mm Glock 17 handgun spread out on the top. Footsteps rang out on the metal staircase and a second later the door opened. Carter continued to concentrate on assembling the gun, the now warm metal pieces familiar in her hands. Her father kicked the door shut, staring at her but Carter didn't acknowledge him.

"That bad of a day, huh?" he asked.

Ignoring the comment, Carter kept working at sliding the pieces together, feeling as they clicked perfectly into place. Her father tossed his coat onto a chair and took the spot beside her on the couch.

"Sarge, you can talk to me," he said.

"Who said I have anything to talk about?" she said, sliding in the tightly coiled spring.

"The fact that you are assembling a gun without a stopwatch."

Carter shrugged. "So I don't have a stopwatch."

Her father placed a large hand over Carter's, stilling her process. After a breath, she looked up at him.

"You fight the punching bag when you're frustrated and you assemble a gun when you're trying to distract yourself from something you don't want to think about. Are you going to tell me what's going on?"

Carter dropped her gaze and her father removed his hand. Setting down the gun pieces, she fingered a flaw in the coffee table wood. "Captain, what do you do when you've made a mistake?"

Her father crossed his arms, studying her hunched shoulders and downcast eyes.

"Are we talking 'blew up my car' mistake? 'Got caught smoking in the school's security tunnels' mistake? Or got a 'belly button ring' mistake?"

Carter curled her fingers, watching the knuckles stick out. "'Ran my mouth and hurt someone' mistake."

Her father nodded thoughtfully. "The best you can do is apologize and work to pick up the pieces. Which, coincidentally, happens to work for the first mistake as well," he said.

When Carter didn't even crack a smile, her father laid a hand on her shoulder. "What's going on, Sarge?"

Letting out a breath, Carter leaned back on the couch, curling her legs up. Instead of meeting her father's eyes, she focused on her knotted hands but didn't see them. What she saw was the way Link looked after she had thrown that word back in his face. She knew punching him would have hurt less.

How did she admit she not only failed Link but her father too? He asked her to be Link's friend, to protect him. But she hadn't been able to protect Link from herself.

"I screwed up," she said. "I crossed a line and now I think I lost my only friends." She closed her eyes, seeing Link's hurt over and over again. "All because I wanted to be right."

Her father hummed in response and Carter sank deeper into the cushions.

"What line?" he asked.

Ashamed, Carter tugged at the fraying end of the cushion, unable to meet her father's penetrating gaze. "One that I knew not to cross."

"Did you physically hurt this friend?"

Carter snapped her head up. "No!"

Her father pointedly stared at her, making her shrink back, knowing the question wasn't unwarranted. "No, I didn't physically hurt him. But I did hit a wound."

"Ah."

Carter crossed her arms, pulling them tightly to herself. "Now I don't know what to do."

When her father leaned forward, she locked eyes with him, noticing the softness around them. "Apologize. A lot of people don't understand that if they admit to their mistakes they could be forgiven." There was a note of sadness in his voice that struck Carter, though she didn't know why.

"What if that's not enough?" she asked.

"Then you learn from this and grow. But don't give up hope. There's a chance this could all be fixed."

Carter nodded, but again remembered the pain in Link's face. She wasn't sure this could ever be made right.

Chapter 15

Rain beat against the glass and darkened the sky outside the school. The constant tapping played as background noise to Mr. Rojas's voice as he droned on. Carter heard neither the incessant rain, nor Mr. Rojas's lecture. Nothing seemed to hold her attention except for the statue of a person beside her.

The bell rang, bringing about a shriek of stools on the tile floor and the rise in voices as conversations were taken up.

"Link," Carter said. "Please."

He didn't glance at her. He wore the same stony expression as when his gaze had landed on her as he walked into the room. A wall of silence had separated them throughout the entire class and Carter found herself at a loss for how to break past it. Shouldering his backpack, Link made for the door, his rigid body screaming his opinion of Carter.

As she watched him storm off, Carter couldn't blame him. If she had taken a second the day before to think about what she was doing, she would have seen how heartless she was being. All because she had to prove she was right. No matter what kind of relationship Link held with his father, Link was still a shameful secret. In forcing him to admit who he was, she had ripped open an old wound and stabbed it, making it bleed fresh. He had every right to be mad at her. She hadn't just crossed a line, she had taken a sledgehammer to a fragile wall.

Letting out a heavy breath, Carter grabbed her bag. By the time she was in the hallway, Link had already vanished into the thick crowds with Donovan. The ruckus of the school: slamming locker doors, pounding footsteps, and happy laughter of friends, grated on Carter's ears. As Carter walked to history class, her thoughts grew darker than the sky.

Donovan was sitting in Link's usual spot when Carter entered history class. Behind him, Link was deep in conversation with Amy and pointedly had his face angled away from Carter. As she took her seat, Amy noticed her.

"Hey, Carter," she said.

"Hi, Amy," Carter said, with a half convincing smile.

When Carter glanced at Link, she found him absorbed with the contents of his notebook. Guilt coiled in her chest.

"I was just telling Link," Amy said. "All of you should sit with my group during lunch."

Link tensed, his jaw twitching as he gripped the edge of the notebook, making the paper crinkle. Carter felt the pit in her stomach grow.

"I know Link and Donovan would love that. I might be busy but thanks anyway," she said.

Nodding, Amy smiled, her face open and untroubled, unable to feel the tension that linked her fellow companions.

"Alright."

As she pivoted back to Link, he raised his head, locking gazes with Carter for a brief second. In his eyes, she read all his hurt and anger his reality held. A reality she had carelessly exposed.

All of Carter's planned words collapsed like sandcastles underfoot. Donovan sat as a silent sentinel beside her, his blank face more impenetrable than ever.

"Donovan," she said, in a quiet voice.

When he looked over at her, there was no emotion in his eyes.

"There's nothing to say, Carter," he said.

As he returned his attention to his homework, Carter sank deeper into her seat. Despite what Donovan said, she frantically searched for how to remedy her mistake but she found her store of apologies empty. The shrill ring of the bell stirred Mr. Philips from his spot and he silenced the class.

"Modern day politics," their history teacher said. "That's our topic for today. Now, something you have to know…"

As he progressed through his lesson, Mr. Philips paced back and forth behind his desk, his gestures assertive when he laid out points. The scratching of pencils scribbled away on paper. Carter heard none of it as she buried herself deeper into her thoughts. Her notebook lay closed and untouched, her pencil tucked away somewhere in her bag.

As the class drew to a close, something a student asked yanked Carter out of herself.

"Did you study politics?" a male voice asked.

A second later, Carter registered that it had been Link who had asked the question. Mr. Philips paused for a breath, then nodded.

"I did, at Georgetown," he said.

"Were you ever part of an election campaign?" a boy asked.

Setting down the whiteboard marker he had been using, Mr. Philips crossed his arms. Carter studied his reaction, the defensiveness in his posture.

"Yes, a few," he said. "Now let's get back to-"

"Which campaign?" a girl cut in.

Mr. Philips rolled his shoulders, portraying

nonchalance. "A couple of senators."

As if that was the end of the topic, he faced the whiteboard again, his shoulders stiff. A frown edged onto Carter's lips. Before Mr. Philips could continue, the same girl blurted out another question.

"Did you ever do more in politics than just help with campaigns?" she asked, leaning on the top of her desk.

Reluctantly, their teacher turned back to them, his features struggling to remain uncaring. "Yes, I worked under a senator for a time before becoming a teacher."

"Which-"

"Enough questions for now," Mr. Philips said, his look chilling.

The girl slid back into her chair, her curiosity reined in.

"Now let me explain your homework. It's a research project, due in three weeks."

Through his explanation, Carter watched him but his manner quickly reverted to its usual formality. The end of class was signaled and everyone jumped into motion. Link bypassed Carter, following Amy out the door along with Donovan. When Carter approached Mr. Philips's desk, he raised his head. "You were blessedly silent today, Carter," he said. "You're not sick, are you?"

"No, not sick."

Dropping his gaze, Mr. Philips gathered up a stack of papers. "Was there something you wanted?"

"Which senator did you work for?"

Mr. Philips's hands faltered before he continued neatening the piles. "It's of no importance."

Carter shoved her hands into her pockets. "If you say so."

He stilled, his fingers clenching the pages. Without another comment, Carter headed out of the room. The hallways were mostly drained as students dispersed to lunch. By the time she reached the mayhem of the cafeteria, her situation had dragged her features into a scowl. The noise of the room and bombarding voices deepened the expression. She scanned the crowd and found Link and Donovan stationed at Amy's table. Looks of excitement coated the faces of Amy's friends as they chatted eagerly with the impassive Donovan.

Carter headed off to her lone table. When she sat, she found that she had no appetite. The empty spots beside her felt like gaping wounds. As she watched the ever-changing scene around her, she racked her brain trying to find a way to bridge the gap that she had made. She was interrupted when a group of guys stopped in front of her table.

"Looks like you've managed to scare off another set of friends. Shocking," Lucas said.

Carter forced her features to relax, feigning unconcern.

"How you haven't managed to scare off your friends with that horrendous excuse you call a face is the real shocking thing," she said, though she felt hollow as the retort came out.

"You know what, Owens?" Lucas said, leaning in, pointing a threatening finger at her.

Carter cut him off as she rose and shouldered her bag. "No, I don't know and I don't care," she said, tired.

She stepped over the bench and left the cafeteria. At the door, she glanced back once to see that Donovan was watching her and Link swiftly ducking his head.

***

Outside, the rain had given up and the clouds were slowly trudging on, leaving behind thin wisps of white and a setting sun. Raindrops slithered down the deli windows. Carter flicked her notebook closed and packed up her bag. Customers' conversations buzzed through the place, giving it a warmth that Carter didn't feel.

"You heading off?" Maggie asked as Carter stopped

at the counter.

Carter nodded and couldn't manage anything other than a blank expression.

"Hon, you sure you're okay?"

Head tilted to the side, Maggie regarded her with concern. The look was a repeat of when she had asked the question the previous five times that day.

"Yeah. Fine."

Maggie pressed her lips together in worry but didn't pry any further. Instead, she handed Carter two sandwiches and Carter stowed them away in her bag.

"See you tomorrow, girly," Maggie said, adding an extra note of affection into her voice.

"Okay."

Tugging the door open, Carter stepped out into the chilly evening. In the distance, a dog barked out a sharp warning. Mist pelted her face and clung to her hair. Behind her cars rushed by with a quick swoosh, splashing murky water over the sidewalk. The air smelled of waterlogged garbage.

Absentmindedly, Carter slid her fingers over the cold, metal trunk of a black car. When she raised her head, she froze.

Standing at her front door were two men in black suits.

Chapter 16

The world crashed in on Carter. She felt her chest constrict as her heart hammered against her ribcage. The men descended the stairs, their movements perfectly in sync.

Carter stumbled back, shaking her head vigorously. Panic and fear slammed into her. She swallowed but her throat tightened, her mouth filling with bile. In her mind, she saw flashes of an empty apartment, an empty bed, a folded black suit.

One of the men hurried towards her and she vaguely recognized Curtis. He stretched out a hand to her but she jerked back.

"No, no, no, no, no, no!" she yelled, swinging a fist at his face.

Her blow never hit its target, shock making her clumsy. Curtis snatched her wrist in his large, muscular hand. Carter strained against him, all the while screaming, "No, no, no, no, no!"

She needed to get out of there, she needed to run, escape him and his words.

"Carter! He's alive!" he yelled, trying to be heard over her panicked shouting. "Do you hear me? Your father is alive!" Carter stilled, eyes locked on his. "He's alive. Okay? He's alive."

Relief swept over her, making her weak. She buckled under the weight of it and Curtis caught her before she could fall. For a long while, all she could manage was to lean against him, trying to find her breath.

He's alive. Over and over the declaration ran through her head, chasing away the images her fear conjured up. When she found she could breathe normally, she gripped Curtis's arm.

"He's alive," she said.

Curtis nodded. The simple confirmation gave her strength and she pushed herself shakily from him. She felt rung out but didn't collapse, though Curtis kept one hand on her arm. He watched her with concerned brown eyes.

"What happened? Where is he?" Carter asked, her voice small.

"He was shot in the right shoulder," Curtis said. Carter took in a ragged breath. "The bullet went through. He's in the hospital. It was a minor surgery. We tried to call but you weren't answering."

Slowly, her panic receded. Alive. Her father was alive. She wasn't alone. Alive. He was alive.

"Take me to him."

In the back of Curtis's car, Carter stared unseeing out the window, Curtis's words playing in her head on an endless loop. Silence invaded the car's interior. The world beyond the window blurred into yellow lights and brick buildings.

As the miles raced past, Carter eventually returned to the world around her. The last traces of her panic and fear burned away under an intense anger.

"How the hell did this happen?!" she demanded. Curtis found her fiery gaze in the rearview mirror. "Captain said that the only reason someone ever got shot is because someone wasn't doing their job."

"Carter, mistakes happen…"

"Bullshit!" she yelled, pounding her fist on the seat. "My father was shot because someone screwed up. I want to know who!"

Curtis's partner shifted uncomfortably, never looking back. "That is something we are not at liberty to tell you."

"That's a joke! There was an attempted assassination, the entire world will know every detail about this."

"No," Curtis said. "The world won't. Since it occurred during a private event, the entire thing is being kept quiet, for the President's sake as well as your father's."

"Then you know who did this!"

"You are not at liberty to know that," Curtis's partner repeated.

Before Carter could rip this man in two, Curtis cut in. "Carter, we have the culprit in custody, that is all we can tell you. That's all you need to know."

Carter growled in frustration. Before she could snap back a retort, Curtis swung the car into the hospital parking lot. He had barely pulled into an open space when Carter exploded from the car. The ER's bright fluorescent light glared at her as she pelted inside, the smell of ammonia filling her nose. Bypassing the sickly pastel furniture in the waiting room, she darted up to the front desk, startling the gray-haired receptionist. "I need to know where Steve Owens is. Now!"

Carter vibrated with impatience as the woman adjusted her glasses and leveled Carter with a peeved expression. "Ma'am, there are procedures that need to be-"

Gripping the counter, Carter leaned in, eyes hard. "Listen, lady, if you don't tell me what I need to know, I will jump over this counter and strangle you with your name tag. Got it?"

The receptionist stared at Carter in horror. Curtis

placed a restraining hand on Carter's shoulder. Carter backed off, shaking with frustration and glaring at the woman. In contrast, Curtis smiled kindly at the woman.

"We're looking for Steve Owens," he said. "I'm Agent Reynolds."

Mollified, the receptionist went to her computer, shooting Carter a disapproving look. "Agent Owens has been moved to recovery. Third floor, room six which is-"

Carter sprinted to the elevators, punching the button. When the lit up number didn't descend fast enough, she spun away, rushing to the stairway, the two agents following her. She took the stairs two at a time, her footsteps thundering in the stairwell. She burst through a door on the third floor, surprising a group of nurses. Looking both ways, she set off again, charging down the hallway, a nurse calling out to her. At room six, she skidded to a halt, breathing hard. She opened the door, blood roaring in her ears.

The room looked plain with a single bed, heart rate monitor, uncomfortable-looking chairs, and a hanging TV.

Her father opened his eyes. He looked worn out. His right arm hung in a sling and a plastic medical bracelet dangled from his wrist. The beeping of the machine expanded in the room.

"Hey, Sarge," he said, raspy.

Carter surged forward. "I hate you. You know that, I hate you."

Her father cupped her face with his left hand. Tears threatened to spill out but Carter held them back with dogged determination.

"I'm fine, Sarge. I'm fine."

"It doesn't mean I still don't hate you, you got that?"

When her father smiled gently, Carter felt as if she would fall apart. All of her anger and panic vanished, leaving behind relief and the fear that would always be with her. Until he left the service, it would be her constant companion: whispering in her ear, staring over her shoulder.

"I got it, Sarge," her father said.

Carter tried to swallow the lump in her throat. "Don't you dare ever leave me."

Her father kissed her forehead. "I'm not going anywhere."

Carter closed her eyes, gripping the white sheets, struggling against the tears. When her father released her, she straightened. Curtis appeared in the doorway.

"Thanks for bringing her," her father said.

Curtis took a spot on the other side of the bed, looking down on his friend. "How are you feeling?"

Carter felt her grasp slipping and knew she couldn't bear to have both her father and Curtis see her crumble. "I need some water. I'll be right back."

Carter made it just outside for the room when her vision clouded with tears and a suppressed sob broke loose. Stumbling, she pressed her hand against the wall, leaning on it as she covered her mouth.

Lowering herself to the floor, she drew herself into a ball, burying her face in her hands. Tears of relief and fear muffled everything around her. Though the floor was cold, she didn't notice. She shook as she let go of all the emotions that had coursed through her that night. The buzz of nurses' conversations and the shuffle of soft-soled shoes faded away. The only thing she heard was the beeping of the heart monitor, reminding her she wasn't alone.

A pair of comforting arms and the whiff of the deli tugged Carter back to reality. She lifted her head and found Maggie offering silent understanding.

"I can't ever lose him," she said, in a choked voice. "He's all I have."

Maggie hugged her. "I know, Hon. And you didn't. He's still here. In one piece. But it's still okay to be scared."

Carter accepted the hug, finding comfort in Maggie's arms. Taking in a steadying breath, Carter forcefully rubbed her eyes, trying to get rid of the evidence.

"Let's go back," she said.

With Maggie as quiet support, Carter re-entered her father's room. Curtis gave Carter's father a nod and headed towards the door.

"Thanks for bringing me," Carter said.

Curtis squeezed her shoulder once before leaving. Dragging a chair up to the bed, Carter sank into it.

"Hi, Steve," Maggie said. "How are you feeling?"

"Like I got shot," he said.

Carter snorted as she rested her battered Converses on the rim of the bed. "That's original."

"I'm on a lot of painkillers, so it's not too bad," her father told Maggie.

Maggie smiled, tension leaving her shoulders. Finally able to see her, Carter noted the red in Maggie's eyes and the crease of worry in her normally smooth brow.

"Good," Maggie breathed out. "I'm glad you're safe. I can keep Carter company tonight."

Shaking her head, Carter slipped deeper into the chair. "I'm not leaving. I'm spending the night here."

"Sarge-"

"Carter-"

"There is no argument you can bring that I won't out-argue."

Her father and Maggie exchanged a glance.

"I can pick her up tomorrow and drive her home," Maggie offered.

"Thank you."

Maggie gave his hand an encouraging squeeze. "I'll leave so you can get some rest." At the door, she paused, sending them both a smile in which her heart was hidden. The door clicked shut, muting the inquiries floating through the hallway. Carter wiggled into a more comfortable position, though in the hard chair it felt impossible.

"You don't look comfortable," her father said.

Carter slouched as if trying to become one with the

chair. "I'm not going anywhere."

"Good, me neither."

He tried to smile but it barely reached the corners of his mouth. He closed his eyes, exhaustion spreading across his face. Curling up, Carter watched him. The constant beeping overtook the room. She flipped off the lamp beside his bed, leaving them in semi-darkness.

After a long moment, she spoke. "I love you, Captain."

Her father's heavy breathing was all the response she received. The only response she needed.

Chapter 17

C arter."

A faint voice tugged Carter from her restless sleep. She stirred, still clinging to the fog of her dreams.

"Carter, hon, it's time to get up," Maggie said, gently shaking Carter's shoulder.

Shifting, Carter slipped out of Maggie's grasp.

"Carter."

Reality seeped into Carter's mind through the beeping of a monitor and the smell of cleaning solutions. The steady beep cut through her sleep. She opened her eyes, instantly awake. She jerked her head towards the bed where her father lay asleep.

She sighed with relief and untucked her feet from beneath her. Every muscle protested the movement, the cramped position she had taken while sleeping stiffening every joint.

"Come on, I'll take you home so you can shower and change," Maggie said.

Carter cautiously stretched, hiding a grimace. For a

breath, she watched her father's chest rise and fall, reassuring herself that he was still okay. He hadn't left her.

"I want to stay," she whispered.

Maggie squatted beside Carter's chair. "I know you do, hon, but he's going to need a lot of time to sleep and recover. I'll bring you back after school."

Carter gripped the chair's armrests, looking at her father. Maggie put a thin hand on top of Carter's. "He's going to be okay," she said.

Relaxing, Carter nodded.

"Let's go before we wake him," Maggie said.

Carter gave her father one last look before following Maggie out.

A shower, change of uniform, and a car ride later, Carter stepped out in front of the school, feeling battered.

"I'll see you this afternoon, all right?" Maggie said.

"Okay," Carter said, her voice hoarse.

Maggie looked at Carter's disheveled hair and ragged face with concern but Carter barely registered it. She climbed the stairs, her body heavy and her mind even heavier.

The hallways lay empty, classes already in motion, the students lost in boredom or in the lesson. Carter's footsteps resounded on the floor as she made her way to history. As she turned the corner, Mason stepped out of his class. Taking in her rumbled state, he smirked.

"Whose bed did you wake up on the wrong side of?" he asked.

Carter glanced at him but kept walking, leaving him stumped by her passivity. Mr. Philips's voice slipped beneath the door as Carter approached her classroom. Outside the door, she halted, weary. With a tired sigh, she opened the door. Mr. Philips fell silent and every head turned to look at her.

"Carter," he said, "I'm glad you could make it. Please take your seat so I can continue."

Carter made no reply, surprising the class. Link

watched her with confusion. Donovan looked over at her but Carter didn't look back.

Mr. Philips picked up his lesson, his voice drawing everyone's attention away from Carter. Everyone's except Link and Donovan's.

When the bell rang, Carter picked up her bag; she hadn't even bothered taking notes. Students poured out of the classroom, flooding the hallways. Carter had just broken free from the initial wave of students when someone saying her name stopped her. She began to turn when Lucas appeared before her, surrounded by a group of his friends.

"Owens," he said. "What happened? I didn't think it was possible for you to look any uglier."

The group let out a round of loud laughs, producing curious bystanders. Lucas accepted a high five from the boy next to him. Carter stared at them, her face unreadable. Lucas pouted in mock sympathy. "What? Did you discover your daddy doesn't love you and left you?"

Anger seared through Carter and she pulled back her hand, curling her finger into a tight fist. She swung. There was a loud smack as her fist was stopped by a strong hand. Looking over, she found Donovan gripping her fist.

"Don't do it," he said.

Carter wrenched her fist free of Donovan's grasp and leveled Lucas with passionless eyes.

"You," Lucas said to Donovan, "should keep a shorter leash on your b-"

The insult died in Lucas's throat as Donovan decked him in the jaw. The crack startled students. Lucas blacked out for a second and crashed into a set of lockers. When he came to, Donovan stood over him. Taking the front of his blazer, Donovan helped Lucas to his feet, saying something too low for Carter to hear, though she saw the result as Lucas paled.

"You should be careful where you walk next time,

running into doors can leave nasty bruises," Donovan said, unconcerned.

Lucas fingered his jaw as Donovan faced Carter.

"And why did you get to punch him and not me?" she asked, glaring at him.

Taking her arm, Donovan led her away from the group of boys, Link following. "Because you couldn't afford another infraction on your school record."

Carter rolled her eyes. "Of course, you read my school file."

Donovan didn't answer. He pushed through the library doors and guided Carter to the furthest corner and released her. Link stopped a few feet away, his arms crossed, betraying a mixture of concern and frustration.

"I just risked a mark on my school record or possible suspension by punching Lucas. Now, you're going to tell us what's going on" Donovan said.

Carter leaned against the wall, crossing her ankles and stuffing her hands into her pockets. She shrugged. She hoped she appeared careless instead of worn out. "Whatever do you mean? I usually get into fights to wake myself up."

"No, you normally belittle people," Donovan said. "Making some comment about their IQ."

"What can I say? Actions speak louder than words."

Link took a step forward. "Cut it out, Carter! The only reason I'm even standing here is because you look like hell and almost got into a fight."

Carter slumped under the intensity of his stare. Fatigue came back to her as the strength her anger had given her disappeared. She dropped her head. With weary sigh, she let the facade of her uncaring demeanor slip away.

"My father was shot last night," she said, in a quiet voice.

"Jeez, Carter, is he okay? What happened?" Link asked, all his frustration gone, pushed away by his worry.

"He's fine," Carter said.

Link watched her with concern while Donovan softened with sympathy. Carter sank to the ground, the weight of her thoughts dragging her down. She rested her head against the wall, staring up at them. "He was hit in the shoulder. The bullet went through clean and he's recovering. I spent the night by his hospital bed in a chair. That's why I look this awful."

Carter focused on her hands as if she couldn't bear the weight of either boy's expression.

"For a second I thought I had lost him," she whispered.

No one said anything, her confession hanging in the still air.

"Look, Link," she started but paused, her thoughts untangling themselves. "Yesterday…I don't know how to do apologies. If you haven't figured it out yet, I don't know how to do friendship either."

Link broke away from her gaze, some of his hurt returning.

"But I am sorry for what I did. For what I said," she said. "For pushing you to tell me and all because I wanted to be right. I hurt you and I'm sorry."

Link let his arms drop to his sides, releasing his barrier.

"You don't have anything to worry about," Carter said. "No one will ever know who you are from me."

She read his hesitancy and finally his acceptance. He offered her a small smile which she returned, along with an outstretched hand.

"Friends?" she asked.

Link settled onto the floor and accepted her hand. "Friends."

Donovan joined them.

After a comfortable pause, Link cleared his throat and scoffed his shoe against the carpet. "So…um… how did you know? About my secret, I mean. No one, at any of my schools, ever figured it out."

Carter sank back against the wall, appreciating the

change of subject, her relief and exhaustion mixing together to leaden her body.

"I knew there was something you weren't telling me; I kept picking up on clues that something seemed off. I finally figured it out when I tackled you," she said. "I saw the freckles in your eyes, same as your father's. With your glasses on they aren't as noticeable. Once I saw that, it all clicked. You have the same nose, mouth, and chin. Then everything else fell into place: your dislike of Mason; avoiding my gaze when I talked about Senator Keller having an illegitimate daughter; your startled reaction when I referred to Donovan as your bodyguard, since that is actually what he is. All of it."

"You figured that all out because you saw freckles in my eyes?" Link asked.

Donovan laughed a low, amused laugh and Carter stared at him, shocked. Miracles did happen apparently.

"My estimation of you was wrong," Donovan said. "After that first lunch, I was convinced you would figure it out sooner."

Carter didn't respond, couldn't respond. All this time, he'd been expecting her to find out. Donovan's face held emotion, real emotion. Would wonders never cease?

"The statue is human," she said.

Donovan smiled, the expression completely foreign on his usually placid face.

"Of course," she said. "The moody persona."

"It was the thing we found that worked the best," he said. "The hard exterior keeps others at bay and draws attention away from Link."

She regarded the pair, feeling as if she were really seeing them as the false personas melted away. She gave the surrounding library a furtive glance, then leaned forward, lowering her voice. "How long have you been his bodyguard?"

"Six years," Donovan said. "Since Douglas became President."

"Did you always know your whole life?" she asked

Link.

"No," he said, unresolved anger simmering beneath his words. "I was told when my dad was running for President." He nodded to Donovan. "For security reasons, I was given a bodyguard. Only a few actually know about it."

"And you and Mason..."

Link rubbed the back of his neck. "He doesn't know. I've only ever met my dad at secure locations."

"It must be terrible having to go to school with him," Carter said.

Link picked at the carpet. "Yeah, it's not the best."

"Well," Carter said. "Let's go to lunch and if we're lucky he'll choke on his chicken."

"I wouldn't mind seeing that," Link chuckled.

"Lunch sounds good," Donovan said.

"Don't want to keep your fan club waiting, I see," Carter said.

Irritated, Donovan shook his head. "Those girls are draining."

Standing, he reached out his hand to Carter. She took it and he easily helped her to her feet, as if she weighed nothing. Link pushed himself up.

"Don't worry," Carter said. "I'll sit with you and keep them at bay with my charm."

"You must have a different definition of charm than I am currently aware of," Donovan said. "Your charm is more on the level of insulting."

"Charm, insults, they amount to the same thing in my book. They are both used for a specific purpose."

"Fair enough," Donovan said.

Before Carter could lead the way, Link stopped her with a hand on her arm. "Hey, I want to say I'm glad your father is okay." He swallowed. "He's the reason my dad is okay."

The maelstrom of the previous night reemerged and Carter fought to keep it away. "Thanks. So how did yesterday with Amy go?"

Seeming to understand her need to move on, Link winced. "It's a work in progress."

"Need help?" she asked.

"You mind?"

She gently punched his arm. "Not at all. What are friends for?"

Chapter 18

Seated between Link and Donovan, Carter didn't feel the weariness of that morning pressing quite so heavily. In only a few hours she would see her father again. A father in the hospital, not the morgue. Though her worry about her father would never go away, being reconciled with her two friends made her breathe easier. For now, for this instant, she could simply be a girl who wasn't alone.

At the moment, not being alone meant that one of her friends was valiantly trying to flirt while the other suffered through a girl verbally harassing him. When the girl giggled, Carter winced as Donovan flexed his jaw in irritation. Carter pitied the girl, her excited nervousness coming off as desperation. From where Donovan sat, she wasn't sure he cared about the difference.

"So there I am, lost in the museum," the girl said, talking fast to cover her nerves. "And they announce they are about to close."

Giggling again, she placed her hand on Donovan's bicep as if to bring him in on the hilarity. Carter saw the humor in the entire thing but the way Donovan pointedly looked at Carter for help, she didn't think he saw it.

It struck Carter then how without Donovan saying anything, she understood what he wanted. Somehow knowing who he was broke down the barriers between them, giving her insight no one else could see. It felt strange and warming.

"I was so nervous, I could barely think," the girl continued.

In response to Donovan's wordless request for help, Carter rested her chin in her hand, suddenly engrossed in the girl's story. Donovan kicked her and she scowled. Behind the passive look he returned her, she had the sense he was smirking.

The girl laughed again, still holding onto Donovan's arm. Despite his physique, it seemed Donovan fit the mold of a damsel in distress. Carter leaned on the table, devoting her full attention to the girl. At Carter's wide-eyed interest, the girl tripped over her story, flushing.

"Please go on," Carter said. "Your story is truly riveting. I want to know how it ends or, you know, I might die of curiosity."

The girl opened her mouth but nothing came out. Carter nodded slowly, waiting for more. "Can you at least let me know if you got out of the museum alive?"

Color flooded the girl's cheeks and she stormed away from the lunch table. Carter only felt a tinge of guilt; after all, the girl had been fondling Donovan's arm for the last three minutes.

"I guess we will never know if she made it out alive. It's tragic."

"Took you long enough," Donovan whispered.

"Why couldn't you have handled it yourself, princess?"

"Because I know any attention, positive or negative, only invites more."

He had a point there. "Well, you ruined my entertainment. Now what am I supposed to do?"

"Anything that doesn't involve my arm being stroked."

Carter raised her eyebrows in shock. "Wait? This bothers you?"

As she reached for Donovan's arm, he shot his hand out and held her wrist. Carter retaliated by pulling back his thumb with her free hand. Donovan countered her move but Link stopped them.

"Guys?" At once, Carter and Donovan released their holds, acting like nothing was out of the ordinary. "Amy wondered if we wanted to work on the history assignment together today, during free period."

Carter scoffed. "I already finished that." Link widened his eyes, pleading. "I mean, sure. I need help with that."

"Okay, great," Amy said. "It will help so I don't have to do it over the weekend. I'll be free as a bird."

Carter saw the hint like a flashing neon sign but Link simply nodded. Carter exchanged a look with Donovan.

"What are you doing this weekend, Link?" Amy asked, leaning in, smiling.

"The usual, homework, video games. I don't know, stuff."

Smile wilting, Amy shrank back. "Sounds like fun. Well, I have to go to the bathroom. Jen, come with me?"

Once the pair were out of sight, Carter socked Link in the arm.

"Ow! What was the for?" he asked, rubbing the sore spot.

"You idiot! She wanted you to ask her out."

Link swiveled around to where Amy had disappeared. "Really?"

With a groan, Carter dropped her head into her hand, pointing an accusing finger at Donovan. "I blame you for this." When Donovan didn't defend himself, Carter focused on Link. "Yes. You would be more prepared for this if your friend over here didn't attract a line of girls wherever he went. Link, how many dates have you been on?"

Reddening, Link fidgeted with his glasses.

"That's what I thought."

"I've been on a few," Link amended.

"Then this should be fine. When Amy comes back, ask her out."

Though Link nodded, he paled at the prospect. Carter placed a hand on his shoulder. "You got this. It will be super easy."

Link didn't seem mollified by this encouragement but the time for a pep talk passed as Amy returned to her seat.

"What were we talking about?" she asked.

Carter sensed Link succumbing to his nerves. Taking pity on the boy, Carter laid laced hands on the table like she presided over a board meeting.

"We were talking about how this weekend is the perfect time for a double date," she said. "What do you say? You and Link, Donovan and me?"

Around them, the other girls at the table froze, trying to understand how Carter's name and Donovan's name were linked with the word 'date'. Link and Donovan snapped their heads to Carter, their eyes boring into her but she remained unconcerned. Amy brightened and Carter took everything in without a care.

"That sounds great," Amy said.

"Really?" Link asked, coming out of his shock.

"Of course." She beamed at him which produced a goofy grin. On Carter's other side, Donovan worked to keep his expression under control.

"Oh, calm down," she whispered.

"What do we want to do?" Amy asked.

The trio all shared glances. The double date suggestion was as far as Carter had thought out. What one did on a date fell out of her realm of expertise.

"How about we go see the new romantic movie, Loving All of You?" Amy offered.

Carter cringed, wishing for a less painful death and

Donovan fought back a laugh at her reaction.

"Okay," Link said.

"This will be fun!" Amy said.

In one breath, Carter could list about twenty different things that would be more fun - including waterboarding in Guantánamo Bay - than sitting through a romantic movie. Before she could suggest anything different, the bell rang. Wrapping her arm with a friend, Amy waved goodbye. "See you in free period."

Still wearing his goofy grin, Link waved. As Carter went to leave, a hand yanked her back. Both Link and Donovan stared her down.

"What?" she asked.

"You know exactly what," Donovan said, folding his arms.

"Seriously? I did you a favor and you get mad at me? Remind me to never be nice again. Insults have better and more entertaining results."

"From where I'm standing this only benefits you."

Carter rolled her eyes. "Yes, I've been desperately longing for a reason to see Loving All Of You, how did you know?"

"Then why suggest it?" Link asked.

Despite the cafeteria being nearly empty, Carter took a step forward. "As far as I see it, it's not possible for Donovan to let you go out with Amy on your own. Instead of him having to explain himself when he is spotted trailing you, I thought this would be a better option."

"You honestly think I'd be spotted?" Donovan asked.

"Oh," Link said at the same time.

Ignoring Donovan's wounded ego, Carter carelessly nudged Link's shoulder. "Yes, that's why. Also, I figured with Donovan and me there we could keep you from doing something stupid. Or make conversation if you run out of topics. I was thinking of you, you idiot."

"Oh. Um…thanks."

Carter spun away, tossing her hands up. "Why I do people favors is beyond me."

Chapter 19

As soon as Maggie parked the car outside the hospital, Carter jumped out. Warm sunlight spread over Carter as she cut through the parking lot. Maggie hurried to keep up with Carter's long strides. "I checked on him this afternoon. He was resting and the doctor said everything looked good. He should be able to come home within the week."

The news made Carter ease up on her pace. The glass doors parted and the noise of the waiting room wrapped around them. At the front desk sat the same gray-haired receptionist from the previous night. When she spotted Carter, she pursed her lips in distaste. Vividly recalling what she'd said, Carter approached the desk.

"I want to apologize," she said, which startled the woman. "For threatening to strangle you last night. Not one of my best moments."

Despite the pointed way the woman peered at Carter over her glasses, Carter knew she accepted the apology in the way her eyes crinkled. Finally, the woman nodded. "Thank you. I looked up who Steve Owens is and understand. I'm glad he's all right."

"Thanks."

With that out of the way, Carter rejoined Maggie. At her father's door, Carter let it swing open and leaned against the door frame. "What are you still doing in bed, old man?"

Her father chuckled weakly while Maggie poked Carter reproachfully. Sauntering into the room, Carter shook her head. "Seriously, Captain, it was a gunshot wound to the shoulder, it's not that bad. I expected better from you." She gestured to the floor. "Where are the nurses I expected you to have running through drills? I'm disappointed. I thought you were made of stronger stuff."

"Sarge, I'm sorry I have disappointed you."

Hooking her foot around the leg of the chair, Carter brought it forward and dropped into it. "See that it doesn't happen again. You're a former Navy SEAL. They don't let bullets stop them."

"This one won't stop me."

A pleased smile broke across Carter's face, relief and vulnerability hidden behind it. "Good."

When her father held up his arm, Carter hurried to accept the embrace. "I love you, Sarge."

A weight lifted from Carter's chest and she let out a small, inaudible breath. "I love you too, Captain."

As Carter retreated to her chair, her father's caring expression shifted and she got the distinct impression she wouldn't like what came next. "Now, do you want to tell me why I've had a nurse and a doctor say that you threatened to bludgeon and strangle to death the receptionist nurse?"

"I did not say bludgeon, that would be overkill."

Her father eyed her, even as he tried to hide his smile.

"I apologized."

"Apologized because I would make you? Or because you knew it to be the right thing?"

Carter lifted her shoulders. "It could be both, we may never know."

"Well," Maggie said. "Either way, she did apologize. Also, we brought edible food."

Carter handed a sandwich to her father before unwrapping her own. As Maggie took a step back, Carter's father stopped her. "Stay with us."

Carter threw him a teasing look, which he ignored.

"I can't stay long," Maggie said. "I have to get back for the dinner rush, but I can stay a few minutes."

"Good," Carter's father said.

"Yeah, we love having you here," Carter said.

This time Carter ignored the sharp look her father sent her as she shared part of her sandwich with Maggie.

"What were you watching?" Carter asked, nodding to the TV.

"Not sure. It was mainly for distraction."

"And how are you feeling?" Carter asked, picking at her sandwich.

"Sore but I'm still on heavy drugs. It's not too bad."

Carter relaxed, guiding the conversation into what the doctors said and how the day had gone. Outside, the hospital kept running: nurses passing their open doorway as doctor's orders wandered in. The heart monitor was the background noise to their voices. Their conversation ended when Maggie stood, announcing she had to leave.

"I'll stop by when the shop is closed and pick you up, Carter," she said.

Before Carter could voice her protest, her father cut in. "Carter, you need to get actual sleep tonight. I'll be fine."

At his tired expression, her arguments died in her throat. "Okay." She looked back at Maggie. "Thanks for the ride. I'll see you later tonight."

Maggie held Carter's father's hand. "I'm glad you're safe, Steve."

"Thanks for being there," he said, returning the look.

After Maggie left, Carter contemplated the door. "Do you think we eat too many sandwiches?"

"I would if I didn't know that Maggie has replaced a

lot of the components with healthier options."

"How dare she! That's it, you can't marry her."

Her father laughed. "I wasn't aware that was an option."

"Wasn't that why you got shot?" Her father arched an eyebrow. "You were afraid Maggie would reject you, so you took a bullet to the shoulder. What woman would say no to an injured man? Tell me now, have you already asked her out?"

"Sarge, I'm not asking Maggie out. Now finish your healthy sandwich."

"Despite what I said early, it seems like a wasted opportunity. This whole invalid act will fade and you'll have missed your chance."

When her father turned up the volume on the TV, Carter smirked. "You shy away from this topic but I am only laying out the facts here."

"Understood," her father said. "But it's not going to happen."

Carter smiled and picked up her sandwich. "If you say so."

Chapter 20

Shutting her locker, Carter stopped short as she found a group of girls blocking her path. Before they even spoke, she knew why they were there. After all, in Carter's mind they were Donovan's Posse: the girls who seemed the most determined to snag his attention. Why they still bothered she didn't understand. She knew all of them but it was only the leader, Sloane Adams, Carter had had the misfortune of sharing classes with.

"Is this where you fulfill my lifelong goal by inducting me into your clique?" Carter asked.

"That's your lifelong goal?" one of the girls asked, skeptically.

"Not at all, I would hope my goals reach higher than a pair of high heels."

The joke flew over their heads and Carter received nothing but blank stares, except for Sloane. She surveyed Carter from head to foot. With a disappointed tsk, she shook her head.

"I don't see it," she said. "You have no social status. You aren't connected to any one of importance. Your hair isn't the right type of messy to be intentional. Your uniform does nothing for your curves if you even had them. Your nails resemble ragged mountains. And you open your mouth too much to be intelligent. Why in the world would Donovan go on a date with you?"

Carter crossed her arms. The insults were nothing new, the disparity between herself and other girls was always apparent in her life.

"Did it ever cross your mind that Donovan finds a brain more attractive than a perfect set of teeth?" Carter asked.

Sloane smiled patronizingly at Carter, displaying her straight, white teeth. "Owens, boys don't want a girl whose looks would improve with a trash bag over her head. They want a girl that they can show off."

"Show off, is that all you're good for then?"

Even with the dig, Sloane held onto her smile. "From one girl to another sad, pathetic excuse for a girl, know that what Donovan is giving you is a 'pity date'. Nothing more."

Tired of Sloane's smug assurance, Carter decided to amuse herself. Rearranging her features into uncertainty, she scuffed her shoe on the floor. "Really? It's only a pity date?"

Sloane sighed in mock sympathy. "Sadly, yes."

Carter lowered her eyes as if embarrassed. "And you know it's a pity date because naturally, you've been on a real date with him?"

Sloane stiffened and Carter milked the moment for all it's worth. "You *have* been on a real date with him, right?"

In answer, Sloane pressed her lips together as Carter stole the patronizing smile from her. "That's right, he hasn't asked you out," she said. "He's talking to me. Has he ever even talked to you? Interesting how you easily jump to the conclusion that it's a pity date when *you* seem to be the one needing pity."

Carter sighed in mock sympathy and put a comforting hand on the leader's arm. "From one girl to another girl, maybe grow a brain and see if that works next time."

The bell rang, giving the group a reason to abandon Carter. As the hallways cleared, she made her way to the library. She rounded a corner and collided with a massive form. She took a step back, steadying herself. Looking up, she met a pair of gray eyes set in a hard-jawed face. The man wore a janitor's uniform, the dark blue material stretching over his muscular shoulders."You alright?" he asked, in a low gruff voice.

Carter nodded, as she took him in, familiarity hovering about his face.

"Okay," he said.

Grabbing his collection of brooms, he walked away. Carter followed his departure, recognition finally clicking.

"Carter."

Link and Donovan stopped in front of her, Donovan studying her face with a slight crease between his eyebrows.

"What is it?" he asked.

"Link, remember that janitor we saw at the Natural History museum talking to Mr. Philips?" Carter asked.

If Donovan thought this question strange, he didn't show it.

"Vaguely," Link said.

"Well, anyways I understand now why Mr. Philips was talking with him: Philips must have helped him get a job here. Joining the other former military employees here."

"Is it normal to have former military men on the janitorial staff?" Donovan asked.

"For a private school with the President's son, yes," she said. "The pay is good and it's a hidden defense against anyone who would try to infiltrate the school and kidnap Mason. If for some reason Smith fails to protect Mason, there are others that could stand in."

"Smart plan," Donovan said.

The trio headed to the library, walking by closed doors, the hum of teacher's voices emanating from beyond. Carter scrutinized Donovan, taking in his strong jaw and prominent cheekbones. Sensing her appraisal, he narrowed his eyes.

"What is it?" he asked.

"Why do girls find it necessary to try and intimidate me over you, when they have received no attention or encouragement from you?"

"What are you talking about?" Link asked.

"I was approached earlier by 'Donovan's Posse' who were trying to convince me the double date is actually a pity date."

Link burst out laughing. "Donovan, I didn't know your group of admirers had turned so aggressive."

"It's not me that makes them act this way," Donovan said.

"You certain about that?" Carter deadpanned. "Because I have enough evidence that says it is."

Donovan stopped walking, bringing the group to a halt. "What you are failing to realize is that it's not me personally but what I symbolize."

Carter and Link exchanged a glance. Donovan ignored it and continued. "I am something they desire."

"Yeah, we got that," Carter said, emphatically.

Donovan leveled her with a hard, unamused look. She held up her hands in mock apology and Donovan's expression reverted to normal. "I am something they desire that they can't have. In a world where they have been granted their every wish, I am unattainable. That is why they act out."

It made sense but Carter simply wished they would accept defeat and leave her alone.

"Really?" Link asked.

Donovan nodded. "Human nature. Attack whatever threatens your way of life."

"I wish they would attack you instead of me," Carter said.

Donovan shot her a challenging smirk. "Can't handle a few spoiled girls, Carter?"

She returned his smirk. "Captain told me I'm not allowed to hit defenseless animals. My only defense is to cut down their ego and leave them with their shattered pride."

"What's wrong with that?" Donovan asked. "Sounds exactly within your skillset."

"I prefer a swift punch. It's faster and sends a stronger message. Nothing says "back off" like a broken nose and thousands of dollars in reconstructive surgery."

Donovan laughed as Link's phone beeped and he dug it out of his pocket. "Amy's waiting for us. We should go."

Glancing up from behind her desk, Diana greeted Carter with a bright smile as the trio entered the library. With a wave in return, Carter followed Link and Donovan to Amy's table. As they approached, Amy looked up and smiled at Link, receiving a blush and nervous smile in response. He took the spot next to her while Carter and Donovan took the seats opposite.

"So," Amy said, "I'm a little lost with this calculus homework. Can you help me?"

She looked at Link with an open, pleading look, her lower lip between her teeth. Donovan and Carter looked at each other, fighting back knowing smiles. Link straightened and edged closer to her.

"Of course, what do you need help on?"

Amy scooted her chair a few inches closer to Link's and leaned on the table, her arm brushing his. She pulled the textbook between them and looked over it, while Link looked at her. Carter looked at Donovan. She gave a nod to Amy and raised her eyebrows as if to say 'she's headstrong.' Donovan nodded.

Carter listened as Link fumbled his way through helping Amy understand the homework. Knowing privacy might help Link be more comfortable, Carter slipped away from the table, trusting Donovan would understand her departure. Wandering through the rows, Carter eventually came upon Donovan as Sloane strode determinedly up to him.

Carter stopped. Clearly her jab about Donovan's refusal to talk to Sloane hit home. Pity she didn't give up, salvaging her pride. Some people were gluttons for punishment.

"Hi," Sloane said. "Looking for something?"

When Donovan didn't answer, Sloane touched his arm and he tensed, shying away. Carter wondered how he ever managed to get through a day without her coming to his rescue. Carter snatched a book off a shelf at random, opened it, and walked into the aisle.

"Donovan," she said, not bothering to look up. "I think I found that reference we were looking for."

She raised her head and froze in pretend surprise. Sloane turned, startled, her hand in mid-air. Donovan relaxed, his annoyance fading at Carter's appearance. With a cool, superior smile, Carter snapped the book shut and held it in both hands.

"Are you done here?" she asked the girl. "Like I predicted, he would make no response and you would be left feeling like an idiot. Give it up and walk away."

All of Sloane's composure snapped, revealing anger and humiliation. "Do you even realize how unimportant you are? You're not worth knowing. Your own mother even tossed you aside."

The book clattered to the floor as Carter raised her fist and swung at Sloane, aiming for those perfect teeth. With a hard smack, Donovan blocked her blow. Sloane took a shocked step back, eyes wide. Donovan tightened his hold on Carter's fist. His calmness pulled Carter from her fiery thoughts.

"Are you in control?" he asked.

He held her gaze, waiting. The understanding in his blue eyes helped Carter bury her hurt and anger. Deflating, she swallowed and Donovan released his hold.

"Just leave," she told Sloane, her voice devoid of

emotion.

Sloane hurried away, casting a fearful glance over her shoulder at Carter. Needing to avoid Donovan's penetrating gaze, Carter retrieved the fallen book and restored it to its rightful place.

When she faced Donovan again, he was leaning a shoulder against the bookcase, his arms crossed. For a long moment, they stared at each other; Donovan silently interrogating her, Carter dodging his questions. He finally let the topic drop, accepting Carter's stone wall.

"Thank you for getting me out of that," he said.

Carter let out a silent sigh of relief at the change of topic. "Sure. She had a determined look other girls have lacked. I figured I should step in before you were tackled to the ground."

Donovan raised an eyebrow. "You underestimate my strength."

"And you underestimate the strength of a determined girl who can't have you and is trying to restore her sense of superiority."

Donovan smiled but the look didn't erase the questions burning in his eyes.

"Has it always been this bad for you?" she asked.

"The first three years were nothing. The last three have been…challenging."

"How so?"

Donovan ran a hand through his hair, dropping his calm mask to reveal weariness. "The main problem is something you probably understand: boredom."

"Of course," she said. "You probably haven't had an intelligent conversation in years."

"I've talked to my brothers from time to time but yes, intellect has been in short supply."

"Come on," Carter said, walking backward to the end of the row. "I'm sure by the time we sit down you'll come up with something that could challenge my brain. If you can."

Chapter 21

As Carter walked to the living room, she slid her arms into her leather jacket. Light from the lamps illuminated the apartment. Her father sat on the couch, his arm in a sling and a computer in front of him. On the coffee table sat stacks of papers and a collection of empty plates and glasses.

When Carter appeared, he looked up and froze. Instead of her usual home uniform of ratty shirt and sweatpants, she wore boots, skinny jeans, and a simple black v-neck t-shirt. Her loose, wavy hair hung down just below her shoulders. At her father's reaction, she scowled and stuffed her hands into the pockets of the jacket.

"Shut up and stop looking at me like that," she said.

Her father shook his head. "I didn't say anything."

"Your face said enough." She held out her hands. "This is what happens when you go away and leave me with Maggie." Carter made a face. "She takes me shopping and buys me pants without pockets."

"You look nice, Sarge."

Making another face, she waved away his comment.

"When you play bodyguard, you have a black suit: that's your uniform. When I play 'fake date to the bodyguard' this is *my* uniform." She snatched her satchel off the hook and she took a seat on the coffee table, studying his worn-out face and tired eyes. "You all right?"

He shifted and winced at the pain but smiled weakly. "A bit sore but it's nothing I can't handle. Where is it you're going?"

Carter shrugged. "Movies and possibly a cage fight if I can convince them."

"Stick to just the movies, I'm not sure I want you fighting grown men on your own."

"Please, like I would take them on, on my own," she said. "Donovan would help me."

When her father gave her a stronger smile, Carter felt the pressure in her chest lighten.

"I don't have to go, you know. I can stay in and we can watch a movie or something."

"Maggie is going to stop by. I'll be fine."

Carter gave him a sly grin. "I see. You want me out of the way so you and Maggie can have some quality time together." Her father's expression fell flat. "No need to look so pissy, Captain. I'll take Maggie as a stepmother any day."

Frowning, her father shooed her away. "Go, before I decide to put you through a set of drills."

Carter kissed the top of his head. "All right, I'm leaving."

A cool gust of wind entered the apartment as she stood in the doorway. "Just know," she said, "If I come home to find you and Maggie making out on the couch, it's dishes for a week."

"Carter!"

She dashed out of the door before her father could rebuke her. Overhead, a pale moon lit her way through the narrow lane to the main road. As she crossed the street to the bus stop, Maggie approached.

"Off to your date then?" she said, gleefully.

"Yup," Carter said, not matching her excitement. "Should be a blast. You know how I love romantic movies with wimpy girl characters."

"It doesn't matter because you're going on a date! That's what is important."

"Sure."

The bus pulled up to the curb and Carter jogged towards it, giving Maggie a wave.

"Have fun!" Maggie called out as Carter climbed on.

The doors shut and the bus took off with Maggie watching till the red tail lights disappeared.

A bus and metro ride later Carter climbed up the concrete steps of the metro station and into a part of the city that was a stark contrast with her neighborhood. Chic cafes and overpriced restaurants lined the sidewalks. Impressive apartment buildings with gleaming glass fronts stretched into the sky. The pedestrians strolling the sidewalks wore outfits that cost more than Carter's entire closet.

A man in a dark green suit opened the apartment door for her as she approached and welcomed her. The decor of the lobby was minimalistic: a polished tile floor, potted plants, and a dark wooden desk at the center of the space.

"Can I help you?" asked the concierge behind the desk.

"I'm looking for the Evans' residence," she said.

"Name?"

"Carter Owens."

The man checked his computer. "9th floor, apartment 32."

A short ride later, Carter stepped out into a wide, silent hallway. A door opened and Donovan exited, dressed casually in converse shoes, jeans, and a black pea coat.

"Where's Link?" Carter asked, stopping next to him.

When Donovan looked over, his normally impassive

face was splashed with surprise.

"Thanks for the compliment," she said, wearing a smug grin.

"I didn't say anything."

"Not in so many words."

Donovan tucked his keys away as Carter glanced around.

"Where is Link?" she asked again.

He pointed down the hall. "Next apartment over."

Carter frowned, puzzled, and the corner of Donovan's mouth curled up.

"No," he said. "I don't live in the same apartment. I have my own, just next door."

When Carter opened her mouth, Donovan laughed. "I'm twenty-two, Carter. What did you expect? I'm close enough to prevent anything from happening. Besides, I needed a different address for school purposes."

"Right, you just look -"

"Like a seventeen-year-old student? That's kind of the point."

Carter backed up and eyed him critically, if not slightly appreciatively as well. "It's a good thing you normally wear a uniform because the casual look ages you."

"Thanks for the compliment," he said.

"I didn't say anything."

"Not in so many words."

A door down the hall opened and Link stepped out, wearing a hoodie tucked beneath a blazer and jeans. He glanced to the elevator before spotting Donovan and Carter standing together. His eyebrows shot up as he looked at Carter.

"You look-"

Carter cut him off with a wave of her hand. "Yes, I know. Let's move past this revelation that I have curves."

Link, still slightly surprised, nodded. "All right."

"We should go," Donovan said.

Link came out of his daze.

"Yeah, right," he said, "I don't want Amy to have to wait."

Carter smiled. "Of course we don't. Let's get this date over with."

Donovan smirked. "Don't sound too excited, Carter."

She shot him a flat look that he returned with a half-smile.

***

The lights in the theater brightened as the credits filled the widescreen. Carter rested her head on her fingertips as she stared at the list of names with a look of wide-eyed disbelief. Amy's light laugh reached her from down the row where she sat beside Link. They stood and Donovan nudged Carter's arm. She blinked herself out of her shocked daze and followed Donovan out of their row. As they reached the bottom of the stairs, she took a spot by his side.

"Is it just me," she said, "or do you feel you lost brain cells watching that poor display of acting? Not to mention the fact that the storyline was so convoluted they forgot to mention how the girl's mother survived the car crash!"

Shaking his head, Donovan ran a hand through his hair. "I'm still trying to understand why the girl went to the father's house. It was a tactical nightmare and an easy spot to get ambushed."

She gestured emphatically to him. "Yes! There was no thought put into her plan of action and she walked blindly into a situation she knew was already dangerous. Especially considering the history of the father's abuse on his son."

"Also, there was the fact that she was unarmed and had avoided announcing her intentions to a superior."

"It's as if she was under the impression that good

intentions would protect her. Completely delusional thinking. Which would also explain why she believed she could reform a delinquent with a serious drinking problem."

They pushed through the theater doors, right behind Link and Amy. The smell of popcorn and melted cheese wafted across the main lobby. Lines of customers snaked their way towards ticket windows and concession stands.

"So," Amy said. "Not the best movie. But still fun, right?"

Donovan and Carter shared a glance, neither expression revealing their thoughts.

"What did you think," Amy asked, lacing her hand with Link's.

Thoughts aligned, Carter and Donovan reacted: Carter stuffing her hands into the pockets of her jacket while Donovan hid his away in his jeans. Link straightened, a pleased grin coming to his lips.

"I thought it was great," he said.

Amy tightened her hold on Link's hand, lost in each other for a long moment. Carter looked at Donovan, barely containing her smile. He looked back with a placid face, a smirk only shown in the twitching of his lips. Carter coughed and the couple seemed to return to themselves.

"So…" she said.

"How about fro-yo?" Amy said, eagerly.

Carter opened her mouth, the objection already between her teeth when Link made eye contact with her. A silent urge to agree was hiding in his hazel eyes.

"Sure, why not?" Carter said.

Amy rose to the tips of her toes, giddy. Carter gave Donovan a look that expressed all of her opinions and which got her a grin in response.

They left the theater, entering the crowded sidewalk. Music spilled out of a bar's open windows, trailed by laughter and conversations. Link and Amy took the lead, their hands still clasped and Amy's bright voice keeping up a steady stream. As they walked, Donovan's relaxed manner dropped away. He surveyed the surrounding crowd with a calculating, intelligent gaze, sizing up those around them.

"Is it just me or did Amy seem more stable during school?" Carter asked, in a lowered voice.

"Being out of the limits of school and under the effects of a romantic movie will change a person," he said. "Especially a girl who is already giving in to her hormones. Add the attention of a boy and physical contact and she may as well be a whole different person."

"So you're saying if you held my hand it would have the same effect on me?"

"No," he said. "You're ruled by logic and have a natural barrier against letting others get close to you. You would mask the feelings the contact would create."

The observation struck a chord in Carter but she ignored it. "Pretty sure of that, aren't you?"

"Yes," Donovan said. He broke from his scan of the surrounding crowd to look at her, searching. "Why you're this way I haven't completely figured out but the main source is your mother and her betrayal."

Ice crawled into Carter's chest. "I would stop yourself, Donovan," she said, in a detached voice, "before you say anything that I will make you regret."

Donovan met her threat unfazed. "My conclusions are well founded, then."

Carter clenched her fists, memories pressing against the barriers in her mind. "I said stop. Now."

Carter didn't remember when they had stopped walking but they stood in the middle of the sidewalk, staring at each other, their breath making small clouds before them. Donovan narrowed his eyes.

"What are you afraid of, Carter?" he said, in a low, ponderous voice. "Being hurt? Or letting someone else in?"

Carter barely raised her fist before Donovan wrapped his fingers around her wrist, stilling her strike.

She seethed.

"Carter, Donovan!" Link shouted back to them.

The tension cracked. Amy and Link watched them, Link wearing a puzzled expression while Amy tried to conceal a mischievous grin at the closeness of the two. Donovan let go of Carter's wrist and the rest of the tension was swept away with the passing crowd. Carter joined Link and Amy, her face devoid of emotion.

"You guys all right?" Link asked, his gaze flickering between her and Donovan.

"Fine," Carter said, cooly. "Let's go get fro-yo."

Amy took the lead again while Carter followed, never sparing a glance at Donovan.

His questions beat against her long after the group split ways, his voice running over and over in her mind as she headed towards home.

The temperature had dropped and Carter balled her fists inside her pockets, glaring at the ground. A burst of laughter caused her to look up, catching a glimpse of a family crowded around a kitchen table. The sound faded away as she entered the lane.

The unfamiliar car didn't register with her as she ascended the staircase. Muffled voices emanated from inside. Pushing aside Donovan's voice, Carter unlocked the front door and pushed it open.

"Captain, I'm home," she said. "You can call off the drone-"

The end of her sentence was caught in her throat as she faced the apartment. Across from her father at the kitchen table sat a woman, in her late thirties with styled, dyed blonde hair, a narrow face, and curvy frame. Carter stared at the scene, every inch of her frozen with shock. The woman stood.

"Hello, Carter," her mother said.

Carter dug her nails into her palms. "What the hell are you doing here?!"

Chapter 22

S arge," Carter's father said.

Carter shot him a fierce look.

"I'm serious!" she said, anger and pain laced in every syllable. "What the hell are you doing here?!"

Her mother took a step forward but Carter's icy glare halted her in her tracks. Her mother glanced back at Carter's father. "I was in the city and I wanted to -"

"Get out," Carter snarled.

Her mother widened her eyes, stunned. Carter felt something inside her snap. Hand shaking, she pointed to the door. "Get. The. Hell. Out."

Her father rose, one hand on the table for support. "Sarge, you have no right-"

"I have every right!" she yelled.

She could see the burden in his eyes and turned her cold, unyielding stare on to her mother. "Leave. Now."

With a nod from Carter's father, her mother gathered up her purse. Carter felt hard as stone as her mother brushed past her. The scent of perfume lingered in her wake. A scent Carter grew up with. A scent clinging to millions of memories, good and bad. As the door had closed, tense silence landed in the apartment.

"Sarge-"

"No!" Carter burst out, switching her glare from the wall to her father. "Why did you ever let her in?"

Her father raised a hand, trying to calm her anger. "Carter you don't understand…"

"How could you possibly be sitting here with her after everything she has done?"

"Carter," he said, tiredly. "I know this is confusing-"

"Confusing! That Thing destroyed our family!"

Her father hardened, shoulders tightening, the weariness burned away. Carter knew she had taken a step too far. But so had he.

"Despite everything, she is your mother," he said, his voice controlled, "and you will not talk about her like that."

Cold hatred seized Carter, not for him but for the third presence that had left behind the smell of citrus.

"No," she said, her voice piercing the air. "That is where you are wrong. I have no mother. Not anymore."

She stormed to her room, the vile feeling of rage coursing through her. Kicking her door shut, she hurled her satchel onto her bed. Everything around her blurred as thoughts battled in her mind. Images of her mother leaving the first time clashing with the image of her mother standing before her moments ago. Conflicting emotions ricocheted through her, suffocating her.

She was never supposed to come back. They had moved on. What right did she have to come back?

Without thinking, Carter ripped off her jacket, threw it onto her bed, and grabbed her boxing gloves. She pulled them on, yanking with unnecessary force on the Velcro straps. Endless scenarios of how the interaction could have gone played through her mind as she pummeled the punching bag.

The sound of her fists hitting the taut leather and the

creaking of the bag as it swung went unheard by Carter, her thoughts drowning out the world. She wasn't supposed to come back. She *wasn't* supposed to come back. Carter forced breath into her lungs, as a vise closed tighter and tighter around her heart. She began to ache with the frantic speed in which she fought the bag but she didn't stop. She landed blow after blow to the tight leather, her movements reckless. The bag swung and she pounded, unaware of the pain in her knuckles.

Tears gathered in her eyes when the strain in her arms and the overwhelming pain in her heart dulled her thoughts. She blinked angrily, causing the tears to spill over and stream down her face.

Her punches became sloppier and slower until she finally stopped, unable to see the bag through her blur of tears. Holding onto one of the chains keeping the bag up, she leaned her head against the cool, black fabric and cried.

Unlike her anger, her sadness was one of deep pain. No tornado of emotion. Just one deep endless pit of grief that threatened to swallow her whole. She didn't hear her door open. She was barely aware of her father's presence until his strong hand pulled her into a one-armed hug.

She yielded to his comfort and buried her face in his shirt, letting loose all the hurt she had bottled up.

"She wasn't supposed to come back," she choked. "Why is she here?"

Her father stroked her head and kissed the top of her hair. "It's complicated."

Chapter 23

The tumult of student voices filled the empty air as Carter opened the car door. Maggie put a hand on Carter's arm, making her pause. Carter felt numb from exhaustion and sadness. Maggie gripped Carter's arm in a gesture that spoke volumes of her concern and worry.

"Carter," she said, softly.

Carter tensed, unable to face anyone's sympathy. Releasing her hand, Maggie settled for an understanding smile. Without a word, Carter picked up her bag and got out of the car.

The full force of spring seemed to have chased the last strains of winter away during the night. The sun's heat penetrated the chill trapped in the breeze. Ducking her head, Carter headed up the stairs, oppressed by the cheeriness of the day.

She had barely taken two steps inside the school when Lucas and his gang of friends converged on her. Instead of taking the opportunity to release some of her pent up pain on someone, who would no doubt earn it when he spoke, Carter found she didn't want to.

"Owens, have you looked in a mirror-"

The rest of the sentence broke off as Carter shoved Lucas aside, walking to her classroom as if he was a ghost.

In front of her first-period classroom, Amy talked with Link, their hands intertwined. Donovan rested against a set of lockers, his gaze roaming over the flow of students. When his eyes landed on Carter, he straightened, surprise and concern flashing through his expression. With an effort, Carter put on a mask of disinterest. The bell rang, sending everyone scattering.

"I should get to class," Amy said, her tone soft.

Despite her best efforts, Carter knew Donovan saw beyond her mask. The small part of her that wasn't numb hated him for seeing her weakness.

"Carter," he said, his voice low. "What's wrong?"

She kept her face blank. "Nothing."

"That's not true," he said. "You can't lie to me."

"Nothing is wrong," she said, tucking her hands into her pockets so he wouldn't see her red knuckles.

He closed the space between them. "Look, Carter. If this is about what I said last night, I apologize. I was out of line."

The double date felt as if it had happened in another lifetime. The conversation with Donovan darted through her mind, the topic pulling up the image of her mother standing in the living room. Pain flicked through her face. Donovan flexed his jaw in reaction, guilty. Carter dragged herself to the present, the feeling equal to pulling a body out of the water. She focused her gaze and she found Donovan watching her.

"It's fine," she said, her voice lifeless.

Donovan opened his mouth to argue but was stopped by Link.

"Are we going to class or are you two going to stand there staring at each other?"

Carter cut around Donovan and Link tossed his arm around her shoulders, his buoyed mood blinding him to hers.

***

At her locker, Carter stared at the interior while behind her students rushed to the cafeteria. Half the day has gone and Carter couldn't remember a single lesson she had heard. Forcing herself to move, she closed her locker. Further down the hallway, Donovan and Link made their way to her. She could see Donovan trying to find the reason for her current mood. She sighed inwardly, a heavy, tired feeling washing over her.

"Carter Owens, please report to the office," a scratchy female voice said over the speakers.

"What did you do?" Link asked.

"Who did you punch?" Donovan asked, noticing her red knuckles.

Carter met their curious expressions with a shake of her head. "I didn't do anything or punch anyone."

"Then why are you getting called to the office?" Link asked.

Without giving an answer, she left them, both boys watching her.

At the office, she opened the wooden door and stepped into the neat, spacious room. Behind the counter were rows of filing cabinets and a woman with a pinched face. She eyed Carter over her oval glasses.

"I was called in," Carter said, stepping up to the desk.

The woman motioned to the right with her pencil. "You have someone here to see you."

Carter went rigid at the sight of her mother, a new wave of exhaustion and emotions crashing over her. Her mother walked forward, wearing high heels, a pencil skirt, and a neat oxford shirt. She looked flawless.

"Carter," she said. "I thought we could have lunch together and talk."

Lunch. As if it were the most natural thing to offer. Hot anger burned away Carter's numbness.

"You thought wrong," she said, "It's not the first time. I'm sure you're used to the feeling."

Shock flickered in her mother's eyes.

"Leave me and my father alone. That shouldn't be too difficult for you; it's what you're good at."

Chapter 24

Carter heard the thrum of students crowding the halls, the sound telling her she should be on her way somewhere but she didn't stir from her corner at the back of the library. She ached from remaining stasis for so long but still didn't get up. Instead, she watched the motes of dust drifting in the sunlight, feeling as if they carried her tangled thoughts and emotions.

The second bell rang through the school and voices tumbled into the library as students settled around tables. Books banged against tabletops and chairs scraped against the floor. Carter took it in without caring, head resting against the wall. On the second level and hidden among the rows of biographies, she felt sure no one would find her there.

A set of footsteps vibrated on the stairs but Carter stayed immobile even as the steps drew closer. When Donovan came into view, Carter gathered up her tangled thoughts and shoved them away. They weren't for him to see and analyze.

"How long have you been here?" he asked.

Carter shifted, wincing at the stiffness in her muscles. "I don't know."

Donovan eyed her as she uncurled her limbs, trying to hide how everything ached. "You didn't come to lunch and from how tense you look, I'm guessing you skipped the last two classes as well."

"What do I care? Not like I wouldn't be bored in them anyways."

"Why did you get called into the office?"

Carter clenched her jaw as the image of her mother swam in front of her eyes. Schooling her face, she shrugged. "It was nothing."

"That's a lie."

Annoyance sparked inside Carter. "You know, just because you can see everything doesn't mean you have the right to know everything."

Donovan stared at her, expressionless. "That's rich coming from you."

She wished he'd go away, leave her to try and make sense of the mess inside. But he stood there, waiting. It didn't matter, Carter didn't plan on giving him anything. Why would she? For the last four years she'd done fine on her own.

"What's wrong, Carter?" Donovan asked.

"Nothing."

Carter stood, cramps in her muscle making it an effort. She leaned on the wall, working to appear nonchalant. She met Donovan's gaze and crossed her arms. The tilt of his head told her he noticed the defensiveness in her posture. It irritated her.

"What?" she said. "What do you see, Donovan? A girl who doesn't want to go to class. That can't be something new."

Donovan said nothing, holding the same knowing look. "Link and I are your friends."

Carter tensed, surrounded by walls she'd created for years. "And, what? That means I share my deepest darkest secrets with you?" She gave a derisive laugh.

"I've known you for only a couple of weeks, what makes you think you have a right to know?"

Bemused, Donovan inched towards her. "Don't you understand that's how friendship works?"

"Then I'm not good at friendship."

"I would have to agree."

Carter scowled at him. "How is that supposed to make me want to tell you anything?"

Donovan stepped closer, challenging. "You pretend you're fine but you're not."

Pushing herself off the wall, Carter strode past Donovan but he halted her with a hand on her arm. "If you force people away long enough they won't be there when you need them."

"I don't force people away," Carter said, yanking her arm free. "They leave on their own."

***

The weather had shifted, whitish-gray clouds pushing out the sunlight as Carter trudged to the deli. Donovan's statement cut into her over and over again: "if you force people away long enough they won't be there when you need them."

From outside the deli, Carter heard the chaos of voices, the noise doubling as she entered. Families, students, and groups of elderly people packed the tables. The scolding of parents to their children clashed with the cheery conversations of friends. Alone, Carter stood just inside the door, surveying the scene.

"Oh, hi, Hon," Maggie said, bits of hair falling out of her ponytail, face flushed from rushing about. "How come you're so late? it's past six."

"I walked a while. Lost track of time."

"You never lose track of time," Maggie said, concerned.

Carter wanted to explain, wanted someone to listen, needed someone to listen. But the bell dinged and a new group joined the crowded deli.

"I'm sorry, Hon, I can't talk. I might see you late tonight but can't count on it."

Smothering her disappointment, Carter sidestepped the new customers and left. Outside felt colder than before and Carter hurried home, needing warmth. As she discarded her keys in the bowl, her father greeted her. On the dining room table around him lay neat stacks of papers and a computer.

"Hi Sarge, how was school?" he asked.

Carter began to drop her bag on the coffee table but stopped, her response trapped in her mouth. The bag clattered onto the wood.

"She was here today," Carter said, smelling her mother's citrus perfume. A scent too fresh to be from the previous night.

"Yes," her father said.

"Why?" Carter snapped. "Why are you doing this? Why did you let her come back here?"

Calmly, her father slid his chair back and rose. "I can explain. I..."

Carter cut him off. "Why are you even letting her into our house? I don't know what she's doing here!"

"I know you don't understand -"

"I don't understand! At all! I don't get why she's back!"

"Carter, if you'd just let me..."

"Don't you see how truly terrible of a person she is?"

"Now, wait a minute.."

"How do you not get that -"

"Enough!" Carter felt hit by the vehemence in her father's tone. "I've had enough of this, Carter. I will not have you talk to me like that."

"But Captain, why-"

Her father's fierce glare cut Carter's rant short.

"I said enough," he said. "I have my reasons. This is

the end of the conversation."

Stunned, Carter couldn't act, couldn't think of what to say. Couldn't make sense of the world pitching around her.

When her father's phone rang, he answered it. "Yes, sir?"

With a last look at Carter, he retreated to his room, closing the door. The heavy silence around her brought Carter back to herself. She spun on her heel and left the apartment. Dropping to the top step she buried her head in her hands. The cold stairs chilled her and the canopy of stars seemed to echo her loneliness. Lost in a troubled storm, she jogged down the steps, unsure where she was going.

Eventually, she found herself back on the wealthy side of the city. Wanting to turn back, but not knowing where else to go, Carter wound her way through the busy sidewalks to Link and Donovan's apartment building. The same doorman welcomed her. The same classical music played in the elevator. The same tan hallway greeted her. Only Carter had changed since the night of the double date.

Uncertain, she walked down the hallway, hearing the hum of TVs within apartments. Time stretched around her as she stood before the smooth wooden door, catching her reflection in the gold numbers.

She raised her hand to knock but hesitated. Stealing herself, she rapped her knuckles against the door. No sound came from within. Cursing, she turned to leave but heard the faint patter of feet and a second later the door opened.

"Carter?!"

Self-conscious, Carter shoved her hands into her pockets. "Do you have a minute to talk?"

Chapter 25

Link blinked in surprise. When Carter fidgeted, Link snapped out of his shock. "Sure. Come in."

Link's apartment had a wide, open layout. A living room to the left held a beige couch and two vanilla armchairs, while the kitchen to the right held granite countertops. Floor to ceiling windows showcased the darkened city and the top of the Capitol building. Carter knew in a glance that her apartment could fit in Link's living room and kitchen.

"It looks like the child support checks are still coming in," she said.

Link flinched and Carter let out a weary sigh, hating herself. "I'm sorry. I didn't come here to insult you. I really didn't."

Link waved the comment away as if it hadn't hit a sore wound. Though Donovan, who sat in one of the armchairs, scowled at Carter for her comment. She didn't blame him, he'd been right. She didn't know how to do friendship.

"Is your mother here?" Carter asked Link.

"She's at the office," he said. "Big court case. I have no idea when she will be home. It's usually never before three." He rubbed his neck, unsure. "Uh..do you want to sit down or something?"

"Sure."

"I can leave," Donovan said, as Link and Carter joined him in the living room.

"No," Carter said. "It's fine."

Both boys watched her. Carter took a deep breath, trying to form the sentences that would explain her presence. When she produced nothing and the silence stretched on, she balled her fists, nervous energy dancing in her fingertips.

How did you release something that had been trapped inside for years? How did someone go about explaining the events that made her the abrasive girl they knew?

"Carter," Link said, "what's going on?"

As Carter cracked her knuckles she looked between them, unable to hold their gazes for longer than a second. Link glanced at Donovan, who shook his head, silently telling him to wait. Carter saw the disassembled handgun Donovan must have been working on, laying on the coffee table.

Needing something familiar to help her gather her courage, she reached for the pieces. Donovan jerked forward but halted as she expertly assembled the weapon. Finished, she gently placed the gun down and pulled back.

"Sorry," she said.

Link stared in astonishment, Donovan's only show of surprise a slight rise in his eyebrows. Carter slid back on the couch and rubbed her hands on her pants, some of her frantic energy appeased.

"I don't know where to begin," she said.

"The reason why you're here would be a good place," Donovan said.

Drawing strength from the steadiness of the boys' presence, she nodded. "I came...because I needed a friend."

She studied her locked fingers. "I don't know how much of this you know," she said, gesturing to Donovan. "But my mom left when I was fourteen."

"What happened?" Link blurted out.

Donovan shot him a look and Link curbed his questions.

"One night she decided that being a mother was no longer what she wanted to do. So she left. In a taxi."

In Donovan's eyes, she could see he wasn't fooled by her impassivity but he didn't call her out. Link bent forward on his knees.

"She just left? Out of the blue?" he asked.

"I was a surprise baby. Unplanned. It was supposed to be the marriage, career, then me." The story rushed forward, the dam in her mind finally broken. "The second year of college my mother got pregnant. They got married. My father went into the military and became a Navy SEAL. My mother left college, left an internship, even passed up job opportunities to raise me." Carter contemplated the spotless carpet. "When I was fourteen, she got offered a position she said she couldn't pass up. She took it. Left my father alone with me. It's been four years since we've seen her. Not once. Until yesterday, when she showed up at our apartment, unannounced. I told her to leave."

Carter relaxed, her past released from her tight-fisted hold. Link had a hundred questions darting through his eyes while Donovan offered quiet understanding.

"You saw her again today," he said. "In the office."

"She wanted to have lunch and talk. She walked into my school and my life as if it was the simplest thing in the world and nothing had changed. I told her to leave my dad and me alone."

Carter buried her face in her hands, suddenly tired.

"Is that what you want?" Donovan asked.

"I don't know. I don't know what I want," she said.

"Why did you come here?"

"Honestly..." She took in a breath. "I didn't have anywhere else to go."

The words hung in the air between them, honest and raw.

"And as far as I can tell, you have gone through something similar," Carter said to Link. "What did you do when you first met your father?"

Carter felt guilty as she saw pain flash through Link's eyes. "I understand if it's too difficult to talk about."

Taking off his glasses, Link stared at them then tossed them onto the table. The aspects of his father's face were so clear in his features. "I almost hit him."

He grinned, noticing Carter's incredulity. "A Secret Service agent stopped me before I could throw a punch. I didn't say anything to him that first time. He was so cold I didn't know what to say."

"How long was it before you saw him again?" Carter asked.

"A few weeks. My mother convinced me that I should at least talk to him. I did. Eventually, we got past everything. Well, almost everything but it took a long time. It's still not ideal. I only see him every few months."

"You forgave him?"

A wry smile came to Link's face. "Not completely. What he did was terrible. But for the most part, I wanted to know him. I was twelve, I wanted a father and I still do. At least, part of a father is better than none."

As Carter sank back on the couch, she mulled over his words. Forgiveness felt foreign when thinking about someone who left so much damage in her life.

"Why did your mother show up now?" Link asked. "After four years?"

Carter rubbed her face as her thoughts ping-ponged back and forth. "I don't know. We were doing fine without her. I want her out of our lives." The last sentence came out as a growl.

"You won't talk to her at all?" Link asked.

"Why should I?" Carter said, angrily. "What has she ever done except abandon me? I owe her nothing and want nothing from her!" When she felt her nails bite into her palms, she forced her fingers to uncurl. "I don't know what to do. This is a rare thing for me."

"I imagine so," Donovan said, softly.

Something in his tone lifted Carter from her troubled thoughts for a moment, the beginning of a grin tugging at her mouth. The moment passed and her face fell.

"Do you plan to shut your mother out until she leaves?" Donovan asked.

"Yes...maybe..." She shrugged. "There is nothing she could say that would change anything. The fact is she left; she picked her career over me."

"That is true," Link said. "But if you don't see her, you don't get to say what you've wanted to."

Carter scowled. "I don't have anything to say to her."

When Link raised his eyebrows in contradiction, she sighed. "Of course I have things to say to her but it will make no difference."

"Then she will leave," Donovan said, "and all the things you have wanted to tell her will be left trapped in your head."

"Yes, but I'd have to see her again to tell her those things. Therein lies the problem. I don't want to see her. I never wanted to see her after she left."

"That's not true," Donovan said.

Carter paced, edgy. "Of course it's not true. But I was fourteen. I forced myself to stop running to the door at the sound of a car. I got over it. I moved on with my life."

Donovan laced his fingers together, eyes trailing Carter's agitated path back and forth.

"What?" she said, glowering at him.

"Carter," he responded, "you say you have moved on, yet you push everyone away." He raised a hand, stopping her arguments. "You became an outcast at school. You fear getting close to people because you fear being abandoned again. You use your intellect and physical force to keep everyone else at a distance. "

Carter wanted to argue it but couldn't ignore that her hands already formed fists.

"Deny it but it's the truth. You tried to force us away."

For a tense moment, she stared at Donovan and he stared back, his face unyielding. Finally, she lowered her eyes, her frustration slipping away.

"Why did either of you ever decide to be my friend?" she asked, quietly.

"You'll have to ask him that," Donovan said, nodding at Link.

Link gave Carter a lopsided smile. "I liked you. You were smart and you didn't like Mason. Having to go to school with my half-brother was never going to be easy. Having someone who didn't fawn over him made it more bearable. Besides, you analyze people and make observations like Donovan and I found that oddly comforting."

Carter felt some of the weight lift off her chest. "I'm glad you didn't give up easily."

Walking back to the couch, she dropped onto it. A comfortable silence settled around them.

"Will you talk to your mother?" Donovan asked, breaking the quiet.

"Honestly…I don't know." The thought of facing her mother again created a tumult of conflicting emotions. Emotions too complicated to figure out. "I don't want to decide now. What I do want is some of that pizza."

"Go ahead but it's cold," Link said, gesturing to the pizza box.

Flipping the lid open, she grabbed a slice and pointed to the gun.

"How fast can you put that together?" she asked.

Donovan smiled and moved towards the gun, quickly disassembling it.

***

A few hours later, when friendly conversations had made the reason for Carter's visit mostly forgotten and the pizza box sat empty, Carter stretched. The lights outside the windows had slowly blinked off, leaving the stars and the street lights the only means of illumination. Carter checked the time. "I didn't realize how late it was," she said.

Link grimaced as he stretched out his arms. "You want to crash here on the couch? Or Donovan has an extra room."

"Two bedroom apartment in this building? You must make more than I thought," Carter said to Donovan.

Donovan slid his hands into his pockets, not responding to Carter's comment. "Are you accepting the offer?"

Despite her best effort to read him, she couldn't tell if the offer pleased him or not.

"As much fun as that sounds," Carter said, "I don't want Captain breaking down your door at four in the morning looking for me. I'll go home."

"You sure?" Link said, cautiously. "It's really late."

Carter laughed. "Link, do you honestly believe a mugger would get the better of me?"

Link gave her a smile that turned into a yawn. "True."

"It doesn't matter either way," she said. "I'll get an Uber home."

After putting in the request, Carter opened the front door then paused. "Uh…thanks for letting me talk." She shifted. "Friends aren't something I'm used to, so I appreciate you not slamming the door in my face."

"Of course, Carter," Link said. "See you tomorrow."

Through the silent elevator and car ride home Carter chewed on the decision that stood before her. Completely lost in her thoughts, the driver called her name twice before she heard him. The car drove off, leaving Carter alone with the street lights.

Every window lay dark as she walked down the lane and ascended the stairs. Moonlight streamed through the living room curtains and pooled on the floor. Carter slipped out of her shoes and eased the front door shut. The click of the lock sounded loud in her ears but no movement came from her father's room. Noiselessly, she snuck to her room.

As she stepped into the hallway, she froze at a sound far more terrifying than her father's anger.

She crept to her father's room. Instead of seeing her father lying beneath the blankets, she found him sitting on the edge of his bed, hunched over. He held his face in his hands, as his shoulders shook with sobs. Despite the conflict earlier, Carter's heart broke with him.

She took the spot on the bed beside him, laying her head on his shoulder. Her father wrapped his arm around her and kissed her hair. They sat together, Carter leaning into him, his head resting on hers. Neither spoke.

Chapter 26

With her eyes closed, Carter listened to the commotion of the school around her. The only part of her that felt connected to the world were the vibrations of the opening and closing lockers that played along her spine. Only when a presence connected with a familiar woodsy cologne joined her, did Carter leave the turning of her thoughts.

"Where's Link?" she asked. A flirty laugh rose above the waves of conversations followed by a bashful chuckle. "Never mind."

A thought struck her and she peered up at Donovan, who lounged on the locker beside her, his body angled towards hers as he surveyed the throng around them.

"That's why Link doesn't wear cologne," she said. "Keeps attention on you." He nodded. "He smells normal. Another way to keep him inconspicuous. Makes sense."

Dropping her head back, Carter stared at the far wall, aware of the conversations spilling gossip undercut with passive-aggressive jabs. "How have you lived so long being surrounded by so much mediocrity?"

"Because I have to," Donovan said.

"I would have gone mad." She palmed her eyes tiredly. "I'm glad I'm almost out of this pit of low intellect."

Finally, Donovan ceased his constant perusal and gave her his full attention, blue eyes curious. "Where do you plan to go after this?"

"I haven't decided yet. Every college accepted me. I haven't figured out how far away I want to go. What follows this for you?"

Donovan inched closer to Carter and dropped his voice. "When Douglas's term ends in two years, I will no longer be required to be Link's friend. We could go our separate ways."

Carter faced him and to any onlooker, the pair looked locked in a talk of conspiracies. "Where will you go? What will you do?"

The bell rang, cutting off Donovan's answer. "An explanation for another time."

"I'll hold you to it."

Link looked as if he were being pulled up from a happy dream when Donovan tapped his shoulder. At the sight of the emptying hall, Link smiled sheepishly.

"I'll see you after class," Amy said, kissing Link on the cheek, bringing color to his face.

"Shut up," he said, not meeting either of Carter or Donovan's laughing eyes.

"Today we're doing an in-class group project," Mr. Rojas said. "I will be splitting you up into groups." Before anyone could protest, he held up his hand. "No, you can not change groups."

Groans and angry mutterings whispered around the room and Carter slumped in her seat, echoing her classmates' sentiments.

"You smile," she hissed to Link, who delighted in her pain. "But I'm going to be stuck with a group of nitwits and end up doing the project alone."

"You get that most of the people in this class are smart, right?" he asked. "It is Advanced Chemistry."

"Smart is relative. Compared to you and Donovan, this class is filled with morons."

"In another group:" Mr. Rojas said. "Carter, Donovan, Link, and Mason."

Carter whipped her head to Link as he tried to control his expression but she could see his dread. The world seemed to be playing a joke on her friend and she didn't find it at all funny. Across the room, Mason locked eyes with Carter, looking like he would rather die. When Carter laid her hand on Link's clenched fists, he uncurled his fingers.

"What did I tell you?" she said. "I get nitwits for partners. Well, one nitwit, to be exact."

Link let out a slow breath and Carter squeezed his hand in silent encouragement.

"Alright class, get into your groups and I will go over what you will be doing," Mr. Rojas said.

Donovan joined Carter and Link at their table, but Mason showed no sign of moving. Carter glared at him which he returned. Naturally, he would assume they would come to him, maybe even bow to him once they got there.

"Mason, you underdeveloped neanderthal! Get over here," Carter yelled over the noise of the class.

A few laughs bounced around the room but quickly died as Mason eyed the culprits. As he made his way over to them, Smith following, Donovan leaned close to Carter.

"Play nice," he warned.

"Fine."

Appraising the group, Mason sat down. "Still managed to hang on to two friends, Owens. Did you buy them off?"

"You would be the one to understand," Carter said. "Keeping you from being friendless is where all the money from the national treasury goes, isn't it?"

"Owens, how you can stand to hear yourself talk amazes me because it gives me a headache."

"Like how your voice with its lack of IQ gives me a headache?"

"Carter," Donovan growled.

Carter raised her hands in surrender while Mason observed the exchange. "What are you? The Owens Whisperer? Do you have a phrase you use to shut her up? Because I'll pay to hear that."

Carter grinned sweetly. "Lean in Mason and I'll whisper that phrase to you."

"Owens, I wouldn't get within a foot of you if there was a gun to my back."

Feigning astonishment, Carter put her hand over her mouth. "There is a brain in that head of yours! And I thought when you ran for President you would be just another walking mouthpiece."

"Class," Mr. Rojas said, keeping Mason from biting back. "I'm going to explain your project for today so pay attention."

At the whiteboard, Mr. Rojas wrote out his instructions, talking as he did so. Mason pretended to listen, his back to Carter. Donovan gripped Carter's upper arm, tugging closer to him.

"For the sake of Link, don't make this any more difficult," Donovan whispered.

Carter turned to him, their faces a few inches apart. When she spoke her breath got tangled with his. "How am I making anything more difficult?"

"Antagonizing Mason will only make this all last longer. Shut up and finish the project so he can go back to his table."

He had a point but making digs at Mason had become such a common pastime it would be difficult to stop. Besides, it was wildly entertaining. Donovan tightened his grip as if reading her thoughts, his blue eyes hard as steel.

"Fine," she said. "I will play nice."

When they shifted away from each other, Carter found Link trying to understand what they said.

"Just exchanging threats and whatnot," Carter said. Puzzled, Link frowned. "It's nothing, Link."

With his directions finished, Mr. Rojas sent the students off to retrieve their materials. Carter stood and carelessly slapped Link's arm. "Come on, we'll get the materials." She pointed to Donovan and Mason. "You two can start working out the equations."

At the back of the line to the supply cabinets, Carter plopped an arm on Link's shoulder, sensing the tension radiating from him.

"How are you doing?" she asked, speaking close to his ear.

"Fine," he said. "What were you and Donovan talking about?"

"He made me promise to stop verbally abusing Mason," she said. She flashed a wicked smile. "He never said anything about lighting his hair on fire with the bunsen burner though."

As Link relaxed, he released a short laugh.

"Personally," she said, "I would love to see whether he screams like a girl."

This image produced a louder laugh from Link and brought about a few curious glances from other students.

"I would too," he said, "even just to see him get carried away by his Secret Service agent."

"Say the word and I'll do it," Carter said.

"Thanks, Carter," he said. He scuffed his foot on the floor. "What's the story behind why you and Mason don't get along?"

For a heartbeat, Carter almost lied, hiding a part of her past behind a careless comment. But she saw the openness in Link and thought of the previous night. He'd been there for her when she needed a friend.

"I transferred to Hamilton Prep two weeks after my mom left," she said, quietly. "When I could have used a table mate like you, I got Mason instead. We haven't stopped butting heads since."

The two students before them finished collecting their materials and left, leaving Carter and Link free to gather their materials. As they were buried in the shelves of the cabinet, Carter looked at Link.

"I can say this with all certainty: you are the better person," she said. "I would give up a hundred Masons to have you as my friend. Your father is lucky to have you as a son."

Link didn't look at her as he reached for a beaker. "Thanks, Carter. The same goes for you." He held her gaze. "Your mother has missed out."

This time, Carter found she couldn't hold Link's gaze and started absentmindedly rearranging gloves and goggles. She cleared her throat. "Thanks. And...uh...thanks for last night."

"What are friends for?" Link said.

They shared smiles, smiles mixed with the lingering hurt of their pasts.

Back at the table, Mason twisted in his seat, flirting with the neighboring girl, successfully distracting her while Donovan worked out the equations. When Carter and Link set their items down, Donovan studied them as if able to see their troubled thoughts.

"You manage to figure out those equations?" she asked, ignoring Donovan's unspoken curiosity. "If not, I can always do them for you."

A flat look was all she received but somehow it was still worth it.

"Okay," she said. "Let's get going."

Mason ignored her and leaned closer to the girl, saying something that made the girl laugh. Picking up her pencil, Carter flung it at Mason's back, making him flinch and Donovan scowl.

"What? You said no verbal abuse."

"Mason, we're working," Donovan said, his deep voice authoritative.

Reluctantly, Mason swiveled around. "Let's get this

over with."

Halfway through the project, after Mason had made his eighth snide comment towards Carter and she had been kept from retorting by Donovan's fierce glances, she managed to unclench her fists.

"For this next part we can split up," she said. "I'm tired of hearing Mason talk so I'll work with Link."

Mason glanced between Carter and Link, smirking. Link went rigid. "You two, huh?"

"Oh, Mason," Carter said, unwilling to let Link take any hits. "I would not go down this line of thinking. You don't want to know what I've heard about you." Mason froze. "It's amazing what details you hear in the girl's locker room."

Swallowing uncomfortably, Mason absorbed himself in the project. Beside her, Link ducked his head, trying to stifle his laughter. When he contained the sound, he gave Carter an appreciative nod.

"What are friends for," she mouthed.

Chapter 27

As Carter cut her way to the library, she passed Mr. Philips's classroom. Seeing the former-military janitor she had walked into talking with her teacher, she backtracked.

"Can you handle all these new repairs?" Mr. Philips asked, holding out a sheet of paper.

The janitor nodded and Mr. Philips clapped the man on the shoulder. Spotting Carter hovering in the doorway, Mr. Philips blinked in surprise.

"Was there something you needed, Carter?" he asked.

Carter twisted to the side as the janitor exited the room. "Essay due Friday, right?"

"Yes, three pages. Please stay within that amount this time. Also, I still need your signed permission slip for the field trip to the Newseum."

"Got it."

When Carter pushed through the library doors, Diana raised her head. Her graying brown hair appeared neater than Carter had seen it and instead of glasses, Diana wore contacts.

"I see things with Mr. Rojas are going well," Carter said.

"What would ever make you think that?" Diana said, coloring.

"You're wearing contacts. And you have a half-eaten sandwich. That means you probably had lunch with him. Also, your shirt is new as well as the skirt, that means you want to look nice here. If you were going out after school then you wouldn't have to worry about it because you could change before you left for the date. If you're having lunch together that means it's going well because you're openly letting the other teachers know you're dating."

Diana gaped at Carter with wide eyes. After all these years Diana still acted surprised at Carter's observation, which thoroughly amused Carter.

"Do you know what the big surprise for this weekend is?" she asked.

Diana snapped her mouth closed. "How did you-"

"He had us do an in-class project which means the homework load will be light this weekend. That way he is free to take you out and do something time-consuming."

"Carter, you are something different altogether."

"Yeah, I know."

Carter bent forward intently. "Could you convince him to do something next weekend as well? I don't feel like doing a lot of homework."

Eyes crinkling with merriment, Diana nodded. "No promises but I'll see what I can do."

"That's all I can ask."

Finding an empty table towards the back, Carter tossed her bag on top along with her blazer. Pushing up her sleeves, she tilted her chair back on two legs and draped her feet on the table. She closed her eyes, hating how the quiet drove her to thoughts of her mother.

A few minutes later, the doors to the library opened and a familiar light laugh entered, joined by a subdued voice and a steady tread. The trio drew closer and Carter showed no sign of awareness. A finger prodded her shoulder and Carter snatched the assailant's wrist. Another hand gently pried her fingers off.

"Good to know you are still aware of your surroundings," Donovan said, in a low voice.

Carter smiled but didn't look at him.

"Carter," Amy said, "are you actually asleep?"

Carter let out a sigh. Link and Amy stood on the other side of the table, eyeing her. Donovan stood next to her, amused. Removing her legs from the table, Carter dropped the chair back to all fours.

"Nope," she said. "Not asleep."

"Good," Amy said, taking a seat. "I was going to say that's probably not the best way to sleep, you could fall."

"Very true."

Amy and Link missed the note of mockery in Carter's voice but from the way Donovan's mouth twitched, he didn't. Amy sidled closer to Link and planted her chin on her hand, staring at him. Link smiled at her but studied his hands more than her.

"What are you doing this weekend?" she asked, offering the question to the table at large.

All three of them exchanged looks before Carter shrugged, summing up all of their thoughts.

"Well," Amy said, "my friend's friend is throwing a party. I figured we could all go. You know, dance, hang out, and stuff."

Link looked at a loss of how to reply. Carter glanced at Donovan, one eyebrow raised in question. After a long second, he gave a small nod.

"That would be great," Carter said. "I assume we will find some sort of entertainment in it, even if it is watching our fellow peers get roaring drunk."

Donovan fought back a smile.

"This will be so much fun!" Amy said.

Link nodded in acknowledgment of this declaration but had no words to match. Amy seemed unconcerned about his lack of enthusiasm.

Though the group fell to work, Amy and Link seemed distracted by the other's presence, to the great entertainment of Carter and Donovan. Eventually, Amy gave up the attempt at work and closed her notebook. "Link," she said. "I have to find a book, will you come help me?"

She grinned sweetly but there was a spark of mischief in her eyes. Link glanced up at her then back at his math homework. "I should probably finish this," he said.

Carter inwardly groaned and kicked Link under the table. He jumped and stared at her in surprise.

"I think the book Amy is looking for is on the second floor. Far back. Where it's secluded. You should help her because it's hard to find anything back there."

Link cocked his head in confusion while Carter seared him with her gaze. Amy took his hand, urging him from his chair.

"Come on," she said.

With one last baffled frown at Carter and Donovan, Link left. Carter laid her head back on the top of the chair. "I never pegged Link for being stupid. That's me wrong for once. Do you think he'll know what to do?"

"Once Amy starts kissing him, I'm sure he will figure out what's going on."

Carter crossed her arms and propped her feet on the table once more. "How can he be so clueless?"

Foregoing homework, Donovan angled his chair back, propping one ankle on his knee. "You have to remember, Link has had very little interaction with girls. It's had to be this way for his safety. He's also a shy sort of person. That hasn't helped."

"He talked to me just fine," she said.

"That's because you reminded him of me, someone smart and straightforward. What he finds difficult to understand are the hidden messages in what girls say. You weren't hard to communicate with because you said exactly what you were thinking. That's why he was instantly comfortable with you."

Carter let out a bright laugh, failing to notice how Donovan struggled against a smile at the sound.

"That has to be a first," she said. "Someone being instantly comfortable with me. Makes more sense why I couldn't get rid of you two."

Afternoon sunlight poured in through the window, lining the walls. Students grouped around tables, heads bent together but no talk of homework passed between them. For a long while, Carter and Donovan sat in companionable silence.

"Do you know what you are going to do?" Donovan asked.

He didn't have to explain his question, it was about the one thing Carter didn't have an answer to. Deciding what step to take with her mother felt like an annoying fly buzzing around her head.

"I honestly don't know," she said. "I don't want to ever see her again but I might never get this chance. I don't know if it's even worth it to tell her what she put my father and me through. It makes no difference, we still end up in the same place. Why bother?"

Donovan didn't reply. Though outwardly he seemed calm, Carter sensed thoughts spinning through his mind.

"What is it?" she asked.

"If you don't speak, you will regret it. This is your chance to let out what you have lived with for years. Nothing will change except you will be free. I've seen soldiers struggle with the same thing. It's not until they talk about what they have faced that they are able to move on."

Though she understood what he said, Carter found an excuse to push off her decision.

"How do you know so much about it?"

Donovan watched her expression change from troubled to curious. "You want that explanation now, I'm guessing."

"Only if you want to give it."

She hoped he would say yes, it felt easier to shove her mother into the corner of her mind.

Donovan ran a hand through his hair, giving the library a check before talking. "I grew up on a Marine base," he said, his voice barely above a whisper. "My father is a commander and my mother is a therapist who works with soldiers dealing with trauma. I have three older brothers and was homeschooled. I started in a public school but when I caused trouble because I got bored quickly, my mother brought me home. It was easier and I learned fast."

At the memories, Donovan smiled, eyes distant. Carter felt drawn in by his low rhythmic tone.

"Growing up around Marines gave me…a very broad education. By the age of ten, I could assemble a gun. At thirteen, I was going through training ops. I jumped grades and finished up high school by the age of sixteen." Something in his countenance dimmed. "That's when I got signed on for the job with Link."

"How did you get it?"

"My father knew President Douglas from when they trained together in the Marines. When President Douglas needed someone to protect Link, he approached my father. My brothers are older than me and looked too much like men already. I was fit but my face made me look younger. I was trained and could blend in: the perfect choice."

A cloud passed across Donovan's face but vanished before it could settle there. "I said yes and like that six years of my life were spent going through school again. Except this time I couldn't cause trouble when I was bored."

Donovan came out of his memories to find Carter staring at him, transfixed. Finally, he made sense to her. The control he possessed, the intelligence, the insight, all of it created in a world of toughened men and a wise mother.

"How have you possibly made it this long?" she

asked, unable to imagine how he could go from training ops to the monotony of school.

"I take college courses to pass the time and go to the gun range as often as possible."

He cracked a smile but Carter could see how the years of isolation by being older and smarter than everyone weighed on him. Right then, she understood him better than anyone. They were alike in their years of loneliness.

"Do you think it will be worth it when you are done?" she asked.

Donovan nodded slowly. "I think it is. I will have a bachelor's degree in criminal psychology and a reference letter that will guarantee me a job at any place of my choosing. Meanwhile, my brothers have been working to rise in the ranks but they have the freedom I do not."

Lacing his fingers, he laid them on his head. "Doesn't mean this job has been easy. There have been enough times of boredom where I would prefer to not be here. But that's the price I paid."

"I guess so."

They fell silent. Snippets of conversations drifted through the air, the words unintelligible by the time they reached the far side of the library.

"You know you'll have to make a decision at some point," he said, gently.

It took a moment for Carter to drag herself out of thoughts of him and his past to her own.

"I know," she said. "And…though it has been years of boredom and times of annoyance with the female aspect, I'm glad you decided to say yes. Not simply for Link's sake, but…for mine."

Donovan held her gaze. "I agree."

The bell rang, knocking them back into reality. Students rose and collected their stuff, their voices blooming the library with bright, careless conversations. Link and Amy appeared, hands clasped, pink in the cheeks, and looking rumpled. Donovan winked at Carter as if to say 'I told you so'.

"How did the book search go?" Carter asked, smirking at Link.

He blinked, puzzled. "What book?"

Chapter 28

The apartment smelled of orange-scented cleaner when Carter entered. Every surface gleamed and the worn couch cushions were plumped up. The coffee table was free of dishes and the dining room table no longer held a fortress of papers. Maggie emerged from the hallway, her hair pulled back, a broom in one hand, and a dirty towel tossed over her shoulder.

"Hey, girly," she said, stowing away the cleaning supplies. "How was school?"

Carter nudged the door shut with her foot. "Fine. I didn't get detention and only insulted a few people." She twirled one finger, gesturing to the whole apartment. "What's going on here?"

Pushing back a loose strand of hair with her wrist, Maggie surveyed her work with satisfaction. "I know it has been a rough couple of days and so I decided to come clean. Help you and Steve out."

A wave of appreciation overwhelmed Carter. "Thank you."

Maggie laid a caring hand on Carter's arm. "How are

you doing with all of this?"

"Fine."

When Maggie gave her a long appraising look, Carter broke away.

"Okay," Maggie said. "But if you're ever not fine, know that you can come talk to me."

"I know."

After a brief hesitation, Maggie hugged Carter. Carter resisted for a second before accepting the embrace. "I love you, Carter. I left food for you in the refrigerator. If you need anything just call."

"Thanks."

With the door half-open, Carter spoke, halting Maggie. "Why do you think she's here?"

Maggie held onto the door handle, expression troubled. "I don't know, Hon," she said, after a thoughtful moment, "but she could have come back to make amends."

When Carter scoffed, Maggie put a loving hand on Carter's arm. "I know that might sound like the craziest thing in the world but sometimes people change. It's possible your mother has realized the mistake she made and wants to do something to fix it."

"She doesn't care," Carter said, not hiding her disdain.

Maggie shrugged half-heartedly. "I know she wanted to talk to you, maybe there is something she wants to say? Maybe she wants to get to know you again."

"I don't care."

Carter wished those words rang true but they sounded unconvincing to herself. When Maggie smiled in understanding, Carter knew she wasn't convinced either.

"I know part of you still does," she said. "You shouldn't close that part off." Carter glared at the ground. "It's okay to still care, Carter. That makes you human."

When Carter didn't reply, Maggie slipped out, leaving Carter alone with the silence and her thoughts. Before she could be unsettled by the lack of noise, she dropped into the couch. She tossed her bag onto the cushions and kicked off her shoes, letting them fall to the floor with a loud thunk. She busied herself with pulling out notebooks and textbooks, fighting the thoughts that Maggie's words had evoked. Her mother wasn't here to fix anything. There was no way to repair the damage of four years of abandonment. Was there?

Frustrated with the tiny fourteen-year-old part of her that dared to hope, Carter dived into her homework, needing to think of something else.

An hour later, her father came home, repeating Carter's actions of hovering in the doorway as he took in the apartment.

"Maggie cleaned," Carter said. She studied his face, noticing the lines that seemed to have appeared overnight and his distracted manner. He was dressed in slacks and a button-down shirt, his arm still resting in a sling. Reaching out, Carter hauled her mess of papers aside, allowing her father access to the couch. He took it without a word. A fraction of the weariness eased from his face as he leaned back. He dragged one hand down his jaw, his gaze lost on something Carter couldn't see.

"You're dressed up," she asked.

"I stopped by the office," he said.

The pit of Carter's stomach dropped out and she forced herself to remain impassive. "When do you go back to full time?"

"Next week. They will put me on desk duty, dealing with cybercrime cases."

Carter sighed with relief, reassured by the safety of her father hidden behind a desk. As her worry subsided, she glimpsed the tension in her father's shoulders and neck. "Was that the only place you went?"

Not meeting her eyes, her father ran a hand through his hair. "No."

Carter picked at a fraying spot on the beige couch cushion. "You saw her?"

"Yes."

They were both silent. The moment stretched on until it felt as if they had been sitting there for hours.

"Why?" Carter asked, working to hold back her anger and confusion.

Letting out a slow breath, her father deflated. Exhaustion spoke in every line on his face as sorrow spoke in his blue eyes. "She wants me to sign the divorce papers."

The statement punched Carter. "What do you mean, 'sign the divorce papers'? What divorce papers? You guys were divorced a long time ago."

"Sarge," her father said, weary.

"Are you telling me this entire time you've still been married?" Carter gripped the edge of the cushion. "She's always been connected to us?" She stood, attempting to fight the anger threatening to drown her. "Did you think she would come back?"

"Carter…"

"You lied to me!"

Hurt stabbed Carter. Divorced or not, the true pain lay with her father withholding this information from her. From years of still being tied to the woman who had abandoned them.

"I hoped." Her father dropped his head. "I thought one day she would come back to her senses and come back to us. I thought that up to the moment she laid the divorce papers in front of me…Clearly, it was a mistake to hope."

Carter hated him for his hope, for thinking the woman who left them could change. Even more, she hated that he hadn't let her be a part of that hope, had kept her at bay.

"Well, your hope was for nothing," she snarled. "She's the same as she always was: heartless. Just sign the damn papers and end this."

Carter stormed out of the apartment, slamming the door. Plagued by riotous thoughts, she walked without knowing where she was headed, only knowing she needed to get away from their apartment, her father, the lie.

Eventually, she found herself at an empty playground and sank into one of the swings. She bent her head into her hands, her furious thoughts crashing against her chaotic emotions. A bitter wind gusted by, biting at Carter. She shivered.

Raising her head, she stared at the old wooden playset. The one as a little kid she'd raced around with shrieks of delight as her father and mother played the roaring monsters chasing her. It felt as if nothing had changed, except it was only her mother who played the monster chasing her.

Carter tugged out her phone.

"Hello?" a deep voice said.

Words choked Carter as she dug her heel into the red wood chips.

"Carter?" Donovan said.

"He never signed the divorce papers," she said biting back her hurt.

Donovan said nothing for a long moment.

"When did you find out?"

"An hour ago."

"Did he say why?"

Carter clenched the phone. "He hoped she would come back. He thought one day she would. But guess what? She finally did come back and it's not for us. She came back to be done with us for good. His hope got him nothing!"

Angered, Carter leapt from the swing and kicked at the wood chips. Donovan didn't answer.

"Aren't you going to say anything?" she yelled.

When he still didn't answer, Carter dropped back to the swing, feeling the fight leave her.

"He lied to me," she whispered.

A long stretch of silence passed before Donovan spoke. "Then he must have loved your mother very much."

Carter saw flashes of images: her father keeping the framed photograph of the three of them, her father's arms outstretched as he begged his wife to stay, her father's dazed stare as the taxi retreated, her father's tight grip as he held Carter as she cried into his shoulder.

With a sigh, Carter smoothed out the mess of wooden chips with her shoe. "Yeah, he did. A lot."

Another beat of silence.

"Where are you?" Donovan asked.

Carter didn't look up, didn't want to see the ghost of happy memories. "A playground a few blocks from my apartment."

"Do you want us to come?" he asked.

She leaned against the swing's thick chain, the metal chilly against her heated skin. "No, I'm fine."

"That's a lie but an understandable one."

Carter had no reply, they both knew he was right. But even as he called her out, it felt comforting that he did. He knew her.

"Donovan..." He waited as she tried to form the right words. "Thanks for caring."

"We both do, Carter."

Despite the invading cold around her, she felt a touch of warmth. "I'll see you tomorrow."

"Night, Carter."

Carter dropped her hand to her lap, sitting motionless. Around her, she glimpsed families in windows as the aroma of dinners floated on the air. She looked to the playset and knew what she had to do.

This time a female voice answered the phone.

"Okay," Carter said, "you want to talk, let's talk."

Chapter 29

Unaware of the clamor of the girl's locker room, Carter laced up her running shoes and headed out into the gray day. As she approached Mr. Danes, he glanced up from his clipboard. "You need something, Owens?"

"What are we doing today?"

Mr. Danes gave her his full attention as if the simple question surprised him. "The usual mile run and then a game of soccer."

"Okay," she said. "Well, you know I'm here."

Leaving Mr. Danes baffled, Carter took off, needing to move. Hours of sitting, listening to lessons had put her on edge. She wanted to outrun her hurt over her father's lie. To outrun the upcoming meeting with her mother. She ran, focusing on the beat of her shoes against the track, her heart beating steadily, the wind chilling her skin, and flicking her hair.

When Donovan fell in beside her, she said nothing. He kept pace, matching her stride for stride. They ran as one entity, even their breath in sync.

"You're meeting her today," Donovan stated instead of questioned. Carter nodded once. "After school?"

Another nod.

"What made you decide to see her?" he asked.

Carter didn't answer right away, her thoughts still racing. "I want to know why she came back now."

They said nothing more. By the time the rest of the class began their miles, Carter felt calmer. As they came alongside Link, Carter and Donovan slowed.

"You two are freaking synchronized when you run, you know that?" he said.

"What can I say?" Carter said. "I've had to run with my dad, so I'm used to slowing my pace for someone else."

"I believe we've already established that I am the faster runner," Donovan said.

"I think those results were wrong because I had already been running at top speed before you decided to race me."

"An excuse worthy of someone who has lost."

Link groaned. "Either race or don't. Just don't make me listen to this anymore."

Donovan and Carter exchanged glances but said nothing else.

***

When Carter exited the locker room she found Donovan and Link waiting. Without a word, they took up positions beside her, as if acting as shields. She savored the feeling of their presence. On the top step of the school entrance, Carter stopped, gazing to the gates and the metro station that would take her downtown.

"Are you driving to meet her?" Link asked.

Carter shook her head. "No, I'll take the metro."

"You want us to give you a ride?" Link asked.

Looking down at the stone steps and back up, Carter shook her head. "No," she said, but she didn't move.

"The car is this way," Donovan said, taking a step toward the parking lot.

After a second's hesitation, Carter followed. They carved their way through rows of BMWs, Mercedes, Audis, and Bentleys in silence as their fellow peers raced for their cars, the guys jostling each other and the girls laughing and mocking their antics.

In the twenty-minute drive it took them to get to the restaurant, not a single word was spoken. Donovan parked in an open spot outside a glass front restaurant, leaving the car idling. Carter searched the restaurant's occupants until she found her mother, talking on the phone.

"She's the blonde two tables back on the left," Carter said, pointing.

Donovan rested one arm on the steering wheel but didn't lean in to see. Link craned his neck for a glimpse. "You okay?"

Carter gave a single nod that neither Donovan nor Link were convinced by.

"I never actually thought I'd have to deal with her again," she said. "After the third year of wishing she would come back, I gave up."

She fell silent, the hum of the car's engine filling the small space.

"You don't have to talk to her," Link said.

"I know," she said. "But I need to." She paused. "Thank you."

"Do you want us to wait?" Link asked.

After mulling over the offer, she shook her head. "I'll be fine."

Gathering her strength, Carter opened the car door. Around her, the wind whipped between buildings, carrying away the persistent honking of horns. When she twisted back, Link offered an encouraging smile and Donovan nodded, as if telling her she could handle this.

Bolstered by them, Carter walked to the restaurant, hiding her emotions away as she opened the door. Classical music floated through the air, mixing with the clinking of silverware and murmur of discussions.

When Carter's mother noticed Carter, she rose. They appraised each other for a stiff moment. Her mother looked as immaculate as always, not a strand of hair out of place. She gestured to the seat opposite.

Taking her time, Carter stared at her mother. In her face, she saw all the features her own face held which she hated: the golden skin, high cheekbones, bow lips. Her blue eyes alone were her father's.

A waiter appeared, a pad in hand. "Are you ready to order?"

"I don't want anything," Carter said.

Her mother smiled apprehensively. "You sure? You just came from school. You must be hungry."

Bitter anger sparked inside Carter at her mother's pretend concern. She had no right to care or act like a mother.

"I don't want anything," she repeated.

Placing her order, her mother touched her necklace. Their eyes met and her mother coughed as if about to say something but the words never made it past her lips. The conversations of their fellow diners drifted around them, a dull buzz of background noise.

"Why are you here?" Carter asked, tonelessly.

Crossing her legs, her mother pressed down her skirt. "I was in town and thought I would see how you were both doing-"

"Let's dispense with the lies," Carter said. "Tell me why you're here."

Her mother brushed back a piece of her hair, her mouth pressed together. In contrast, Carter sat like a pillar of stone.

"I'm sure your father has told you," her mother said.

Carter didn't reply, waiting. Her mother clasped her hands, placing them on the cream tablecloth. Her nails were perfect half-moons, painted pink. "I came to have him sign the divorce papers and settle things with our lawyer," she said.

The confession formed a wall between them. Carter rested her elbows on the armrests, keeping everything hidden.

"Why did you need to talk to me then?" she asked.

Her mother leaned forward. "I wanted to see how you were doing."

Carter plastered on a mocking, disdainful smile which made her mother blink. "You wanted to see how I was doing..." she said, slowly, condescendingly.

"Alright," she said, her tone carefree. "You want to know how I'm doing so it will ease your conscience? Then know this: I'm fine, mother." She flashed her a wide fake smile, waving a flippant hand. "You may now go and live your life knowing that your only daughter is doing...just...fine."

"Carter," her mother said, her voice flooded with emotion, "please let me explain-"

"No need. You clearly decided your happiness was of greater importance than that of your family's."

"Carter, that's not why I left," she said.

Carter raised one patronizing eyebrow. "No? Why then, was my father beating you? Was he drinking into all hours of the night and coming home drunk to pass out on the couch? Was he unloving? Was he uncaring? Did he not provide everything we needed? Please, do tell."

Her mother's uncertainty was plainly written on her features. On the table, her phone dinged and she glanced at it, something softening in her gaze. One hand went to her necklace. Everything clicked and Carter pounced.

"Who is he?" she asked, her voice smooth as glass.

At her mother's startled eyes, Carter read the denial. "Don't lie to me."

"He is just someone-"

"I said don't lie to me!"

Shifting, her mother reached up to the necklace again

while she crossed one arm over herself as if trying to build a shield against Carter. "Someone from work."

Carter checked her mother's left ring finger, spotting a faint tan line. "You're engaged."

Despite wishing to see guilt, Carter only saw happiness in her mother's eyes. "Yes."

A new pain cut through Carter as the image of a faceless man consumed her. It became tangled with the image of her mother laughing at his words, kissing him like she had kissed Carter's father, building a life with him. The images tore into her, angering her at the thought of her mother finding happiness.

"Did you tell Captain?"

Her mother gave a half-smile at the nickname. "I remember the first time you-"

"No." Her mother stopped talking. "We're not talking about the past. You forfeited your right to those memories."

Stunned, her mother opened and closed her mouth.

"Does he know?" Carter asked again.

Her mother shook her head. "No. He doesn't know."

"Good, then you will not tell him," Carter said, leaning forward. "Understood? I think one hell is enough to put him through, don't you?"

Her mother hardened, eyes blazing with fury. "You can not talk to me like this. I am still your mother."

Standing, Carter regarded her mother coolly. "That is where you are wrong. You stopped being my mother the moment you walked out that door."

"Carter, I...this...it's better this way," her mother said.

"Sign the papers and leave," Carter said. "Don't try and see us again. You haven't been part of our lives for four years and you're right, it is better this way."

Her mother swallowed.

"Enjoy your meal," Carter said, hollowly. "I told you I didn't want anything and I meant it."

***

The apartment lay quiet when Carter entered, the silence feeling like a physical weight. In her room, she dumped her bag on the floor. Without turning on any lights, she climbed into bed and curled up against her pillows, staring out the window.

The sun drifted away for the night and she sat there, unseeing, numb with a constant pain in her chest. The front door opened and her father called out. Carter made no response. Her father moved about the living room, his even treads ringing on the wooden floor. A minute later, her door squeaked open.

"Hey, Sarge," he said.

Carter didn't answer. Her father sat on the edge of her bed. With his good arm, he pulled her into a hug. Carter went willingly, resting her head on his shoulder, staring blankly at the floor.

"You talked to her, didn't you?" he said.

She nodded. He kissed the top of her head. "Did it help?"

She found she couldn't reply, the empty feeling eating her from inside.

"I'll sign the papers and we will be free of her for good," he said.

"Yeah. Free."

Chapter 30

As the dull morning light crept across Carter's bed it found her already awake, laying completely still. Carter heard her father bustling around the apartment but she didn't get up. Other than the ache in her chest, Carter felt numb. When her door swung open, she didn't stir.

"Time to get up, Sarge," her father said.

Carter showed no sign of hearing him.

"Sarge?" he asked, peering down at her.

"I heard you."

Her father waited for her to sit up but she didn't. All the things Carter had said the previous day lived in the room, no longer in her head. Instead of making her feel better, they made everything worse.

Her father affectionately jostled her shoulder. "I'll have something for you to eat when you're done with your shower."

"Okay."

When her father drifted away, Carter swung her legs off the bed, the carpeted floor cool beneath her feet. The scalding water of the shower roused the blood in her veins but did nothing to alleviate the numbness. Exiting her room dressed in her uniform, damp hair darkening the blazer, she smelled toast and eggs.

"We don't eat breakfast," Carter said, looking at the plate of food before her. "Not unless it comes in the form of a power shake."

Her father didn't bother answering, instead eyeing Carter over the rim of his coffee cup, taking in the shadows under her eyes. "Do you want to talk about it?"

Despite her hurt over his lie, Carter felt words of confusion, anger, and pain rise into her throat. But she never said a single thing, because she could see the burdened, weary shadow in her father's face. She took a bite of eggs, forcing it down with her jumbled confession.

"No," she said. "There's nothing to talk about."

All through their drive to school, neither of them spoke, instead letting the patter of news reporters fill the emptiness. Only a few other cars lined the school drive when her father stopped the SUV. Father and daughter met each other's gaze. Behind their eyes, they could read the thoughts that neither of them knew how to voice.

"Have a good day," Carter said, climbing out. "Try not to get shot again. I hear offices can be dangerous places."

The joke lacked heart as did her father's chuckle. "You too. Stay out of trouble. I love you, Sarge."

"I love you too, Captain."

For half a second, Carter lingered but closed the door and walked away. Rather than entering the heated halls, Carter hoisted herself onto the low stone wall that ran along the ramp to the parking lot. The rich scent of espresso floated around her as students passed. In the distance, storm clouds crashed into each other.

From her perch, Carter watched as the parking lot filled, waiting.

A silver Bentley swerved into an open space and Lucas climbed out. As he teamed up with his friends, he recognized Carter and grinned in anticipation. The black Mercedes settled into a spot and Donovan stepped out, surveying the scene around him with no reaction. Only when his gaze lighted on Carter did he narrow his eyes. Even from where she sat, Carter felt the force of his scrutiny.

"You know, Owens," Lucas said, detaching from his friends to lounge against the wall next to Carter. "It doesn't matter how long you stare at the cars, you're never going to be able to afford one." Donovan quickened his pace as if sensing a fight. "Did you hear me, Owens?"

Numb, Carter barely heard Lucas.

"Mind moving aside?" Donovan asked, his deep voice cutting through the air.

Lucas spun around, glad for a willing target. When he saw Donovan, his mocking reply died.

"Not like there is anything here I care about," Lucas said, unconsciously touching his bruised jaw as he sauntered off.

In one smooth motion, Donovan swung legs over the wall, sitting beside Carter while Link scrambled up on her other side. The rumble of car engines and chatter of students wrapped around them.

"Were you waiting for us?" Link asked, breaking their silence.

"Would you believe me if I said 'no'?"

"No," Donovan said.

She made no reply.

Though the bell rang, emptying the parking lot, none of the trio gave any indication of leaving.

"What happened?" Donovan asked.

Squinting out on the parking lot, Carter didn't see the rows of expensive cars but instead, she saw her mother's flawless appearance, her perfect pink nails, her hand with the shadow of an engagement ring.

"Nothing," she said. "We talked. That was it."

"Look at me," Donovan said.

The request sounded so odd that Carter did as he requested. He studied her face with intelligent eyes. "That's not it."

She broke away. "There's nothing else."

Link looked between them, not seeing what Donovan saw but knowing to stay silent.

"You don't have to tell me," Donovan said, "but I would prefer it if you didn't lie to me."

Carter rounded on him. "Why do you even care? What makes you think that you'd understand?"

Despite her outburst, Donovan kept his cool. "Because, despite what you think, I do know what is going on. I thought I could help."

"Well, you can't! Okay? There is nothing you can do that would help."

Donovan dropped down from the wall and straightened, his arms hanging loosely by his side.

"There is one thing," he said. "Punch me."

Carter forgot her frustration as Link fought back a surprised laugh.

"What?" she said.

Dropped his bag to the ground, Donovan slipped his hands into his pockets.

"Punch me," he said. "You feel like hitting something, right? Hit me."

Carter twisted around but didn't climb off the wall. "I'm not going to hit you."

"No, you're not. You're not even going to get close but you can give it your best shot."

For good measure, he smirked. Galled into action, Carter hopped down, forming fists. With mocking casualness, Donovan drew his hands out of his pockets. Link clambered off the wall, appointing himself as a lookout.

Carter swung at Donovan's jaw. With a speed that startled her, he ducked her blow. When he righted, she came out at him with her opposite fist. He blocked this shot with his forearm and caught her wrist with his other hand. She broke from his hold and attacked again. Again he parried the hit.

Gritting her teeth, Carter jerked her knee up to his side. Donovan retreated a single step, avoiding the impact. A surge of frustration rose in Carter and she darted in quickening movements. Every jab, strike, and punch she threw, he blocked, his counter moves swift and sure.

The second bell rang but neither of them heard. Carter became more frantic and less coordinated as her thoughts pounded away in her head. Sweat beaded on her forehead as she struggled to move faster. Images of her mother flashed in her mind, affecting her concentration. The pain in her chest expanded. Donovan blocked another one of her hits and her anger exploded.

"She's happy! Okay?" she yelled. "She's engaged and she's happy!"

Depleted, Carter sank to the ground, pressing her back against the rough stone and burying her head in her hands. Donovan lowered himself beside her, his hands draped over his knees. Link sat across from them, sympathy filling his eyes.

"She is moving on with her life," Carter said. "Making a new family. Why does she get to have happiness? She doesn't deserve it. She abandoned us. She was supposed to be miserable. But she's happy. Where is our happy ending?"

She leaned her head back, the numbness that had been dragging on her finally gone. Before Donovan could say anything, a woman appeared from around the corner, her mouth forming a tight line.

"The bell has rung," she said. "To class, all of you."

As Link shouldered his backpack, Donovan held out a hand to Carter. When she took it he easily lifted her to her feet. "I do understand." Carter stared at him, skeptical and he nodded at Link. "He might not have gotten as close to hitting me as you did but he tried just as hard."

Carter cast a glance at Link and he shrugged, wearing

a half-smile. Finding out who his father was, facing the fact that his mother had lied to him all his life. Yeah, she imagined Link would want to hit something.

"I get it, Carter," Donovan said.

"He really does," Link said.

Before she had the chance to respond, the woman cleared her throat. "Class. Now," she commanded.

As they all walked into school, Carter glanced at Donovan and he met her gaze.

Chapter 31

Thunder clouds clashed outside and lightning streaked across the sky. Rain pummeled the cafeteria windows, a constant drumming in Carter's ears. She sat with her back pressed against the cold pane, the chill leaching into her. But she didn't move. She felt trapped in the day before, everything she'd said, everything she didn't say.

Amy's bubbly voice traveled to the table a second before she came into view, Link beside her. The couple sat next to each other, talking happily. When Donovan slid in next to Carter, his arm brushed hers. He eyed her uneaten sandwich.

"It's yours if you want it," Carter said.

"Not hungry?"

She shook her head. Somehow it seemed easier to be numb because now all she felt was lost.

"Are you going to tell me what actually happened yesterday?" Donovan said, angling toward her.

"I did. I talked to her. Found out she is engaged and left."

Donovan continued to study her, which irked Carter.

"What?" she snapped.

"Yesterday. Did you talk to her or did you badger her?"

Carter straightened. "What's that supposed to mean?"

"Exactly what I said. Did you talk or did you go in looking for a fight?"

Right then, Carter wanted to hit him. "I went to talk."

"But you ended up looking for a fight," he said.

"How could you possibly know that?"

"Because," he said, "regardless of what you think, I know you." Donovan stared at her like she was a puzzle he could easily solve. "And I know if you had talked to her, actually talked to her, you wouldn't look this way."

"Yeah," Carter scoffed. "And what is that? Still pissed over what she did?"

As Donovan regarded her with a touch of pity, Carter felt her defenses rising up to protect her. "No. Lost."

He struck home and Carter hated him for it. "I'm not lost," she hissed. "I know exactly what is happening and who she is."

Donovan didn't back down, his face close to hers. "Do you?"

The question poked at Carter's self-created walls. "You are the one who doesn't know anything."

To her annoyance, Donovan eased back and shrugged. "You're right. I only know what you've told me and what I see. Maybe you should find out if you are the one not seeing clearly."

Furious with Donovan, with herself, with everything, Carter snatched up her bag. "Don't assume you know everything."

"Maybe you should listen to your own advice."

Carter stormed out of the cafeteria, a startled Link calling after her.

***

Donovan's accusations beat against Carter like the rain pelting her face as she disembarked the bus in her neighborhood. His statement taunted her: "Maybe you should find out if you are the one not seeing clearly". Soaked and numb from cold, Carter walked into the cheery embrace of the deli. Maggie rushed over with a towel, brows pinched with concern. "Hon, you're all wet."

Only then did Carter register her current state. Accepting the towel, she dried her jacket, bag, and wiped off the rain that clung to her hair. Maggie watched her all the while, worried.

"Come sit," Maggie said.

In the booth, Carter stared out on the storm, clouds battling, thunder roaring, lightning spiking. Maggie set down a plate with two cookies, prodding Carter's arm to get her attention. Without speaking, Carter broke the cookie into pieces, crumbs falling onto the plate.

"Steve said you talked to your mother yesterday," Maggie said cautiously. Carter nodded. "How did it go?" Carter shrugged. "I know it must have been hard but did you at least get closure?"

Carter pulled back: closure was the last thing she felt. Inside her still felt like a gaping wound. She dropped the cookie. "I have to go."

Maggie stood but didn't follow. Yanking the door open, Carter raced into the icy, battering rain. She pounded up the apartment stairs, taking them two at a time. With the damp, the door swelled and Carter had to shoulder her way into her own home. The door shut as she leaned against it.

Carter shook with cold surrounded by emptiness. Forcing herself to stand, she stumbled into her room, discarded her layers of wet clothes, and changed to the first dry thing she found. But the warm clothes did nothing to dispel the storm within.

In her father's room, Carter unlocked her father's gun case and took out the first gun her eyes landed on.

Sinking to the floor, she disassembled it. There was a chill over the apartment but she didn't feel it. As she worked the chaos in her mind calmed as she focused on something that she could control. Something she could understand. Something that made sense.

Over and over again, she tirelessly tore her work apart only to rebuild it again. The light shifted and melted from the sky. Still, she assembled and disassembled the gun, her fingers fitting the pieces together by memory more than by sight.

Her father found her in the same spot hours later, her fingers bruised from pressing the metal too hard. She didn't see how he stopped in the doorway, a pain beyond grief came over him at the sight of her.

What she did see was his hand as he dropped it gently over hers, stilling her frantic movements.

But she didn't look at him. In the silence of the room, the rain continued to hit the window

"What am I not getting?" she said, barely audible.

"Sarge..." her father said, gently.

"What am I missing?!" she said, unable to hold back her hurt and anger. "What is wrong with me? Why did she leave me ...What did I do wrong?"

Carter's voice cracked on the last question. She dropped her head. She couldn't bear to see the truth in her father's eyes, that it was her fault. Her father let out a weary sigh and sank to the ground. "Look at me, Carter"

When she didn't, he rested a hand on her shoulder. "Sarge, look at me." Finally, she met his eyes. "It wasn't your fault. Your mother left because she decided to leave. It had nothing to do with you, you hear me?"

He held her gaze in the dim light for a long moment and Carter knew he hoped his words got through. "You can't take on this guilt. I don't fully know why she left but it had nothing to do with you."

"If I'm not the reason she left, then why?" she whispered.

Her father wrapped her in his protective arms as if he

could shield her. They stayed silent, neither knowing what to say next, trapped in emotions they hadn't felt for years.

Chapter 32

Carter jammed her fists deeper into the pockets of her jacket as she sat huddled on the trunk of a car. The world smelled fresh with the scent of damp grass and wet cement. On the horizon, sunlight poked holes in the barrier of gray clouds. A gentle breeze played with the ends of Carter's loose hair. As students passed by, they gave Carter odd looks.

When the black Mercedes pulled into the empty space in front of Carter, she saw through the tinted front window Donovan's flicker of surprise and Link's blatant bafflement.

"You can't convince me this time that you weren't waiting for us," Link said. Carter almost smiled at that. "How did you know we would park here?"

"You've parked here the previous two times. Humans are creatures of habit."

Link laughed, lightening Carter's mood. Donovan gave Carter a studying look, as usual reading her unsaid thoughts

"You don't have to say it," Donovan said.

"How do you know what I'm going to say?" Carter asked.

"The way you're sitting. Your face. If you wanted a fight, there would be more tension in your body. Since it's not a fight, there is only one other reason you would be waiting for us."

At his thorough deduction, Carter did smile slightly, though it quickly faded.

"You don't have to say it," Donovan repeated.

"I know, but I need to."

Link ran a hand through his hair. "Should I know what is going on?"

Neither of them answered him.

"I'm sorry," Carter said, quietly.

"I know."

Scratching his jaw, puzzled, Link darted a glance at both of them. "Is that what happened yesterday, you two fought?"

"Yeah," Carter said, as Donovan rested back on the hood of the car.

"What was it about?" Link asked.

When Donovan said nothing, Carter knew he was letting her be the one to share or not. The fact that he wouldn't reveal her outburst struck Carter. He was being a good friend to her even when she hadn't been. Right then, she knew she didn't deserve his friendship.

"Donovan told me," Carter said. "That I wasn't seeing everything clearly in regards to my mother. I got kind of mad at him."

Donovan raised one mocking eyebrow. "Kind of mad?"

Despite herself, Carter breathed out a laugh and Link took this as a sign he could take the spot beside her on the trunk.

"What did Donovan say that made you so pissed?" he asked.

"He said I wasn't seeing things clearly in regards to my mother," she said, bitterness entering her voice. "He was wrong."

Link softened with understanding while Donovan held his peace.

"Carter..." Link said. He met her gaze for a second then dropped it to his clasped hands. "I know it's going to sound...odd..." He wiggled, uncertain. "But have you ever thought that...I don't know, you've painted your mother as a monster for so long you've forgotten she's human?"

Carter closed her eyes, seeing too clearly the unyielding way her mother told her father she was leaving. The way she met Carter's eyes but still walked out the door. Tangled with those were the good times when it had been the three of them, together.

"Making her human," Carter said slowly, "makes it possible for me to rationalize what she did. It would mean somehow it was okay."

Link shook his head adamantly. "Carter, no. No matter what, leaving you was messed up. You can still be mad at what she did. I still have times of being mad at my dad." He sighed. "Whether that will ever change or not, I don't know."

The vehemence in his tone comforted Carter. Not only was she not alone but he understood her.

"Did you see your father as a monster?" she asked.

"First few years of my life," he said, "he was this faceless man that had abandoned me. When he showed up and wasn't this monster, it took me a while to deal with that. In the end, what mattered was I got to say the things I had always needed to say." Carter stared at the ground in thought. "What happened yesterday with your mother?"

Embarrassed, Carter didn't look up. "I insulted her."

Link bumped his shoulder with her. "At least you didn't try to punch her. Did you say what you needed to?"

"I thought I did. But no, I didn't."

"Do you think you'll see her again?"

That was the question. Could she face her mother again after what she'd said? Would it change anything if she did? Did she want to?

"I honestly don't know."

"Carter," Donovan said. "Saying what you need to doesn't change anything. How much you see her or don't, interact with her or don't, will still be in your hands. She doesn't have the power to control the situation."

Carter regarded him, mystified. "How do you understand so much about this? I know your mother was a psychologist but this seems like more than what you would pick up just chatting with her."

In answer, Donovan dipped his head toward Link.

"This is ancient history to Donovan," Link said. "He was the only one who I could tell all my problems to. Your situation is nothing new."

"And Link turned out all right," Donovan said.

"As far as you know," Carter said.

Link shoved her shoulder, eliciting a chuckle from her. They fell silent for a moment, both boys appraising her.

"What are you doing after school?" she asked.

"You need a ride?" Donovan asked.

"I think I might."

Behind them, the bell called out to them, telling them to head to class.

"You guys don't feel like ditching first period and going somewhere, do you?" Carter asked.

Donovan shook his head. "You've missed three classes in the last two weeks. You can't afford to miss another. You do still have to graduate."

She scowled. "I'm not sure I like how you pay attention to details."

He shrugged, unconcerned. As Carter slid off the trunk, Link followed. In companionable silence, they headed toward the front doors. Inside the halls were quickly emptying as groups disappeared into doorways.

Outside their chemistry classroom, a dark-haired blur flung her arms around Link and he stumbled backward.

"I didn't see you come in," Amy said, keeping her arms draped around Link's neck. "Hi."

The soft note in her voice teased out Link's goofy grin. "Hi."

"Are you ready for the party tomorrow?"

Link looked at Carter and Donovan.

"Sure, I guess," he said.

"Good." Amy gave him a quick kiss. Retreating a step, she focused on Carter. "What are you planning on wearing?"

Carter stared at Amy, incredulous. "I was planning on clothes but that's only if I don't come up with a second option."

Amy laughed. "Alright, well, I'll see you in History."

She left, joining the last remaining students.

"What would your second option be?" Donovan taunted. "Going naked?"

"Please," Carter said scornfully, "it's far too cold to go naked. Nudity is for summer events only."

Chapter 33

At the top of the school's front steps, Carter stood unmoving with Link and Donovan, forcing students to branch around them. She gripped her messenger bag strap.

"It changes nothing," Donovan said.

Carter found courage in his steady blue eyes.

"It changes nothing," she repeated.

Since the morning, the sun had made more breakthroughs in the clouds, sending patches of golden light onto the city. The trio wound through the rows of cars and piled into the Mercedes.

"Where to?" Donovan asked, starting the engine.

"The Sofitel hotel. It's in Lafayette Square."

Donovan navigated the car out of the chaos of the parking lot and headed for downtown Washington D.C. The monuments looked like white beacons against the gray sky. Passing the White House, Carter instinctively glanced in the rearview mirror at Link. He stared out the opposite window but flexed his jaw once.

At the hotel's entrance, Donovan parked at the curb.

Tall buildings crowded the sidewalks, pressed up against each other in camaraderie. Pedestrians in coats walked with determined steps to their final destinations. Carter reached for the door but Donovan stopped her with a question. "Do you want us to wait?"

Carter didn't know how to respond. Reading her hesitation, Donovan glanced back at Link. "You want to get something to eat?"

"Sure," Link said. "I know a place around here."

Carter felt like she could breathe a little easier. "Thank you."

With the encouraging weight of their eyes on her, she crossed the sidewalk. A sense of calm came over her as she pushed through the revolving door into the hotel. A lavish lobby lay before her: black and white patterned carpet covering the floor, high-backed couches lining the walls, a front desk of gray stone topped with glass. Beyond the entrance, an archway led to a low lit restaurant and bar. Everything about the place spoke of money.

Through the archway, Carter glimpsed her mother perched on a barstool, holding a half-empty glass of amber liquid. For a moment, Carter studied her. In the dim light, with her face perfectly made up, she didn't look like the mother Carter had grown up with. She looked like a stranger. Though she felt a twinge of pain in her chest, she no longer felt her original anger.

As Carter cut through the tables, her mother noticed her and froze. Carter stopped before her. Her mother reached for her necklace, seeking comfort. Sliding her hands into her pockets, Carter eyed the pendant. At the pointed gaze, her mother lowered her hand.

"I didn't think I would see you again," she said.

"I know."

"How did you know where I was staying?" her mother asked, groping for something to say.

"I called around."

Her mother's put together persona was cracking,

showing nerves. Something about seeing her mother so unnerved by her sudden presence put Carter at ease.

"Why are you here?" her mother finally asked.

"I need to say something," she said.

Surprise flicked in her mother's eyes. She swallowed the rest of her drink and gestured for another. Carter recognized a woman who needed a drink to face her past.

In that moment, Carter found clarity. She saw a selfish woman, one who always took the easy way out. The weight of Carter's imagined guilt lifted. Along with that realization was the truth that the love and strength in her life had always come from her father. Even before her mother left. That had never changed.

Nervous, Carter's mother shifted in her chair, clutching the tumbler.

"I needed you," Carter said, calmly. "I was a fourteen-year-old girl. I needed a mother to help me, to guide me." Her mother's face flushed. "I needed you." A sad smile slipped across Carter's lips. "At least, I thought I needed you. Turns out, I didn't."

Dazed, her mother could only stare at Carter.

Carter took a step back, boxing away her emotions. "If I ever want to see you again, I'll let you know. Goodbye, mother."

She walked away, not looking back. Not seeing her mother motion to the bartender and hold out her glass, shaking.

Carter pushed through the doors and into the night, relief slowly washed over her. She texted Donovan and waited by the curb. Closing her eyes, she tilted her head back and breathed in the evening air. The gray clouds had drifted away with the sun and above her, the first dots of stars popped into view.

A few minutes later, Donovan swung up to the curb and both boys studied her as she climbed in. She met their curious gazes with a peaceful one of her own.

"Thanks for the ride," she said. "Mind taking me home?"

Relief loosened all three tongues, they talked about school and listened as Link voiced his nervousness over the upcoming party.

When Carter spotted the windows of her apartment glowing, she felt a sudden sense of urgency. She gave a hasty goodbye and sprinted up the stairs.

"Hey," her father said, seated on the couch. "It's later than usual. Where have you been?"

Carter didn't answer as she sank beside him and hugged him. He put an arm around her and kissed the top of her head.

"I love you, Captain," she said.

He tightened his hold on her, understanding without needing to be told. "I love you too, Sarge. I'm not going anywhere."

She smiled. "I know."

Chapter 34

Carter scowled at her closet, hands on hips. A neat line of clothes lay before her, hues ranging from black to dark blue. There was no way around it: she didn't know what to wear. And she hated it. Behind her, her punching bag hung tantalizingly, teasing her to forget the party and beat out her frustrations of not knowing how to be normal.

The front door opened and Maggie's sweet voice floated through the apartment. A low murmured conversation took place followed by two taps at Carter's door. Apparently, her father thought she needed reinforcements.

"Hey, Hon," Maggie said peeking in and noting Carter's ratty t-shirt and sweatpants. "What's going on?" Carter huffed. "Steve heard mutterings."

Traitor. "Yeah, well, Captain has nothing to be worried about." Carter crossed her arms, jutting out her chin defiantly. "I'm completely fine."

Maggie flopped onto the edge of the neat bed and crossed her legs. "Is that so?" she said, a teasing note in her voice.

"Yup."

"So you're glaring at your closet because…"

Carter didn't answer. She would not be defeated by this. Holding in a smile, Maggie made to leave. "Alright, since you are completely fine. I will let you get back to it."

"Wait!" Carter said as Maggie reached for the doorknob.

"Yes?"

Carter wanted to punch something. Scowling again, she dug her hands into the pockets of her sweats, hating the gleeful light in Maggie's eyes. When her tongue remained securely behind her teeth, Maggie lifted an eyebrow. "Carter?"

Carter groaned, her head falling back. "What does someone wear to a party?"

A smile instantly jumped to Maggie's face and Carter raised her hand. "Laugh at me and I'll never talk to you again."

Reigning in her delight, Maggie nodded.

"I thought I would wear what I just wore to the date, but...I don't know..." Carter growled and ran a hand through her damp hair. "This is stupid. I don't know why I even care? Amy just asked what I was wearing, so that made me wonder if I should actually be thinking about it. Which led me to wonder, if I had a mom would I be more aware of this stuff? Which led me to a complete blank on what to wear. And this is stupid. I sound like a pissy teenage girl."

"Well, Hon, you still are a teenage girl. It's alright to sound like one," Maggie said, rifling through the clothes, eyeing certain items. "And yes, if your mother had been here when you were entering teenage life you would have been more aware of this stuff. But she wasn't and now you have me to help you." She gave Carter a soft smile. "I hope you don't mind."

Carter felt some of her annoyance vanishing. "No, I

don't mind."

"Good, because you're stuck with me." Maggie handed Carter a blue shirt, jeans, and a pair of her nicer looking Converse.

"This looks almost exactly like what I wore for the date," she said.

"Well, that makes sense because you don't own a lot of variations. This will have to do. The blue is nice because it works well with your eyes." Carter accepted the items and Maggie planted her hands on her hips. "Now, what did you plan on doing with your hair?"

Carter blinked. "You say that like I had a plan at all instead of just letting it dry, or putting it up in a ponytail."

"Either works. If you want to do something different, I'll just be outside."

"What do you mean different? I'm not letting you curl my hair."

"No, I was thinking of just blow drying it."

"I don't know if we own a blow dryer."

"You do because I gave you one for your birthday two years ago."

"Good luck finding it. It's probably still in the box."

Maggie left the room to hunt for the once gifted hairdryer. As Carter finished changing, she heard a cry of triumph from Maggie.

"It was still in the box!" Maggie said as Carter stepped into the bathroom.

As Maggie tried to wrestle the hair drier out of the box, Carter opened a drawer and located a switchblade. "Here."

Amused, Maggie accepted the knife, cutting the plastic ties.

"I probably never thanked you for the hairdryer," Carter said.

"You did and now you will get to use it."

"Did your mother teach you what to do?" Carter asked as she plugged in the hairdryer.

"Yes and since I don't have a daughter yet, I get the honor of teaching you."

Ten minutes later, Carter's hair fell gently over her shoulders. For a moment, she looked at herself in the mirror. For the first time, she wasn't aware of all her mother's features in her face but her father's, realizing she had his round chin.

"What?" Maggie said.

"Nothing. I just think I look a little bit like Captain."

Maggie laughed. "Of course you do, Hon. No one could deny that." She clapped her hands, eager. "Now makeup?"

"No!"

The gut reaction hit Carter harder than she thought it would. Her mother's flawless face bursting into her mind.

"That's fine," Maggie said, startled. "You are beautiful just the same."

Carter took in a breath. "I'm going to grab my jacket."

On her nightstand, her phone dinged with a message from Donovan, telling her that they were outside. She pocketed the phone, snatched her jacket, and walked out into the family room. Maggie sat at the table next to her father. He looked up as Carter pulled her satchel off the hook by the door.

"My ride is here," she said, pointing to the door with her thumb.

Crossing to her, her father placed a hand on her shoulder. "Do you know what I'm going to say?"

"If I get high, drunk, or pregnant, it's military school for me."

Her father grinned. "Correct."

He hugged her and kissed the top of her head. "You look beautiful, Sarge."

"Thanks, Captain."

"Have fun tonight."

"Do you actually mean that? Because my idea of fun is not a party but seeing if I can break into the Ukrainian

Embassy."

"Either way, I will find you if you don't come home by midnight tonight."

Carter touched her necklace and saluted. "Got it. American soil it is." She slipped out the door but popped her head back inside. "Oh, and have fun you two." She sent her father a wink and disappeared.

His annoyed utterance followed her down the stairs. In the lane sat the black Mercedes. At the sight of her, Link stepped out and took a spot in the back. Carter slipped in and looked back at him, unaware of Donovan's blue eyes taking her in.

"You ready to partake in this night of teenage debauchery ?" she asked Link.

Link looked like he might be sick. "Are you?"

"No," she said. "Let's do this."

***

Even in the elevator, Carter could feel the thundering bass emanating from the penthouse.

"Pretty much everyone from school will be here, so it should be interesting," Amy said, her voice growing in volume as the elevator rose.

Carter and Donovan exchanged looks. When the doors slid back, a wall of noise slammed into them. Following Amy, they headed into the chaos of loud conversations and dancing bodies.

"Let's get a drink," Amy said, tugging Link toward the kitchen.

Before Donovan could follow, Carter grabbed his arm. "I have a better plan than you playing puppy dog tonight."

Donovan eyed her. "Puppy dog?"

"Because you would be following the two of them like a puppy. Come on."

Carter pushed her way through the grinding mass in the living-room-turned-dance-floor out to the balcony. The cool night air felt pleasant compared to the overheated interior. Carter walked along the balcony until she found a viewpoint of the kitchen. Amidst the ever-changing scene, she picked out Amy and Link pouring drinks.

"Now you don't have to be an overbearing friend," she said, lounging against the railing.

As he claimed the spot beside her, Donovan brushed his arm with hers, sliding his hands into his pockets. "Have you ever been to a high school party before?"

His voice seemed quiet compared to the deafening noise that pushed against the glass. The scene before them was a clash of flirtations, arguments, break-ups, and make-outs.

"Nope," she said. "I didn't have any friends to ask me to any."

At the admittance, Donovan peered down at her. "Link and I are really your only friends?"

Not meeting his gaze, Carter shoved her hands into her jacket pockets. "Yeah, you are." She didn't say anything else for a moment. "Before my mom left I went to a public school and had friends. But when I transferred to Hamilton, things were…different."

"Your mother left and you were below everyone around you in money and status."

Carter let out a small breath. "Even if I had a mind to make friends, I wasn't in the place to do so." She looked up at him. "Have you been to a party?"

"Yes," he said. "We went to a couple at our old school. They were more low key than this."

"This isn't a common occurrence for you?"

Donovan shook his head. "The weekends are usually pretty quiet. Except for once every couple of months."

"Seeing his father. When does he get to see him next?"

"Sunday."

Carter found where Link bent close to Amy, smiling, for all appearances a normal teenage boy. He said something and Amy threw her arms around his neck, laughing up at him.

"How does he feel about it?" Carter asked.

Donovan didn't answer right away, his eyes trained on Link. "It's never an easy thing. But I think he prefers to have the visits rather than not."

Carter pulled her jacket tight around her. It was cold so many stories up but she didn't suggest they go back into the party. Out of their line of sight, they heard a shout as a pair of drunk teenage boys decided to beat each other up. Link and Amy remained unfazed by the commotion.

"You want something to drink?" he asked.

"Are you sure you can go in there and make it back alive? Some of these girls look wasted and their aggression and hormone levels are probably high."

"I've taken down 250 lbs Marines, I can handle a few wasted teenagers."

Carter waved her hands towards the doors. "Then, by all means, go get me a soda. This should be fun to watch."

Without commenting, Donovan slipped inside, the volume rising and spilling out over the city. Carter tracked him through the party, avoiding girls and teasing hands. Captivated by his progress, she wasn't conscious of Lucas approaching.

Lucas leaned against the railing and eyed her up and down. When Carter looked at him, her expression fell into boredom. Along his jaw, she could see the fading bruise from Donovan's fist.

"Owens," he said, the reek of alcohol on his breath. "You look hot."

"Could you be any more of a cliché at this moment?" she asked.

He sidled closer, one hand sliding on the railing and inching along her back. "Come on, you know everyone knows we have a 'will they, won't they' thing going on."

"Lucas, I didn't find you attractive when you hit on me in freshman year and since then you've only managed to repulse me further. The fact that you cling to this fantasy that we will hook up someday is a little disturbing. Especially when all you do is insult me. I suggest getting some help."

It spoke to the level of alcohol in Lucas's system that all he did was grin. "You have fantasies about me too?"

"Am I interrupting something?" Donovan asked, holding two Pepsis.

"Interrupting implies that something is even going on," Carter said. "Lucas, are you going to leave, or do you want to make an idiot of yourself one more time? I'm sure Donovan would be amused and I'll get a kick out of it."

When Lucas faced Donovan, he paled a little, clearly not drunk enough to get into a fight. He shouldered his way past Donovan and disappeared into the party.

"What did he want?" Donovan asked, resuming his spot beside Carter.

"If you have to ask that question, you clearly are not as smart as I took you for."

He chuckled. "Asked you to bear his offspring, did he?"

"Yes. But he didn't put it as eloquently as that." Carter shook her head in exasperation. "Teenage boys." She took a sip of soda. "Thanks for the drink."

"Sure. Not big on alcohol, I take it?"

"Are you kidding? There is not enough mouthwash or breath mints that would keep my father from knowing I was drinking."

"What would he do? Ground you?"

"Please, I would take grounding over what he would do. He would have me up at four in the morning to do military drills."

"Harsh punishment."

Despite the idea of the punishment, Carter grinned.

"Not really. I've done it before. He would just be making me do it while hungover. And he has a really loud whistle. But it's what you get when you grow up under a Navy SEAL."

"Must have made for an interesting childhood."

Flashing him a wry smile, she focused back on the party, speaking to the window. "It mostly started when my mother left. He didn't know how to handle a teenage girl and fell back on what he knew. A month after she left, he bought me a punching bag. When I found something frustrating with homework or school he taught me to assemble a gun. He taught me to focus my frustration and energy into something productive." She laughed. "I've spent the last four years assembling guns, running through training courses, throwing knives, and learning how to defend myself. Definitely makes for an interesting life. But that's something I figure you know something about."

He smiled. "You just described the first sixteen years of my life. Except I was competing against men and brothers who were a few years older than me."

Carter looked up at him. "Tell me about it."

As Donovan talked, Carter both heard and saw the affection he felt for his life, his family, his brothers. His half-smile drew her in, as did the wild adventures he and his brothers had gotten themselves into. The time drifted by as they exchanged war stories. When Donovan commented about Link's teetering state, they rescued him. He fell asleep in the back of the car, his snores the background noise to Carter and Donovan's continued stories.

"Thanks for...whatever tonight was," Carter said, holding the car door open. "I'm not sure I would have had as much fun if you weren't there beating off girls...and telling me about your life." Link let out an abrupt snort. "Will you be able to get him back to his apartment?"

"Carter, he weighs about 160 lbs," he said, his tone

patronizing. "Yes, I can get him to the apartment just fine."

"You're saying that so I know how much you bench. Well, I'm not that impressed. Find some other way to impress me."

Carter smiled to herself when it took Donovan a minute to drive away.

Chapter 35

As Carter entered the school halls, she noted the effects and regrets of the weekend written on student's faces. Upperclassmen winced at the slightest noise and glared at the freshmen who hadn't yet been hooked by their vices. Halfway to chemistry, Amy halted Carter in her tracks, her dark eyes worried.

"Do you know what's going on?" she asked.

Carter saw Amy's friends a few feet away, all standing back, helpless. "Link?"

Amy nodded, swallowing down her apprehension.

"What happened?"

"I'm not sure. I said hi to him when he arrived but he seemed distant. Yesterday when I called him he didn't answer or respond to any of my texts. I thought he had fun at the party...But maybe he didn't. Maybe we shouldn't have gone. I don't know what's wrong-"

Carter held up a hand, cutting off Amy's tsunami of words. Amy closed her mouth, choking back her worries. The bell rang, sending everyone scattering to their respective classes.

"Look, I'll find out what's going on with him," Carter said.

"Thanks," Amy said. "I'll see you in history."

As Carter headed off, she mulled over Amy's description of Link and found it accurate when she found him at their table. He sat with his notebook open, unseeing, the edge of his mouth turned down. Carter looked to Donovan for answers but he only shook his head.

"Hey," Carter said, as she took her seat.

The second bell rang, bringing Mason into the room trailed by Smith. Link watched his half-brother, hands clenched. Carter felt her heart sink into her stomach.

"I have a surprise for you," Mr. Rojas said. "Pop quiz."

A round of groans echoed through the classroom. A girl slumped into her folded arms and a boy tossed his pencil onto the table as if already resigning himself to a bad grade. Link didn't seem to hear the announcement as he stared at his notebook. Laying her folded arms on the desk, Carter rested her chin on top, bringing her into Link's line of sight. "Hey, how are you doing?"

"Fine."

"Come on, Link. It's me."

Link narrowed his eyes. "Carter, I said I was fine."

Carter saw his unspoken pain but she let the subject drop. Tests were passed out and Mr. Rojas said they could begin.

Half an hour later, Carter finished off her test. As she walked to Mr. Rojas's desk, she earned glares of annoyance and jealousy. Mr. Rojas checked the time as Carter set the test down before him. "Seems a bit slow for you."

"I got bored halfway through and got distracted."

Mr. Rojas gave her a genuine smile. "I hope you don't waste your talents in life. You truly have a great mind."

"Don't worry. I don't plan to."

When she swiveled away, she came face to face with

Donovan. "What took you so long?"

He reached around her and laid his test on top of hers. "Your writing is hard to decipher from such a distance. I think your answer to five lacked real thought."

Carter started to smile but it never found completion. "What happened?"

Mr. Rojas cleared his throat. "Get back to your seats. The rest of the class still has to finish."

When the bell finally rang Carter was the first up, though she waited for Link as he slowly gathered his things. In the hallway, Link began to walk away but Carter snagged his arm.

"Donovan," she said to his obvious confusion.

He retreated from Carter's hold only to bump into Mason.

"Watch it!" Mason said.

Carter leapt in front of Link. "Mason, why don't you make someone else's day miserable for once?"

"Oh look, Carter Owens," Mason said. "Defender of the Weak." Link tensed behind Carter. "Long live the girl who knows how to cut you down with a single word. Don't you have any other tricks?"

"I can knock you down with a single hit. Does that work?"

"Try it, Owens. It would make my day to see you get tackled to the ground."

"And it would make mine to see you hit the ground. How about I tackle you and we'll both get what we want?"

Before Carter could make good on her offer, Donovan stepped between them but only focused on Carter. "Not today," he whispered.

Mason strode off and Carter spun around. Link stood motionless like someone had punched him. Donovan gripped Link's shoulder in comfort. "Come on."

Outside history, the trio found Amy waiting. "Hey." She smiled brightly but dimmed when Link barely acknowledged her and went to his seat.

"He's having a bad day," Carter said.

The reassurance didn't seem to mollify Amy and she took her spot with tight lips. As Donovan moved to the door, Carter blocked his path. "What is going on? What happened this weekend?"

"It's what didn't happen this weekend."

"He didn't get to see him. Do you know why?"

"All they told me was something came up."

Despite knowing that was how the life of being the President worked, she disliked the man for missing time with his son.

"Has he been like this ever since?" she asked.

"Yes."

Inside the classroom, Carter knew a storm was building as Amy sat ramrod straight, staring dead ahead. Link observed none of the subtle signs.

"Continuing on with our study of Presidents and their administrations we move next to Bill Clinton, the 42nd President," Mr. Philips said, quieting the room. "Though there are many things that Clinton did to improve the country, what he is remembered for most are his indiscretions." Mr. Philips paced, serious. "Which in a way is fitting because Presidents are the embodiment of the country. They are held to a higher standard. For them, to err is a reflection of the state of our government."

Carter raised her hand and he acknowledged her, reluctantly. "Yes, Ms. Owens?".

"You're saying that despite what Clinton's positive accomplishments were, it's okay that he be forever remembered as an adulterer?"

Mr. Philips nodded. "He had a position to uphold and failed to do so. Anyone in his place should be held accountable for their actions and transgressions."

Mr. Philips glanced quickly past her shoulder, before returning to her.

"Even if those actions don't affect the country and only play a role in their private life?" she asked.

"Yes, because no matter what they have done, when

they hold a title with such honor they know that they could be exposed. Nothing can be kept a secret forever." He straightened. "Now, let's start off with Clinton's campaign and what means he took to be elected..."

Mr. Philips started pacing again and Carter slid down in her seat, his last words still playing around in her head. Beside her, a frown also marred Donovan's face.

Chapter 36

As history class dispersed, Amy started to walk out without looking back but had a change of heart at the door. "So," she said, the words clipped. "Are you going to sit with me at lunch?"

Link dragged himself out of his troubled thoughts, confused. The expression looked angrier than he knew. "Yeah, why wouldn't I?"

Disbelief ignited in Amy's eyes. "Why wouldn't you?" she said, everything about her gearing up for an argument.

"Yeah, that's what I said," Link said, puzzled.

Amy took a step forward, hot words burning her tongue. Before they had the chance to singe Link and cause serious damage, Carter stepped forward. "Oh, Link, I forgot, Mr. Rojas wants to see you about that test."

She spun him in the opposite direction. "See you at lunch, Amy. Save Link a seat," she called back.

Link stumbled along, completely lost. Amy stared after them. Donovan spoke low to her and she calmed down. Carter continued to guide Link through the river of students. When they found an empty corridor, she released him.

"I thought you said we were going to see Mr. Rojas?" Link asked.

"That was a lie. I had to get you away from Amy before you destroyed your relationship."

He frowned, reaching a new level of confusion. "What do you mean? We were just talking. Although, she seemed pissed for some reason."

Carter carelessly slapped his arm with the back of her hand. "That's because you have been completely distant with her."

"What?"

"And she thinks it's her fault"

He waved his arms around. "I never said it was. Why does she think that?"

"Because when you don't pay attention to her, she doesn't know what to think."

"I said hi to her this morning and nodded to her."

"Yes, how anyone would take that badly is beyond me."

Link raised his hand. "Please don't. Not today, Carter." He ran a hand through his hair as he stared at the floor, worn out.

"You didn't answer her calls or texts," she said. "Add that to the distracted state you're in today and she's worried."

Link lifted his head as understanding dawned on him. "She thought...ah..." Link swore under his breath. "That had nothing to do with her."

Carter took a step forward and laid a hand on his shoulder. "I know."

Link ran his hands over his face as if he could erase his problems with the gesture. With a frustrated breath, he dropped to the ground, Carter lowering herself beside him. For a long moment, neither of them spoke. He took off his glasses and let them dangle from his hand. In the distance, they could hear the jumbled sound of voices but no one found them. Donovan paused at the sight of them on the floor. When Carter shook her head slightly, he made himself scarce.

"I'm sorry," she said.

The glasses twirled in Link's fingers as he managed a vague nod. "I don't like these glasses. They're large and annoying. Sometimes I manage to forget about them but they are always there. For another two years, I will have to wear these. I will have to look like I rolled out of bed."

With his face completely unobscured, Carter could see his father in his features and wondered how she hadn't seen it at the very beginning.

"Did you know I can't get a specific type of haircut?" he asked. She didn't respond knowing the question was rhetorical. He laid his head against the wall. "If I cut it too short and style it just right, then I really look like him."

He chewed on his words, glaring at the opposite wall. "Seriously! My life is dictated by another's. I'm a..." He gave a smile that lacked any humor. "What did Mr. Philips say? I'm a transgression." He waved his hand as if batting something away. "I'm a son with a parentage no one wants to acknowledge. I'm a mistake."

"Looks like we're in the same boat," Carter said. "I was never supposed to happen. Link, I know they won't acknowledge it but I will. I think, mistake or not, this world is better with you in it. My life is better with you in it." She nodded back down the hall. "So is everyone else you've met. Especially Amy."

Link widened his eyes. "Crap, Amy." He slid his glasses back on. "How badly did I screw up?"

Carter helped him up. "It won't be too bad. Apologize for being distant, tell her it was a bad day, and then ask her out on a date for tomorrow. Not a double date."

Link brushed off his uniform and ran a hand through his hair, nervously. "That will work?"

"Yes."

Link stopped his fidgeting. "Thanks, Carter."

She nodded, knowing his words held more meaning. "Let's go break the bad news to Donovan that he has to sit through another romantic movie. Maybe I'll help him out. I can go with him and shoot him to put him out of his misery."

Link laughed, pushing away the thoughts that would never leave but had been made lighter. They rounded the corner and found Donovan leaning against the lockers, his phone in hand.

"Link is going to ask Amy out on a date,'" Carter said.

"That should help smooth things over."

"I know," she said. "Have fun watching a wimpy girl do nothing for herself and rely entirely on the man."

"I will since you are going with me. I accept your offer."

Carter rolled her eyes. "I should have known you were listening. What do you want to be shot with: a 9mm Glock 17 or 9mm Sig Sauer P226?"

His expression was unreadable, only his eyes betrayed his emotions. She smiled. "Navy SEAL father, remember?"

As they passed by the front entrance, Carter's father stepped inside, shadowed by two other men in black suits. Carter felt her stomach drop as the worst reasons for his presence raced through her mind. Without a word to either boy, she hurried over to her father. "Captain," she said, "what are you doing here?"

Her father smiled, easing some of her nerves. He motioned with his good hand to his companions. "Head to Principal Withers's office and I'll be right behind." The men walked away. "I'm not here to deliver bad news. Everything is fine." Carter relaxed and she glanced over her shoulder at Link. Her father followed her gaze. "He does look a lot like him."

"Yeah, he does. Now why are you here?" she asked.

"It's a simple check. Your tracker went off the grid for a minute and I got an alert. It seems all signals around the school were blocked for a full minute. I'm here to make sure everything in the system is running smoothly."

Carter studied her father, searching for signs of worry or nerves. She found none. "Is that something that happens?"

"Not often but sometimes things shift with satellites and you get a dead spot for a moment. I was sent to double check."

"Okay."

He accompanied her as she returned to Link and Donovan.

"You must be Link," her father said, his deep voice made both boys straighten.

Link nodded and shot a look at Carter. Her father held out a hand. "I'm Agent Owens," he said. Link shook his hand. "It's a pleasure meeting you."

"Likewise."

"Donovan, correct?" her father said.

They shook hands, both grips strong and steady.

"Yes, sir," Donovan said, for once sounding like Link's bodyguard instead of a teenage boy.

The subtle shift in Donovan's demeanor almost made Carter laugh. If she hadn't known he wasn't capable of it, she would've sworn Donovan seemed nervous.

"It's a pleasure meeting both of you," Carter's father said. He gave Carter a sideways hug. "I'll see you at home, Sarge."

Carter hugged him back and watched as he disappeared into the main office. Link grinned at her. "You make a lot more sense now."

She playfully punched his arm. "Shut up and let's go make sure you still have a girlfriend."

Chapter 37

I have a question for you," Carter said to Donovan. She sat leaning back in her chair, her crossed ankles on the library table. Across from Carter, Link and Amy's notebooks and textbooks were open and strewn about but the couple was nowhere in sight. She had no doubt they were in one of the second story rows, exchanging apologies. Donovan sat beside her, writing out long, complicated equations.

"Is there a reason you feel the need to announce that you have a question?" he asked, not bothering to look over.

She flung her pencil into the air and watched as it twirled before catching it again. "No."

"What's your question?"

"What is your opinion on Mr. Philips?" she asked.

"Who says I have one?"

"Because you're human, everyone has an opinion on everyone and everything. What is your opinion?"

"Not on everything."

"Try telling the internet and social media that. So tell

me."

Donovan glanced at her. "Do you want my opinion or impression?"

"Impression."

"Why say "opinion" if you meant "impression"?"

Carter held up the pencil. "Stop being pedantic and tell me or I will find somewhere to stick this pencil that will be very uncomfortable."

Donovan snapped the pencil in two. "Make a more realistic threat next time."

Carter didn't point out the fact he had delivered two weapons instead of one. As Donovan went back to his equations, Carter secured another pencil and tossed it again.

"Is there a reason why you don't want to tell me your impression?" she asked.

He stayed motionless for a second in thought. "He is a teacher with vast knowledge of the inner workings of the political system. Teaching was not his first choice of occupation. He was probably blackballed from politics and for that, he has a bitterness towards anyone in office.

What he did, I don't know and this is merely an educated guess based on what I've seen and heard him talk about."

"That's what I came up with as well."

Carter threw the pencil in the air, watching it flip over and over along with her thoughts. The library settled back into silence, only whispered words breaking it. Diana bustled through the rows pushing a book cart.

"Did Mr. Philips's mood strike you as odd today?" she asked.

"Not in the least. He was in the same mood that he is always in."

"But what about his whole speech of Presidents and the weight they hold and their secrets will be found out crap." The pencil spun upward. "That didn't hit you as unusually hostile, even for him?"

She caught the pencil and then let it fly. As it fell,

Donovan snatched the pencil from the air. She raised an eyebrow. "Well?"

"Well, what?"

"Did his talk of Presidential transgressions strike you as odd?"

"He was bringing up a valid point."

"You believe that he was correct?"

Donovan nodded. "I do. Men in leadership positions should be held to a higher standard for the mere fact that their mistakes, if ever made public, could cause a lot of unnecessary problems. In this day and age, nothing stays secret."

"You think eventually the truth of..." Carter gestured to Link's open backpack, "will come out?"

Cautiously, Donovan scanned the library and lowered his voice. "For his sake, I hope it never does. But there are enough people who have problems with Presidents that it might. For now, no one knows and he is safe."

"Do you think if someone knew they would try to act on that knowledge?"

Resigning himself to the conversation, he tossed his pencil onto the table. "It depends on the person and what sort of history they have with the president."

Carter gave him a thoughtful look and snatched his pencil, resuming her previous occupation. "Do you think anyone here knows?"

Donovan rocked his chair back on two legs, placing his laced fingers behind his head. "As far as I'm aware? No, no one besides you."

She pursed her lips, skeptical.

"What?" he asked.

"Nothing."

"Carter," he said, dragging out her name.

Catching her pencil and pointing it at him. "You don't think Mr. Philips possibly knows?"

"What is it with this interest in Mr. Philips?"

"I'm making conversation."

"No, you're making speculations."

"Fine, I'm making speculations. But I don't think they are unfounded."

Doubtful, Donovan folded and Carter held up her hands blocking his thoughts. "Hear me out. When he was talking about transgressions he looked at Link."

"He's a teacher, he looks at everyone while he is talking."

"When you first arrived, he was surprised to see Link. Doesn't that strike you as something?"

Donovan regarded her. "Do you feel the need to give everyone ulterior motives?"

"Only those who have them," she said. "I was right about the both of you, wasn't I?"

"Now that that mystery is solved, you find the need for a new one?"

Pulling her legs off the table, Carter dropped her chair to all fours, twisting to face Donovan, earnest. "I'm not out to solve some mystery. I could care less whether Mr. Philips has ties with the Russian mafia. What I care about is what I saw and heard and whether it holds any weight."

"That's all you want to know?"

"Yes," Carter breathed out. She might not have the title of bodyguard for Link but that didn't stop the protective instinct she felt for him.

He gave a slow nod, relenting. "Alright, I understand that. The thing is, there is not a lot he could do even if he did know."

"You mean besides exposing Link and the President."

"How?"

"Documents."

"There are no hard copies that tie them together."

"Even money?"

"They're run through different channels."

"Photos of Link."

"What would that prove? One, there are ways to alter photos so no one could completely believe it. Two, you have a lanky kid with brown hair and glasses, who vaguely looks like his father when he isn't wearing them."

At Donovan's quick answers, she guessed these were all aspects and weaknesses he'd visited before. But still, she wasn't ready to let the subject drop just yet.

"Photos of them together," she said.

Donovan raised a patronizing eyebrow. "Need I remind you he hasn't seen him since we've been going here and even if he had, there is no possible way to get those pictures. I don't even know the destination until half an hour before. The places have all been enclosed and impossible for snipers to get a clear aim. How could he?"

Quietly, Carter ran through every possible scenario she could but found counter-arguments for each one. Donovan watched her, a small smile on his lips. When Carter came out of her head, his smile disappeared, replaced by his normal impassivity. "Come up with anything else?"

"Yes. But for it to work Mr. Philips would have had to have some sort of military training."

"Which he doesn't have."

"Which he doesn't have," she echoed.

Looking down at the floor then back up at Donovan, her eyes held hints of worry. "He's safe?"

"He's safe. Even if something happened, I'm here to get him to a secure location."

They didn't speak, Carter gazing out at the library, Donovan gazing at her.

"What brought this on?" he asked.

She shrugged, forcing herself to seem unconcerned. When she started to respond, he held up his hand. "If you're going to lie to me, don't say anything."

Embarrassed, Carter dropped her eyes, fighting a grin. But as she searched for the answer to his question, her expression sobered. "Today I saw how vulnerable he is. And it's strange to admit it but I care about him. I don't ever want to see him hurt."

"It's not crazy," Donovan said gently.

Carter held in a laugh. "For you, maybe. But the sensation is something new to me. If you haven't noticed, I don't have any friends to spare."

"True. But the ones you have aren't going anywhere."

She didn't say anything, everything she felt in the moment conveyed in her small smile. Suddenly unable to hold her gaze, Donovan reclaimed his pencil and ran it over his fingers. "So what brought your father here today?"

Carter waved her hand flippantly. "Oh, some signal going out. It was a glitch, that's all."

Donovan stopped twirling the pencil. "How is he doing?"

The question warmed Carter, hearing the touch of compassion in his voice. "Good. The sling came off the other day. Physical Therapy is starting up today and the doctors say he should be fully recovered in three months. Honestly, I'm happy that he is still behind a desk for now."

"Will he be there for long?

"Hopefully, for the rest of his time in the service."

"How much longer does he have?"

Carter let out a low breath as if the time were a physical weight that she always held with her. "About four months." A myriad of emotions swirled in her, each of them playing across her face, the final one being worry.

"What does he plan to do afterward?" Donovan asked, trying to tear her from her burdening thoughts.

"I don't know. But something where he's not taking bullets for someone else. He has mentioned taking up a training post in the Navy SEALS but he hasn't settled on anything yet."

"Well, I'm glad he is recovering."

She dipped her head, accepting his sincerity. The rattling of wheels grew louder as Diana stepped out from one of the rows with a half-empty cart. A thought struck

Carter.

"Diana," she said, barely needing to raise her voice in the quiet.

Diana redirected her cart and stopped in front of the table. She pointedly stared at Donovan's tilted back position and he lowered the chair and crossed one ankle on his knee

"Diana, do you know how long Mr. Philips has been at the school?" Carter said, saving Donovan from a verbal rebuke.

Donovan shot her a look, which she ignored.

"Mr. Philips," Diana said, her voice distant as she sorted through memories. She brightened as the right memory clicked into place. "He started working here about five years ago. I remember because it was the fall when Douglas was announced as the next President."

"Really?" Carter asked.

"Yes. Why?"

She shook her head and slid back in her chair. "No, reason. Just curious."

Diana pushed on, leaving Carter with Donovan and his very loud thoughts. "I was merely curious," she said. "It just makes your point more clear. He couldn't have even known about Link if he was out of politics by the time Douglas was getting elected."

"Are you happy now?"

Carter nodded, though doubts tugged at her mind.

Chapter 38

The rowdy shouts of boys welcomed Carter as she entered the deli. At the counter, Maggie scrawled on her notepad, letting the family be as boisterous as they liked since they were the only customers.

"Hey," Carter said, announcing her presence.

Maggie offered her a tired smile. "Hey, girly."

"You free to talk?"

At the question, some of Maggie's weariness melted away. "I need a break and you are a perfect reason to take one." Carter scuffed her shoes on the floor so Maggie didn't see her smile and how much her words affected her. "I'll grab cookies."

Dodging shouts and called names, Carter took her usual booth in the back. Sliding in across from her, Maggie laid down a napkin and a cookie. She let out a breath and sank into the booth.

"Long day?" Carter asked.

Maggie dramatically widened her eyes. "It wasn't too bad, just constant. I'm ready to be off my feet."

"You should come over to the apartment tonight. We

could watch something."

"A romance?" Maggie teased.

"Or I could teach you how to assemble a gun."

"Don't worry, Steve already taught me."

That brought Carter up short. "When did this happen? That wasn't what you were doing last Saturday, was it?" She put her elbow on the table and rested her chin in her hand. "You never did tell me what you were doing over so late."

Maggie looked unamused even as she flushed. "I was spending time with an overprotective friend as he waited for his daughter to come back from a party. Her first party, I might add. He doesn't know how to handle you going off to events. This is uncharted territory. I was giving him moral support."

Carter broke her cookie in half with a half-concealed smirk. "Sure, if that's the story you're going for. We'll see what Captain says and whether your stories line up."

Though she joked, Carter hoped there was more to it. Her father deserved someone as kind and loving as Maggie.

"Grown-ups can be friends," Maggie laughed.

"Alright, but you should know he is now a free man and won't be available forever."

"I'm willing to debate that, you're his daughter. I'm not sure any woman could come within ten feet of your father without you interrogating them."

That was definitely true. "Good thing you've already made the cut. You should use that to your advantage."

Maggie sobered as she leaned forward on the table. "Hon, you understand that I care for you and your father deeply, right?"

"That was never a question."

A piece of Maggie's smile returned. "Then know that I put both of your happiness first. Your father is not in the place to be with anyone new, not with what just happened with your mother."

Carter knew Maggie had a point but Carter wanted

nothing more than for her father to move on, to let go. But she also knew a man who had waited four years in the hope his wife would return wasn't going to let go quickly. She only hoped Maggie would still want him when he finally decided he was ready to find happiness again.

"Joking or not," Maggie continued. "Know that I will do nothing about this. Not until he is ready for it. And you are ready for it."

"I'm ready. You can date Captain whenever you want. You have my full approval."

The smile came home to Maggie. "I'm happy to hear that." She propped her chin on her fist. "Now, you never told me all about the party. And how it went with Donovan."

"Yes, I did. I said it was loud, crowded, and full of unintelligible drunk high schoolers. What more did you need?"

"You didn't say how it went with Donovan."

"We didn't go together in that sense."

"Still, you like him, right?

What type of question was that? Of course she did. Him and Link were the only people at school she did like.

"You know I do."

Maggie pressed her lips together, trying not to laugh. "I mean do you like him more than a friend?"

"Do I prefer his company over the majority of the male populace at school? Yes. Do my hormones go into overdrive and my brain takes a nap when he is around? No."

Grinning, Maggie did a small dance, seeming more like a best friend than a mother figure. "You do like him."

Carter fought viciously to keep her smile in check. "Did you not hear what I said? I don't like him. He just doesn't make me feel like punching him every time he opens his mouth."

"Oh, I heard what you said. But my hearing is selective and I translate things differently."

"That is obvious."

"What I heard is you found a man that meets your standards."

Carter scoffed. "I don't have standards."

"You do, girly. High standards. Your father set them and no one will ever meet them. But it seems Donovan is getting close."

Carter did smile at that, thinking of how Donovan could read her, how he was trained to defend himself, and how he could assemble a gun in under a minute.

"I see that smile," Maggie said.

Though Maggie's love life was an acceptable topic to discuss, Carter decided hers was not. Not that she had one. Because she didn't. Donovan was only a friend.

"That was for no reason at all," she said.

Though Maggie smiled more reservedly, her eyes still beamed with mischief. "Sure, you smile like that about every peer you talk about."

Carter ate the rest of her cookie so her face wouldn't betray her further. Someone called out to Maggie, ending her break.

"I'm glad you are letting people in," Maggie said. "Even if it's only to the point where you aren't inclined to punch them."

When Maggie left, Carter stared out the window, forcibly not thinking about Donovan. When her attempt failed, she waved goodbye to Maggie and hurried home. Her father's car sat in the driveway and when Carter opened the door, she found him at the dining table. His suit jacket hung over the back of a chair and he wore a look of fatigue. Her heart clenched as he lifted his head and wiped away his obvious exhaustion.

"Are you okay?" she asked, taking a seat at the table.

Her father straightened, his face unreadable. "Of course, I'm fine. How was school?"

Carter tried to ignore the prick of hurt at his

concealment. "Fine. Are you sure?"

"Sarge, I'm fine."

Though he offered a reassuring smile, it appeared brittle to Carter and she didn't understand why.

"Did you get everything worked out at the school?" she asked. "Was it a glitch?"

"Yes, we believe so. We are sending in a tech crew to double check."

"Was that the only reason you were there?" She wondered if something else in the school was suspicious but he didn't want to alarm her.

"What other reason would we have?"

She sensed him holding back. "I don't see why there needed to be three of you for a simple check-up job."

"We were also checking the security tunnels and updating something in the system," he said.

"Which was...?"

"None of your concern."

Carter sent him a challenging stare that he met.

"How did physical therapy go?" she asked.

When her father abruptly rose and moved to the kitchen, Carter felt a sinking in her gut.

"It was fine," he said.

Carter twisted in her chair, observing the tension in his back. "What's wrong? Did everything go all right? Nothing bad has come up, has it?"

Without turning around, he answered. "Sarge, I said it was fine."

Something was wrong. "You might have said that but your body language says otherwise. Captain, what's going on? You can tell me-"

"Carter!" The curt tone cut through Carter.

Carter sat stunned, feeling as if someone had punched her heart. Letting out a breath, her father ran his good hand through his hair, without looking at her.

"I said it was fine," he said, quietly.

Even in the quiet tone, Carter heard the defensiveness and felt lost. She didn't know what could have changed between seeing him at school and now. She'd never felt this distance from her father before.

"I have some calls to make," her father said. "I'll be in my room. Eat without me, I'm not that hungry."

Pain crawled up Carter's throat as her father walked away. "Me neither."

Chapter 39

The apartment lay completely quiet around Carter the next evening. On her nightstand, her phone buzzed. She scanned Donovan's message, confirming where they were meeting. After dashing off a reply, she tucked the phone into her jeans. She unhooked her jacket from a hanger and shut her bedroom door. Across the hall, her father's door stood open but she didn't spare it a glance.

As Carter descended the stairs, car headlights lit up the front of the building. Her father wore his black suit and everything about him appeared its normal military neat self. Carter felt her heart twist with uncertainty. That morning when she'd woken up, he'd already left for the office, not giving her time to ask him more questions. Leaving her to take a lonely trip to school.

Meeting at the bottom of the steps, they observed each other, trying to read thoughts that were hidden behind masks of impassivity. Her father looked down at her bag.

"Where are you going?" he asked.

Carter vaguely pointed towards the street. "Amy and

Link are going on a date tonight and I'm keeping Donovan company."

"It's a school night," her father said with a flickering frown.

"I finished my homework."

"What time will you be home?"

"Eleven at the latest."

The exchange sounded normal for a father and daughter but to Carter, it felt like they were talking to each other from opposite sides of a wall.

"Maggie said you didn't stop by the deli today," her father said.

"I had homework to get done. How was PT?"

Her father's controlled expression mirrored Carter's. "Fine."

Again Carter felt that prick of hurt, sensing something he wouldn't share. For a beat, neither of them moved, neither of them spoke. Carter waited for her father to say something, to make the wall between them disappear but he didn't.

"I have to go," she said. "I have a bus to catch."

Her father let her pass by without a word but as she hit the lane, he stopped her. "Carter, stay safe." She nodded and turned away. "I love you, Sarge."

She stuffed her hands into her jacket pockets. "Yeah," she said. "Same."

She walked away, her father watching until her shadow disappeared.

Carter slid down in her seat on the bus, letting the constantly changing scenery keep her thoughts captive: buildings, cars, houses, trees, buildings, cars, houses, trees. When the bus rumbled to a stop, Carter swung herself out, landing in a busy office block. Around her, businessmen in suits headed out to relieve their weary minds with a strong drink. Women, who during the day wore sensible shoes, now walked in high heels with laughter on their lips and freedom in their eyes. Each unfamiliar face was easy to read. But the face she'd known all her life was a closed book.

In the mall, across from the movie theater entrance, Donovan rested against a wall, hands in his dark jean pockets and ankles crossed: the picture of ease. As Carter neared, she noted how he took in every face, his eyes never settling. But when she stepped around a group of younger teens, he settled his gaze on her.

"Are they already in there?" she asked.

"They're in line at the concession stand."

In the theater lobby, Carter found Link and Amy waiting in line, their hands locked together. Link spoke and Amy's hand flew to her mouth as she laughed. Their happiness seemed so simple, everything they thought and felt written plainly for the world to see. Carter watched, mesmerized, unaware her inner turmoil played out for Donovan to see.

"What's going on?" Donovan asked, nudging her elbow.

Carter frowned. "What do you mean?"

"You've been distracted all day."

"It's nothing-"

Donovan's flat glare halted Carter. Without answering, she studied the tableau before them without really seeing it. Donovan took her silence in stride and continued his appraisal of the surrounding crowd.

"You don't have to be here," he said, after a few minutes.

"Do you not want me to be here?"

"Do you want to be here?"

Carter thought of home and her father. "Yeah, I want to be here."

He pulled out two tickets and handed one to her. "Link told me what they were seeing and I got it when we showed up early."

She read the movie title. "It's a horror movie."

"Apparently Amy has a liking for them. Or is looking for an excuse to cling to Link."

"And Link?"

"He has a stronger stomach than you'd think. I don't think he'll mind Amy clinging to him."

Carter managed a rough smile that didn't last. Link and Amy made their purchase and took off towards the theater. Donovan and Carter moved in sync, handing their tickets to the attendant and joining the stream of moviegoers.

Towards the end, they entered their auditorium. Donovan stopped Carter before she could round the sloping wall. She glanced down at his hand on her arm, then at him. He let go of her.

"Link is going to text when it's clear," he said.

Carter listened to the whispered conversations and crinkling of candy wrappers. Donovan's phone vibrated. They spotted Link and Amy towards the back and off to the right. Carter led the way up the stairs, taking a spot far from the couple but still in view.

When Carter sat, her arm brushed against Donovan's as they both went to claim the middle armrest. Carter took her arm away first, silently conceding to him. Commercials played on the screen as the seats continued to fill.

"You don't have to be here," he said.

She looked at him, surprised to find him closer than she expected but she didn't back away. "Why are you asking me again? If I didn't want to be here, I wouldn't be."

"I don't doubt that but you have to be the quietest date I've ever had. And I didn't expect that. Especially not from you."

Crossing her arms, she studied him. "First: this isn't a date. And second: do you have a problem with silence, Donovan?"

"I know it's not a date. It was a slip of the tongue. And silence with you, yes, because it holds too much weight."

"I don't imagine you've ever let anything slip, let alone a word like 'date'. And my silence has nothing to do with you or this situation. So why should it bother you?"

Donovan put his elbow on the armrest. "In this instance it's true. I don't think of you as my date and don't plan on letting the word 'date' slip again. And the fact that your silence doesn't involve me doesn't bother me but it is affecting me. In that manner, you have put me in the situation."

"For the record, I don't think of you as my date either. Just in case that thought crossed your mind." Carter angled towards him, her brow furrowed. "And whether my silence affects you or not is none of my concern."

"The thought of you being my date never crossed my mind," Donovan said. "And you can be as silent as you want. I no longer care."

"Good, because being your date never crossed mine. That's fine with me. I don't need you to care."

"Fine."

"Good."

They stared at each other then faced the screen. Conversations filled the silence. Carter rested her elbow on the unoccupied armrest. She cast a sideways glance at Donovan. He sat with his arms crossed and one foot balanced on his knee, his eyes flickering to Link and Amy every few minutes.

"You had other dates," she said.

A flash of a smile skidded across his lips. He spoke without looking at her. "I grew up on a Marine base not a monastery, Carter." Donovan studied her profile. "Why do you ask?"

"You said I was your quietest date-"

"Slip of the tongue."

"I was just curious. That's all."

"How many dates have you been on?"

Despite herself, Carter chuckled and looked down at her hands.

"That many, huh?" Donovan said.

"I have a Secret Service agent as a father, transferred

schools, and my mom left when I was fourteen. You figure it out."

"That means the double date was technically your first date then."

"If you could even call it a date."

"Do you?"

"No."

Donovan nodded, his expression almost teasing. "Then you have yet to have a first date."

"It would seem so."

"You don't seem that broken up about it."

"I'm not run by my hormones. Besides, there was never anyone worth dating."

The lights dimmed in the movie theater and the crowd fell silent. Donovan leaned close to Carter and whispered, his breath falling across her neck. "Who constitutes someone worth dating?"

She eyed him in the darkened theater. "Why do you want to know?"

He gave a half convincing shrug. "I was just curious. That's all."

As she threw him a flat look, he smirked. She shook her head and focused back at the screen. As the characters on the screen started talking, Carter leaned back over to Donovan. He shifted closer.

"Honestly," she whispered, "I would take anyone who could last five minutes in hand to hand combat with me."

"Good to know," he whispered, a faint smile touching his lips.

Only ten minutes into the movie she noticed Amy shift closer to Link, wrapping her arms around his, her hand finding his. When the first scare occurred, she buried her head in his shoulder, letting out a small squeak. Carter fought back a laugh as Donovan grinned.

As the movie progressed Carter and Donovan inched closer to each other. When a side character was brutally murdered, the theater seemed to cringe. All except the two of them.

"He should have taken the crowbar with him instead of the ax," Carter said, in a hushed tone. "The ax was too heavy and his aim would have had to be precise to even do damage."

"Where are his natural fight instincts?" Donovan said.

"Obviously he wasn't born with any."

"His death was unavoidable."

"Clearly. No one that stupid could live."

"Not in this movie," he said.

As Carter looked back at the screen, she jumped with the rest of the crowd as the killer popped up. She gripped Donovan's arm, muttering something under her breath. Instantly, she let go.

"Surprised me," she said, not looking at him.

"Of course," Donovan said, a smile in his voice.

For the rest of the movie, Carter forced herself to remain unfazed by any sudden scares. As the credits began to roll, the house lights brightened. Under the cover of the rising mass, Donovan and Carter quickly exited. They broke away from the chatting group, finding a spot out of sight.

"That was an impractical ending," Carter said.

"As well as predictable," Donovan said.

"That too."

Link and Amy appeared, their hands clasped and her head buried in his shoulder. He said something and she beamed up at him.

"Do you know where they're headed?" Carter asked as they tailed the couple to the exit.

"For frozen yogurt."

At the brightly painted fro-yo palace, Donovan secured a table where they could see the couple but wouldn't be seen while Carter bought two cups of frozen yogurt. Young couples and groups of girls filled the space with a hum of voices. As she ate, Carter scanned the surrounding crowd, roaming over a muscular man, who sat alone a few tables down from Link and Amy. She toyed with her spoon.

"Donovan," she said. "Wasn't that man watching the same movie as us?"

Donovan followed her gaze. "Yes," he said, unconcerned.

"That's not something worth noting?"

He dug into the yogurt. "Not at all."

"How come you're so sure?"

He used his spoon to point to a couple two tables past Link and Amy. "Because they were also at the same movie. It's not odd for people to come here after a movie, Carter."

Carter let the subject go, her caution alleviated. Link and Amy slowly inched closer and closer toward each other, taking scoops from the other's frozen yogurt cup. Couples whispered to each other, as groups of girls giggled.

Carter ate absentmindedly as her thoughts reverted to her father. Donovan eyed her as Link and Amy found other occupations for their mouths. He studied her for a long moment.

"Thanks, Carter," he said.

It took her a second to respond, dragging herself from her thoughts. "For what?"

"Coming with me."

"Oh, that. It wasn't that big of a deal."

"No. But I found it amusing to see you pretend to get startled just for the excuse to grab my arm."

"Get over yourself, Donovan. Or go find some other girl to cling to you."

He laughed, the sound deep and genuine. Stretching his back, he ran a hand through his hair. "I'll pass on that offer."

Setting aside her yogurt, Carter laid her arms on the table. "Are you telling me in all this time you've never dated?"

"No," he said.

"Why not? They seem willing."

Donovan spun his spoon in his yogurt. "I don't get involved because it could affect my focus." Carter didn't say anything. "And because it would be a lie. They are drawn to something that isn't real."

"Interesting."

"Did you want a different reason?"

"Most every guy fakes who they are to get exactly what they want. It's interesting to meet someone who doesn't think the same way."

"You forget I am a few years older than these girls and can see how a relationship with me would affect them. I care, that is the difference between those tools and me."

"I would have to agree."

Amy checked her phone and said something to Link, making them both rise. Carter started to stand but Donovan stuck his hand out, stilling her. Sitting back down, she watched as Link and Amy exited. Trashing their remaining yogurt, Carter and Donovan followed. They waited by the glass front doors, looking out until Amy kissed Link and climbed into a car. Link was still watching the car drive off when Carter and Donovan appeared at his side.

"Have a fun night?" Carter asked.

Link started, cleared his throat, and tried to contain his smile.

"We should head home," he said, forcing a frown that didn't seem to stick.

She exchanged grins with Donovan as they walked towards their car. Looking back at the frozen yogurt shop, she noticed the muscular man casually walked out. He glanced at them before heading off in the opposite direction.

Chapter 40

Carter stared out the window onto the football field. But she wasn't looking at the line of students as they made their way around the track, none of them working very hard. Hints of dark circles lived beneath her eyes. Link sat beside her, scribbling away on the latest project. A project she had already finished.

"Carter," Link said.

Only after another nudge and a call of her name did Carter answer. "Hmmm?"

"What's going on with you? You've been, I don't know, distracted or something."

"I'm surprised you left 'Amy and Link world' long enough to notice that."

Link fidgeted, betraying himself as he cast a glance to Donovan, who worked on his calculus homework. As he ran a hand through his hair, a flash of irritation flickered across his face. He paused, feeling Carter's gaze. Their eyes met for a split second before Carter turned away.

"Well, what did he say?" Carter asked, rubbing her eyes.

"Only that you've been distracted and I should see if I can find out why."

"Did he mention anything about subtlety in your approach?"

Link shrugged carelessly. "Yes, but I figured you would see through it and would prefer if I was straightforward."

For the first time in the last four days, Carter smiled. Link fiddled with his pencil. "Are you going to tell me?"

"It's nothing."

"Should I believe that without question or do you want me to push past it?"

Despite the weariness that clung to her, Carter laughed. A few students turned to her, puzzled. Donovan lifted his head at the sound but Carter didn't notice. Mr. Rojas eyed Carter. "Miss Owens is there something you find amusing about the project?"

"Besides the misspelling on the second page and the way in which it was frustratingly easy? No, not at all, sir."

Mr. Rojas sighed, caught between amusement and annoyance. "If that is the case, please remain quiet as the rest of your peers lack your frustration."

As he returned to assist struggling students, Carter inched closer to Link.

"It seems you're learning from dating Amy," she said, lowering her voice.

Flushing, Link rubbed the back of his neck. "Yeah, she is confusing at times but I have learned the response 'nothing' actually means something is going on."

"Then the next problem is figuring out whether she wants you to accept it or not."

"Yeah. I still don't know that one." He twisted his pencil between his hands. "So what's with you?"

Carter didn't speak. The last few days had been filled with stiff conversations with her father and unreadable expressions. She didn't know what was going on with him. Each day she grew more afraid that he would never let her know. She feared that the wall between them might never come down.

"I don't know," she said. Link showed genuine concern. "But you don't need to worry. How has it been going with Amy?"

"Okay," Link said, accepting the change of subject. "Well, it's..." He smiled, bashful. "It's going well. She's not mad at me about what happened Monday. The date seemed to take care of that."

"She looked like she had fun," Carter playfully elbowed him, "buried in your shoulder."

Link went red as he made a face at the floor, his smile conquering. "Uh...yeah, it was good. Did you know she smells like sunshine and peaches?" he asked in a rush, the words seeming to come crashing out of their own accord.

The comparison made no sense but Carter knew that it did to Link. It also told her that her friend was happy. Something she didn't want to dampen with her problems.

"No," she said. "I was not aware of this fact."

Link leaned partially on the desk, intent. "Yeah, and when she's excited about something she'll hold onto my arm. She also does this thing where she plays with the end of her hair when she's studying. She tied it into a knot once without even noticing..."

Link's litany of Amy's attributes ended when Mr. Rojas called for the class's attention. "Alright, if you're not finished with your project, take it home. It will be due tomorrow," Mr. Rojas said. "For those of you who did manage to finish, drop it on my desk."

With the shrill of the bell, students tucked papers away and departed.

"Sorry," Link said. "I kind of...lost track of my thoughts."

"I'm guessing," Carter said. "Donovan doesn't thoroughly enjoy bit by bit breakdowns of Amy's every movement."

Link chuckled. "I've never even bothered to say

anything."

"It's not his thing. And don't worry, I'm glad you're happy, Link. If anyone deserves it, you do."

He bent over to grab his backpack. "Thanks."

Outside the classroom, Carter took up her normal spot against the lockers as they waited for Donovan. He stopped outside the door, quickly finishing up a message.

"Is that James?" Link asked, nodding to his phone.

"Yeah," Donovan said.

Carter felt a tiny spark of curiosity. "Who's James?"

"One of my older brothers," Donovan said. "He's in town and I'm seeing him this weekend."

Carter didn't press for more, her curiosity fizzling out. At the lack of more prodding, Donovan eyed Carter.

"Want to go to History?" Link asked before Donovan could say anything.

"Why?" Carter asked. "You feel like ditching? Because I'm okay with that."

Link tugged her off the lockers. "Not today. Come on."

When he slung one arm around her shoulders, she smiled at the comforting gesture as something flashed in Donovan's eyes. As they rounded the corner to the history classroom, someone shouted Link's name. Amy bounced forward and wrapped her arms around his neck, kissing him. The four slipped into their seats as Mr. Philips sent a look over the room, quieting last minute words and giggles.

"Before we get started," he said. "I would like to remind you that our field trip to the Newseum is a week from today." He surveyed the group before him. "I know some of you still haven't turned in your signed permission slips. You need to have that done by the beginning of next week or you won't be able to go. This field trip is something to help benefit you. Don't waste it." He started writing on the whiteboard. "Now, let's move on with our study of the last five presidents."

***

In the cafeteria, Carter claimed the first spot at Amy's table as everyone else headed to the lunch line. Laughter collided with the slamming of trays on tables, the noise a dull roar in Carter's ears. She revisited every conversation, every interaction with her father, trying to see what she was missing. Trying to understand why he was shutting her out. She folded her arms and dropped her head on top of them.

"Carter."

She jerked her head up and she read in Donovan's face how hard he was working to keep his thoughts and questions at bay. Across the way, Link and Amy sat lost in a happy bubble that included no one but themselves.

"What's going on with you?" Donovan asked.

She shook her head. "Nothing."

Donovan settled back against the wall. "Alright. Don't tell me."

Carter didn't reply. How could she? What was there to tell when she didn't know herself. She buried her face in her hands. How did she not know what was going on? This was her father, the one person who she knew better than she knew herself. Now he felt like someone else. Overwhelmed, she sighed heavily.

Before Carter knew what was happening, Donovan stood, bringing her with him. She didn't protest as he guided her a few feet away to an empty corner with Link still in view. "What's going on, Carter?"

"I don't know."

He crossed his arms. "Come on, something is going on. You're distracted and you look like you need sleep."

"Look, I can't tell you."

"Why not?"

Letting out another frustrated breath, Carter tossed up her hands. "Because I honestly don't know." She pressed her shoulder into the wall and crossed her arms. "Captain is keeping something from me and I don't know what it is. He's been working late nights and he's avoiding me. Maggie might be avoiding me as well but I can't tell either. She might just be that busy. I saw her leaving our apartment the other day but she never told me why she was there." She rubbed her eyes tiredly. "I'm not sleeping. It's like every time I fall asleep my brain is trying to puzzle out what's going on but it's coming up short." She closed her eyes, worn out. "I keep going over everything Captain says and does and yet nothing comes of it. I've always been able to figure him out before. I'm not sure what to do."

"How long has it been like this?" Donovan asked.

"Since Monday. Why?"

"Your father started physical therapy Monday, correct?"

She assented. Donovan nodded to himself. The tornado of voices spun around them, words like bits of debris, flying in the air. They ignored it.

"What are you thinking?" she asked.

"Okay," Donovan said, holding up his hands as if to ward her off of getting her hopes up. "I'm not going to pretend to know for sure what is going on with your father. But sometimes soldiers struggle with shock after being shot. Your father could easily be dealing with PTSD."

Carter frowned. "But he could tell me."

Donovan shook his head. "Men usually find the need to face things like this on their own and in their own way. He may not even realize that's what he's dealing with. I've seen countless soldiers deal with it, post-trauma therapy was one of my mom's main areas. Everyone works through it differently."

Frustrated, Carter straightened. "But why now? He was shot weeks ago."

"Trauma hits at different times. He's started physical therapy and that could have triggered it."

Carter soaked up his words, trying to make them match with the way her father had been acting.

"I don't know if that is what's wrong," he continued, "but I do know there are more possible answers than it being about you."

Part of her had been worried it might have to be about her, so Carter held fast to the reassurance, needing it to be true.

"If PTSD is the reason for his distance I wish he would tell me," she said. "I've been driving myself crazy trying to figure what is wrong."

"In time, he might. For now, give him space."

Space was the last thing Carter wanted to give. But if her father was facing something she didn't understand then she would try to give him space. Even if it hurt.

"Okay," she said. "And thanks."

Donovan tilted his head towards her. "Maybe next time you can just tell me what's going on so I don't have to pester you."

She found compassion - along with something else she couldn't fully comprehend - brimming in his blue eyes. "I'll work on it."

Chapter 41

By the time Carter bent forward to tie her Converses, half the girl's locker room had emptied, the bell making girls hurry to freedom. Carter looped the laces slowly, wanting to put off going home as long as she could. Even with her decision to give her father space, she hated the unknowns that underlined every conversation. When she left the locker room, she found Link and Donovan waiting for her.

"We wanted to see if you needed a ride home," Donovan said, answering Carter's unspoken question.

"Thanks," she said, "but I don't feel like going home at the moment."

"Want to come home with us?" Link asked.

The fact that she didn't have to even ask, warmed Carter. "Yeah, I do."

Link's apartment appeared as neat as it had been the last time Carter was there. The faint smell of lemon-scented cleaner lingered in the air and she wondered how recently the cleaning lady had left. The spotless windows displayed rows of buildings and other lives of the wealthy. The light of the late afternoon sun streamed into the apartment and elongated the shadows.

Link took off his glasses and tossed them onto a table beside the door. A routine that felt similar to Carter dropping her keys into the ceramic bowl. Donovan settled his bag down on the ground near the couch. Carter noticed Link's hesitancy.

"Do whatever you normally do," she said, waving a hand to dismiss his uncertainty. "I'm fine."

"I was going to take a shower and change," he said.

"Yeah, go ahead."

Link headed to the hallway but paused. "Eat anything you want. There's not much in the fridge but I think we have something."

"Thanks." As he left, Carter let her eyes roam over the long narrow table beneath the hanging TV, lined with silver framed photographs. She picked up the closest one. A woman in her late thirties with dirty blonde hair and hazel eyes had her arms wrapped around an eight-year-old version of Link. It was a version of Link that still had blonde hair and didn't wear glasses. Even young, the resemblance between him and his father was uncanny.

In the next photo, a 14-year-old Link wore glasses and his hair was brown. Carter continued down the table, inspecting the pieces of Link's life. A frame towards the end held a photo of Link and Donovan, with Link holding a rolled-up scroll tied with a blue ribbon. Link's face was dotted with the beginning of acne. Donovan's face still held a boyish look, though Carter knew he must be seventeen at the time.

"You look young," she said, studying the way Link had his arm wrapped around Donovan's shoulder and the faint smile on Donovan's face.

Donovan tore his attention away from his spread of homework. "What did you say?" Carter held the frame up and he stared at it for a moment before returning to his work. "I was."

"Do you ever regret it?" she asked.

Donovan stilled, his pencil hanging in the air. After a second's hesitation, he answered. "No."

Carter spun around to challenge the hesitation just as Link appeared, toweling his hair. Without his glasses, in his own home, and dressed in casual jeans and a t-shirt, he looked more self-assured. "What are you doing?"

"Watching you grow up," Carter said.

He joined her, taking in the collection of his life, the snapshots of memories. "My mom likes having them out," he said, picking up the photo of him and Donovan. "I don't know why. They're kind of embarrassing."

"I like them." She tapped the frame. "Your eighth-grade promotion, right?"

He nodded, then pointed to another photo, and his past unraveled before them. When he finished, he stood there lost in his memories.

"How does your mom feel about you leaving for college?" Carter asked.

"I'm going to Georgetown so I'm not going far. We've talked about me living at home for the first year. We haven't decided yet. Where are you going?"

"I haven't made up my mind. Georgetown is a possibility, as well as Brown or Stanford. I don't know whether I could leave Captain."

Before Link could comment, the apartment door opened and a flood of voices spilled inside. Link's mother dressed in a trim business suit led the parade of lawyers.

"Hi, sweetheart," Link's mother said as she hugged Link and kissed his cheek. The affectionate greeting spoke volumes of the bond between mother and son. Something Carter knew in the bond she shared with her father. Well, usually did.

"Sorry to barge in here," Link's mother said, "but something was going on with the heating in the office so we decided to finish up here."

"It's fine," Link said.

Donovan flipped his textbook closed. "We'll move to my apartment, Monica."

"I appreciate that."

"Mom, this is Carter," Link said, gesturing from Carter to his mom.

"It's wonderful to meet you. Sorry about kicking you out," his mother said, her tone light. "Link has told me wonderful things about you. I hope the next time we meet we'll have a longer time to talk."

"Me, too," Carter said.

With a last apology, Monica joined the crowd of men and women, making themselves at home on the dining room table. Link, Carter, and Donovan gathered up their things and left the apartment. The arguments died down as they slipped into the hallway. Donovan pulled out his keys and unlocked three different locks before opening his door.

The apartment before Carter surprised her. It looked like an apartment out of a home decoration magazine, immaculate in dark browns and blacks. The only sign that Donovan lived there was the punching bag hanging in the corner and the shooting range chart on the fridge. Carter remained in the doorway, as Donovan hung up his keys on a small hook and Link settled into one of the chairs.

"You live here?" she said.

Both Donovan and Link looked at her.

"Yeah, why?" Donovan asked.

"It's not what I expected," she said.

"What were you expecting? A mattress on the ground and a water canteen?"

"Not exactly. But definitely not a setup from Crate and Barrel."

"Monica had all this done," he twirled his finger, " I think she felt sorry I was living on my own at sixteen and wanted to make it feel homey."

"So it would have been a mattress and a water canteen if she hadn't helped."

"And a gun case and a couple of computers with video surveillance," he said, a smile tugged at her mouth.

Link's phone rang and color came to his face. "Mind if I talk in your room?" he asked, standing up from the table.

Donovan nodded as Link answered the phone.

"Hey," he said, in a tone that meant it could only be one person.

His voice trailed off as he walked down the hallway and closed the door. Carter surveyed the living room. Instead of a TV, the other wall of the apartment held a bookshelf crammed to bursting with books. Dotted along the shelves in front of the books sat picture frames. When Carter looked at Donovan, he was watching her, the corner of his mouth curled. "Do you want my life story as well?"

"Do you mind?"

He hesitated then shrugged and leaned back in his chair. In the first photo, Donovan was in his mid-teens and surrounded by his family: His parents and his three brothers. Though they all shared their mother's Greek, tan skin tone and dark hair mixed with their father's sharp features, compared to his older brothers' large frames, Donovan looked like a skeleton.

"I didn't know you were the runt of the family," Carter said. Wincing, she dropped her head, wishing the words back but found Donovan impassive. "I'm sorry. You just are so much smaller than them."

"That was right after I got the job with Link and lost twenty pounds of muscle."

"You lost twenty pounds of muscle?"

"I had to, I needed to look like a middle schooler."

In the next photo, Donovan's mother had her face pressed against a squirming, ten-year-old Donovan. Her brown eyes were laughing, countering his determined blue ones. Carter let out a laugh. Curiosity getting the better of him, Donovan joined her. A flicker of a smile betrayed him, as he looked at the photo.

"What's the story here?" Carter asked.

Donovan crossed his arms, still staring at the picture. She sensed his reluctance. "My mother said this photo summed me up."

He went silent, the rest of his thoughts trapped behind a door he didn't want to open. Carter stared at the photo and waited.

"I was a difficult kid," he finally admitted. "She said I was as stubborn as a mule and as talkative as a clam."

"A clam?"

"Sometimes when I was struggling with a problem the only way to get me to talk about it was to use force and pry it out of me. It was a contrast to the rest of the time when I talked freely."

A slow smile took over Carter's face as she imagined the type of kid Donovan must have been. "Does that still hold true?"

Donovan shook his head and said nothing. In his apartment, surrounded by the evidence of lonely years in the hundreds of books, Carter understood his resistance to share freely. Besides Link, who was there in his life that he'd let in? Always hiding who he was, who could he share his life with? Maybe letting her glimpse his past in pictures was all he could offer to her. Accepting this small gift, she continued to look without comment and Donovan didn't return to the table.

A photo of Donovan in his early teens stopped her in her tracks. He had one foot on his older brother, who laid on the ground. Donovan's arms were crossed triumphantly, his expression smug. She glanced at him.

"It was the first time I beat James in hand to hand combat," he said.

"James is..."

"Two years older than me. Then it's Clint and Brock. We're all two years apart." His words came a little easier, less guarded.

"What do they do?" she asked.

"Brock works at the FBI. Clint's a security detail for

a senator, and James works with a private security company."

"Do they know about Link?" she asked.

"Yes, they would have asked too many questions when I went back to middle school after already graduating high school."

Carter shifted to the next photo but Donovan retreated a step back, drawing her attention. "If you're fine, I'm going to take a shower and change."

"I'm fine. Thanks for sharing."

He left the living room. Carter perused the photos but felt her energy waning as the silence of the apartment grew. Eventually, she left Donovan's past and settled on the couch. She mentally urged herself to start her homework. But couldn't bring herself to do it.

The nights of broken sleep rushed upon her. Giving in to the tired feeling, she slumped on the couch, resting her head on the armrest. Exhaustion slowly overtook her and her mind slipped from reality. The last thing she was aware of was approaching footsteps and the faint scent of a familiar cologne.

***

"Carter."

Her name spoken by a deep, smooth voice teased Carter back to reality. She stirred. A hand gently shook her shoulder.

"Carter," Donovan said again.

She cracked her eyes open, staring up into Donovan's face. Panic spiked through her at the sight of him bent over her. She jerked away, heart stuttering in her chest. Donovan held up his hands in a calming gesture. "Hey, you're fine. You just fell asleep on my couch."

Whipping her head around, Carter tried to get her bearings. The apartment was washed in yellow lamplight.

The smell of Chinese food lingered in the air. Everything righted itself and she remembered where she was.

"Right," Carter said, burying her face in her hands, willing her heart rate to return to normal. "Sorry about that. I don't usually fall asleep in other people's apartments."

"It's fine," Donovan said, perching on the edge of his coffee table.

Taking in a deep breath, Carter dropped her hands. Donovan sat with his elbows on his knees, hands clasped. As he read her weariness, she broke from his gaze, feeling too much weight in his scrutiny of her.

"I woke you because your father called twice and texted three times."

He held out her phone.

"It's still a school night. Come home," the message said.

Checking the time, Carter realized it was a little past eleven. She stood up abruptly. "I didn't realize I slept so long."

Donovan didn't speak as Carter quickly collected her bag and put away her untouched homework. As she sent off a text to her father, Donovan fetched his keys. Pulling the door open for her, he followed her out. She halted as he locked his apartment.

"I'm fine," she said. "I'll take the metro home."

Their gazes battled each other and Donovan's won out.

"Thanks," she said.

Donovan nodded beside her.

"Where's Link?" she asked, as they rode down in the elevator.

"Monica finished after we had dinner and he went back to his place."

"What have you been doing the last few hours?"

"I was working in my room. I only came out when I heard your phone going off for the second time."

Carter ran a hand through her hair and realized the mess it was in. "I didn't even hear it." Absentmindedly, she dragged her fingers through the tangled strands, bringing it back to a semblance of order. Donovan gazed at her as she shook it out. When she looked over, he coolly turned away, not at all fazed that she had caught him watching her.

In silence, they got into his car and drove but the silence didn't feel weighted. There was a comfortability about it. Donovan edged the car down the narrow lane, stopping outside Carter's apartment. She reached for her door but paused as he spoke.

"Remember, it might have nothing to do with you, Carter," he said.

She locked eyes with him. "Thank you, for everything." She chuckled softly. "And for the use of your couch."

Donovan smiled gently. "Goodnight, Carter."

"Night, Donovan."

As Carter climbed the stairs, the car disappeared. When she stepped inside the apartment, Carter found her father sitting at the dining table. Though this scene felt like a hundred others they had shared, something about it wasn't the same. Nudging the door shut with her foot, Carter tried to read any of her father's thoughts in his calm face.

"Where were you?" he asked.

"With Link and Donovan," she said, sitting down. "Doing homework."

He nodded, his expression completely closed. "Let me know next time if you won't be home by eleven."

It was Carter's turn to nod. "All right. I will."

Silence descended between them but it was a different silence than the one she'd shared with Donovan. This silence was layered with things unsaid. Her father stood, breaking the quiet with the scraping of his chair along the tile floor.

"There is some dinner left in the fridge if you're

hungry," he said.

"Thanks." The words felt as hollow as her stomach.

"I'm going to turn in for the night," her father said. "It was a long day."

Carter responded with another nod. As she studied her father, she tried to see some of the things Donovan talked about but could read nothing.

"Captain," she said. He paused. "Are you okay?"

"I'm fine. Just tired." She sank back in her chair, trying to ignore the ring of a lie. "I love you, Captain."

Her father worked for a smile but barely managed. "I love you too, Sarge."

He left her and closed his door. Carter hugged her leg, wishing she'd imagined the tone of regret.

Chapter 42

Carter rolled over in bed and checked the time, wincing at the light from her phone. It was a little past six and the sun was just cresting the horizon. Carter waited. Waited to hear the telltale signs of her father waking up and preparing for their usual Saturday run.

When she heard nothing, Carter tossed aside her covers and climbed out of bed. Changed into her workout clothes, she crossed the hall to her father's room, tying her hair back as she went. She knocked gently before opening the door. Her father sat on the edge of his bed, his back to her, his hands pressed into the mattress.

"Come on old man, it's Saturday. We have a run ahead of us," Carter said.

Her father studied the floor. "I'm going to skip the run today."

Carter waited for her nickname but he never said it. Cautiously, she took a step into the room. "What's wrong, Captain? You no longer have your sling, let's celebrate with a run."

He didn't stand up but he straightened and looked at

her. For a breath, it seemed he would say the thing that had been building a wall between them all week. "Not today, Sarge." He stood. "You'll have to go without me."

As he walked past her, Carter felt like reaching for him and demanding to know what was going on. But she didn't move. He left, leaving Carter in a storm of questions. Feeling trapped by her thoughts, Carter bolted from the apartment.

The metal staircase was slick with cold morning fog. She clambered down the stairs and started running the minute she hit the pavement. All around her apartments lay quiet, their occupants still tucked into beds and in dreams. Carter was alone.

As Carter hit the main road, she ran faster, wanting to outrun all the unknowns that lived in the apartment. Mist hit her face and got stuck in her hair. Car lights flashed by, as their tires ran through puddles. As she ran, she focused on the even rhythm of her breathing. The steady beat of her shoes on the pavement. The thump of her necklace as it bounced off her chest.

The world shifted around her. Faint sunlight began to burn away the mist. More cars took to the street. Apartment buildings shifted to storefronts. Then Georgetown itself drifted away as she moved towards the center of D.C.

Sweat gathered on Carter's forehead as she headed towards the Lincoln Memorial. The Mall was mostly empty, the only people there were joggers and cyclists. It wasn't until she lapped the Reflecting Pool she became fully aware of her surroundings. Aware of the fact that it was the same route she always took with her father.

Her body was reaching the peak of its energy as she rounded the narrow pool. She came face to face with the empty Lincoln Memorial steps, topped by the towering columned building. She sprinted. She raced down the stretch of water, beating away the fatigue she could feel coming on. She pelted towards two men running, giving them a short, 'on your left' signal before bolting past them. Reaching the stairs, she charged up them, two at a time. She pushed away the weariness in her muscles, relishing in the one thing she could control.

At the top, she turned and headed back down, her steps light and quick. She focused on the white, clean steps, keeping her balance. At the bottom, she ran half the length of the pool before settling into a slow jog, aching. She rounded the end of the Reflecting Pool when she heard something that made her stop.

"Carter?"

She halted, seeing Donovan and a man that could only be his brother. At the sight of Donovan, she felt her tornado of thoughts quiet down. Taking deep, even breaths, she put her hands on her hips and walked to meet them, her heart still banging away inside her chest.

As they closed the distance, she saw Donovan's expression was impassive, though his brother wore an intrigued smile. James stood a few inches taller than Donovan, his build wider and more muscular. Where Donovan came off serious, James came off friendly. The brothers breathed evenly; Carter figured that they had only just started their run.

"You must be James," Carter said, holding out her hand.

James shook it, impressed with the strength behind the slender fingers. "I am," he said, his voice deeper than Donovan's. "You're Carter?"

"Carter Owens, I go to school with Donovan."

She pointed to Donovan, who stood with his arms crossed and his face inscrutable. Something about the tension in his body told her this interaction wasn't something he wanted, which threw her since he'd called her name.

"It's nice to meet you," James said, placing his hands behind his back out of habit. He smiled, softening the power of his stance. "It's a pleasure knowing anyone Donovan goes to school with. We don't hear a lot about his day to day life, so it's good to know he is making..."

"She knows, Jay," Donovan said.

"Knows what?" James asked.

"About everything. Me. Link."

James regarded Carter with a new sense of curiosity. "Really?"

Carter gave him a smug smile. Before James could ask questions, Donovan held up his hand, stalling his brother. "It's a long story and I'll explain later."

"Donovan says you work with a security company," Carter said, diverting the conversation.

"I do," James said. "Recently promoted. He mention anything else about me?"

"Only that you were in town this weekend."

James glanced back at Donovan, who wore a neutral look, though again Carter sensed his discomfort.

"Well, that's my brother for you," James said. "He keeps things close to the vest but expects to have everyone tell him everything." Donovan flexed his jaw but said nothing. "I'm sure you already know this about him."

"I know a little something about that," Carter said. "I'm still trying to figure him out."

James laughed. "He gets better the longer you know him. But there are still times I have to beat information out of him."

Carter threw Donovan a teasing smile but when he remained stiff, she offered the smile to James. "Good to know that method works."

Donovan met her gaze but wore the blank mask she'd seen when she'd first known him. Reading his resistance to the conversation but not understanding where it came from, she took a step back. "I'll let you get back to your run."

"Carter, we're going to breakfast after this," James said. "You want to come along?"

Carter wanted to say yes. Getting a chance to know more about Donovan, his brother, and his life as well as avoid her apartment for a little longer felt like a gift. But she noticed the tightness in Donovan's jaw. "Thanks for the offer but I'm going to have to pass. It was a pleasure meeting you, James."

He smiled. "Likewise."

"See you later, Donovan."

"Carter."

The goodbye felt too formal and she took off, adding one more interaction into the list of things she couldn't make sense of.

***

As Carter drew closer to her street, she envisioned ways to talk to her father. But she came to a dead stop outside her apartment building.

Her father's car was gone.

A hundred new questions slammed into her as she stared at the empty spot. It was Saturday. He never had work on Saturday. Why was he gone? Where would he go? A dog howled from a window, breaking her from her daze. A silent apartment was waiting for her. She leaned against the door, sitting in the emptiness. A slip of paper on the coffee table snagged her attention. She quickly snatched it up, reading her father's words.

"I had a meeting to go to. I'll be back before lunch."

Balling the paper in her fist, Carter moved to her room. What meeting? Why didn't he tell her about it that morning? Why was he keeping things from her? Why wouldn't he let her in? Question after question dive-bombed her as she showered and dressed and left the apartment. Even in open space, her thoughts ricocheted around her head.

The growling of her stomach brought her back to reality. In the early morning, the deli was empty. The ding of the bell seemed to float through the space. Maggie appeared from the kitchen, carrying a large box.

"Hey, Hon," she said, with a smile, though something dampened the expression.

Placing the box on a table, she set about refilling napkin dispensers. Carter joined her. Maggie glanced at her but quickly averted her gaze. "Steve isn't with you?"

"No, he had a meeting. I thought I would come have breakfast here."

"Of course, girly, what do you want?"

"Anything."

"All right, stay here and I'll fix something up for you."

Maggie left before Carter could thank her. As she waited, Carter filled the napkin dispensers, surrounded by empty tables and booths. By the time Maggie returned, Carter had finished. Maggie set down a plate of food before Carter. She noticed the refilled dispensers and smiled, a true smile. "Hon, you didn't have to do that."

"I figured I could help. Can you sit?"

Maggie looked at the kitchen, reluctant to agree. Carter felt a clamp tighten around her chest. Unable to think of a reason to leave, Maggie sat. "Of course I can," she said. She rested her arms on top. "How is school going?"

As Carter took a bite of her food, she shrugged. "Fine. It seems like the deli has been busy this last week. I haven't seen you."

Something flashed across Maggie's face but she covered it up before Carter could read it. It didn't matter though, Carter caught it. She set down her food. "Is something going on between you and my father that neither of you want to tell me about?"

Maggie widened her eyes with real surprise. "No, Hon. I told you where I stood on that point."

"So you're not sleeping with him?"

Maggie straightened with shock. "Carter! No!" She flushed with embarrassment.

"But I saw you leaving the apartment the other day?"

Carter said, confused.

"Is that what all this is about?" Leaning forward, Maggie rested a hand on Carter's arm. Carter slipped out of her hold, still staring at her. "Hon, your father needed a friend to talk to. That's all. Nothing happened. You understand? Nothing happened."

As Carter picked at her food, she watched Maggie. "Nothing happened?" Maggie nodded. "What did you talk about?"

Maggie cleared her throat, suddenly not as comfortable. "Just some stuff."

Carter frowned. "What are you not telling me? Do you know what's going on with him?"

"Carter, your father is going through a lot of difficult situations with the divorce, his shoulder PT, and adjusting to a different job... He could just need space."

"I know this. Why doesn't he just talk to me about this? Why is he shutting me out?"

"He's not shutting you out-"

"Yes, he is!" Carter said. "I know Captain and I know when he isn't telling me something. Do you know what he isn't telling me?"

"Carter, it could be...a number of things-"

"Do you know what it is?"

Maggie faltered. "Whether I do or don't, it's your father's business to share with you."

"But he's not telling me."

Maggie gave her a sympathetic smile. "Then he has a reason for it. You have to trust him."

For a moment, Carter studied Maggie, needing the truth but not certain Maggie had it. "So you don't know what it is?"

Collecting the napkin dispensers, Maggie rose. "Hon, I have to get back to work. Thanks for the help." She pointed to the barely touched plate of food. "Finish up your breakfast."

As Maggie bustled away, Carter stared at her food, her stomach in tight coils. Pushing the plate away, she walked out of the deli. At the sound of the bell, Maggie looked up. A flash of guilt crossed her face.

The world was awake and fully alive with the voices of families chattering as Carter walked back to the apartment. Her stomach no longer grumbled, a sour feeling had taken the place of hunger. She kicked the front door shut. Her bag lay on the floor, a reminder of the homework she had but she ignored it.

Instead, Carter grabbed her boxing gloves, tucking them under her arm. She hit play on her music and hoped the pulsing sound would cloud her thoughts. As a pounding bass filled her room she wrapped up her hands, pulled on her gloves, and assaulted the punching bag.

Maggie's words still hummed in her ears, the avoidance of her last question loudest of all. Maggie knew. She knew and wasn't telling Carter. But why? Why wasn't anyone talking to her? Why were her father and Maggie shutting her out? What had she done wrong? With every unanswered question, she beat the taut leather. The metal creaked, the sound drowned out by the music.

She kept swinging away, battling the things she didn't know. She became more forceful, her speed increasing. Sweat beaded on her forehead and ran down her temples. Every muscle in her hand and arms ached but she didn't stop. She couldn't stop.

The front door opened and only because she was waiting for it, did she hear it. She kept hitting the bag, listening as her father wandered about the apartment. She waited for her door to open and her father to walk in.

When she heard his bedroom door closing, she stopped. The bag continued to sway. She wrapped one hand round the chain and laid her head on the stiff material as weariness enveloped her. It was a feeling that had nothing to do with the ache in her arms.

Chapter 43

Hands jammed into her pockets, Carter climbed the school stairs. Weariness hovered around her as unanswered questions sat heavily on her shoulders. She pushed through the school doors and entered the fray of voices ricocheting off walls.

When she found Link and Amy huddled together in the hallway, Carter looked across the way, knowing she'd find Donovan there. Despite the strange interaction of Saturday, the sight of him made Carter breathe a little easier. But as she took the open spot beside him, she became aware of the rigidity in his posture that contradicted his passivity.

"Hey," she said.

He gave a single nod but nothing else, his lips a thin line. A group of sophomore girls passed by and sent bashful smiles to Donovan. A second later, a round of giggles swept over them. Carter noted a subtle tightening of his jaw.

"How did it go with your brother this weekend?" she asked.

"Fine."

His voice was toneless and Carter could detect none of his thoughts. Fighting off a sense of unease, she tried again. "It was nice meeting him."

Donovan made no indication that he had heard. Before she could push further, a petite, redheaded girl appeared before them.

"Hi, Donovan," she said. "I don't know if you know this but we have A.P. Lit together. I sit two seats over from you."

Even though Donovan didn't react to the girl's statement, Carter had no doubt he knew the girl's full name and extensive personal information. The girl wasn't hindered by his silence. "Look, I don't know if you had a partner for the project due this Thursday, I thought I would just ask -"

"I have a partner," Donovan interrupted.

Though he spoke with very little inflection, Carter heard an undercurrent of irritation. A deep blush bloomed on the girl's cheeks. "Oh…okay. Well, if it doesn't work out...I'm free..."

When he said nothing, she hurried away, her heels clicking on the tile floor. Carter glanced from the retreating girl to Donovan, whose jaw was still clenched.

"Are you alright?" she asked.

The bell rang, stirring people from their own worlds.

"We should get to class," Donovan said.

Carter stopped him with a hand on his arm. "Hey," she said, searching his face for any clue to his thoughts. "What's wrong?"

Every thought and emotion were closed off from her, blocked by an impassive mask. Carter reflexively tightened her grip, as she felt another wall being built against her. She couldn't let it happen. Not when she needed him. Not when everyone else around her was closing her off.

Donovan slipped his arm from her hold. "Nothing."

Retrieving Link, Donovan avoided Carter's probing

gaze by guiding Link into the classroom.

"Is Donovan alright?" Carter asked Link once they were both seated.

"Yeah, why wouldn't he be?"

Carter ignored the question and studied Link. He was an open book, his unconcern easy to read. "He didn't say anything about how it went with his brother?"

Link pulled a notebook from his bag. "No. He doesn't tell me stuff like that. Why? What's going on?"

"I don't know. But something is."

Link glanced back at Donovan who already had the homework laid before him and worked, displaying no emotion at all. "He looks fine to me," Link said. "Did he say something to you?"

"Not in words, no."

"You might just be reading into it too much. He's quiet at times. We know this."

Carter didn't agree. The longer she thought about it the more she knew something was wrong.

***

Carter positioned herself against the wall by the boys' locker room, waiting. From behind the door, she heard the muffled shouts of laughter and yells as boys joked around.

Every interaction with Donovan that day had been worse than when they'd first met. His responses were monosyllables and his lies repetitive. Brick by brick she felt him walling her off. She couldn't let him shut her out.

The final bell rang. Doors banged open as students streamed out, their chatter absorbing the quiet of moments before. Carter waited. The boy's locker room door opened and Link walked out, sliding his blazer on. Carter grabbed him and he let out a surprised yelp as she hooked his arm and pulled him into the closest bathroom. Donovan moved faster this time. He darted inside as Carter closed the door and flipped the lock.

"What is it with you and bathrooms?" Link asked, checking for other students.

"They have locks," Carter said. She focused on Donovan. "You want to tell me what's going on?"

Donovan flexed his jaw as he realized the ambush was for him. He crossed his arms. "Carter," he said, in the same emotionless voice he'd used all day. "I told you, nothing is going on."

She scrutinized him, watching as he struggled to remain neutral. In his blue eyes, she could see flashes of frustration.

"I know something's up. Talk to me," she said. "Or at least don't lie to me."

"Carter, why do you feel the need to drag guys into bathrooms to confront them?" he asked, patronizing.

"Why aren't you answering my question?"

He lost his composure for a fraction of a second, revealing irritation. "Was my silence bothering you?" he asked. "Maybe I didn't feel like playing therapist to you. You should find someone else to annoy with your problems."

The words hung in the air, stunning Link and stinging Carter. Donovan made no sign that he regretted it. Without looking away, Carter removed her blazer.

"Look, I never asked you to care. You pushed me to tell you," she said, rolling up one sleeve of her shirt. "You didn't have to give me advice, so don't throw that back in my face."

"What are you doing?" Link asked, hesitant.

Carter started rolling up her second sleeve and stared at Donovan. "I'm going to kick Donovan's ass."

Donovan looked at her with humorless eyes. "No, you're not."

She waved her hands out to her sides. "Does it look like I'm joking?"

Rolling her shoulders, Carter raised her fists. Uncertain, Link looked from Carter to Donovan, then back. "Carter, you can't be serious?"

She ignored him. "Put 'em up, Donovan, or you won't recognize that pretty face of yours in the morning."

"You couldn't hit me the last time."

"I wasn't focused."

"That will change nothing."

She smirked, took one step forward, and swung at his face. Donovan's instincts kicked in and he caught her fist before it hit him. But before he prepared a defense, Carter kneed him in the side. Wincing, he bent over as she brought her elbow around, clipping him in the jaw. He snapped his gaze to her as he touched his jaw, shocked. Link's eyebrows shot up. Carter took a step back, indifferent.

"That looked like it hurt," she said. "You all right?"

Donovan straightened and said nothing. Carter held her hands out. "Either you're going to talk to me or you're going to get punched. Your decision."

Donovan stared at her, his face hard. "What do you think you are doing?"

"Taking your brother's advice."

Carter came at him again. This time he was ready. She swung and he caught her fist. He used his hold to spin her around, pulling her into a lock, pinning her back to his chest.

"I'm not going to fight you, Carter," he said.

"Don't worry, I've spent the last four years fighting guys twice your size. You won't hurt me."

She tried to break out of his hold but he countered her.

"I'm serious," he said. "Stop this."

"You're the one that can make it stop. Just talk to me."

When he said nothing, she elbowed his side and jerked her head back. He avoided the impact of her head but wasn't fast enough to dodge her elbow. She twisted the wrist holding her and broke away. She faced him again. Donovan held his emotions in check, but she could see something sparking in his eyes.

"Come on, Donovan, what's it going to be?"

"I'm not doing this with you."

"Fine. It's your face."

He blocked her next attack but she used his forward momentum to get in a hit to his side. He grimaced but blocked her next move. She quickened her blows, getting in one for every three he blocked.

"Feel like talking?" she asked after she landed a hit to his ribs.

"I'm not fighting you, Carter. Now quit it."

"Just talk to me."

He responded with silence.

They kept going, Donovan shielding himself from her blows but not retaliating. At one point, he countered too fast and Carter took a punch to her left side. She winced at the spike of pain. Instantly, Donovan took a step back, his hands raised. "Carter, I'm sorry. But this is enough."

"Are you ready to talk?"

"I'm serious."

"So am I!"

She stared him down, determined. She wasn't going to let a wall form between them. She wasn't going to lose him too. In an instant, Donovan let go of his passivity, displaying the myriad of his emotions.

"I need to get out of here," he said.

She saw a storm of frustration, disappointment, and desperation.

"Keys," she said to Link. He tossed them to her and she deftly caught them in one hand. "Come on, I'm driving."

Chapter 44

Carter swung the Mercedes into a wide parking spot. Before them was a gray stone building, on the outskirts of the city. The trio climbed out of the car, making sure not to hit the pickup trucks on either side. Donovan looked over the building, a note of recognition in his passive gaze. Carter had a feeling he'd been here before. After all, he was a Marine.

The burly man behind the counter, with a dark beard and a scar down his left temple, didn't blink an eye as he saw Carter walk in. His surprise showed as Donovan and Link followed her. "Hi, Carter, where's Steve?" the man asked, in a voice fit for a bear.

"At work," she said, stopping before the glass counter.

Link swiveled his head from one side of the place to the other. Every inch of the walls were covered in guns, ranging from sniper rifles to handguns. The wall behind the man displayed an assortment of selected handguns as well as tacked up photographs.

Carter gestured between the man and Link and

Donovan. "Mark, meet my friends. Donovan and Link, this is Mark."

Donovan took Mark's outstretched hand and gave a nod in acknowledgment. Mark narrowed his eyes. "You look familiar. You've been here before?"

"Few times," Donovan said.

Mark shook Link's hand but barely gave him a second thought. "What will it be today?"

"Three ear muffs, glasses, and two guns. I'll take the usual." Carter looked to Donovan.

"I'll take an M45," he said.

"You got ID?" Mark asked.

Donovan handed it over and Mark checked it before going to work. He pulled out three large ear muffs - which looked like bulky headphones - three sets of plastic glasses, two target sheets, and then grabbed two different handguns off the wall.

"How many clips do you want?" he asked.

Carter raised an eyebrow at Donovan.

"Two," he said.

Carter wondered what was eating away at him that it would take two clips to help release. Whatever it was, she hoped this would help break down the wall between them.

Carter tossed Link a pair of ear muffs and glasses, then grabbed her stuff. She guided them to a side door. Putting on her ear muffs and glasses, she directed Link to do the same. She pushed through a door into a long rectangle room. One long metal table ran the width of the room. Spaced out along it were metal partitions, dividing the table into stalls. Gunfire rang off the walls, the sound muffled in their covered ears.

At the last stall, Carter stopped, wanting to stay away from the room's other occupants. She didn't bother setting up her own target but stayed with Donovan. In a matter of minutes, the black outline of a human torso raced in the distance and Donovan had his gun in hand. Link and Carter gave him room. Donovan set his stance, loaded his clip into the gun, and brought it up.

In quick succession, he fired at the target. The shots exploded as the paper quivered as each bullet tore through it. Before the shots had time to die away, Donovan released the first clip, reloaded, and emptied the second clip. Carter couldn't deny being impressed with the ease in which he handled the gun.

When Donovan lowered his weapon, Carter joined him in the stall. Link remained positioned against the wall, watching the other gunmen. Carter noted that some of the tension in Donovan had vanished. She nudged his shoulder with her hand.

"Are you going to tell me what today was about?" she said over the noise of bullets tearing through the air.

Donovan retreated behind an indifferent mask. "It's nothing, I just needed to let off some steam."

Hurt and anger shot through Carter. "Don't stonewall me! I've had enough of that. Tell me what's going on!"

He pressed his lips together, trapping in his words. Carter planted her feet and crossed her arms. She had no intention of leaving until he talked. She didn't say anything, only stared him down, challenging him to let her in. When she caught a flicker of emotion in his eyes, she relaxed a fraction.

"My brother got promoted," Donovan said, raising his voice enough so she could hear it.

"I know. So?"

Irritation flashed through Donovan's face. He stayed silent. Despite the fact Carter wanted to shove him, to shake his thoughts out of him, she held herself back. Instead, she tried a tactic that didn't come easy for her: gentleness. She laid a hand on his arm, a gesture Maggie used so often to comfort Carter. "Donovan, talk to me."

Something cracked in his expression and all his emotions came crashing out: annoyance, disappointment, jealousy. The sight of it startled her.

"He got promoted and I'm stuck! In high school! Babysitting!" Donovan cast a glance at Link then away.

"Babysitting was how James put it yesterday." He ran a hand through his hair, each confession releasing a bit of his frustration. "My brothers are surrounded by people who can respect them for their work. I have to spend my days entrenched in empty-headed girls and egotistical boys." He balled his fists and shook his head as if he couldn't believe where he was. "For two more years, I have to deal with a complete lack of freedom." He met Carter's gaze. "Do you understand how aggravating that is?"

She didn't respond for a long moment. The ringing of gunfire continued on around them. Link had taken to looking at his phone, oblivious to their talk. She did understand. She understood in a way she never imagined she could. They were both locked in a world that felt too small, too confining, too empty.

"I find it irritating and I'm not you," Carter said.

Donovan took a deep breath, letting it out slowly.

"I know it's frustrating but this will be worth it in the long run," she said.

"Yeah, I know," Donovan said, though he didn't sound convinced. "The problem is I spent hours with my brother, having to listen as he tells me about how great his job is. And the mature adults he works with, not whiny teenagers"

Carter affectionately shook his arm. "You're going to get that. Donovan, at the end of this you get to walk into any place and get whatever job you want. You have to remember that."

He nodded but stared down at the ground, lost in his own thoughts. "He talked to me about some of his coworkers whom I realized could be parents of my 'classmates'."

Throughout high school, Carter had dealt with the immaturity around her, knowing that after high school it would get better. She didn't know how hard it must be for Donovan to hear from his brothers exactly how much better it was and knowing he still had to wait another two years.

"I'm sorry," she said. Donovan rested his head back on the metal partition, contemplating the ceiling. "What you're doing matters."

He said nothing.

"Link is able to have a normal life because of you." Finally, Donovan met her gaze. "With all the crap he has to deal with, that's a gift. Don't forget that. He is grateful for it and so am I."

Carter waited, hoping he could hear her conviction and accept the truth. After a minute, he straightened his shoulders and she could see his renewed resolve.

"Maybe next time you can just tell me what's going on and I won't have to pester you."

Donovan grinned. "I'll work on it."

"Now move aside," Carter said, elbowing him out of the stall. "I'm not wasting a chance to shoot something."

Chuckling, Donovan backed away to watch. Carter replaced the target sheet and she picked up her gun, loading the clip. Taking in a deep breath, she raised it. Exhaling, she squeezed the trigger. The gun recoiled but she kept her arms steady and continued to shoot in a planned out formation.

With the clip emptied, she lowered the gun. She pressed a button and the target rushed back. Donovan walked forward, followed by Link, his gaze trained on the target sheet. He remained indifferent but when he looked at her there was a hint of intrigue in his eyes. In the target's chest was a smiley face made from bullet holes. Link laughed as Donovan stared at Carter.

She shrugged. "I thought it would cheer you up,"

He smiled at her, which she couldn't help but return. She unclipped the sheet as he gathered up his items. They left the echo of bullets and walked back to the quiet storefront.

"How did it go today?" Mark asked as they set their gear down on the counter.

Carter held up her target sheet. "I'm feeling pretty

positive."

Link chuckled as Mark shook his head in amusement. Donovan surveyed the photos on the back wall, stopping at one in particular. "Is that the first day you came?" he asked Carter.

Carter found the photo in question. In it, she was a gangly girl, standing by her father, gun out to her side.

"He took me here when I was sixteen." A quiet smile appeared on her lips. "It was a birthday present."

Another photo caught her attention. Narrowing her eyes, she stepped closer to the counter. She pointed at it. "Mark, who is that man? The one in the center of the group, with the scars on his neck."

Mark lumbered over to the wall and studied the photo. "That's Ben," he said, tapping the curled picture. "He comes here a lot with this group. They are all former Army men. Sad story. He was in an ambush with three other platoons years back. That's how he got those scars. Half of the men didn't make it."

Carter felt her throat tighten as she thought of her father and of the new scar he wore on his shoulder.

"You know him?" Mark asked.

She found she couldn't speak.

"He works at our school," Donovan said.

Mark gave an approving nod. "Well, he is a good man to have around."

As they exited, the sun was nowhere in sight, leaving the sky dark. Link got into the back of the car but Donovan stopped Carter with a hand on her arm. "You alright?"

"I'm just glad he's at a desk and not in the field."

Donovan softened with understanding. Carter started towards the car but he stopped her again.

"Thank you," he said.

"For what exactly?"

"Listening."

"Anytime." Carter cocked her head. "Is that why you were...off, yesterday?"

Donovan didn't say anything, hiding his thoughts. After all it had taken to get him to open up, Carter felt stung at his continued rejection. She took a step back, sliding her hands into her pockets.

"My brothers haven't ever met the people I've made friends with, doing what I do," Donovan said. "I wasn't sure how I felt about them getting to know you."

Carter relaxed. At least that explained some of the tension she'd seen.

"I get it," she said. "It's hard to be taken seriously when your friends are high schoolers."

"Yes."

They stared at each other for a moment before she spoke again. "Well, if it would ever be fun to surprise them by having a high school girl beat them in a race, let me know."

Donovan smiled. "I'll keep that in mind."

He opened the driver's side door as Carter slipped into the passenger's seat. Her phone dinged but she ignored it.

"It's nice that you remembered me," Link said, putting his phone down.

Donovan started the car as Carter gave a half chuckle.

"Home?" he asked.

Her phone dinged for a second time. Retrieving it, she read over the text. A slight frown came in to play as she read over the words a second time.

"Everything alright?" Donovan asked.

"Captain is staying late for a meeting." She glanced between the two boys. "Either of you have space on your couch I could borrow for a couple of hours? I'm tired of a quiet apartment."

Before Link could even open his mouth, Donovan replied, "Yeah, I do."

Chapter 45

Two days later, Carter stepped out of the girls' locker room into a chilly afternoon. A thin curtain of clouds swept across the sky and the air smelled of coming rain. Carter moved off to one side of the track and began to stretch. The volume of voices steadily rose as more students trickled out. As Donovan and Link approached Carter, she twisted and winced.

"What's wrong?" Donovan asked.

Carter started to deny her discomfort but stopped. Instead, she lifted up the edge of her shirt. Besides a toned stomach, she revealed a fist-size bruise on her left side, right below her ribs. "That's thanks to you," she said, dropping her shirt.

Donovan frowned in distaste.

"I thought she was the one hitting you?" Link said.

"She was," Donovan said. "It was an accident. Carter also doesn't protect her left side."

Carter jabbed a finger at him. "This is not my fault. My left side is perfectly protected."

Donovan pointedly flicked his eyes down to her side

and up at her. "You left your left side wide open. How do you explain that bruise, if you were protected?"

Carter scowled. He had a point but that didn't mean she had to admit it. Donovan raised a questioning eyebrow. She jutted out her chin, hands placed challengingly on her hips. "Fine, it's something to remember the next time I take you on."

"Remember it but I'll never fight you again. I don't want to leave any more bruises."

"I'm more resilient than I look."

"Don't worry, that's something I am very aware of."

"So I'll just protect my left side."

Carter fought against a smile, noticing as Donovan did the same. Link regarded them with pure puzzlement. "I can't tell if you two are flirting or not."

The smile broke free of Carter's hold as Donovan's hid away in his eyes.

"Anyone tell you that you have a mean right hook?" she asked.

"What about your elbow?" He absentmindedly ran a hand over his jaw. "Where did you learn that move from?"

A memory darted through her mind, widening her smile. "My dad," she said. "I nearly took out his eye the first time I tried it."

Link chuckled while Donovan grinned. The amusement dropped away as a question appeared in his eyes. Carter felt her own smile fall, as she read the expression.

"How's it going?" Donovan asked. "With your dad?"

He pinned her down with his gaze as if he knew she would try to lie and he would need to get the real answer from her expression. He didn't have to try so hard. She'd learned the lesson: nothing slipped past his notice.

"The same," she answered. Before he could say anything, she shot him a taunting look. "Are you ready to find out once and for all who's faster?"

She knew he was aware of what she was doing but

he accepted the change of topic all the same. Which she was grateful for. Right then she didn't want to think about all the things her father wasn't telling her.

"Now?" Donovan asked.

She raised a mocking eyebrow. "Why? Do you want a week to prepare?"

"No, I wasn't sure if you needed one."

"I don't need to prepare to beat you."

"We'll see about that."

Mr. Danes eyed Carter and Donovan over his clipboard as they stopped before him, cautious.

"Can we borrow your two stopwatches?" Donovan asked.

Mr. Danes straightened, his curiosity piqued. "What for?"

"We're going to prove that I'm faster than Donovan," Carter said.

Mr. Danes reached into his pocket and pulled out two stopwatches. "Knock yourselves out," he said, handing them over. "I mean that in a figurative sense, Owens."

With a wink, she strode back to Link

"You sure this is a good idea?" he asked.

Carter and Donovan looked at each other then back at him.

"Why wouldn't it be?" she asked.

"I just have this feeling you'll never talk to each other after this."

"Don't worry," Donovan said. "I'm sure Carter won't be too broken up about losing."

She elbowed him and handed Link one of the stopwatches.

"What do you say? Keep it easy and do a mile?" she asked.

"Sounds good," Donovan said.

They recruited a second student to work the other stopwatch and lined up at the starting mark. A few of their classmates watched with a mixture of intrigue and confusion. Mr. Danes took up a position beside Link, his curiosity getting the better of him.

Carter shook out her arms and rolled her shoulders. Donovan brought one knee up to his chest then switched. By the time their muscles were ready, the rest of the class had begun to wonder what was going on.

"Ready?" Link asked.

Donovan and Carter both sank down into a crouch, their fingertips barely resting in the red turf.

"Don't punch me if you lose," Donovan said.

"Don't pout if I win."

Link raised the stopwatch and the second student followed suit. "All right, on your mark."

Carter focused on the track, body humming with energy.

"Get set."

She took in a breath, every nerve rearing to go.

"Go!"

They shot off like bullets from a gun, rounding the first turn at a dead sprint. Carter found her rhythm and sank deeper into it. She knew this, knew the power in her body as she propelled herself forward. Knew the rush of the wind in her ears. Knew the pounding of her shoes on the track. Knew the beat of her heart.

As Donovan lengthened his strides, Carter followed, pushing every muscle to work harder. On the edge of the track, students watched as the two runners shifted back and forth, neither gaining any distance on the other. More and more students dropped their conversations to watch. Link clenched the stopwatch without knowing, his own breathing coming in shallow breaths, his gaze riveted on the speeding figures.

As Carter and Donovan started the final lap, Carter felt every inch of her burning with exhaustion. Fire seemed to engulf her body. Her heart rammed itself against the inside of her chest. Adrenaline coursed through her, fueling every part of her that felt like stopping.

They rounded the last corner and Carter pushed

herself, forcing her body to give everything she had. She surged forward but Donovan didn't let the lead last very long. He charged after her, with renewed determination.

A few students besides Link started yelling as Carter and Donovan pelted towards them. Carter's vision blurred into a single spot past the starting line. With a fierce growl, she threw herself forward, crossing the line a split second before Donovan.

Link shouted, throwing his hands in the air. Carter stumbled a few more feet and collapsed onto the field. Donovan crashed down next to her a moment later. They both laid on their backs, sucking in deep lungfuls of air. Carter closed her eyes, every muscle feeling as if it were simultaneously on fire and made of lead. Her heart still jackhammered against her ribs. Blood pounded in her ears, muffling the noise of the class.

She turned her head to Donovan. His chest was working like a bellows, gulping down as much air as possible. Sensing her gaze, he looked over. They exchanged weak smiles.

Mr. Danes blew his whistle and started everyone on their own miles. Link ran over to Carter and Donovan, skidded to a halt, and dropped to one knee. "Want to hear the results?"

Carter and Donovan locked eyes again as if they just remembered they had been racing to prove something. Carter waved a floppy hand. "Sure...what are...the results?" she asked, still working to get enough air back.

"Carter came in first with 4 minutes, 38.47 seconds. Donovan is second with 4 minutes and 38.9 seconds."

Donovan reached over, tapping Carter's arm with the back of his hand. "Congratulations."

She gave a breathless chuckle. "I think I'll celebrate...by passing out now."

"Really? I feel...fine."

She punched his arm but the blow had little force behind it.

"Evans!" Mr. Danes barked.

Link jerked his head up. Mr. Danes gestured for him to get running. Link returned the stopwatches before joining the slow progression of students. Carter didn't move, her muscles feeling as if they had melted. Slowly, her breathing eased. But still she didn't move, having no desire to leave her spot. Donovan rose into a sitting position and glanced over his shoulder at her.

"You still feel like passing out?" he asked.

Her heart had quieted down and she shook her head. He stood and held out a hand. She took it, their fingers gripping each other. Even after the taxing working out, he easily lifted her to her feet. Their hands dropped away. Donovan pulled up the edge of his shirt, showcasing an impressive set of abdominal muscles as he wiped the sweat on his forehead.

Despite herself, Carter betrayed her thoughts with raised eyebrows. Then she spotted the softball-sized, purple bruise above his left hip bone. A few girls, passing by, stumbled into each other as they tried to walk and gawk at the same time.

"Careful, Donovan," Carter said. "You might send the girls in this class to the nurse with fainting spells."

He dropped his shirt. "Do you number among that lot, Carter?"

Crossing her arms, she gave him a flat stare in response. His smile grew. She pointed to the spot where she had seen the bruise. "I see you have some nice coloring.“

"I have your knee to thank for that."

She smirked. At least he wouldn't be so quick to underestimate her next time. If there ever were to be a next time. Which she hoped there would be.

"You want to jog to cool down?" Donovan asked.

"I feel like I want to throw up but sure, let's cool down."

They started jogging. The slow, rhythmic pace relaxed Carter and she found her muscles relishing the simple movement.

"Do you plan on hiding out with us again today?" Donovan asked.

"I think I've avoided my apartment enough this week."

"Well," he said, "if you ever need to hide out, my couch is available."

She looked at him, a teasing smile on her lips. "Is that an open invitation?"

There was no joke in Donovan's eyes and his seriousness stole away her playful manner. "It is."

She didn't smile or make a single mocking comment. "Thanks." Not wanting to think about how much his offer meant, Carter lengthened her stride. "Come on, I'm sure Link is lonely."

"Let's go keep him company then."

They quickened their pace, their strides perfectly in sync.

Chapter 46

Donovan pulled the Mercedes to a stop outside Carter's apartment. The windows were dark, letting Carter know her father wasn't home. A mix of relief and disappointment swirled inside her.

"You really didn't have to give me a ride," she said.

Donovan shrugged carelessly like driving miles in the opposite direction wasn't a big deal. "We don't mind."

When Link didn't confirm his statement, Donovan checked the rearview mirror while Carter twisted around. Link typed away on his phone, oblivious to his friends. Donovan and Carter shared a knowing look. She opened her door. "Don't take it too badly that I beat you."

"How long do you plan on gloating?"

"Until I beat you at something else."

Grabbing her bag, she climbed out. When she closed the door, Donovan was watching her, struggling against a smile. She fought her own smile as she walked away. The apartment held the same silence as it had the last two weeks but Carter found it didn't bother her in light of her buoyant mood. Still fighting her smile, she kicked off her shoes and settled onto the couch.

The sun gradually lowered into the distance as papers and notebooks expanded from where she sat. Her mood hadn't dimmed by the time she heard her father's car. As he climbed the stairs, she raised her pencil in preparation.

But she lowered her hand as she took in her father's serious countenance. Mechanically, he shut the door and left his keys in the bowl. When he faced Carter, her buoyant mood vanished.

"Hey, Captain. What's going on?" She cleared aside a spot on the couch. He didn't take it. Instead, he stood before her.

"Carter." At the sound of her name, she clenched her pencil. "I need to tell you something."

"Is it something about why you have been distant the last two weeks?"

He nodded once and crossed his arms. Though Carter knew she should feel relieved she would know what was going on, she couldn't ignore the tension she saw in her father. Something wasn't right.

"I know this is going to be hard to hear," he said.

A part of Carter screamed in her mind for him not to say whatever it was. All the worst possibilities of why he shut her out beat inside her head.

"It's not going to be easy to understand either," he said, slowly.

"Captain, say it," she said, with forced calm. "I trust you."

Her father held her gaze for a long moment, too many emotions flashing through his eyes for her to read.

"I signed back on with the Secret Service for two more years."

Carter turned to stone, her heart freezing inside her chest. She couldn't think. Couldn't breathe.

"After the attempted assassination," her father said. "Five agents on the President's detail were fired. With that many senior agents laid off, President Douglas asked if I would be willing to stay on until the end of his term.

And I accepted."

Carter stared at him, unmoving, unblinking. She had dropped out of the world and everything kept moving, except her. Even still, she could read her father's resolve in his stance and expression. Now…now she could read him. Now when she didn't want to. Didn't want to know that there was no changing his mind.

"Four more months," she said, the quiet words thawing her and cutting off her father. "Four more months and then you would be safe." She spoke as if the reality of his decision still lay beyond her grasp.

"I know this is difficult to understand, Sarge, but it's something I need to do. I needed to-"

"Captain, you had four more months to go. Four months."

Sighing heavily, her father took a seat on the coffee table before her. He leaned over his knees, his hands clasped. "Sarge, this was not a decision I made lightly. With everything that happened, I realized I was still needed."

"You were shot," she said.

With the statement came a fresh rush of fear. The image of her father in the hospital bed. The sight of Curtis on her doorstep. The gray-haired woman working at the reception desk. The smell of antiseptic cleaner. The beeping of the heart monitor.

"Sarge, I know-"

Carter bolted upright, the pencil snapped in her grip. "You can't do this to me! I've had to live with the reality that you could not come home every night for most of my life. You can't put me through this again!"

She tried to take a deep breath but her lungs seemed to be collapsing. Her father rose, holding up his hands in a placating gesture. "Sarge, this is something I need to do."

"No, it's not! You've already given enough to this President. You promised me this would be over soon. You were going to be safe." The words tumbled out with no filter.

"I know. But circumstances have changed, I'm needed…"

Carter gripped the two pieces of the pencil tighter. "We had a plan! You were going to be safe. You can't leave me."

"Sarge-"

She ignored his sadness and plowed on "These last two weeks. That's why...You were deciding whether you would..."

"Yes."

The distance and stiff conversations made sense. Carter staggered back, shaking her head.

"Sarge, I need you to listen to me," he said, taking a step forward.

She shook her head more adamantly, her eyes glassy.

"You need to understand it wasn't an easy decision but I made it for a reason."

Carter focused on him, her eyes still wide with shock. "It makes no difference. You can't stop a bullet with reasoning."

Before he could say anything, she raced towards the door.

"Carter!"

She clambered down the stairs, the pencil falling from her hand. When she hit the last step, she took off running. Where she was going she didn't know but she needed to run away. Her father's declaration chased after her, nipping at her heels.

Breathing hard, she stumbled to a halt, bending over her knees, gulping in air. She squeezed her eyes shut, wishing away the night. Wishing she could return to the race at school when she felt in control. When her father wasn't marked for death.

As Carter straightened, she realized where her legs had taken her. To the playground she'd grown up on. She entered and dropped into one of the swings. It swayed beneath her. She bent her face into her hands. The cold wind bitterly shouldered its way past her. The harsh tones of voices drifted out into the night. As she sat, Carter felt all her emotions mesh together and sting her eyes. The tightness in her chest doubled and she fought for each lungful of air.

The metal fence squeaked out a warning and Carter shot her head up. Parades of tears traveled down her face. A thin figure approached her.

"Hi, Hon," Maggie said, concerned.

Carter buried her head into her hands again. "He's signed up for two more years," she choked out.

Maggie crouched down, resting one hand on Carter's knee. "I know, Hon."

"Why would he do that? Why would he do that to us? To me?"

Maggie rubbed Carter's arm comfortingly. "I know it was a hard decision for him to make," she said. "He didn't make it on a whim. We talked about it for a long-"

Carter jerked up. "You knew?"

"Your father needed a friend, Carter."

Carter made no sign that she had even heard Maggie, her tears receding. "You knew and you didn't tell me about what he was planning to do? Didn't warn me? Didn't give me the chance to talk him out of it?"

"Carter, it was your father's decision, so it was his choice when to tell you, not mine."

For the second time that night, Carter felt her heart getting punched. Maggie with her caring brown eyes, friendly smile, comforting manner. She knew. All this time she knew and lied.

"You were my friend," Carter said.

"It was not my place to tell." Maggie reached to stroke Carter's hair but Carter pulled away. "Hon, you have to-"

Carter stumbled up from the swing, backing away from Maggie. "Stop. Don't call me that. You are not my mother. You were supposed to be someone I trusted." She shook her head, her eyes hard as steel. "Turns out you're as much of a let down as she was."

Tears jumped into Maggie's eyes but Carter didn't see as she spun away. She left the playground and kept walking.

She was a block away from her house when she took in the world around her. All her fiery emotions had fallen away with each step, leaving her depleted. She stared at the lane, frozen by the question of what to do. Accepting Donovan's offer of his couch came to mind but without her phone or wallet, she couldn't get there.

Numb with cold, she ascended the apartment stairs. Her father was on the phone and pacing when Carter walked in. He stared at her, his worry clear. Without a word, she shut the door and moved to her room.

"Carter," he said, stopping her. "We need to talk about this."

She didn't turn around as she responded. "You haven't talked to me for the last two weeks. Why start now?"

Chapter 47

Carter woke to her father moving about the apartment. A renewed stab of shock hit her as the announcement from the night before came back in full force. She listened to her father's even tread as he walked from one room to the next, eventually stopping outside her door.

"Sarge," he said. "You awake?"

Not answering, Carter flung aside the blankets and stood up. She knew he would hear her bare feet on the thin carpet. After a second, he walked away. As she got ready, Carter managed to avoid him. The smell of frying eggs and partially burned toast drifted through the apartment but she took no notice.

When Carter stepped into the living room, she halted. Her father stood with his back to her as he pulled on his black suit jacket. At the sight, she felt like someone broke through her chest and squeezed her heart with their hand. She needed to get out.

"I have breakfast for you," her father said, stalling Carter.

"Not hungry." Her stomach had been replaced by rope tangled in a million tiny knots. The thought of eating seemed impossible.

"I can give you a ride," her father said, as she grabbed the door handle.

"I'm fine."

"Carter, don't shut me out."

Tense with anger, she twisted back to him. "Don't you know? Children learn all of their habits from their parents."

She was halfway out the door when her father's words stopped her dead in her tracks.

"I love you, Sarge," he said, quietly.

An invisible enemy used Carter's heart as a punching bag. "No, you don't," she said. "If you did, you wouldn't be doing this."

Slamming the door shut, she hurried down the stairs. Her father didn't call after her. A bank of eerie clouds loomed on the horizon. As Carter entered the lane, Maggie came into view. Carter turned to stone, her battered and bruised heart shrinking away.

"He's inside," she said before Maggie could speak.

"I'm here to talk to you," Maggie said, blocking Carter's path

Carter stared at her, all her emotions battling in her eyes. "That's new."

Maggie reached for Carter but reconsidered it and retracted her hand. "Carter, this isn't fair. You know I couldn't tell you."

"Nothing is fair," Carter said, her tone hard as rock. "I thought life would have taught you that by now. I have a friend who betrayed me and a father who is once again a human bulletproof vest."

She left Maggie rooted to the spot.

Carter shouldered her way through the dense crowd of students in the school hallway. Gossip was handed out like paper notes in lowered voices, accompanied by smirks and sidelong glances. Everything around Carter seemed heightened as if all the noise of the world beat against her eardrums. New waves of emotions washed over her as she continually replayed her father's words: "I signed back on with the Secret Service for two more years."

She felt as if pieces of her were cracking. She balled her fists, trying to keep herself together. When Lucas crossed her path with a taunting grin already in play, she felt her nerves snap. It took everything in her to hold herself back from knocking him out, simply for his look.

"Owens," he said, "punch anyone lately?"

"Is that an invitation?" she said.

He barked out a mocking laugh. "You know what your problem is?"

"Currently it's the sad excuse for a human being in front of me."

He cast her a patronizing smile. "You think you're above everyone else but really you're just the daughter to the President's throw away human shield."

Before Carter's fist could make contact, a sharp voice called her name. "Carter!"

Fingers still clenched, Carter lowered her hand, staring daggers at Lucas. His smirk widened until Donovan took a spot beside Carter.

"How's the jaw?" he asked.

There was still a fading sign of Donovan's right hook on Lucas's face.

"It seems you still have a master," Lucas said, locking eyes with Carter.

This time Donovan wasn't fast enough.

Carter punched Lucas, a loud crack sounding as her fist collided with his cheekbone. His head jerked to the side as he stumbled into a group of juniors. A couple of girls gasped. Donovan grabbed Carter's arms and held her back from going at Lucas again. But his hold wasn't necessary. The fight had left her, her need to lash out mollified. Lucas cupped his cheek.

"I guess that changes my answer to your original

question," Carter said.

"I'll have you expelled for this," he snarled.

"And what will you do when I tell the principal who has been dealing steroids in the boys' locker room?"

"You have no proof."

"Try me."

Principal Withers split the group around them, fighting back a look of severe anger. Donovan let go of Carter's arms. The Principal glanced between Lucas's face and Carter's scowl, assessing the situation. "You two. My office."

Without looking back at Donovan, Carter followed Mr. Withers as hundreds of eyes followed her. Lucas grudgingly walked with her.

"Sit," Principal Withers ordered.

Lucas and Carter sat down in the two chairs before the Principal's desk. Mr. Withers gripped the back of his leather chair, regarding them.

"Mr. Benton," he said. "What part did you play in this ordeal?" Lucas opened his mouth but Mr. Withers cut him off. "Let me remind you, son, there was a hallway full of eyewitnesses. I do not have time for falsities. If you lie to me, I will see that you receive a punishment equal to Miss Owens."

Lucas slouched in his chair. Mr. Withers tightened his hold on the chair. "Respond, Mr. Benton, or I will assume you physically assaulted Miss Owens and she was defending herself."

Lucas sat bolt upright. "I didn't touch her!" he yelled.

"Then what, pray tell, did you do to bring about this altercation?"

Lucas ground his teeth, his eyes fiery with defiance. Carter didn't even bother to look at him. His gaze flickered to her, menacing.

"I insulted her," he said, through clenched teeth.

"Very well." Mr. Withers shifted his gaze to Carter, not concealing his frustration. "Miss Owens, was I not clear when I said that a second infraction could result in suspension or expulsion?"

"You were very clear, sir," she said, her voice lacking any note of submission.

"I also remember a meeting with your father, where he promised me this sort of occurrence would not happen again."

Pain burst in Carter's chest. "Yeah, well, he's breaking a lot of promises lately so don't think you're special."

Mr. Withers narrowed his eyes, seeming to read more than Carter wanted him to. She crossed her arms, shielding herself.

"Is he available to take my call?" he asked.

"Not likely, he's probably with the President."

Carter knew it wasn't true but in her mind, that's where she saw him. Right beside the President, a single step away from diving to take the bullet.

Mr. Withers nodded. "I see. Mr. Benton, I'm assigning you a week's worth of detention-"

"What?!"

"-starting next Monday. Don't skip or I will make your last two months of school here unbearable. Good day, close the door on your way out."

Lucas stormed out of the office, slamming the door, making the pane of glass rattle. Mr. Withers didn't even flinch, accustomed to the dramatics. In Mr. Withers's eyes, Carter could see understanding and sympathy. Neither of which she cared for at the moment.

"Miss Owens," he said, "how is your father's recovery going?"

The question threw Carter off guard. "Fine."

"I understand that having such an event happen to someone-"

Carter shot up, cutting him off. A new flare of anger coursed through her. "I do not want your pity or sympathy," she said, trying to rein in her emotions. "I understand that punching Lucas was a serious infraction and I will suffer what consequences you see fit. But I didn't do it without just cause. Give me my punishment, I have a field trip to get to."

Mr. Withers studied her with old eyes. "All right. Have a good field trip, Miss Owens. I think you've had enough punishment with Mr. Benton's insults"

Carter stared at him, baffled. He waved a hand towards the door. "I believe you have somewhere to be, Miss Owens."

Carter nodded dumbly. She opened the door but paused at Mr. Withers' voice.

"Miss Owens," he said. "This is not a free pass that you will have again. Assault another student again and I will have you expelled." He smiled. "Enjoy the rest of your day."

Without a word, Carter left the office. The hallways were empty, a low hum of voices coming from behind closed doors. Outside a thick darkening layer of clouds overran the sky. By the time that Carter rounded the corner to her classroom, her flare of anger had died down to smoldering embers, leaving her raw.

She stopped short at the sight of a man in a black suit standing outside the chemistry room. When he shifted, she realized it was Smith. "Yes, sir. I understand," he said. He glanced at his watch. "I will. Same to you, Mr. President."

He hung up as Carter closed the distance.

"Mason all right?" she asked.

"He is."

"Carter, I heard about your father," Smith said. Carter froze, feeling sick. "It's an honorable thing that he is doing, stepping back in when the President needs him."

She couldn't look at him. Couldn't breathe.

"Many men in his situation would not be as brave to sign up for two more years."

Carter found all she could do was nod, her guts twisting as she clenched the door handle.

"You should be proud," he said.

It took all Carter's willpower not to snap at him. As

she stepped into the classroom, she schooled her features into a mask of indifference. Mr. Rojas fell silent.

"Miss Owens, it's good to have you with us," he said.

She said nothing as she carved her way to her seat. She felt Donovan's penetrating gaze on her like it was a hot brand. As she settled onto her stool, Mr. Rojas took up his lesson once more.

"Hey, you all right?" Link whispered. "I saw you deck Lucas."

"I'm fine," Carter said, bending over her bag to hide her emotions. "Guy just gets on my nerves. That's all."

Even Link's concerned gaze felt oppressive and she tried to ignore it.

"Carter, that didn't really look like he was just-"

"Mr. Evans?" Link jerked his attention to the front of the class. "Did what you were saying to Miss Owens have anything to do with the current topic?"

Link squirmed, embarrassed. "No."

"Then I will ask you to stop talking during my class."

Link nodded, his cheeks receiving spots of pink. Overhead the school speaker clicked on. "Good morning, students," Principal Withers said. "This announcement is for all the seniors signed up for the field trip to the Newseum. Please make your way out to the buses at the front steps. Thank you."

The speaker clicked off and more than half of the classroom rose to their feet. Carter immersed herself in the gathering throng, slipping out of Link and Donovan's sight. Outside large charter buses stood idling. Carter cut through the mass of students to Mr. Philips, who stood with his clipboard ready.

"I'm here," she said, and climbed onto the closest bus, hiding in a seat in the back.

When the buses pulled up to the curb outside of the Newseum, Carter was the last one to file off. She continued to avoid Link with his worry and Donovan with his scrutiny. The class entered the museum through darkened paned doors into the gallery level.

The Newseum – a museum dedicated to displaying history as told through the news - rose six stories with rooms displaying sections of the Berlin wall, to theater rooms showcasing newsreels that shook the world. But inside the gallery level, the museum resembled a low lit maze of narrow hallways and dim rooms, lit only with spotlights over Pulitzer prize winning photographs. As with the National Museum of American History, only Hamilton Prep students occupied the place since Mason was present along with four Secret Service agents.

"All right, listen up," Mr. Philips said, calling over the murmur of voices. "We have seven hours here. You'll spend an hour on each floor, starting with the gallery. There is a cafe and we'll break there for lunch. Remember you are required to write a full essay on something that catches your interest here today, so don't mess around. But you are free to move about as you please. In an hour, I'll call you all together and we'll move on. If you have questions, I or some other museum assistant will be around." He waved them away. "Go explore."

Students broke away and spilled into the surrounding space. Carter distanced herself from the crowd, winding her way through hallways and around unconnected sections of walls that stood there only to display large photos. All she could think about was avoiding as many students as she could, not wanting to fall apart or lash out. With each passing minute, she felt herself splintering, her father's words hanging over her, chipping away at her composure.

Her phone beeped, the message another punch.

"I'll be home late. We need to talk. I love you, Sarge."

Carter stood in the middle of the hallway, staring down at the message. Behind her, she heard Link's voice but she didn't move. Every part of her felt battered.

"Carter, there you are," Link said. "So, something happened with Amy."

It took everything Carter had to stow away her phone

and face Link and Donovan while her mind spiraled. She tried to appear to be listening but she felt on the verge of shattering. As each second passed she wanted to scream, every nerve tight to the point of breaking.

"Now she's avoiding me. What do you think, Carter?" Link said, nudging her arm.

Carter exploded. "Link! For crying out loud! Man up and deal with your own problems for once!"

Link stared at her, stunned, while Donovan looked furious. Carter tried to find it in her to care but she felt spent. Link shuffled back a step, clenching his backpack straps.

"Link, stay here," Donovan said, firmly. "Do not move. Carter, come with me."

Taking Carter's arm, Donovan led her into one of the dim empty rooms. Carter yanked her arm free and spun on him.

"What the hell was that?" he asked.

Carter glared at him. "Don't. I don't want a lecture from you."

"Then tell me why you lost it on Link."

"Because he needs to deal with his problems. Some of us have bigger things to deal with than not understanding a girlfriend."

Donovan stared her down. "What's going on?"

"Nothing. Back off!"

His look dissected her, reading the emotions that warred on her face.

"Let me leave," she said, angry.

He crossed his arms, blocking the entrance. "No. Tell me what's going on and don't say 'nothing'. You punched Lucas."

Carter clenched her fists, belligerent. The words sat trapped in her mouth. An irrational part of her didn't want to say them, feeling that if she spoke them then they would be true.

Donovan softened and raised one hand as if to reach for her. "When will you learn you can trust me?" he asked, his voice more gentle than she ever imagined it could be.

"Trust you?" she said. "How could I possibly trust you when everyone I know betrays me?!"

Understanding passed over Donovan's face. "What happened with your father?"

She looked away, unable to handle the intensity of his stare.

"Carter, what happened?" Donovan asked, more forcefully.

The truth rattled around Carter's head, eating away at her. She sagged as the reality hit her again. It beat against her like waves crashing against a mountain, wearing it down. She shook her head as if already denying what she hadn't yet said.

"Carter..."

Donovan took one step closer. She finally met his gaze, vulnerable.

"He signed on for two more years," she whispered.

Donovan moved as if he was going to hug her but something held him back.

Carter dropped her head.

"I don't know what to do, Donovan," she said. His name came off her lips gently, carrying more of her emotions than she knew.

Donovan rested his hands on her shoulders. "Look at me."

When she didn't, he tilted up her chin with his fingers. Their eyes locked.

"You're going to get through this. You're going to take this one day at a time," he said, soothingly. "Because you are one of the strongest people I know." He almost smiled. "I have the bruises to prove it."

Their eyes held each other, emotions plainly written on their faces. In that instant something coursed between them.

Carter shifted towards him...and then the world went dark.

Chapter 48

A startled scream punctured the air. Questioning voices jumbled together. An unfamiliar metallic clang echoed through the hallways. Carter whipped her head around. Though the main gallery lights were dark, the small spotlights over photos remained on, giving weak illumination. Voices built with cries of confusion and fear ricocheting off the walls. When Carter looked back to Donovan, he was already gone. Carter hurried after him and nearly collided with him in the hall.

Link wasn't there.

Donovan pulled out his phone but froze. "Carter, there's no signal."

Carter felt her stomach give a sickening lurch. Before she could say anything, a loud bang and a burst of light exploded near the gallery entrance. Pandemonium broke loose. Momentarily blinded by a flash bang, students crashed into each other as they tried to run away. Screams crowded the air. Silhouettes scattered, not knowing where to go. Donovan sprinted down the hall. Switching on her phone flashlight, Carter chased after him. Figures came out of nowhere, knocking into her. She staggered, running into another student. Terrified faces popped into view as she swiped her light all around her, searching.

Two more flash bangs erupted in different sections sending more terror into the building. Someone careened into Carter and she hit a wall, smacking the glass of a photo. Shaking herself, she straightened and swept her light around her but in the near darkness couldn't find Donovan. Yelling his name, she shoved her way through the crazed mass.

Entering the main foyer, she saw the front entrance sealed off by a metal barrier, and dread drenched her. The main exit blocked, she spun around, trying to find Donovan or Link in the chaos of dark figures and ghostly faces. When she spotted a prone body, she sprinted, falling to her knees. She rolled the body over and horror twisted her gut.

It was Curtis.

Swallowing down the bile that rose to her throat, Carter checked his pulse. He still had one. She let out a shaky breath. Using her light, she surveyed him. In his chest, she found a tranquilizer dart.

Above the scared screams, Carter heard a pop of a gun. She swiveled her light around. Down a long corridor, she spotted another prone body and a flash of blonde hair. She took off running, her phone creating arcs of light along the floor, momentarily highlighting an unconscious Smith before moving on. Carter approached a boulder-like man picking up a blond boy. Mason struggled against his captor but the muscular man continued to drag him towards an unassuming doorway. Flooded with adrenaline, Carter dropped her phone and launched herself onto the kidnapper's back. She wrapped her arm around his thick neck in a chokehold and hooked her feet around his stomach.

The man let go of Mason and stumbled back, smashing Carter into a wall. Her head smacked against the hard surface and she felt her grip loosen. In that instant, the man grabbed her by her neck and bent forward, throwing her off him. Carter tucked into a ball as she collided with the floor. A spasm of pain skidded through her spine. She rolled and pushed herself up, as a new stab of pain shot through her. She ignored it, her heart rate spiking.

The man whipped out a gun but Carter rushed forward; using both of her hands she snapped the wrist holding the weapon. The gun skittered across the ground. The man punched Carter in the side and she grimaced.

Carter spun, putting her back to the attacker and brought the man's forearm down hard against her shoulder. She heard the crack of bone as the elbow rammed upward. The man grunted in pain. Carter smashed her elbow into the man's face, breaking his nose, blood bursting from the extremity. He staggered and Carter jumped onto his back, wrapping him in a chokehold again.

With his one good arm, the man pulled out a knife and sliced Carter's bicep. She cried out but managed to hold on, though her hold weakened. The man rammed her into the wall again and she winced.

"Mason...get...the gun..." she grunted.

Mason didn't move, petrified. The man slammed Carter again but she sensed him tiring. She felt her strength waning and didn't know if she could outlast him.

"Mason," Carter panted. "You are...completely... useless."

A sharp bam sounded and the man sank to his knees before falling back on Carter. Donovan raced forward, tranquilizer gun in hand and dragged the kidnapper off of Carter. She lay there, breathing hard. "Thanks."

Somewhere further in the gallery, Carter heard a few pop-pop sounds but saw no flashes of blinding light. She pushed herself up, grimacing. Donovan knelt beside her, noticing the stain on her arm in the low light of the spotlighted photos.

"What happened?" he asked, reaching for her arm.

"Guy had a knife."

Donovan gently tugged her arm out of her jacket sleeve. Carter forced her face to remain stoic.

"It's deep, you'll need stitches," he said. "For now all we can do is patch it up."

Carter slid the rest of the blazer off and let it fall to the floor. She eyed the wound and the blood that already coated her shirt.

"Hold still." In one easy move, Donovan tore her sleeve off and used it as a makeshift bandage. He removed his school tie and added it, knotting it securely.

"Link?" she asked, already knowing the answer.

Donovan clenched his jaw. Carter silently prayed Link was mixed with the horde of panicking students instead of in a kidnapper's hands.

"Whoever they are, they don't have him yet. But they're looking," Donovan said. Carter started to ask how he knew but he held up a comm set and earpiece. It seemed Donovan had already taken another man down and now listened to their communication. "They are releasing canisters of knockout gas."

Grabbing the discarded tranquilizer gun, Carter slid it into the back of her pants then moved to the unconscious attacker. She rifled through his pockets, finding two gas masks, a comm set, lighter, cigarettes, gum, zip ties, a security key card, and two photos. One was of Mason, the other of Link.

"Why does he have a picture of that Evans kid?" Mason asked, leaning over Carter. She jerked her head up in time to see Mason's eyes harden. "I knew it," he growled. "I knew there was something familiar about him. All this time! Why that son of-" Mason spun around, swearing and slamming the side of his fist into the wall. "This is his fault!"

Carter jumped to her feet and grabbed the front of Mason's shirt front, shaking him. "Hey! Link is innocent!

You got that."

Mason shoved Carter's hand off of him. "I wasn't talking about Link, I was talking about my father! That lying, cheating a-"

"Mason!" Carter shouted.

"No!" Mason jabbed a finger at her. "You don't get to cut me off! My father lied to me! Lied to my mom! To our entire family! That scumbag slept with some b-"

Carter slapped Mason and he staggered, clutching his cheek. "Shut up! We don't have time for you to have an emotional breakdown. If you haven't noticed, there are people who want Link and *you*! So pull yourself together! Got it?"

Despite the fury in Mason's eyes, he nodded.

"Good, now let's go find Link."

Chapter 49

No," Donovan said.

Carter spun around to face him. "What?"

"I'm taking you and Mason to a secure location beneath the gallery and then I'm going to find Link. Alone. "

Carter glared up at him. "Like hell you are. You need backup and we don't have time to get to a secure location. We need to find Link now. Wonder Boy will simply have to come with us."

Mason let out an indignant 'hey' but Carter ignored him, staring Donovan down.

"This is not up for discussion," Donovan said. "I'm getting Mason and you to a secure location."

For a heartbeat, Carter thought about slapping him as well, hoping it would knock some sense into him. Instead, she took a steadying breath. "That's great. How will I be able to protect Mason when there are only two gas masks and you need one?"

"I have another one and it doesn't matter; the archive

tunnels are on a separate ventilation system. You'll be fine."

"And you won't," Carter said sternly, crossing her arms. "Tell me this Donovan: what happens when you get Link? How are you planning to cover your back as you carry an unconscious boy to safety? Huh?"

Fire ignited in Donovan's eyes. "Don't be stupid about this, Carter."

She shoved his chest, furious with him for being obtuse. "You're the one being stupid. You're planning to go into an unknown situation with zero backup and think you'll be able to protect Link once you find him."

Mason huffed. "And you said I didn't have time to have an emotional breakdown."

"Shut up Mason!" Carter snapped.

He raised his hands in mock surrender and leaned against the wall like he didn't have a care in the world.

"He's right," Donovan said. "We don't have time for this. I'm taking you and Mason-"

"With you to find Link."

"Carter, Mason is a high profile risk and you are a civilian!"

Carter pointed at him. "Don't you dare call me a civilian! I just took on a two hundred pound man. You're not leaving either of us behind. Mason will be safer with the both of us." She saw Donovan rearing for another counter argument but she cut him off. "Standard tactical protocol: a Marine never enters an unknown situation without backup. The longer you fight me on this the longer Link is in danger."

Anger and indecision warred through Donovan but Carter knew she'd won when he unclenched his hands.

"Mason stays between us," he said, regaining his control, though she sensed the anger he struggled to suppress. "Put on the masks. We use the tranquilizer guns as a last resort. Our only advantage here is that they won't think anyone is against them. Follow my lead. You know basic hand signals?"

"That's a stupid question."

"Good. Mason, you don't make a sound and do exactly as Carter instructs."

Mason looked like he wanted to argue but Donovan narrowed his eyes threateningly and Mason reluctantly nodded. Carter handed Mason one of the masks and strapped the other one on. It was different from any mask she'd seen: sleek rubber that covered the lower half of her face with a filter in the center.

Carter checked her tranquilizer gun but paused. Only now that they'd stopped arguing did she hear it: the absence of screams and stampeding feet. Even the walls no longer rang with the echoes of chaos. A shiver raced down her spine and she thought only of Link, unconscious and alone.

"Are you ready?" Donovan asked.

In that moment, Carter felt the full weight of their reality hit her. This was not a training course and Link was not just some dummy waiting in a chair. He was one of the few friends she had and someone she could trust. Someone she would do anything to protect.

Out in the museum lay a minefield of variables they had no clue about. She met Donovan's gaze, noting his strong features and a fight brightening his eyes. In that instant, one thing struck her.

She realized her heart banged against her ribs for an entirely different reason.

There was no one else she wanted more by her side than him in that moment.

"I got your six," she said, cocking her gun.

In Donovan's eyes, she found a look she couldn't quite decipher. Before she could question it, he nodded. Retrieving her phone, Carter took Mason's arm and steered him in front of her, right behind Donovan. In a single file, they headed back into the main gallery. They moved in the center of the hallway, out of the spots of illumination from the photo lights. Adrenaline coursed through Carter. She squeezed the gun handle, fingers tingling. A white haze from the knockout gas lingered in the air, distorting the little bit of light, creating phantom shadows.

As they approached the foyer, Carter saw outlines of students passed out on the floor. They began to pick their way through the maze when Carter heard a steady tread. Donovan snapped his head back, listening. The heavy footsteps drew closer and Donovan waved back to a solitary wall. Carter grabbed the back of Mason's blazer, hurrying him after Donovan. They slipped behind the wall and Carter pressed Mason into a crouch.

"I'm in the foyer," a gravelly voice said. "Robinson isn't responding." The voice was muffled by a mask but Carter heard every word and tensed. "I'm going to make sure he has the kid."

"Roger that," Carter heard through the earpiece.

Carter locked eyes with Donovan. When Robinson was found, whoever was behind this would know someone had taken him out. This man needed to be taken down. Thinking the same thing, Donovan nodded.

The footsteps neared and Donovan signaled for Carter. They would perform a pincer tactic: Carter sweeping around the front and Donovan the back. Taking a deep breath, Carter willed her nerves to calm but every part of her vibrated with anticipation. Every tap of the man's boots wound her tighter. A faint shadow crossed the floor and Carter popped out of her hiding spot.

"Hey," she said.

The man faltered and Carter chopped his throat with the side of her hand. He reached for her neck but Donovan appeared behind him, circling his arms around the man's throat. The man was taller than Donovan and seventy-five pounds heavier but Donovan didn't lose his hold.

The man clawed Donovan's arm with two massive hands. Before Donovan's hold could be broken, Carter punched the man in the jaw, elbowed him in the stomach, and kicked the side of his knee, popping it out of its socket.

The man buckled, dropping him deeper into Donovan's chokehold. Frantically, he grappled with Donovan's arms, unconsciousness pulling the man under. Carter watched as his eyelids sagged and Donovan gently lowered him to the ground. Taking off his blazer, he wound it around the muzzle of the tranquilizer gun to muffle the sound and shot the man in the leg, assuring he'd stay down.

"Let's move," Donovan said.

Grabbing Mason, Carter pushed him back into line and they crossed the foyer avoiding arms and legs while sweeping their phone lights over the students, searching. Agonizing minute by agonizing minute they proceeded to check every student. Each time, Carter prayed it was Link and felt a new sickening dread when it wasn't.

They made it to a secluded section of the gallery when Carter finally spotted a familiar mop of unruly brown hair. Her heart plummeted to the ground before being wrenched back up and lodged in her throat. Rushing forward, she flipped the boy over. Relief poured over her. Though unconscious, Link was okay. Carter saw her own emotions echoed in Donovan as he knelt by Link, checking him for any signs of damage. But there was something else as well, an edge to his face she didn't fully understand. Near them, Mason stared at Link with unabashed curiosity and disbelief. When Carter rose, Mason met her eyes. For the first time since knowing Mason, he looked uncertain. She shook his arm. "I need you to keep it together, okay?"

He yanked his arm free, reverting to his petulant state. "Yeah, got it."

Donovan hoisted Link onto his shoulder.

"Follow or lead?" Carter asked.

"Follow. Take us back to the hallway where we found Mason. Don't worry about noise, if you see someone, shoot."

Carter urged Mason to follow in behind her. With

Link safe in their care, Carter felt every sense heightened, fear that he could be taken even now putting her on alert. She gripped her gun handle, its metal imprinting her palm. Every breath she took sounded like cannon blasts in the stillness. Her heart spiked every time she detected distant footsteps. Through the earpiece, she heard men confirming their search pattern. Each time one of them spoke, Carter felt her breath freeze in her throat.

They crept back through the gallery, pausing briefly at each corner, before hurrying on. They made it to the hallway without a mishap but Carter felt her nerves fraying, fearing their luck would run out. Only once they all passed through a secure door and it clicked shut behind them, did Carter finally breathe easier.

Chapter 50

S trips of emergency lighting ran along the edge of the floor, illuminating the stairwell. Donovan ripped off his gas mask and Carter followed, gratefully filling her lungs. Link's arms bounced lifelessly against Donovan's back as they hurried down the stairs. Their footsteps resounded off the stone walls. None of them spoke as Donovan led them down a corridor lined with pyramids of crates. With every breath, Carter felt her heart return closer to a normal rate.

What didn't stop running were her thoughts, spinning off in every direction, sprinting through theories and speculations. She replayed the details of the altercation with the two men, trying to form answers.

Donovan was a stone wall beside her, his face looked like a storm cloud. He showed no signs that carrying around a one hundred sixty-pound Link was any effort. Carter glanced at him, trying to get a read on where his mind was taking him. He flexed his jaw with anger.

At a door marked Restoration, Donovan flashed a security key card at the scanner and the door's lock clicked open. More emergency lighting showed a large room ringed with work tables and cupboards nestled between them. Photographs in the throes of repair lay on the countertops. The room smelled of strong chemicals.

"How does the security keypad still work?" Mason asked.

"Security systems are always on a different power source for reasons like this," Carter said, standing by Donovan.

Gently, they lowered Link to the rough ground. Unconscious, he looked younger, an innocent kid who needed protection. Seeing him safe lifted an invisible weight from Carter's chest. The sight did not have the same effect on Donovan. Fury radiated from him, his hands clenched.

"I'm sealing you three in here and I'm going to get those bastards," he said.

He stalked to the door but Carter darted around him, pressing her hands to his chest. "No, now it is not the time to play the hot-headed-illogical card again."

"Carter-"

"What's your plan this time, Donovan? Take on a pack of unknown opponents with one hand tied behind your back?"

"Get out of the way, Carter," he said, his tone deadly calm.

"No! You are not playing the lone ranger!"

"I'm leaving and you aren't going to stop me."

"You wanna bet!"

"I can't stay here!"

"And you can't leave without backup!"

Donovan glared at her, vibrating with pent-up emotions. "Get. Out. Of. My. Way."

"No! I'm not letting you do something stupid."

Donovan stared her down. "They came for Link! I have to make this right!"

"Link is safe!"

"But he wasn't! I failed! Something almost happened

to him and it was my fault."

Beyond the anger at the enemy, Carter saw the anger at himself. "If you want to blame someone, blame me. I yelled at him. But guess what? None of that matters right now. What matters is that you can't go out there alone and get yourself killed. We don't know how many men are there. Or who is even behind this."

Growling in frustration, Donovan paced looking like a caged animal. "Oh, I know exactly who is behind this. And when I find Philips I'm going to snap his neck."

Carter blinked, in that instant everything clicked into place. The photos the kidnappers carried were school IDs. Student records were sealed. The only way those pictures could be obtained was if someone had clearance, like a teacher. Phillips was the one to set up the field trip. But why kidnap both boys? To what end?

"If he had the both of us together, he could expose my father," Mason said, quietly.

Donovan paused and Carter glanced at the First Son. He sat on the ground, a few feet from Link, looking at his half-brother like he still couldn't wrap his head around the revelation.

Seeing the two brothers together, Carter realized it didn't matter what Philips' goal was. What mattered was keeping both boys safe.

"We have to get a call out to the Secret Service," Carter said.

Donovan focused on her and she could see him shoving his emotions to the side, rational thought coming back into play. "They're using a signal jammer. We can't make a single call out."

Carter's heart sank but a thought flashed in her mind. Yanking her necklace off, she dropped it and slammed her foot down on the pedant. Donovan eyed her.

"There's a tracker embedded in it," she said. "That means that right now my father just got an alert that it went offline."

Donovan started pacing again, this time furrowing his

brow in thought rather than anger. "Even if that works, it might not be fast enough. We have to get a call out to the Secret Service or the military."

"That means we have to take out the signal jammer. Which would most likely be in the security booth. I'm guessing you know where that is?"

"First floor, outside the gallery."

Carter nodded, already formulating a plan. "Can these archive tunnels get us there?"

Donovan grimaced, hating his next words. "I didn't memorize the archive tunnels. Only the way to get to the archive tunnels and the floor plan of the rest of the museum."

Mason scoffed. "Lazy."

"Mason, shut up," Carter said.

Mason shrugged and draped his arms over his legs, now unable to look anywhere near Link.

"The only route is back through the gallery," Carter said.

Donovan faced her, both of them thinking the same thing. He couldn't go without backup but they couldn't leave Mason and Link unprotected. But if neither of them went, a rescue team might never come. Carter tensed with indecision, unwilling to let Donovan go alone and knowing he'd feel the same way if she suggested leaving.

"You could give me a gun and leave," Mason said, seeming to understand the dilemma.

"No!" both Carter and Donovan said.

"I don't see how you have any other plan," Mason said. "Before you found...Evans...you made a big deal about not going places without backup. But we need protection."

"Mason, do you even know how to handle a gun?" Carter asked.

Mason faltered and Carter tugged at her ponytail, irritation building. "I'm annoyed with Smith sleeping on the job, right now."

Mason straightened. "Wait, he's not dead?"

"No, merely knocked out."

Mason wilted with relief, burying his face in his hands. "I thought…"

Despite everything that happened, Carter found the most unsettling thing to be Mason showing human emotions, such as fear and compassion.

"That means Smith can watch over us," Mason said.

Carter pinched the bridge of her nose. "Yes, Mason we'll leave you with an unconscious man as your protector, that sounds brilliant."

Mason scowled at her, which felt normal. "If there is ammonia in one of these archive restoration supply cupboards, then you can use it to wake him up and he *won't be* unconscious."

At the reasonable suggestion, Carter and Donovan exchanged a look then stared at Mason.

"You can both stop looking at me like you're shocked I have a brain," he said.

"Not that you have one," Carter said. "That you know how to use it."

"Oh, ha ha. You know I take all the same advanced classes as you do, don't you, Owens?"

Carter wanted to snap a retort but Donovan pointed. "Check for ammonia."

Leaving Mason to look smug, Carter searched the cupboards, finding an array of familiar chemicals.

"I found some," Donovan said, holding a bottle.

When Carter met Donovan in the middle of the room, she paused. Donovan locked eyes with her and she knew he'd already come to the realization she had. He would be going to get Smith alone.

"Smith is a couple of yards from the stairwell entrance," Donovan said, reading her mind. "I'll be back in less than ten minutes."

Carter hated everything about this. They still didn't know how many men searched the gallery for Link. They didn't know how the men would act when they discovered two members of their team were down. They didn't know what force the men would use on anyone who tried to stop them. There were so many unknowns and Carter hated it.

"I know that," she said, with forced calm.

Donovan didn't linger, grabbing his gun and hurrying out the door. When it locked shut behind him, Carter swallowed, fear and concern crawling into her throat.

"So, are you two dating or something?" Mason asked.

"Shut up, Mason," Carter snapped, grateful to release some of her tension.

But it wasn't enough, she needed to move, needed to act. But all she could do was pace, staring at the door. To distract herself, she worked through what their next play would be. Together, they could get through the gallery but she didn't know how many men would be stationed in the security booth. Would they have the element of surprise on their side? Or would someone notice them on the security feeds? Would Donovan be noticed as he helped Smith? Had they already been noticed? The enemies' comm sets had been suspiciously quiet for the last few minutes. Anxiety created a vice around Carter's chest. She tried to fight it as she scanned the room around them, looking for a distraction. Her gaze stopped on the cupboard full of chemicals. Chemicals she recognized.

She crossed to the cupboard and pulled out ingredients as well as a glass beaker. Surprised or not, this would give them a small advantage. Using the gum from the man she'd taken down, Carter secured a lighter to the bottom of a beaker, zip tying the lid of the lighter open before rifling through the chemicals. As she searched for one in particular, Mason handed it to her.

"Flash bang, right?" he said. Carter stared at him. "You forget, I'm in chemistry with you and I was there the day you set off a flash bang in the classroom." He shrugged. "I went home and researched how you did it."

Carter took the ingredient from him and shook her

head, this had to be the strangest day of her life. Dumping out Link's backpack, Carter carefully stored the beaker and supplies at the bottom of it. She froze as she slid the straps on, a rough voice speaking into the comm set.

"Holcom, what is your status on Robinson?" Static. "Holcom." Silence. "Holcom?...Ramirez go find Holcom."

"Carter?" Mason asked.

Carter didn't answer, staring at nothing, her heart pounding in fear as Ramirez responded in the affirmative, his order took him to Donovan and Smith's location. Every disastrous outcome flooded Carter's mind. Every nightmare that she'd had about her father in danger was replaced with Donovan.

"Trent, I found Holcom, he's unconscious. Someone shot him."

Carter couldn't breathe, in her mind she screamed at Donovan to hurry, to get out of the gallery, to get to safety. Trent swore and Carter shuddered at the vehemence in his voice.

"Kennan, what do you see on the security feeds?" Trent asked.

Carter ground her teeth, picturing Donovan and Smith's silhouettes spotted in the darkness. Hearing the shots fired by Ramirez. Seeing as Donovan and Smith crumpled to the ground.

When the door to the Restoration room opened, Carter spun, gun raised, nerves screaming. Before she could fire, Mason knocked her aim off course. "Don't shoot, you idiot."

Donovan halted in the doorway, Smith upright but leaning on Donovan's shoulder. Carter released a shaky breath. To her annoyance, Donovan almost smiled.

"Worried?" he asked.

"You took your time," she snapped.

Smith lifted himself off Donovan's shoulder, more in control. "Is backup on its way?"

"No," Donovan said. "But it will be. Are you stable enough to handle this end?"

Though a little pale, Smith straightened and nodded. He unholstered his gun. "Go get help."

Carter and Donovan both checked their weapons and headed for the door. Before she slipped out, Carter gave Link one last glance. Donovan closed the door and the lock clicked. Instead of leaving, Donovan grabbed a fire extinguisher from a holder on the wall and smashed it against the keypad, shattering the screen.

"Now only the backup will be able to get in," he said. "Let's go."

Carter raced behind Donovan as he guided them back through the corridors. With each step, her heart picked up speed, adrenaline coursing through her. By the time they reached the stairwell, Carter buzzed with energy. They climbed, drawing closer to danger. They stopped outside the security door. Their presence was no longer concealed. The men responsible for this mess would be on alert.

"You don't have to do this," Donovan said, meeting Carter's eyes.

A sudden surge of emotions overtook Carter, heightened by his closeness.

Without thinking, she kissed him.

Before he could react, she broke away. "That's in case something happens to one of us."

A charge set off in Donovan's eyes. He grabbed her waist and kissed her.

He pulled her against him, his other hand holding the back of her neck. Instinctively, Carter wrapped her arms around his neck, deepening the kiss. His hold on her tightened, electrifying every one of her cells. Behind his lips was an undeniable need as if he had been drowning for years and she was oxygen. A different sort of adrenaline shot through Carter.

The intensity of the moment made it seem timeless. But when they broke away it had only been seconds.

Donovan stared down at her.

"Well," Carter said, slightly breathless. "Let's make it out of this alive, 'cause I want to do that again."

Chapter 51

Carter's words snapped them back to reality. They broke apart and strapped on their gas masks. Carter tried to ignore the sparks coursing through her, focusing all her thoughts on the task at hand, not the feel of Donovan's lips.

When Donovan pressed his back to the wall beside the door, Carter moved to stand behind him. As he reached for the handle, he stretched his other hand back, resting it against Carter's side, shielding her from what lay beyond. Carter curled her hands around her gun, fighting off the chain reaction of sparks his touch set off. Already every nerve in her coursed with adrenaline.

Gently, Donovan eased the door open, his muscles straining, simultaneously alert and still. Carter could see nothing, only his back. But she read the empty hallway in the release of his shoulders.

As he slipped out, Donovan waved her forward. Carter followed him, her senses alive and burning with awareness. On whisper treads, they crept down the hallway, closing in on where Robinson's body still lay unconscious. Halfway down the hall, they halted as they heard footsteps. Donovan didn't hesitate, grabbing Carter's hand and pulling her into action. They darted behind a single paneled wall.

"I found Robinson," Ramirez said in their ears.

Donovan went rigid and Carter could tell the minute he stopped breathing. It was the same minute her lungs stopped working as well.

"We have a problem. He's unconscious too. Shot with a dart." A beat. "The boy isn't with him."

Swearing spilled over the comm set.

"Kennan, Hutchins," Trent said. "What the hell is going on?! Who is doing this?"

Ignoring the responses, Carter signaled to Donovan, questioning whether they should take out Ramirez. After a second, Donovan shook his head. Carter mulled over the refusal, seeing Donovan's conclusion. If they acted now they'd for certain be seen on the surveillance cameras.

"Ramirez," Trent said. "Go check on the Secret Service agents. If one of them managed to wake up, this could be their doing. No one on the outside knows what's happening and I want to keep it that way."

Carter felt a twinge of disappointment, hoping that by now there'd have been some sign of her father coming to her aid. She smothered the emotion as Donovan shifted, peering around the side of the panel. All clear, they slipped into the hallway staying in the shadows, praying that the darkness hid them on the security feeds.

At the end of the hall, Donovan paused, surveying the next corridor. He ducked around the corner, Carter on his tail. Like clockwork, every two seconds, she checked behind them. Together they navigated their way through the labyrinth of the gallery. Their footsteps sounded as one.

As they exited the gallery, they heard the continued call of men giving out their positions and statuses on their search. The atrium beyond the gallery lay as dark as the hallways Carter and Donovan had left. Donovan guided them along the wall, keeping his eyes trained on the security door across the way, his gun raised. As they approached, Carter aimed her gun behind them. She kept her breathing steady, willing her heart to remain calm. The gun's handle was imprinted on her palm as she rested her finger on the trigger.

The steel security door lay locked, only a few feet before them, surrounded by concrete walls. The only way in was passing a security scanner. What lay inside was anyone's guess but Carter had an idea that it was more men built like mountains with military training.

Donovan slowed their pace to a crawl as they covered the last few feet. He took one side of the door as Carter took the other. They squatted, getting into position. Donovan made eye contact with her. He pointed to himself and then to the right. She mimicked the gesture, pointing to the left. As he slipped out the key card, he leveled his gun at the door. He waited, his hand hovering over the scanner as he looked to Carter. Her heart hammered in her chest, blood pumping in her ears. Tugging off Link's backpack, she removed the beaker and combined ingredients. She clicked the lighter and a flame burst out, licking the air above the beaker's lip.

As Donovan flashed the key card over the scanner, Carter set the mesh over the beaker's opening. The keypad blinked green, Donovan pushed the door open and Carter slid the glass beaker inside.

"What-"

Both Donovan and Carter twisted away, shielding their eyes. A flash of brilliant white light exploded in the room. Shouts of surprise echoed. Before the light dissipated, Carter and Donovan raced inside. Before rows of computer screens sat two men, trying to rid themselves of their momentary blindness. Carter fired a tranquilizer dart at the man on the left, while Donovan took the right. Both men were unconscious before their eyes had time to clear.

Donovan closed the door, locking it. They tied up the two men, storing them against a far wall. At the computers, they went to work. Donovan pawed through the multiple machines on the desk looking for the signal jammer. Carter took a seat in one of the vacant chairs, looking at the wall of screens.

"Found it," Donovan said, pulling out a metal device from behind one of the monitors.

He yanked the cable out and reached for his phone. "Now let's get the military here."

Carter reached for him. "I don't think that's necessary."

"Why?"

"Because they're already here."

Chapter 52

Donovan jerked his head up. From the video feed covering the front of the museum, they watched as a line of SUVs and SWAT cars created a perimeter around the front entrance. Carter felt a flood of relief. Donovan stared as if he wasn't sure what he was seeing.

"How'd they know?" he asked.

Carter shook her head, her eyes still glued to the screen. "Must have been my tracker. It's the only explanation."

The line of cars fanned out, making a barrier in the street. Car doors flung open and hordes of men in full-body gear clambered out. All Carter and Donovan could do was stare, the pressure of their solitude lifted.

A man in a black suit, wearing an FBI bullet proof vest, stepped out of one of the SUVs, followed by more hard-faced men dressed in similar attire. From the moment his foot hit the ground, the man barked out orders that neither Carter nor Donovan could hear. But one thing was clear: this was the man in charge. Within minutes, stations were up and troops of men were formed into packs and ready to move.

As the scene continued to unravel, Carter became aware of the pain in her arm. The dull throbbing pulled her from her mystified stupor. With the return of her thoughts, she noticed the time, shocked to realize it had been less than an hour since the power went out.

She shifted back in her chair, wincing. Donovan broke from his daze. "Your arm?"

She nodded. She looked down at it, eyeing the sleeve that was now thoroughly ruined.

"You mind?" she asked, looking to her arm.

Donovan rolled his chair closer to her, his legs bumping against hers. She leaned towards him, offering up her other sleeve. In one smooth motion, he ripped it off and moved to her wounded arm. Carefully, he unknotted the tie, his fingers warm as he held her limb in place. He wrapped the new bandage around the old one and secured it again. Carter peered down at her bare arms then up at Donovan, his face only a few inches away from hers.

"I don't think the ripped shirt is my look," she said.

"I don't know," he said, his voice low. "I could argue a few points in its defense."

He stared at her. In his blue eyes, Carter saw all the emotions she felt. Her heart stuttered a few beats before quickening its pace. The feel of his fingers on her arm still lingered. In that moment, she had the strongest urge to tear both their gas masks off and kiss him. She saw in his face the same thoughts playing through his mind.

They both shifted closer.

The sharp buzz of a radio in the room shattered the moment.

They froze, jolted from the intensity of emotions racing through them. Donovan backed away first, breaking their connection.

"Porter come in," a baritone voice commanded.

Carter and Donovan searched for the radio. The command came once more as Donovan found it.

"Porter is currently unconscious," Donovan said, rushing to answer, "as well as the rest of the security team."

At the statement, Carter noticed the other set of men zip-tied and comatose in the far corner of the room. On screen, the gray-haired man glared at the front doors, as he held a radio similar to the one in Donovan's hand.

"Who am I speaking to?" the man said, iron in his tone.

"This is Agent Donovan Keller of the Secret Service," Donovan said.

The gray-haired man spoke rapidly to a man beside him. Together they consulted a screen and the man in charge focused back on the museum. "Agent Keller, this is Associate Deputy Director Townsend with the FBI." His face was hard as stone. "I have no record of you. You have one minute to explain to me who you are."

Donovan didn't show any concern. "With all due respect, sir," he said, confident though respectful, "it's because you don't have the right clearance. Now if you will connect me to-"

Townsend's eyes narrowed. "I am second to the Director of the FBI," he said, cutting Donovan off. "I can assure you I have the right clearance."

Donovan flexed his jaw, annoyed. "Deputy Townsend," he said, trying to hold in his impatience. "We do not have time for this. I'm currently in a museum that has been hit with knock out gas and filled with an unknown amount of hostiles. I need-"

"No! Understand this. I am standing outside a museum with its entrance barred and talking to a so-called agent by the name of Donovan Keller that we have no record of. There is nothing you can say-"

Townsend cut himself off when a faint voice spoke. Carter looked to Donovan but his eyes were fixed on the screen, his fist clenching the radio. From the speaker, they heard someone talk.

"Did you say, Keller?"

Chatter filled Carter's ear but she wrenched out her earpiece, needing to hear what came next. Beside her, Donovan did the same. From behind Townsend, a man in his late twenties with Donovan's similar facial structure stepped forward. Donovan relaxed.

"Yes," Townsend said, unaware that he still held down the talk button.

Donovan's brother looked at the Deputy Director with the utmost respect, his posture military straight. "If he said Donovan Keller, sir, you can trust he is telling the truth. One call to Director Joseph will confirm it."

"You know him?"

"He's my brother, sir. His current position is highly classified."

Carter waited as the Deputy Director made a call, a bubble of nerves playing in her stomach. They were unable to hear what was said, the Deputy Director finally releasing the talk button.

"That's Brock?" Carter asked.

Donovan nodded once. The static from the radio filled the room as they waited.

"Agent Keller," Townsend said, his voice no longer harsh.

"Yes?" Donovan said.

"What's your status?"

Donovan dropped his tense shoulders and the crease in his forehead vanished. "Knock out gas was released and the entire class of students is unconscious as well as three of the four Secret Service agents on The Falcon's detail. The Falcon is secure in the Restoration room and both he and Lancer are protected by Agent Smith. Four hostiles have been neutralized. I'm positioned in the security booth, along with a civilian. Carter Owens. Her father is Agent Owens of the Secret Service."

Townsend took all of this information in with a straight-faced expression. At the name 'Owens' he called out something. A second later, Carter's father walked around a van and into view of the camera.

At the sight of him, Carter felt every fear and knot of tension dissipate. She sagged as a weight was taken off her shoulders. Her father was impassive but she could tell from the stiffness in his posture that worry ate away at him. Townsend spoke to him. He gave a single nod and a one-word response. Carter's heart ached to run out of the security booth and find the familiar comfort in her father's strong arms.

"Agent Keller," Townsend said, "my men are preparing to breach the main doors. I need you to vent the museum."

"Tell me what to do," Donovan said.

Carter watched as he followed Townsend's instruction, typing away on the computer. He worked with the assurance of someone confident in their place. He spoke to Townsend as a soldier would a commander.

Deep respect came over Carter as she studied him, seeing a man she had only glimpsed. She liked this version of him, someone who had earned his title and deserved to keep it. She felt a tired smile tugging at her lips.

Donovan hit enter and a faint whirring sound came on above them breaking Carter from her thoughts. She glanced up at the vents, imagining she could see the gas being sucked away. Thirty seconds later the computer flashed a message. *"Venting complete."*

"Deputy Townsend," Donovan said, removing his gas mask, "you're clear to breach."

"Copy that."

Townsend nodded to a group of men beside him. The men approached the museum with swift, calculated movements. Carter pulled off her mask and took a deep breath. The air tasted clear and seemed to strengthen her aching muscles. Donovan watched the group's progress, expressionless.

From the corner of her eye, Carter spotted movement on one of the other screens. What she saw made her burn with anger. In the stairwell to the archive tunnels was a group of five men, Philips in the lead. Carter glanced at the team at the front doors and knew they wouldn't move fast enough to catch the escaping group in the tunnels.

"Donovan," she said.

Instantly, he knew something was wrong and she motioned to the screen. He came to the same conclusion as her and grabbed his gun. "We have to go."

Forcing her weariness away, Carter picked up her gun and dashed out of the security room after Donovan. Despite her best efforts, Carter felt a dragging sensation she couldn't shake off.

As they crossed the atrium back to the gallery, they kept their guns trained in either direction. They retained the same form they had before, Donovan taking the lead as Carter brought up the rear. They moved quickly and efficiently, accustomed to each other's thoughts and pace. By the time the FBI team managed to get the front doors open, Carter and Donovan had covered the distance to the stairwell.

Slowly, the pair descended and snaked their way down the corridor, slipping from the cover of one set of crates to the next, inching closer to where voices emanated from. Crouched around a corner, Donovan spied on the now stalled group.

"Still five hostiles," he whispered. "They are outside the Restoration room. We need to move now."

Carter nodded, her heart jackhammering her rib cage. The pain in her arm weighed her down but she did her best to ignore it. Donovan pointed to himself and then to the right. Carter nodded, knowing they would be going in the same formation as last time. Her stomach knotted as he rose from his crouched position, fist raised. Blood pounded in her ears, deafening her. The metal casing of the gun dug into her palm as she squeezed it to help her remain alert.

Donovan dropped his fist and they burst from around the corner, guns raised, targets already in sight. The men barely had time to turn around before Carter and

Donovan fired. Carter's first dart took down Mr. Philips. Donovan got two quick shots into two of the men before he was attacked.

As Carter shifted her gun to her next target, she knew something was wrong. Her movement wasn't fast enough, even with the boost of adrenaline. By the time she had her gun leveled at the other man, he was before her. He wrapped one bear-sized hand over the gun. Carter let it go, narrowly missing having her fingers crushed.

She kneed the man in the side and swung at his face, battling against sudden exhaustion. Only her knee made contact, the man easily batting aside her fist.

A trickle of dread set in.

The man reached out for her. In his eyes, she could read his resistance to harm a girl and she managed to duck away.

Taking a step back, she twisted and grabbed the fire extinguisher. With all her remaining strength and more speed than she thought she possessed, she brought it up and smashed it against her opponent.

The blow grazed his temple, sending him stumbling back but didn't have lasting damage. As he regained his footing, blood dripped from the cut on his forehead and he snarled. In a blink, he stood in front of Carter before she could devise a plan of attack. She aimed a fist at his jaw but the blow never landed.

The man slammed his fist into Carter's ribs and she cried out at the explosion of pain. He sent a second blow to her face and Carter felt as if she had been hit by a semi-truck. The force of the hit threw her back into the wall. Stars popped before her vision as pain pierced her brain.

She heard a gunshot, the sound seeming to come from a distance.

Donovan's name rose to her lips, right before her world went dark.

Chapter 53

Carter regained consciousness, laying on the ground. Her brain felt swollen and crammed with a jumbled mess of thoughts. Gradually, the shuffling footsteps registered. Everything came into focus as Donovan smashed the butt of his gun into her attacker's face. The sheer force of the blow sent the man crashing to the floor. Donovan shot him in the leg to keep him there, his face a mask of fury.

Carter tried to move but a flash of pain nearly brought the blackness back. A cry escaped her lips. She closed her eyes, fighting to remain conscious. Donovan rushed to her side, his features contorting into deep concern.

"Carter," he said, unable to hide the worry in his tone.

The initial shock of agony subsided, leaving her with an intense pain that was bearable. Her breath came in shallow gasps as she focused on Donovan. He bent over her, his blue eyes dark with roiling emotions. Tucking his gun away, he gently cupped the back of her head and caressed the side of her face.

"Hey," he said, tenderly.

She took in a deep breath, the pain ebbing away. At the look of worry on his face, her heart smiled.

"You're right," she said, her voice raspy. "I don't protect my left side."

Donovan dropped his head and gave a shaky, relieved laugh. He leaned forward and kissed her forehead, his breathing ragged. His lips were warm and soft. The feel of them lingered on her skin.

Carter closed her eyes, every inch of her felt battered. But with each steady breath, she became more and more accustomed to her injuries. From the aches in her body, she knew at least a couple of ribs were bruised, if not cracked. Her face felt sore but nothing was majorly damaged. It was possible she had a concussion because of the fuzziness in her brain. Slowly, she propped herself on her elbow.

"Can you get up?" Donovan asked.

Carter started to nod but stopped when the hallway tilted, dizziness washing over her. Donovan caught her before she hit the ground, one arm holding her around her shoulders.

"I'll take that as a no," he said.

She blinked, trying to clear the haze from her mind. "I just need a minute."

Donovan didn't respond. Instead, he slid his other arm under her legs. Instinctively, Carter wrapped her uninjured arm around his neck as he lifted her off the ground.

A stab of pain hit her as his hand pressed against her injured ribs. She sucked in a breath, gripping the back of his shirt, the spike bringing tears to her eyes. Donovan quickly shifted his hand. "Sorry. You okay?"

She rested her head in the crook of his neck, taking a shaky breath, her eyes closed.

"Yeah," she said, her fingers still clenching his collar.

Moving cautiously, Donovan took a couple of steps over to the crates and sat down. His grip on her didn't loosen as he leaned his head back against the wall. There was a quiet strength in his hold as if he was scared that if he let go she might disappear. The adrenaline-induced energy of the past hour drained from him.

For a long moment, neither said anything. Carter let her body relax fully against Donovan. She found strength in his hold as well as the steady drumming of his heartbeat in her ear.

In his arms, she felt small and vulnerable but beneath that was a sense of safety. She breathed him in. He smelled like sweat with a faint scent of his cologne. Her breathing synced with his as she moved with the rise and fall of his chest.

Slowly, her dizziness vanished and her thoughts righted themselves. She carefully raised her head. Donovan had his eyes closed. He looked tired and bruises played along the side of his face, from his cheekbone to his jaw. She lightly touched his injured jaw. He gazed down at her. An exhausted smile pulled at the edge of his mouth.

"How are you feeling?" he said.

"Like I got beat up by a two hundred seventy-five pound militarily trained guy." Donovan chuckled weakly. "What about you?"

"Only a little better than that. I have a bruised rib or two but that's about the worst of it. I've had worse encounters."

Carter raised her eyebrows in surprise. "Really?"

"You live with Marines, you're bound to be black and blue for a good part of it. I learned how to take a hit."

"Seems I could stand to learn that sort of lesson."

"You shouldn't have to if I'm around."

She closed her eyes as he kissed her forehead. The heat of his lips seemed to engulf her and send her aching body humming.

Down the corridor, they heard the soft patter of footsteps. A second later, a team of men rounded the corner and Donovan whipped his gun out from behind his back aiming at the leader. The man dressed in full-body gear and armed with an automatic gun raised it along with his other hand. He then quickly flipped up his visor. "Good to see you're still in one piece, Donny," Brock said, grinning

Donovan let out a tired breath and dropped the gun. Brock waved the men forward and they began tying up the unconscious attackers.

"I have Agent Keller and the civilian," Brock said, into a comm set. "I'm escorting them out now. Have a medic standing by."

Carter shifted as if to stand up but Donovan didn't release her. Without a word, he stood, still holding her in his arms, his hold on her making it clear that he wasn't about to let go.

Brock led them back through the tunnels and up the stairwell. Inside the gallery, the lights had been restored and men in body gear moved through the hallways, clearing the area. As they approached the museum entrance, Carter looked up at Donovan.

"I'm going to have to walk once we hit those doors," she said.

"Why?"

"Because if my dad sees you carrying me, he will most likely shoot you."

This comment received a smile. "Understood."

They stopped just inside the front doors and Donovan lowered Carter's feet to the ground but kept a firm grip on her side. She kept her arm slung over his shoulders, testing the steadiness of her balance. When convinced she wasn't going to fall over, she loosened her hold. Donovan caught her hand before she could pull it away.

"I'll risk being shot," he said, "I don't want you collapsing."

"Okay."

Brock stepped forward and pushed the door open, holding it for them. They emerged into the gray day, the cool air scented with coming rain. Beyond them lay the perimeter of cars with the addition of ambulances.

The scene teemed with people constantly in motion, preparing for the onslaught of hysterical parents and the reviving of dozens of students.

They had barely stepped out when Carter's father appeared. He hurried forward, a tidal wave of emotions playing across his face. Before he could sweep Carter up into a hug, Donovan took a step forward and raised his hand.

"She's injured," Donovan rushed to say. "Bruised ribs, possibly fractured, a cut that needs stitches, and a minor concussion."

Her father swallowed down his emotions and stepped over to Carter. Tears of relief sprung to her eyes.

"Sarge," her father said, gently encasing her in his arms.

Carter leaned into him, a fresh wave of exhaustion hitting her.

"Come on, Donny," Brock said. "Deputy Townsend wants to meet you."

Donovan gave Carter one final look and left with his brother. It seemed hours before Carter's father let go of her, even then she didn't want him to. The rim of his eyes were red. Carter shivered as a breeze whispered past her bare arms. Her father quickly slipped off his jacket and wrapped it around her shoulders. It smelled clean and familiar.

"You got my message," Carter said.

She felt utterly weak and knew if it weren't for her father's strong hands gripping her arms, she would most likely crumple to the ground.

"I was worried you were running away for a moment. Especially after..." A lump lodged itself in Carter's throat. "Come on, let's get you to the ambulance."

Carter let herself be guided by her father's unyielding hold on her shoulders. Inside her was a hurricane of exhaustion, pain, and sadness. All three things seemed to battle for the top spot, the weight of them all clouding her mind.

A medic waited at the back of an open ambulance. The sight of the open van and the gurney snapped Carter from her thoughts. She pulled away from the man as he stepped towards her.

"I'm not leaving," she said. "Not until Link is okay."

Her father stared down at her, his refusal ready in his eyes.

"Sarge," her father said, her name a warning.

"No," she said, determination giving her a spark of energy. "I just dealt with men twice my size to make sure he was okay. I'm staying until I see that."

A shadow passed over her father's face and his mouth became a thin line. "You shouldn't have been put in that situation in the first place."

Carter knew he was talking about Donovan. "Captain, I was the one who forced him to take me along. I wasn't about to let him go into an unknown situation without backup."

"But he let you get hurt."

She smiled wearily. "I'll heal."

Her father stared at her, all his worry and fear plain in his eyes. He tightened his hold on her arms as if to reassure himself that she was there.

"I'm okay now," she said. "Thanks for coming for me."

He softened. "I will always find you. That's a promise -"

"And a threat," Carter finished for him.

Someone approached them.

"Agent Owens," he said. "Deputy Townsend is ready for you."

Her father nodded but spoke to the medic. "Take care of her."

"Yes, sir."

Her father kissed the top of her head and left. Carter watched him disappear around a car and a horde of moving workers. Carefully, she climbed onto the lip of the ambulance and sat down to wait.

Chapter 54

The medic checked Carter's vitals, cleaned and stitched the cut on her arm, and did a preliminary check of her injured ribs. Finished, he bandaged her up, gave her something for the pain, and wrapped a blanket around her shoulders.

Carter tugged the edges of the thick blanket closer to her, watching the hive of activity. Beyond the cordoned off area, she glimpsed TV vans and the lights of filming equipment. Reporters stood before cameras giving general facts about the state of the museum and their speculations.

Donovan appeared from the busy crowd, his posture upright but his expression worn out. When he spotted Carter, he lightened. Carter felt the beginnings of a smile as he stopped before her. From her perch on the back of the ambulance, they were almost at eye level.

"Link?" she asked.

"They are still doing a sweep of the museum. I won't be able to get in until they are done. I came to see how you are doing." He studied her. "How are *you* doing?"

For a second she didn't reply, taking him in. "Better now."

A quiet moment slipped by as the world continued to rage on around them. It was as if they were a stone in the center of the stream, untroubled. A breeze gusted by whipping up stray pieces of Carter's hair. Donovan caught the strands, sweeping them away from her face. He held them down, his fingers becoming tangled in her hair. With his other hand he lightly traced the bruise on her cheek, then the one on her jaw.

"Does it hurt?" he asked.

"Hmmm?" With her eyes locked on his, the world was a blur. Nothing else seemed real except the feel of his fingers.

He smiled, brushing his thumb over her lips. The feel of it sent sparks of electricity coursing through her.

"If you don't kiss me now," she said, "I'll punch you."

He grinned wider and leaned in, hovered just above her lips, their breath intertwining.

He kissed her slowly as if he knew he had all the time in the world to savor the moment. Everything disappeared and nothing else existed except Donovan and his lips pressed against hers. His lips were caring and they sent the pain and exhaustion away. He broke from her, resting his forehead on hers.

"I've been wanting to do that since the second day I knew you, when you almost broke Finch's wrist," he said.

A breathless smile tugged at Carter's lips. "Then why didn't you?"

"Conflicting interests."

"Well," she said, "since I just got beat up trying to protect Link, I say the interests are no longer conflicting."

He kissed her again. This time there was a smile behind it. She placed her hand on his chest, gripping his shirt, and drawing him closer. Donovan dropped his hand to her waist, tightening his hold.

A deep, angry growl made them both freeze. "Get away from my daughter before I shoot you."

Donovan jerked away as if Carter was made of fire. Before he stepped out of reach, she grabbed his hand, lacing her fingers through his.

"Captain, you know Donovan," she said, her tone light, "He's a Marine."

Her father's scowl deepened. Carter grinned as Donovan tightened his hold on her hand.

"Do you hate me, Sarge?" her father asked.

"I say we give him a chance," she said. "He did just save my life. I say if he can't last five minutes in a fight with you, you can shoot him."

Donovan looked at her. "Thanks."

"Don't worry, he will probably only shoot you in the shoulder. Not a big deal. Besides, you'll have a cool scar and all girls love that."

With his eyes captured by hers, Donovan seemed to forget about her father. "Does that include you?"

"It does."

He shifted closer to her.

"Then I'll shoot you now," Carter's father said, "and you can have that scar."

Donovan jolted back into the awareness of her father. The scowl was there but it lacked any true malice.

"I came to collect you," Carter's father said. "The museum is cleared. We're about to go retrieve your charge." Dropping Carter's hand, Donovan cleared his throat. He straightened, trying to regain a sense of professionalism. Carter's father did not look impressed. "On the way there, we'll have a little chat."

Donovan glanced at Carter. She tried to give him a reassuring smile but knew it didn't help that she was laughing on the inside. Steeling himself, Donovan walked towards her father. Steve placed a hand on his shoulder. Carter could tell by the shift in Donovan's stance that her father's hold was bone-crushing.

She smiled to herself and wrapped the blanket tighter,

watching as they disappeared. A minute later, a group of men, including her father and Donovan, entered the museum. She kept her gaze trained on the doors, waiting. The minutes passed with no movement from the entrance but a steady flow of activity around her.

An increase in volume from beyond the wooden barriers caught Carter's attention away. A convoy of cars, bearing the Presidential flags, arrived. As they passed beyond the barriers, reporters shouted for attention, eager for more information. The line of vehicles stopped but no one emerged. Deputy Townsend walked over to the center car and spoke with someone inside.

The museum doors opening snapped Carter's focus back. A pack of men in black emerged, their bodies closely pressed together, forming a shield. Carter craned her neck, wanting to catch a glimpse of Link or Donovan. When they were under the cover of the makeshift city of vehicles, the unit separated.

Donovan and Carter's father led Link away, blocking him from the prying cameras. The trio stopped before Carter. A wide grin split her mouth as she looked into Link's groggy face. He blinked a few times, still trying to wake himself up. Removing his glasses, he palmed his eyes. He focused on Carter and a matching smile pulled at his sleepy expression.

"Who managed to beat you up?" he asked, replacing his glasses.

"Some guy I insulted," she said.

"It was bound to happen at some time."

His voice and his lighthearted expression made the last bit of worry in Carter's chest vanish. Seeing him unconscious and vulnerable was something she never wanted to witness again. "I'm glad you're okay."

"Thanks for making that possible."

She nodded. Her father and Donovan talked quietly a foot away. Though she couldn't hear what they were saying, she could tell that the antagonism between them was no longer there.

In the convoy of cars, doors opened and men in suits climbed out. Following behind one of them was the President. Instantly, a barrier of men formed a circle around him. All eyes landed on that point, including Link and Carter's.

The group surged toward Smith and a tired-looking Mason. When they were close, the circle parted and the President embraced his son. But even as he did, Carter noted the tension in Mason. If Mason's anger at learning the truth about Link was any indication, a storm was brewing for the two of them.

Carter's thoughts on the relationship vanished as she noticed Link wilt. She took hold of Link's hand, gripping it. The pressure brought his gaze to her. The look of sadness in his eyes nearly sent her marching over to the President to give him a slap equivalent to the one she'd given his son. She let her thoughts play out across her face. The sight of her righteous indignation made Link smile. He squeezed her hand back.

"It's life, I guess," he said.

"It doesn't mean it's okay."

"No. It doesn't." The words were weighed down with sorrow that Carter understood.

As Mason was led to one of the cars, the President cut a path in their direction. At the sight of his father walking toward him, Link tightened his hold on Carter's hand as if he needed to steal some of her strength. She echoed his hold, letting him know she was there. The solid group of black suits split and the President stepped forward. Instead of going to Link, he directed his attention to Carter's father.

"Agent Owens," President Douglas said. "I was told you lent a hand in helping this situation not turn out as terrible as it could have been. I want to offer my gratitude."

He stretched out his hand and Steve shook it. Carter saw the respect that passed between the two men. But it didn't change how her heart sank at seeing them together.

Knowing her father would be a shield once again for two more years.

"I played a very small role, sir," her father said. "Agent Keller and my daughter were the ones who did the most."

Douglas shifted to Donovan. But before he shook Donovan's hand, he looked at Link. In his face, he betrayed a strong desire to hug his son. The President didn't act on this instinct, knowing enough people were watching him. His eyes told the story of the shame, grief, regret, and love that lay between them. Link held Carter's hand firmly, needing something to anchor him to the spot. Something that would stop him from reaching for his father.

When President Douglas reached out his hand to Donovan, the moment broke. Link loosened his grip on Carter's hand and his shoulders sank.

"Agent Keller, thank you for all that you did," President Douglas said, his gratitude heavy with meaning.

"Thank you, Mr. President."

When President Douglas released Donovan's hand, he thanked Carter. She restrained herself from breaking his wrist. Link standing beside her was the only thing that held her back. With one final look at Link, the President nodded. "I'm glad you are all safe," he said. He glanced at Carter's father. "I look forward to your return, Steve."

"As do I, Mr. President," her father said.

The words laid a burden on Carter's heart and dropped sadness into her eyes. Douglas became enclosed in the circle of men and guided away to the car. Link stood there staring after him, lost. Donovan placed a hand on his shoulder.

"I'm sure your mother is going out of her mind with worry," he said. "Let's get you to her."

Link nodded, unable to talk.

"You should get your ribs checked out," Carter said

to Donovan.

"I will, once he is safe at home." Donovan looked as if he wanted to kiss her before leaving but was all too aware of her father standing only a few feet away. "Thank you," he said instead. "Good-bye."

Impulsively, Carter reached out and cupped the back of Donovan's neck. She brought his lips to hers, ignoring the growl from her father. When she let go, Link gaped at them.

"So...you two...kissing...and..." He widened his eyes. "Are you sure this is wise? I hate to think about what happens if it ends. Someone is likely to die."

After facing dangerous odds together, Carter knew that would never happen.

"I guess it's a good thing I'm a great shot," she said.

Donovan smirked but he sobered when Carter's father came into view. He nodded to him. "Sir."

Donovan led Link away, glancing back once at Carter. Her father stood before her and their eyes met. For a moment neither of them spoke, the air electric with conflicting thoughts and emotions.

"You're going back," she said. "Two years?"

The quiet sadness in her father's eyes was all the confirmation she needed. She dropped her head with renewed weariness.

"Carter," he said, a note of conviction in his voice, "I know you can't understand this but I'm not only trying to protect the leader of our nation but also a friend, someone I have spent the last six years serving. If I didn't see President Douglas through his term and something happened to him, I would feel it was my fault. It's not about honor or sacrifice, it's about doing something in my gut I know I have to do." Though his face remained calm and serious, she caught the glint of determination in his eyes. "I know that won't make sense to you but it's what I need to do."

Carter said nothing. She understood what he was talking about. The feeling he described was the same one that had sent her looking for Link, sent her diving into an unknown situation without a second thought. Her best friend had been in harm's way and she would have done anything to keep him safe. Though she now understood why, it didn't mean her heart wasn't aching. In that moment, she still felt like a battered girl with a bruised heart.

Tears pooled in her eyes. They slid from beneath her closed lids and plopped onto the ground, darkening the gravel.

"Sarge," her father said, gently.

It took her a long minute to raise her head. When she did, looking back at her were the same caring, blue eyes that she grew up trusting.

"I get it, Captain."

"I love you, Sarge," he said, fiercely.

"I know."

Her father hugged her and she rested in his steady hold. Tiredness crept up on her and her eyelids dipped. Her father laid a hand on her shoulder, keeping her from falling over. He called to the medic. "What's the verdict?"

"Her second, third, and fourth ribs on her left side are bruised, not broken. She suffered a minor concussion and her cut is taken care of."

"Can I just go home then?" Carter asked.

Her father looked about to protest but the medic spoke first. "You could. At the hospital they would tell you the same thing, advise plenty of rest and ice packs to help reduce swelling. You can take a basic painkiller to help with the pain."

"Let's go home, Captain," Carter said.

Her father studied her, debating. When she started to lean to the side, fatigue dragging her down, he decided. "Okay." He nodded to the medic. "Thank you."

Carter slipped off the edge of the van, leaving the blanket behind. Her father wrapped a steadying arm around her shoulders and guided her to the car. Opening the door for her, he helped her into the passenger seat.

"I'll be right back," he said.

He shut the door and Carter rested back against the headrest. By the time her father returned, she was fast asleep.

***

The gentle call of her name roused Carter. She blinked. They were back at their apartment. A light rain had started and the patter sounded soothingly on the car roof. Carter shifted and pushed herself up. Pinpricks of pain darted through her body and she closed her eyes. Her father rested a hand on her shoulder.

"Can you walk?" he asked.

She nodded. "Yeah."

Slowly, she unbuckled and as she reached for the door, her father opened it. Exhaustion hung from her every limb. Her thoughts felt sluggish. Every injury sent her reminders when she moved. Her father half lifted, half helped her out of the seat.

The misty rain felt refreshing. The air smelled clean, the toxins from the city getting washed away. They made a slow progression up the stairs, the tapping of their shoes on the metal echoed in the quiet neighborhood. Her father went to insert his key into the door as it swung open. Maggie stood on the other side, a bundle of worry and tears. As they entered, the light fell around Carter's face.

"Oh, Hon!" Maggie choked, seeing the red bruises along Carter's face. She covered her mouth. "Steve told me something happened."

Despite the fatigue and ache in her body, Carter couldn't help but smile. "It's not as bad as it looks."

Happy, relieved tears spilled over Maggie's eyes. She gently hugged Carter and Carter accepted the embrace, allowing it to be the end of their conflict, letting her anger and hurt melt away. Maggie stared at Carter with motherly, red-rimmed eyes.

"I'm so sorry," she said.

"I am too. For everything I said."

Maggie managed a quiet smile. "What do you need?"

"Sleep."

Nodding, she tucked a hair behind Carter's ear. Behind Carter, her father watched the exchange with a soft expression. Maggie held his gaze and her words, tones of love, and small affectionate gestures stirred something in him. Carter glanced back and saw it all.

A weary smile tugged at her mouth as she followed Maggie to her room. Her father waited outside as Maggie assisted Carter with changing her clothes. She winced as her shirt was removed, the pain dragging her further into exhaustion.

When she crawled into her bed, she could barely keep her eyes open. Her father entered her room and kissed the top of her head. "I love you, Sarge."

"I love...you too...Captain," Carter said, drowsily.

"Sleep well, girly," Maggie whispered.

The nickname succeeded in producing a small smile from Carter. The last thing she saw before she closed her eyes was her father taking Maggie's hand.

"Thank you for being here," he said.

"I'm here for you both."

The promise followed Carter as she drifted off.

Chapter 55

The mahogany clock in the corner of the Principal's office ticked on, as it had for many years and would continue for many years to come. The morning light cascaded through the windows and washed over the desk and the office's occupants. The sky was clear, a vivid blue color holding the promise of summer and freedom. Carter sat straight in her chair, calm as she gave Principal Withers her full attention.

"Mr. Owens," Mr. Withers said, "I understand you're busy and I appreciate you giving me a minute of your time. I was told that you and your daughter were one of the reasons why the incident that occurred at the Newseum didn't become a major catastrophe." When he looked to Carter, she found respect mingled with his gratitude. "I want to offer my thanks to both of you."

"We were glad we could help," Carter's father said.

Carter smiled, a mixture of playful and unconcerned. "Of course. What's a couple of bruised ribs when it comes to dozens of lives?"

Despite himself, Principal Withers grinned good-naturedly. Carter still wore the purple bruises of her fight across her cheek. When she moved too quickly, her ribs yelled at her but the worst of the pain was over.

"As you are probably aware," Principal Withers said, "This last week without students has given us a chance to update all of our records and have the FBI re-vet all remaining staff members. They all checked out."

Steve nodded. "That's good to hear." He stood and buttoned his jacket. "I hate to be rude but my time is limited."

Principal Withers stretched out his hand. "I completely understand. Thank you again."

Carter grinned at him. "Does this mean I get a free pass to skip fourth period?"

Though Mr. Withers scowled, there was a touch of amusement in his eyes. "No, it does not. And please refrain from challenging Mr. Harris on every point. He needs to be able to finish teaching his calculus lesson."

She gave a nod and caught, from the corner of her eye, a faint smile on her father's face. "Got it."

As they left the office, the hallways slowly began to fill with students. The tones that pinged off the spotless walls and gleaming floors were ones of speculation and intrigue. Over the week, the news stations had given contradictory stories on what had occurred. None of it the truth.

Carter's father pushed through the front doors and sweet, spring air greeted them. Lines of sleek cars trickled in through the gates and down the gravel drive. Despite the incident, there were only half a dozen transfers. Most parents assumed that if the President still allowed his son Mason to attend the school, it was safe to send their children as well.

Carter avoided passing students as she followed her father to the parking lot. When they reached the black SUV, he faced her. She gave him a small smile, despite the conflicting emotions that suddenly crowded her chest.

"Maggie says Friday works for going out to dinner," he said.

Carter leaned against the car. "You know it kills the mood on a date if you bring your daughter."

Her father narrowed his eyes dangerously. "I'm not leaving you in an empty apartment. Not now that you have a Marine boyfriend."

"We haven't officially put labels on it."

"He was kissing you. I'm putting a label on it. 'Boyfriend' will have to do since it can't be 'Deceased'."

Carter grinned but her father didn't lighten.

"That also reminds me," he said. "I need to install security cameras."

"Like I don't know how to disable those."

Even as her father frowned, it held no anger. When he dug into his pocket, retrieving his keys, the smile slipped from Carter's face. "You're still at a desk today."

"Still at a desk."

"I know many of those paper pushers are gung-ho but there's no need to get shot. Again."

The joke didn't land, her worry taking the joviality out of it. Her father hugged her and Carter held onto him, gripping his black suit jacket.

"I love you, Sarge."

She tightened her hold on him. "I love you too, Captain."

The sentiment seemed to hurt as it came out. When he released her, Carter schooled her expression into something resembling calm. Her father smiled, seeing through it. Kissing the top of her head, he climbed into the car.

"You know you'll have to take Maggie on a date that's just the two of you eventually," Carter said.

"I'll do that once I know I can trust this Marine boyfriend of yours. Till then it's the three of us."

"You're just using me to avoid commitment."

"I'll see you at home."

A joke rose to Carter's mind but she couldn't manage

it. Instead, she said a single word. "Promise?"

He nodded. "Promise."

***

The volume of voices had risen considerably when Carter re-entered the school. Gossip tripped off people's lips and buzzed from phone to phone. Students swapped stories, none of them true and constantly growing further from the truth. Carter made her way through the excited throng, heading towards her first period. No one looked her way. No one knew what part she had played a week ago.

As she approached her classroom, she spotted Link and Amy huddled close together, whispering to each other. Carter glanced across the way and a familiar sight made her stop.

A sight that lessened some of the tightness in her chest and calmed her storming thoughts. Donovan leaned against a set of lockers, his hands tucked away in the pocket of his slacks, his ankles crossed. The four adoring girls formed a semi-circle around him. He wore a blank look, though his eyes never settled on anything for longer than a second.

Unnoticed by him, Carter indulged herself, regarding him as everyone else did: dark blue eyes standing out on a handsome face and a lean, built physique. Even the ugly purple bruises on his jaw and cheek added to his captivating image.

"Where did you get the bruises?" one girl asked. "Was it from the people who attacked the museum? Did you fight them?"

"Why would I be fighting people who attacked the museum?" Donovan asked, patronizing.

She tossed her hair over her shoulder. "Because clearly, you're strong enough to do that."

He leveled a look at her that was so flat even she would have had a hard time misreading his thought of 'stupid'.

A half-smile on her lips, Carter crossed the hallway and tapped one of the girls on the shoulder. When the girl twisted around, Carter slipped into the circle. Donovan straightened. For once, his gaze held still.

The girl closest to him let out a huff. "Owens, don't you have somewhere better to be? I don't know, like detention or juvie?"

Donovan brought his hand up to Carter's face and gently caressed her bruised cheek.

"I don't think so," Carter said. "I'm happy right where I am."

Taking hold of the edge of Donovan's blazer, she leaned in and kissed him. He cupped the back of her head. Around them, girls let out startled gasps. The retreating of shoes made Carter smile.

"That was way too much fun," she said.

"What? Kissing me? Or making those girls jealous?"

"A little of both."

With a spark of mischief, he kissed her once more.

"Technically," he said, so quiet only she could hear, "I'm working."

"And I'm helping you keep your cover," she said, matching his volume. "Besides, from the reflection of that classroom window," she nodded to a pane of glass beside an open doorway, "I can see Link. So far, still alive."

Donovan shook his head in disbelief, chuckling. "Then I can kiss you again."

"If you don't, you'll have bigger problems on your hands besides Link's safety. Your safety for instance."

"Carter, are you always going to be threatening me when it comes to acts of affection?"

"Are you always going to analyze everything I do?"

"Are you going to constantly question my motives?"

"Are you ever going to shut up?"

"Is this going to be difficult?"

"Donovan, did you want it to be easy?"

The edge of his lip curled as a challenged gleam deepened the color of his blue eyes. He kissed her in response. His lips were soft and seemed to drive all thoughts from her mind.

When they broke apart, she left her hands resting against his chest for a second longer then drew back, sliding her hands into her pockets. Donovan dropped his hands, cocking his head. "What?"

"Captain has given you the label of 'boyfriend'."

Donovan raised his eyebrows. "Does this mean I have his approval? I know we left on good terms but I still had the feeling I should sleep with a gun under my pillow."

"Don't you anyways?"

"Yes. But now I would have the safety off."

She smiled. "He still has his reservations about you. But I believe that will change with time."

Donovan suppressed a smile but turned serious. "How do you feel about the label?"

"It depends," she said.

"On?"

"On how you feel about dating me? I am still a high school girl after all."

"True. But it depends."

Carter narrowed her eyes in suspicion. "On?"

"On whether you can hit a target from twenty yards with a 9mm Glock?"

As she fought back a laugh, her cheeks colored. "I can."

Donovan held her face and kissed her. "Then I have no problem dating you."

The bell rang bringing their reality back. All around them groups split and slipped into doorways, down hallways, and up stairways. Link kissed Amy, then watched as she walked off. Before she rounded a corner, she sent him one last wave. The sight of it brought a rebellious grin to his lips. When he spun towards the classroom, he froze seeing Carter and Donovan. He smothered his telling look.

"Happy?" Carter asked.

"Yeah. You?"

In her mind, the image of her father driving away popped up, making her still. But Donovan's steady presence beside her didn't let her dwell on the thought too long.

"Yeah," she said. "Let's get to class, if we're lucky there will be a pop quiz."

They took their normal seats and Link nudged Carter's arm with his elbow. "How are you doing?" He eyed the side of her face, wincing as if feeling the pain of the blow.

"I'm okay," she said. "I can take a few punches."

As Mason walked through the doorway, followed by Smith, both Carter and Link glanced over. The two brothers' eyes met. A strange uncertainty passed between them. For a breath, Mason's usual cockiness fell away, revealing something almost kind. After giving the barest nod to Link, Mason sauntered to his seat, once again The First Son. The only son.

"Did you two talk?" Carter asked.

Link shook his head, fiddling with a pencil. "No. I don't know if we ever will. He knows and there is not a lot to say on the matter. It changes nothing about our situations."

At the resignation in his voice, Carter said nothing but took his hand and squeezed it. He held her gaze, understanding shared between them. As the bell rang again, Mr. Rojas stood up.

"All right," he said. "I know it's been a week since you've been here but you know how this works. Phones away. If it rings or dings, it's mine."

***

Carter pushed through the library doors, the hushed interior a vast contrast to the hectic hallways outside. Only a few students had made it in before her. They sat quietly at tables, entrenched in their thoughts or forms of distraction.

"You haven't been causing fights on field trips, have you?" Diana asked.

Carter pointed to herself, feigning surprise. "Who me? Never."

Diana smiled like she knew a secret. "It's been rumored around the teacher's lounge that it was a couple of students who aided in preventing the worst of the incident. You wouldn't happen to know anything about that, would you?"

"I'm just a student," Carter said, shrugging innocently. "How would I know such things?"

Diana leaned on her desk and peered at Carter through her round glasses. "Because you seem to know everything."

"Like the fact that it's going extremely well with Mr. Rojas and you spent most of the break with him?"

Flushing, Diana shuffled a stack of papers, confirming Carter's deduction.

"For instance, things like that," Diana said. "I would ask how you know but I'll stop myself."

Grinning, Carter backed up a step. "Actually, I made a guess."

The librarian shook her head, bemused. When Donovan and Link strode in, Carter waved to Diana and fell into step alongside the two boys.

"Time to talk?" Donovan asked.

Instead of answering him, Carter glanced at Link. "Is Amy coming?"

"No, she had a test she needed to look over."

"You two work everything out?" she asked.

He nodded. "Yeah, waking up from being knocked out kind of erased our argument."

"Good."

Carter guided them to the second story and a far back corner where they wouldn't be overheard. She sank to the floor, her back pressed against the wall. Donovan took the wall adjacent to her, Link plopped into the spot opposite.

"Did either of you find it strange how the details from the attempted kidnapping were kept quiet?" she asked.

"It was in the President's best interest," Donovan said. "As well as ours."

"I've heard so many different theories today," Link said. "About what happened and none of them were close to the truth. I'm not mad about that. It means I'm still safe. But it's weird no one knows. Even the excuse for Mr. Philip's absence was a 'life emergency'." He scratched the back of his neck. "Do we even know what happened?"

Carter and Donovan exchanged a look, both of them revisiting the incident.

"I know you two know," Link said, "but do you know why?"

Donovan held Carter's gaze, his look a question.

"Yeah," she said. "I finally managed to get my dad to tell me. Did you get anything from Brock?"

Donovan shook his head. "He isn't in a high enough position to be in the know. And I was told I would be notified if there was any information that was pertinent to my job."

"So basically, they aren't going to share anything with you?" Carter said.

"Exactly."

"I guess it's a good thing that my father is trying to make up for crushing my heart."

The comment came off carefree but when she looked at Donovan, he was studying her. In a single glance, silent words of encouragement and reassurance passed between them.

Link leaned over his crossed legs, unaware of the

unspoken conversation taking place. "What *did* happen?"

"Mr. Philips," Carter said, "was your father's assistant back when your father was still a Senator and making plans to run for President. And your father was the reason Philips was blackballed from politics." She shrugged. "My dad didn't go into details about what happened but Philips knew about you. It seems you were the source of their conflict."

Link scowled at the news. "You think he knew who I was when I showed up?"

"Yes," Carter said. She locked eyes with Donovan. "You don't have to say it."

"I know, but I need to."

Annoyed, Link frowned. "Are you doing that thing again where you both understand each other without actually saying anything?"

Carter chuckled but didn't look at Link.

"I should have listened to you," Donovan said.

"It's okay. He's safe," Carter reassured him.

Link rolled his eyes and shook his head. "This is going to get old fast."

Carter bumped his knee with her shoe. "You and Amy have your way of silently communicating."

Link pointed at her, defiant. "No, it's not the same. I can tell when she wants to say something or kiss me but that's about it. You two have full-blown conversations without saying anything. It's not natural."

"Do you want to hear the rest of my information or keep nitpicking over the oddities of Donovan's and my relationship?"

"Information," he said, "But it's still odd."

Carter fought back a smile. "Philips also knew Ben, the former-military janitor, from his days of working with Douglas." She softened with regret. "Apparently Douglas sanctioned an Op even after knowing the high level of risks involved." She paused for a breath. "Twenty men were killed."

Link swallowed and nodded slowly, the pain of the

news clear in his eyes.

"When Ben came back from the Op with only half of his platoon," she continued, "he was broken. He returned home to find the man that was responsible for the lives of his friends was now the President. Philips made contact. Both men had something against Douglas."

Link dropped his head, tugging at the carpet. "They came for me, not just Mason. Why?"

Carter shifted, uncomfortable with the answer. Donovan read the meaning behind the movement. "It's because you're the same age as Mason and illegitimate," he said, gently.

Clarity hit Link and he gave a self-loathing chuckle. "Of course. I'm the thing that breaks my dad's image of being upstanding and wholesome. Put Mason and me together and you expose my...our father." He hunched his shoulders.

"I could just punch him," Carter said, low and menacing, her fingers forming fists as she took in Link's sadness.

Link raised his head. Her pure outrage on his defense made him smile, a smile full of amusement and sorrow. "Then I would have a black-eyed father and you would be arrested. It's probably not the best plan of action."

"But you deserve better," she said, her tone heavy with conviction.

He shrugged. "And so do you. And so does Donovan for that matter but that doesn't change facts."

"Yes," Carter said, sadly, "but it also doesn't mean I don't wish better for you."

"You mean that, don't you?"

"If I didn't mean it, I wouldn't have said it."

After a moment's pause, Link spoke. "What were their plans then?"

"It's like you said, they wanted both you and Mason together so they could use you to expose the President for being adulterous."

"Would simply exposing the President be worth it for

them if they were caught?" Link asked.

"I don't think they had plans of being caught. Remember the false alarm lockdown? My tracker going offline? It was all purposeful, testing the school's security. They probably initially planned to take Mason and you here but when that wasn't an option, they devised the field trip. A museum where only our class would be and multiple exits where they could escape with you."

Link stared at her for a long moment but didn't see her, absorbing the information. She could see he felt the weight of the scenarios that didn't end up with him sitting on the library floor. Carter and Donovan remained silent. They watched as he processed everything.

Eventually, Link looked between them. A thought tugged at the corner of his mouth. He rubbed the back of his neck. "Thanks for making sure that didn't happen."

Donovan nodded and Carter sent him a warm grin.

"Really, I should be thanking you," she said. Both boys regarded her curiously. "It gave me an excuse to slap Mason, something I've wanted to do for a long time."

Link burst out laughing, the gesture releasing his burdened thoughts.

"Well, it's a good thing you're fast on your feet," Donovan said. "Or the whole situation could have had a different ending."

"So what you're saying," Carter teased, "is that you would have failed without me as backup?"

Donovan tried to glare at her but her taunting grin didn't let him manage it and he softened. Link rested his chin in his hand.

"Are Amy and I this annoying?" he asked.

"Yes," both Carter and Donovan said.

Link shrugged, unconcerned. "All right. Then I won't complain." A thought struck him. "Wait, earlier you said that your dad told you all of this because he crushed your heart. What did you mean?"

An ache returned to Carter's heart and she couldn't hold onto her smile. Donovan held her gaze, caring and understanding pouring through it. She found solace in his eyes.

"He signed back up for two more years with the secret service," she said. "He will be finishing out his protection detail by your father's side."

"Carter, I'm sorry," Link said.

"Yeah, well, that's life, right?" She smiled, dispersing the cloud that had formed over them. "At least it makes my choice of college clear."

"How come?"

"Well, I want to be as close to him as I can be in case anything happens. So Georgetown it is."

Donovan's quiet smile betrayed his feelings on the matter. Link perked up, excited.

"You'll be with us!"

Carter felt her heart lighten at the thought. "Yup, it looks like you're stuck with me."

"That doesn't sound too bad," Donovan said.

"Not at all," Link said. "Because clearly, it takes two of you to keep me out of trouble."

Carter laughed, the sound affectionate as it drifted away into the library's silence.

"That's true. I can be your second bodyguard," she said, winking at Link. "It will be my secret service."

Epilogue

Early evening sunlight poured over the street, encasing Carter and Donovan in warmth. The day was cloudless and summer filled every mind. Buildings of staggered heights lined the sidewalk, casting shadows down on the couple. They moved as if in a separate world, not seeing the things around them.

"I don't understand," Carter said, "why holding a guy's hand has such a strong effect on girls?"

Donovan looked at her, his eyebrows raised, his lips curling into a smirk. The bruises along his jaw had shifted to a yellow, brown color.

"Are you saying that this has no effect on you?" he asked.

He brushed his fingers along the inside of her palm before lacing his fingers between hers. Carter felt her heart lurch and her nerves begin to hum. Despite this, she kept her face blank, fighting against the rush of heat climbing into her cheeks.

"None whatsoever," she said, her voice controlled.

Donovan leaned close to her ear. "You forget, you

can't lie to me."

His voice was low and touched with a teasing note. When he pulled away, Carter scowled but didn't let go of his hand. A smile slowly overtook his face, the sight enticing one from her.

"You know, if you want to hold my hand," he said. "You can. It is your right, with me being your boyfriend."

"A label that is still in question by my father, though he did give it to you."

"I plan on making it more permanent."

"We'll see if that's possible."

In response, Donovan squeezed her hand. The feel of his fingers locked in hers felt new and familiar all at once. It was a feeling she didn't plan on losing.

They were passing a dark alley when she spoke again. "How's Link doing with being alone to -"

A pair of rough hands grabbed Carter and yanked her from Donovan's hold. She let out a cry of surprise. But a hand clamped down over her mouth and nose, cutting her off. The other hand closed around her in a vise-like grip, carrying her back into the alleyway.

Donovan rushed after her but another muscular man appeared. He caught Donovan by the shoulder, hauling him back. Carter struggled against her attacker but the man was three times her size and she dangled from his hold. Still, she tried to kick at his legs and butt his face with her head. All of her efforts had little effect as the oxygen drained out of her.

Her lungs screamed for air and she could only watch as Donovan efficiently rendered his opponent unconscious. Before the man hit the ground, he raced for her. The world was going blurry and she felt her thoughts unraveling. The hand over her face disappeared. Carter gasped, sucking in air. She leaned her head forward and Donovan took the opportunity to land a blow to her captor. The man released her. She went stumbling to the ground, fighting to get air into her lungs.

Her mind was slow to clear, her lungs working furiously. A second later, Donovan knelt by her side. He took her arm and lifted her to her feet. His face was tight with concern but his eyes blazed with adrenaline.

"Can you walk?" he asked, urgently.

Behind him, the man lay unconscious. Carter didn't glance at the prone figure. She nodded, the world still hazy.

"Good," he said. "We have to move."

They hurried to the mouth of the alley, Carter leaning on Donovan for support. As they hit the sidewalk, he kept her positioned away from the street, his body blocking hers from view.

They had barely gone a few steps before a gun fired.

The window of the bakery next to them exploded in a shower of glass. Chaos erupted, leaving Carter's ears ringing, the world muffled. The window shards rained over them and she raised her arms, blocking her face.

Everything was a storm of confusion as she fought to regain clarity. Another shot cut through the air, landing in a second window above them. Donovan flipped over a deserted table on the sidewalk and they both ducked behind it.

He shielded her body with his own, his arms wrapped tightly around her.

More gunfire pelted the sidewalk and beat against the wooden table. Carter's mind crystallized as adrenaline spiked her system, the fuzzy thoughts of a second ago burned away. In its place was a sharp focus. Donovan leaned close to her, his lips hovering over her ear.

"We need to make a run for the bakery and take cover on the other side of the counter."

Carter twisted her head so she could see him. His blue eyes were serious, his lips a determined line.

"I'll follow you," he said.

She felt her heart race and her body buzz. Even in the intensity of the moment, she was overly aware of him. The feel of his chest pressed against her back, and his arms securing her.

"On the count of three," he said.

Carter nodded, shifting her stance.

"One."

Blood pounded in her ears.

"Two."

Another volley of gunfire ricocheted off the sidewalk and brick buildings.

"Three!"

Carter sprinted forward, Donovan hot on her heels. She leapt through the shattered window. Clearing the length of the shop in a few steps, she vaulted over the counter and landed hard on the floor. Donovan slid over the top and dropped down beside her.

She looked at him, her breathing fast and energized. Donovan met her gaze, his eyes bright like burning candle flames.

A smile spread across her face. He was quick to return it.

She laughed, peering over the top of the counter and then back at him.

"Well," she said, "Captain has had a good many opportunities to hit you with a bean bag bullet and hasn't. I say this is a good sign."

"Good," Donovan said, "because I wanted to take you out tonight."

Carter couldn't stop the happiness she felt with that statement. "Then let's get me through this with no injuries and you only mildly wounded."

"I'll take mildly wounded for a date with you."

They smiled as another round of bullets pinged off the counter and tile floor. Carter twisted to peak over the counter. From the low view, there wasn't much to see.

"What's our next move?" she asked.

Donovan pointed to himself. "You mean my next move. Technically, you weren't even supposed to struggle against Curtis."

Carter frowned. "You try playing the helpless damsel

after years of training and see how easy it is to do nothing." A thought struck her. "You didn't hurt Curtis too badly, did you?"

Donovan shook his head. "He might have a headache tomorrow and a bruise or two but he'll be fine. Now, come on. Let's move. And no attacking the men. That's my job today."

As Carter rolled her eyes, Donovan chuckled. He rose to a crouch and took her hand as he passed by. She suppressed a smile at the feel of his hand in hers.

Pulling a gun from the back of his jeans, Donovan raised it. They crept along the counter and ducked into the empty back room. Dust layered the floor. They left footprints as they made their way to the back door. Donovan released Carter's hand and reached for the handle. With a backward look at her and a nod in response, he eased it open.

He edged his gun out, checking the alley. Satisfied it was clear, he pushed the door all the way open, swinging his gun around to check the other end. Before Carter stepped out, he scanned the rooftops.

"Let's move," he said

She followed his lead as he moved down the alley. Every few feet, she glanced back.

"I still think I should have taken the gun from Anderson," she said. "He was unconscious and I feel completely helpless."

Donovan smiled but didn't look back, his focus on the opening. "That's not what this is about. Today is about me proving, again, to your father that I can protect you."

"I can protect myself."

"I know that."

Carter swallowed her next comment when a man appeared at the entrance. Donovan fired twice. Two red paintballs exploded on the man's chest. Smirking, the man stuffed his hands in his pockets and leaned against the wall. Carter looked back but saw no sign of danger from that end. They slid along the wall until they reached the corner.

"The car is only a block away but this is the end of our cover," Donovan said. "You ready?"

"Give me a gun and I will be."

He chuckled but made no response. "Okay, stay with me."

"I don't plan on leaving." The words slipped out before Carter had time to realize what she had said. Donovan halted.

"We have to go," she said, trying to erase the words.

A touch of a smile tugged at his lips as he sharpened his focus once more. "All right."

He checked that the street was clear and hurried out, Carter close behind. A storm of gunshots rang out the second they hit the pavement. Donovan pulled Carter to cover against a rusty car. She huddled close to the ground, Donovan's hand keeping her as small as possible.

"This is stupid, I want a gun," she said.

Donovan made no reply, his focus elsewhere. He spun around and aimed three shots at a second-story window. Two of the three met its target and the gunfire ceased. "Move!"

Carter was already rising as he took hold of her arm to help her up. They sprinted for the next street, ducking around a car and sliding into a kneeling stance. The upper torso of a man popped up from a roof across the way. Donovan took him down with a quick hit to the chest.

"We need to make it to the car soon," he said, "because I only have one bullet left. After that, it's just me between you and bullets. And I don't feel like getting hit with a bean bag round."

"I heard those hurt worse than a real bullet."

"You see why I want to avoid it then." He nodded to the street. "Come on. Almost there."

Giving the lane one final check, he took the lead. They hurried down the sidewalk, Donovan scanning the rooftops as they went. They stopped at the corner, the

Mercedes in sight, parked across the way. Donovan whipped his head out and back in. When nothing happened, he peered out again, examining the sidewalk. Carter could see the determination radiating from him, his body tense with energy.

When he stepped out, she followed, keeping close. He swiveled one way and the next, his mind alert for a trap. The street remained quiet.

Just as they reached the car, sunlight glinted off something metal protruding from a window. Before the shooter could fire, Donovan aimed and squeezed the trigger. His final shot took out a man that materialized from the shadows. The sequence was over in less than a second.

Carter couldn't help but smile, admiring the speed and certainty in which he had moved. Though empty, he swung the gun around, searching for last minute attacks.

None came.

A moment later her father walked out of a building. The men who had been shot stood and gathered together. Her father's face was serious as he looked at Donovan, who straightened under his gaze.

"Good," he said. "But you are out of bullets, so it would only take a single shot to end you at this point."

Donovan gave a curt nod. "Yes, that is if I were still standing here. By this time I planned to be a mile away in the car."

Her father frowned. "Life doesn't go as you plan. Remember that."

"I will, sir."

Joining the group, Curtis clapped a hand on Carter's father's shoulder. "Steve, lighten up. You've put him through three different scenarios and he's proven he can protect Carter in each one. I say it's time you trust him."

Carter smiled at Curtis and he sent her a grin. She focused on her father, who still wore a convincing frown. "Well, Captain?"

After a long minute, the frown broke.

***

Carter stood in front of her closet, her freshly blow-dried hair falling over her shoulders. She stared at the dark assortment of clothes, her hands hidden away in the pockets of her sweats. The apartment lay quiet, the question on Carter's mind the loudest thing.

"I really have no variety," she said.

"Your closet could stand to expand, yes."

Carter waved a frustrated hand at the ensemble. "I think I have five shirts that are all the same. Even the same color."

Maggie restrained her laughter. "I think you're right."

Leaning her head back, Carter groaned. "This is stupid and I know it, yet somehow I care what I wear tonight. And what Donovan thinks."

Maggie placed a consoling hand on her shoulder, bringing Carter's attention to her. "Hon, it's not going to matter what you wear. He will be happy just to be taking you out."

"You say that like I could go in my sweats."

Maggie's laughter burst out, wiping away Carter's annoyance for the moment.

"How about this," she said, "you'll wear what you usually do and tomorrow I'll take you shopping."

Carter grimaced. "Even the word 'shopping' makes me want to shoot something."

"It's that or wear the same thing every time you go out with Donovan."

Carter's eyes narrowed on the closet, her mouth a thin line. "Is the sweats option off the table?"

"Yes, I can't let you leave the house on your first date in your father's old training t-shirt and ratty sweatpants." Frustrated, Carter palmed her eyes. "Is it always this annoying being a girl?"

Maggie shrugged and moved to the closet. "It feels annoying because everything is new but you'll get used to it." She pulled out a simple dark green shirt and a pair jeans.

Carter took the items and shook her head. "I hope it gets easier or I'll break a hole in my punching bag."

Maggie chuckled and picked up Carter's discarded towel. As Carter was about to change, they heard a knock on the front door. They froze, listening as her father crossed the living room. A deep, familiar masculine voice drifted through the apartment. Carter couldn't help the smile that appeared. Maggie shot her a cheeky grin. In response, Carter scowled.

"Don't worry, girly," Maggie said. "Your secret is safe with me." She waved her hands at Carter. "Hurry up and get dressed, I don't want Steve torturing him for too long."

Carter quickly changed, straining to hear anything beyond her door. Before leaving, she allowed herself a quick glance in the mirror. Even as she scrutinized herself, there was a brightness in her eyes she couldn't avoid noticing. A grin pulled at the edge of her mouth.

When she stepped into the living room, Donovan's attention instantly jumped to her and he cut himself off mid-sentence. Right then all the annoyance of her closet and clothes were worth it for the appreciative look in his eyes.

"Oh, Hon," Maggie said, "You'll need a jacket. Stay here, I'll get it."

As she passed Carter, she whispered, "He's cute. Good job."

Carter laughed as Maggie winked.

"What kind of weapons are you carrying?" Carter's father asked, using Maggie's absence to his advantage.

Donovan forced his gaze away from Carter. "I have an ankle holster with a switchblade and in my glove compartment is an M45 with two extra clips."

Her father nodded in approval. When Maggie returned, she handed Carter her jacket. Thanking her, Carter slipped it on. With an ease that made her stomach flip, Donovan took her hand.

"I want her home by ten," Carter's father said.

"Captain, seriously?" Carter deadpanned.

He shrugged, his face even. "Fine, don't go on a date."

"Ten it is, sir," Donovan said.

He squeezed Carter's hand, keeping her from voicing any more arguments. Her father smiled, the look more welcoming as he looked at Donovan. "Hurt her in anyway and I will shoot you. Connections or no connections. And it doesn't matter where you go. I'll find you."

Now it was Carter's turn to squeeze Donovan's hand, sensing the touch of fear that sank into his stomach. Maggie laughed and took Steve's arm.

"What he meant to say is 'have fun'," she said.

He shook his head. "No, I meant what I said."

Carter pulled the door open. "We're leaving now."

Before she took a step, her father spoke. "I love you, Sarge."

She smiled at him. "I love you, too, Captain."

"Have a good time," he said. Then his face went serious. "But not too good of a time."

Shaking her head, Carter left, taking Donovan with her. They remained quiet as they descended the stairs, waiting for the click of the door. It finally came when they made it to the car.

The night was cool, the glow of house lights spilling into the drive and alleyway. Donovan looked back at the apartment. "What are the chances your father has a sniper rifle trained on me and will shoot me if I kiss you now?"

"Very low. He prefers a Glock and close quarters."

Donovan took a step towards her. He took her face in his hands, brushing his thumb along her cheek. She rested her hands against his chest, feeling the faint beating of his heart. He stared at her. In his blue eyes, she saw a feeling she knew her own eyes held. A feeling that coursed through her.

He kissed her, the feeling sending roots deeper into

her chest.

"Look at that," she said, "kissed me and still alive."

"I say that's a good sign." He laced his fingers through hers. "Where do you want to go tonight?"

"As long as I'm with you, I don't care."

"How does a romantic movie sound?"

She angled away from him and eyed him doubtfully. "Like you don't want this relationship to last very long."

"Shooting range and dinner it is."

"Good," she said. "It will give me a chance to beat you at something new."

Donovan gave her a serious look. "Carter, you understand I was assembling a gun by the age of ten, right?"

With a taunting expression, she cocked her head. "Are you scared of a challenge, Donovan?"

He kissed her. "From you? Never."

Turn the page

for a glimpse of when

Link and Mason met

Two Weeks Later
After The Attack

Link paced the length of the classroom and spun around to make the journey back, nerves carrying him from one end to the next. Carter sat on top of a table, her feet propped on a stool, watching Link's progress. Donovan rested against the table beside her, his arm touching her. Breathing out, Link ran a nervous hand through his hair. His mind was a frantic mess and he couldn't seem to gain control of it.

The classroom lay empty except for the three occupants. Outside the closed door, the muted sounds of students could be heard. No one tried to enter the classroom. If they had, they would have found the door locked. The minutes ticked on and no one said anything. The wait felt like it had lasted an eternity when they finally heard a knock. Carter and Donovan looked to Link, who stared at the door. What waited for him behind that door was something he didn't know whether or not he wanted.

"You sure about this?" Carter asked.

Link nodded but he knew they would see it wasn't the

truth. Rising, Donovan went over to the door and flipped the lock. When he opened the door, Mason was on the other side, shadowed by Smith.

The two newcomers walked in and Donovan engaged the lock again. Silence settled over the room as Donovan took up his position next to Carter. Link stood frozen near the table, eyes glued on his half brother. In turn, Mason seemed unable to look at Link. All his bluster and posturing were nowhere to be seen.

"Why did you want to see Link?" Carter asked, getting bored of the quiet.

Mason stuffed his hands into his pockets and finally made eye contact with the boy who appeared to be his opposite. Mason was blonde, built, and bold. In comparison, Link looked like a little kid still growing into his teenage body.

"I don't know," Mason said. "I guess I wanted to see you now that...I know. And...talk."

Link nodded, his gaze dropping like he was the one to blame for who he was.

"Talking is fine," Carter said. She leaned forward, eyes boring into Mason. "But if you say anything remotely unkind, I will attack you so hard and so fast it will take both Smith and Donovan to stop me. Got it?"

Link held back a smile, drawing strength from her loyalty. Mason nodded but didn't seem scared. His demeanor was subdued and he looked uncertain. Link wondered if he had ever been uncertain in his entire life.

"Did you really not know?" Link blurted out.

Cautious, Mason rubbed the back of his neck. "I wasn't sure, but..." he dropped his hand. "You look a lot like him."

Link crossed his arms, building a shield. "Yeah, I know."

Mason pointed to Link's hair. "But you don't have his hair color."

"It's dyed."

"Oh." A stretch of silence. "The glasses?"

Link took them off and laid them on the table. "Fake."

"Makes sense."

The two boys stood regarding each other. The boy who was known by everyone, talked about, and loved for being part of The Family.

And the boy who lived in the shadows, seen by few, and truly known by even fewer.

"Did you always know?" Mason asked.

"No, I found out six years ago."

"That must have sucked."

The sympathy caught Link by surprise.

"Yeah, it did," he said. "I hated him for a long time."

Mason chuckled. "You're not the only son to feel that."

The binding word of 'son' seemed to crack another layer of tension that hung between the two brothers.

"Why do *you* hate him?" Link asked, curious.

Mason leaned back on the closest table, crossing his arms. The posture was relaxed, like he had found common ground. "There are too many reasons. He became President. He cheated on my mom. His job comes before me."

Link shuffled his foot, staring at the ground.

"At least you see him more than I do," Link said.

"What delusion are you under?" Mason said. "I'm lucky if I see him once a week."

"I barely see him once a month and even that doesn't happen sometimes."

Mason looked away, holding in his thoughts. The room filled with a new sort of tension, one built from trying to decide who had it worse.

"I thought..." Mason started. "I thought I was the only target." The statement cracked the wall between them. "I'm the face everyone knows. I thought whatever was happening would only be about me. I had no reason not to believe it." Mason broke his gaze with the wall and locked eyes with Link. "Then you were mentioned and I was so confused…and then pissed."

"Were you scared?" Link asked, wanting to reaffirm that the person before him wasn't 'Wonder Boy'.

"I was terrified."

Link smiled and Mason's mouth curled upward. Before the smile could settle, Mason turned serious. "I'm sorry you were involved. Doesn't seem fair to me."

"Nothing ever is."

Something like acceptance passed between the two brothers.

The bell rang, ending lunch and ending the meeting. Mason rose and took a step towards the door but stopped. For a moment he hesitated, debating. Link felt the same apprehension but fought it and extended his hand. Mason paused, then took it.

"I always wanted a brother," he said.

"Me too," Link said. "I guess we both got our wish."

When Mason and Smith slipped out the door, Link turned to Carter and Donovan wearing a dazed smile. Carter and Donovan exchanged a look, then Carter gave a heavy sigh. "I guess this means I can't hate him now, doesn't it?"

Acknowledgements

First and foremost to Jesus Christ for the gift of imagination and the ability to use it and for the gift of dying on the cross for my sins that I might spend eternity with Him. That is the greatest gift and story!

To Grace, for loving Carter from the first and sending me texts after every chapter encouraging me to keep going.

To Kelly, for telling me to make Link illegitimate and not make Donovan a cliche bad boy. Gosh, I can't imagine how bad the book would have been without those two changes. Also for being my editor!

To mom, for telling me to keep the mahogany grandfather clock. And for spending two months on the first chapter equipping me with the tools I needed to move forward.

To Trisha, (Trisha Van Cartier) a wonderful sister-in-law who, when I asked if you'd copy edit my book, you didn't hesitate to say yes!

To Kevin, for loving Gabby, a character that is now cut (RIP Gabby) but that you loved and made me laugh by loving. Also for being amazing and giving me the money to pay my cover designer.

To Murph, for inspiring the observational side of Carter.

To Joel, for giving me the money I needed to see this project to completion!

To Benjamin DeHart. Working with you on the cover was a dream! I could not have asked for a more understanding and amazing cover designer, thank you!

To Rachel Butler for being a bomtastic beta reader!

To Thea Bank, Gloria, Mia, Bianca Brümmer, Richard Kigo, Taysia Smith, Anupama Iyer, and for supporting me for so many years! You have my love and thanks!

To Nigel and Sushil, becasue when I needed help you both jumped in and blew me away. Thank you!

To Ally Carter for inspiring this Gallagher Girl.

To those people in my life who won't understand that you had an impact on my life and will most likely never know or never see this: Brooke and Brenna Brean, Alex Bautista, Dylan Blakenbaker, and Jason Laws.

To the readers who were with Carter since the beginning. You are the reason that this book is a reality! From the bottom of my odd author's heart thank you, Noodle! *hands you ice cream*

And finally to You, the one reading this book! The one that decided to buy it and go on the journey with Carter despite the fact that she can be a bit prickly. Thanks for giving her (and me) a chance!

Joy Jenkins came late to the reading game,
due to vision problems. She holds a
strong love for Young Adult since
it's where her love of reading began.
Now she writes Young Adult hoping to
inspire the next generation.
When she isn't creating in her little writing
studio outside of Boston, Joy can be found
buried in a book or discussing literature
and drinking tea with her family of artists.

JoyJenkins.com
instagram@joymoment
twitter@_joymoment_

Support the author, leave a review on Amazon and
Goodreads.

Made in the USA
Middletown, DE
14 July 2021